THE YEARS

Memoirs of a Member of the Russian Duma,
1906–1917

THE YEARS

**Memoirs of a Member of the Russian Duma,
1906–1917**

V. V. Shulgin

TRANSLATED BY
Tanya Davis

INTRODUCTION BY
Jonathan E. Sanders

Hippocrene Books
New York

TRANSLATOR'S NOTE

The Library of Congress transliteration system was used, with certain modifications. For ease of reading, ligatures were omitted, the soft sign (') was omitted in surnames, and the anglicized form of Russian first names was used.

For information, address: Hippocrene Books, Inc., 171 Madison Avenue, New York, N. Y. 10016.

Printed in the United States of America.

Design by Ardashes Hampartzoomian

Library of Congress Cataloging in Publication Data

Shul'gin, V. V. (Vasilii Vital'evich), 1878–
    The years.

    Translation of: The years.
    Includes bibliographical references and index.
    1. Shul'gin, V. V. (Vasilii Vital'evich), 1878–
2. Soviet Union—History—Nicholas II, 1894–1917.
3. Statesmen—Soviet Union—Biography. I. Title.
DK254.S5A3213   1984   947.08'3'0924   84-19765
ISBN 0-88254-855-7

Contents

Part III • THE YEARS   199

Part IV • THE EVE OF DESTRUCTION   239

Introduction

VASILII VITAL'EVICH SHUL'GIN'S memoirs provide a unique vista for understanding the fateful years between Russia's 1905 and 1917 revolutions. There are many accounts of this intense period, but few from the pens of genuinely conservative figures. Even fewer were written by rightists elected to public office. Shul'gin is not only very representative of these nonrevolutionary and antirevolutionary elements, but he possessed a rare combination of qualities. Intelligent, well-educated, and articulate, Shul'gin actually participated in the seminal events of Russia's brief experiment with semiconstitutionalism. No blind reactionary yearning for a mythic past, Shul'gin gradually began to understand that Russia would move in the direction he wanted only if men like himself stood for election to the Duma. He eventually became a skilled practitioner of the political arts and tried to come to terms with some of the changes wrought by Russia's modernization. He wanted to preserve the monarchial Russia that he believed in, a Russia untainted by the influence of Poles, Jews, or other minorities, a Russia permeated with the spirit of a duty-oriented nobility not corrupted by the selfish values of a crude and materialistic working class. However, in order to preserve this old, hierarchically ordered world, he was willing to make use of the new institutions that had been created in response to the forces of change.

Shul'gin's personal evolution adds to the importance of these memoirs. Indeed, insights gained from following his development as a Representative in the Second, Third, and Fourth Dumas compensate for the rambling, almost stream-of-consciousness nature of this volume. From a starting point as a leading writer for a reactionary newspaper, the *Kievlianin* (a paper started by his father in 1864), Shul'gin emerged onto the national scene as the leader of the moderate-right Nationalist Party in the Duma. An open anti-Semite, Shul'gin attracted world attention for his opposition to the notorious Beilis trial. On the eve of the First World War Shul'gin found himself defending the freedom of speech of his ardent enemies in the Duma, the supposed agents of revolutionary unrest, the Social Democrats. His transformation from an ardent supporter of the Tsar and opponent of those leading the country's intelligentsia-dominated liberal movement to a member of the Duma's "loyal-opposition" Progressive Bloc and a friend of the quintessential liberal Pavel Nikolaevich Miliukov provides evidence of the flux evident in Russia's new public political life. Finally, the irony of Shul'gin's role as one of the two politicians detailed from revolutionary Petrograd to receive the Tsar's abdication decree highlights the drama and contradictions of past assumptions so evident during the last years of the old regime.

The Years is preeminently a political memoir. Observation of Russia's cultural, social, and intellectual life appears only as incidental sidebars. Even the vivid and nuanced picture of heroic chaos engulfing the Russian army in the First World War—scenes painted with a sensitivity for detail and insight on the level of those provided by a contemporary Russian conservative and fervent nationalist, Alexander Solzhenitsyn, in his masterful *August 1914*—serve only as a backdrop for the drama of high politics being played out in Petrograd.

Unlike so many writers of accounts of the revolution's right-wing enemies, Shul'gin does not dwell on court gossip. He was a devoted monarchist, but the royal family did not obsess him. His belief in the principles of monarchism did not cloud his perception of the last Romanov Tsar. He saw Nicholas II, in whose presence Shul'gin always felt uncomfortable, as weak-willed and ill-suited for his role. Subsequently, he would lament that Russia's tragedy consisted in its being ruled by a man who was unwilling, or perhaps unable, to assert his personal authority and fully utilize his imperial power, his institutionalized charisma, to preserve his own regime—aptly summed up in the phrase "autocracy without an autocrat." Adroitness in legislative initatives and party maneuvering concerned Shul'gin more than conspiracy theories or gossipy speculation about the unnatural influence over the Tsar and Tsarina exercised by the "holy-devil" Rasputin. Shul'gin concentrated his attention on the arena of popular representation, the Duma. For the most part his memoirs follow the traditional approach of viewing politics from the top down. However, at times he escapes this convention. His account of the election maneuvering in his home province of Volyn is revealing and demonstrates the connections between local and national politics.

The first Russian revolution (1905) formed the touchstone of Shul'gin's political experience. Shul'gin, like so many other of the old order's defenders, was suddenly swept from his moorings by the All-Nation Struggle Against Absolutism that culminated in the October 1905 general strike. He found himself living a life he had not sought, in a world filled with new rules of conduct, and imperiously called upon to restore order.

Shul'gin conceived of post-1905 Russia as a peculiar mixture of autocratic and representative government. The Tsar's October Manifesto, which promised a democratically elected Duma together with a series of personal and political freedoms, was not a constitution. Shul'gin saw the Duma as an institution created by the autocrat, who was free to change it as he saw fit. The Duma's existence did not diminish the Tsar's autocratic powers. On the other hand, in contrast to the most extreme rightists, Shul'gin accepted the Duma as a genuine and legitimate legislative body.

Never a believer in true democracy, Shul'gin abhorred the radical composition of the first two Dumas. Both were elected under a broad franchise and relatively unfettered election procedures. He felt that the overly liberal policies of S. Iu. Witte created too many possibilities for the leftists.[1]

Appalled by the confrontational approach of the Russian liberals, the Constitutional Democrats (Kadets), and the leftist parties (especially the Socialist Revolutionaries, whom he disdained as mere terrorists), Shul'gin regarded the first two Dumas, dominated by them, as seditious. They trespassed on rights that historically belonged to the autocrat. Thus Shul'gin applauded the "coup d'état of June 7, 1907," in which the Duma was dismissed and the election laws manipulated to produce a more conservative Duma.[2]

Shul'gin felt confident and comfortable in the Third Duma, elected under the new system. He claimed that it was a real Russian parliament. He gloried in it as the embodiment of political freedom because those elected enjoyed the right of free speech within its walls. Shul'gin stubbornly defended this privilege for all members of the elite club of Duma deputies. But his views of the qualifications for membership in this club were decidedly discriminatory.

Shul'gin's respect for and contentment in the Third Duma grew out of his successes. In Prime Minister P. A. Stolypin he found an ally. Stolypin became more heroic as Shul'gin's historical perspective grew. Stolypin's coup d'état delivered the Duma from the wrathful antimonarchists into the hands of a majority made up of respectful upholders of traditional values. His intervention assured the realization of projects dear to Shul'gin.[3] In his memoirs Shul'gin praised Stolypin for attempting to save the Romanov dynasty through a program of reforms.[4] Stolypin's law-and-order approach held great appeal, as did the image, enhanced by events subsequent to his assassination, of him as a practitioner of realpolitik using Russia's new political system to save its old institutions. For a conservative of Shul'gin's stripe, this was a legitimate use of politics about which he could be enthusiastic.

Shul'gin professed a reluctant involvement in politics. He held and expressed very definite views, but his was an activism of opinion only. He did not create national policy, he responded to it. Before the

shattering changes of 1905 he claimed to be interested only in journalism and the local public-welfare functions traditionally performed
by service-oriented Russian nobles. After 1907, when he had completed his term in the Second Duma, Shul'gin tells us that he still
hated politics.[5] How did this reluctant participant become so totally
engrossed in politics? In part the answer is that before 1905 political
activities were regarded ipso facto as illegitimate. Only radical fanatics
working in the revolutionary underground engaged in such activities.
Shul'gin had contented himself with being a wordsmith, marshaling
ideas, but not engaging in policy-shaping in any activist sense. At best
he reacted to events rhetorically; he did not transgress propriety and
try to devise political programs for the nation. The Duma legislation
of 1905 and 1906 legitimized public politics. More important a sense
of duty and national honor impelled Shul'gin to act.

Shul'gin had internalized the long-standing noble tradition of service. He felt duty bound to serve the nation (and his fellow nobles, the
country's real and worthy Russians) in the hour of need. Unlike tradi-
tionalistic conservatives who contemptuously viewed politics as something dirty, this noble with a professional background as a
newspaperman saw public politics as an avenue for advancing his
causes. The Duma provided him with a great forum for articulating
his views. He could display his oratorical talents, pose as a true democrat appealing to the court of public opinion, and propagate his
ethnocentric and authoritarian ideas. Legislative work gave him op-
portunities to develop talents verging on the demagogic.

Russian nationalism was Shul'gin's lodestar; he was obsessed with
the idea of enhancing the power and dominant status of the country's
Great Russian ethnic majority, especially the Great Russian nobility.
The stunning military defeats that the Japanese had inflicted in 1904–
1905 wounded his national pride.[6] The rising tide of civil strife that
followed these defeats threatened the monarchy's very existence. In
the *Kievlianin* Shul'gin strongly opposed the Liberation Movement.
The declaration of the October Manifesto, hailed by some as a constitution, shocked him, at least initially, as a betrayal of Tsar and
Fatherland. He believed that the very idea of a constitution was "un-
Russian." The pogroms that swept cities such as his native Kiev in
October were seen as a natural reaction to this "unnatural" govermen-
tal act. Foolish Witte (and by implication the weak-willed Tsar who
listened to him) had broken the "ecological balance" of autocracy; the
intelligentsia and the Jews paid the price in blood. For Shul'gin, a
strong believer in the rule of law (he had graduated from Kiev University with a law degree), such spontaneous actions were seen as
regrettable but natural and understandable. Uneducated fellows
from the underclasses reacted against foreign concepts by attacking

the alien elements corrupting Russia.[7] The active involvement of members of various national minorities—Poles, Finns, Lithuanians, Jews (but curiously few Ukrainians)—in the Liberation Movement and the frenzy of activity that followed the October Manifesto confirmed Shul'gin's view that real Russian values, leadership, and hegemony had to be reasserted in order to return to normalcy.

Equally important, as the unrest stirred up by urban-based revolutionaries and liberals reached the countryside it touched off peasant disorders. These threatened the property and the very lives of Russian nobles.[8] The immediate response of many, including those associated with the *Kievlianin,* was to launch a vituperative antiintellectual, anti-Semitic, anticosmopolitan campaign and to push for the election of members of the reactionary Union of Russian People to the First Duma. Those elected, outnumbered and ineffective, failed to have much impact in the quest for an unconditionally supported autocracy. Moreover, the union's thuggish image, born of its conception and its involvement in pogroms—the essence of anachronistic conservatism—precluded this group from attracting widespread noble support.[9]

Shul'gin adapted himself to the new circumstances of Russia's national life as he tried to use the Duma's legislative powers to promote and to protect the interests of noble Russian landowners. Not unlike many members of the nobility (*dvorianstvo*) whose estates were located in territories annexed from Poland following its partition in the late eighteenth century, Shul'gin was caught in a double bind. Class as well as caste barriers, biases, and enmities separated him from the peasantry. An equally unbridgeable chasm kept him apart from the Polish nobles who were his neighbors. To complicate matters further, when men like Shul'gin retreated to nearby cities for intellectual stimulation, cultural uplift, or simply to relieve their isolation in the company of their peers, they confronted the social instability born of working-class discontent and nurtured by the dissatisfaction in the teeming Jewish ghettos. In these circumstances Russian nobles from the western provinces, Shul'gin prominent among them, seized on politics as a means of self-preservation. As they became more adept at legislative procedures and public political life, such men joined together in the Nationalist Party.

The moderate-right Nationalist Party, with Shul'gin as its outstanding orator, played an outsized role in the Third State Duma (1907–1912). In cooperation with Prime Minister Stolypin, the Nationalist Party worked for the promotion of the quatrapartite formula of Autocracy, Orthodoxy, Nationality, and Private Property. Significantly, the Nationalists tempered their enthusiasm for autocracy with a clearly expressed commitment to the country's new representative institutions. This commitment contrasted sharply with the position of the reactionaries who constituted the extreme right in the Duma.

The Nationalists' primary goal was the introduction of units of local self-government (zemstvo institutions) into the western provinces. Under the leadership of Shul'gin and others, the Nationalists promoted a Western Zemstvo Bill which would guarantee the minority Russian noblemen of the affected regions a predominant role in the new institutions. In keeping with the party's overt anti-Semitism, the bill denied Jews equal rights and denied their recognition as citizens. For the new zemstvo institutions Shul'gin urged the tutelage of all groups by the Russian nobles. Giving them an outsized role obviated the need for anything approaching true democracy.[10]

Shul'gin's part in the Duma debates over controversial issues such as the Western Zemstvo Bill added to his prominence. However, nothing on the Russia scene generated so much national and international attention as the prewar cause célèbre, the Beilis case, which came to trial in the autumn of 1913. Shul'gin shocked almost everyone involved in the country's public life by denouncing this incarnation of the blood accusation (ritual murder) against a Jew as a fantasy and a gross perversion of justice. He exposed the sham and groundlessness of the charges brought against the hapless Kiev resident Mendel Beilis for the alleged ritual murder of a young Russian. What made Shul'gin's stand so sensational was that, like his Tsar and the ministers involved in prosecuting the case, he was an anti-Semite, and because of his writings a well-known one.[11]

The contradictions in Shul'gin's denunciation are more apparent than real. He had not become a Judeophile. He retained his prejudices and dedication to militant Russian nationalism. However, the picture of perjury, government conspiracy, false evidence, absurd charges, and general prosecutorial incompetence offended Shul'gin's sense of justice and his belief in the integrity and independence of the courts. Violations of the rule of law outraged him. The Minister of Justice's conduct underlined his belief that bureaucrats posed almost as grave a threat to the old regime as non-Russians.[12]

Moreover, Shul'gin had become a practical politician. He realized that the witchhunt in Kiev, however emotionally satisfying to some, distracted Russia from far more vital issues. At that very moment disintegration threatened his own Nationalist Party. More important, a thoroughgoing revolutionary upheaval that threatened to overturn everything was in full swing. Only the outbreak of the First World War would delay it.[13] Thus Shul'gin felt duty bound to speak out.

Russia's many military defeats in the First World War tested Shul'gin's leadership abilities. By 1915 he understood that the government would have to pay for its defeats on the battlefield through concessions to society, by offering a chance for involvement in the war effort. His experiences in the army changed Shul'gin's approach to politics somewhat. While his nationalism would never fade, the particularism of serving his caste and constituency paled. In his earlier memoirs, *Dni* [The Days], a work largely devoted to recounting Shul'gin's role in and reaction to Russia's revolutions, he recalled, "I was at the front and saw everything . . . I arrived in Petrograd feeling no longer like a representative of one of the southern provinces. I felt that I was a representative of the army."[14] Soon Shul'gin joined with Duma moderates and liberals, whose admiration he had won in the Beilis affair, in forming a Progressive Bloc. Shul'gin brought a faction of renegade Nationalists (the "Progressive Nationalists") with him into this broad alliance for greater participation by the Duma in the conduct of the government and the war. From this new position of loyal opposition Shul'gin eased into a more confrontational position vis-à-vis his monarch. From here it was only a few short steps, dictated by events and circumstances, that sent Shul'gin to accept the Tsar's abdication in 1917.

The Years ends with the dissolution of the Duma and Nicholas II's abdication. Yet if anything the twists and turns of Shul'gin's life became even more dramatic after his years as an elected politician ended. Right after the February Revolution Shul'gin became extremely worried about the great polarization developing, especially in the cities. He was among the first to call attention to the menacing potential of the Bolsheviks' popular appeal.[15] After the October Revolution he joined the White forces. Shul'gin organized the White secret service, the so-called Azbuka. When it ran out of money at the end of 1919, Shul'gin, bitterly disappointed by the political and psychological short-sightedness of the Volunteer Army, abandoned his part in the anti-Bolshevik military effort.[16]

Shul'gin emigrated to the West, where he participated in rightist émigré circles in Berlin and other cities. He wrote for the diaspora press, attended their meetings, and became famous as an unwitting dupe of the Soviet secret police. Purportedly to see his son, whom he had left behind in Sevastopol in 1920, Shul'gin arranged for the underground Monarchist Union of Central Russia to smuggle him back into his homeland. Unbeknownst to this former leader of the Whites' own spy organization, the Soviet secret police had thoroughly penetrated the Monarchist Union. Agents of the union, which was known under the code name "Trust," permitted him to spend more than half of 1926 visiting Leningrad, Moscow, and Kiev. Trust agents posing as ardent foes of the Soviets (some really were) impressed on him the strength of their organization and the mounting opposition to Bolshevik rule in Russia. In an act of bravado they encouraged him to publish an account of his adventures. Shul'gin not only complied, but before he published the book he forwarded the manuscript to Moscow for approval by his "friends" in the Trust. Shul'gin's book *Three Capitals: Travels in Red Russia* made its sensational appearance in 1927. In it he optimistically explained how the rule of the kikes was ending, that the real Russia was reasserting herself, and that communism was nothing permanent, it was only an episode.[17] Soon after the book's publication the real nature of the Trust became public knowledge in the West. In a series of articles in the émigré press (primarily Struve's *Vozrozhdenie*), Shul'gin explained how he had been lured into the country and fed contrived information. One article that appeared in an English scholarly journal was sensibly titled "How I Was Hoodwinked by the Bolsheviks."[18] The Soviet secret police had bested the anti-Communist émigrés, publicly exposing the ineptitude and naiveté of the conservatives. The Trust's halo of power, ability, and solidarity vanished; the hopes of the right-wing émigrés diminished; the emigration was demoralized and Shul'gin was made to look exceedingly foolish.

Shul'gin continued his involvement with émigré activities for almost a decade after being hoodwinked and humiliated. He appeared at public forums to discuss his role in the Tsar's abdication. He wrote for Strvue's *Russkaia mysl'* and *Vozrozhdenie,* including at least one article endorsing fascism as the only effective means of fighting the criminality of communism.[19] For much of this time, into the mid-1930s, he was apparently living in Belgrade. Shul'gin then faded from public view. His brief biography in the latest edition of the *Great Soviet Encyclopedia* states that he abandoned political activities in 1937. He was living in the small Yugoslav town of Sremski Karlovci when the Soviet army swarmed into Yugoslavia in 1944. He was taken prisoner and shipped back to the USSR, where he was sentenced to a long prison term for aggressive anti-Soviet activities.[20] He remained in prison until Khrushchev's de-Stalinization campaign freed him in 1956. Shul'gin then settled in the ancient Russian town of Vladimir, where his wife joined him from Yugoslavia.

Back in the traditional Russian heartland in his old age, Shul'gin's previous unmitigated hostility to communism and the new Soviet regime changed or was changed. We know nothing about the circumstances, motivations, or reasons for his conversion. Shul'gin wrote a pamphlet, *Letters to Russian Emigres,* urging them to abandon their antipathy toward the Soviet Union. He declared that communism was the salvation of all mankind.[21] Besides such overt displays of loyalty, Shul'gin devoted much of his time to reflections on the past. He was a consultant for and appeared in the 1965 film *Before the Court of History.* Before he died, on February 15, 1976, at the ripe age of ninety-nine, he completed these unusual memoirs, *The Years,* covering his service in the prerevolutionary Duma.[22] They provide unusual insights into that short but event-filled period in twentieth-century Russian history.

JONATHAN E. SANDERS
W. Averell Harriman Institute for
Advanced Study of the Soviet Union,
Columbia University

February 1984

NOTES

1. In point of fact he believed that the chaotic "Days of Freedom" that followed the October Manifesto, as well as the Moscow armed uprising in December 1905, resulted from Witte's concessions. He wrote, "The liberal reforms only incensed the revolutionary elements in the nation and pushed them to greater activity." See below p. 85. For a more detailed reaction to the October Manifesto and the events that followed, especially the pogroms, see Shul'gin's previous memoir *Dni* [The Days] (Leningrad, 1926), pp. 11–40. For other views on the reaction to the October Manifesto, see Laura Engelstein, *Moscow, 1905: Working-Class Organization and Political Conflict* (Stanford: Stanford University Press, 1982), pp. 136–225, and Jonathan Sanders, "The Union of Unions: Political, Economic, Civil, and Human Rights Organizations in the 1905 Russian Revolution" (Ph.D. diss., Columbia University, 1983), chaps. X, XI.

2. On the changes in the electoral law, see Samuel Harper, *The New Electoral Law for the Russian Duma* (Chicago, 1908) and Leopold Haimson, "Introduction: The Landed Nobility," in *The Politics of Rural Russia, 1905–1914,* ed. Leopold Haimson (Bloomington: University of Indiana Press, 1979), pp. 10–18. The charts drawn by Ronald Petrusha are especially helpful. Also of interest is Gilbert Doctorow, "The Russian Gentry and the Coup d'Etat of June 3, 1907," *Cahiers du Monde Russe et Sovietique,* no. 1 (1976): 43–51, and the classical Soviet work, A. Ia. Avrekh, *Tsarizm i tret'eiiunskai sistema* (Moscow, 1966).

3. See Robert Edelman, *Gentry Politics on the Eve of the Russian Revolution: The Nationalist Party 1907–1917* (New Brunswick: Rutgers University Press, 1980), especially the insightful section on the Western Zemstvo crisis, pp. 116–127; also Geoffrey A. Hosking, *The Russian Constitutional Experiment: Government and Duma 1907–1914* (Cambridge: Cambridge University Press, 1973), pp. 106–149. The best Soviet work on this is A. Ia. Avrekh, *Stolypin i Tret'iia Duma* (Moscow, 1968).

4. See below p. 95.

5. "When the Second Duma was dissolved, I hoped that I was through with it forever. I hated politics, and the drudgery of the past 102 days had not altered my feelings. But man proposes and God disposes. For a variety of reasons that I won't go into here, I ended up taking part in the elections

again. I purposely use the term 'take part in,' not 'stand for election.'" See below p. 49.

6. In fact, projecting his own views onto his monarch he concluded, "The memory of Tsushima was the main stimulus to his [the Tsar's] decision to renounce the throne, which he made after conferring with his five commanders." See below p. 55.

7. See Shulgin, *Dni*, pp. 11–38.

8. In point of fact few nobles were killed, although rumors of such events panicked many. On this and other aspects of the nobility's response to 1905, see Roberta Manning's excellent book, *The Crisis of the Old Order in Russia: Gentry and Government* (Princeton: Princeton University Press, 1982).

9. See Hans Rogger, "Was There a Russian Fascism?: The Union of Russian People," *Journal of Modern History,* 1964, no. 5, pp. 398–415; V. Levitskii, "Pravyiia partii," in *Obshchestvennoe dvizhenie v nachale XX-go veka,* ed. L. Martov et al. (St. Petersburg, 1909–14), vol. 4, pp. 366–395.

10. I take my understanding of the Nationalist Party and Shulgin's role in it from Robert Edelman's fine book, *Gentry Politics on the Eve of the Russian Revolution.*

11. Maurice Samuel, *Blood Accusation: The Strange History of the Beilis Case* (New York: Alfred A. Knopf, 1966), pp. 163–167.

12. See A. S. Tager, *The Decay of Czarism: The Beiliss Trial* (Philadelphia, 1935); Hans Rogger, "The Beiliss Case: Anti-Semitism and Politics in the Reign of Nicholas II," *Slavic Review,* 1966, no. 4, pp. 615–629; Heinz-Dietrich Lowe, *Antisemitismus un reaktionare Utopie: Russischer Konservatismus im Kampf gegen den Wandel von Staat und Gesellschaft, 1890–1917* (Hamburg: Hoffman und Campe Verlag, 1978), esp. pp. 121–124, 137–145; Andrew M. Verner, "Nicholas II and the Role of the Autocrat" (Ph.D. diss., Columbia University, 1983).

13. See Leopold Haimson, "The Problem of Social Stability in Urban Russia, 1905–1917," *Slavic Review,* 1964, no. 4, pp. 619–642; 1965, no. 1, pp. 1–22.

14. *Dni,* p. 44.

15. See Robert Paul Browder and Alexander F. Kerensky (eds.), *The Russian Provisional Government 1917: Documents* (Stanford: Stanford University Press, 1961), vol. 3, pp. 1261–1267.

16. See the somewhat unreliable, D. O. Zaslavskii, *Rytsar' chernoi sotni V. V. Shul'gin* (Leningrad, 1925), esp. pp. 68–71; Peter Kenez, *Civil War in South Russia, 1919–1920: The Defeat of the Whites* (Berkeley: University of California Press, 1977), pp. 65–71. Kenez, the most sophisticated Western historian of the Civil War, observed, "Shulgin alone among the major figures of the anti-Bolshevik movement could be described as a proto-fascist. His passionate nationalism, his demagogy, his willingness to exploit anti-Semitism, and his ability to experiment with unconventional methods of political warfare made him appear a modern figure among conservatives and reactionaries. It is ironic but not very surprising that he was among the very few White leaders who ultimately made their peace with the Soviet regime." Op. cit., p. 66. It is interesting that Shulgin, though a full-blown nationalist, never became part of the Russian fascist movement. On this peculiar grouping, see John J.

Stephan, *The Russian Fascists: Tragedy and Farce in Exile, 1925–1945* (New York: Harper & Row, 1978).

17. V. V. Shul'gin, *Tri stolitsy puteshestvie v krasnuiu rossiiu* (Berlin, n.d. [The Columbia University Library copy is hand dated March 1927]), p. 137.

18. Basil Shulgin, "How I Was Hoodwinked by the Bolsheviks," *Slavonic Review* 6 (1927–28): 505–519.

19. *Vozrozhdenie,* no. 73, August 14, 1925, p. 2.

20. V. Vladimirov, "O knige 'Gody'i ee avtore," in V. Shul'gin, *Gody: vospominaniia byvshego chlena Gosudarstvennoi dumy* (Moscow, 1979), p. 8.

21. V. V. Shul'gin, *Pis'ma k russkim emigrantam* (Moscow, 1961).

22. An excerpt from these memoirs was first published in 1966. See "Glavyi iz knigi 'Gody,'" *Istoriia SSSR,* 1966, no. 6, pp. 65–91; 1967, no. 1, pp. 123–159. The Soviet publishing house Novosti published a fuller text with notes and commentaries by G. Ioffe and an introduction by V. P. Vladimirov in 1979.

Part I

THE DUMA

The Elections

ENCOURAGED BY THEIR relative success in the First Duma, where the Polish circle consisted of about forty deputies, the Polish landowners planned to increase their representation in the Second State Duma. To this end a congress of Poles was convened in Warsaw, with delegates attending from provinces throughout southern Russia, Lithuania, and the Kingdom of Poland. In order to bring the greatest possible number of Polish deputies into the Second Duma, so that there would be a Polish bloc of one hundred deputies, the congress decided to prevent Russian candidates from winning seats in the Duma in any district where Poles and Russians were voting together.

Surprisingly, the Poles announced their decision in the newspapers. This was "a bit much," as they say, and aroused a protest. The sleeping Russian landowners woke up. Those from Podolsk Province took the initiative and summoned a congress of Russian landowners from the Southwestern Region—the provinces of Kiev, Podolsk, and Volyn—to meet in Kiev. This occurred in October of 1906. All the landowners were invited, but only fifty attended.

In our district (Ostrozhsk) there were more than fifty men who had the right to participate in the qualifying elections. Two went to Kiev—Senkevich and I.

Only two out of fifty! That meant that only four percent were awake. I should add that I first became acquainted with Efim Arsenevich Senkevich at the congress, although Lisiche, his estate, was only fifteen kilometers, or an hour's drive in good weather, from Kurgany, my estate. Nor was I acquainted with any of the other landowners who attended the congress.

As chairman, the congress elected a huntsman of His Majesty's court, Marshal of Nobility Peter Nicholaevich Balashev. Balashev was a former guardsman and hussar who had retired at an early age, having attained the rank of lieutenant. He belonged to the Petersburg aristocracy both on his father's and his mother's side. One of his ancestors had been a comrade-in-arms of Peter the Great. The maiden name of his mother, the Countess Catherine Andreevna, was Shuvalov. Her sister, Elizabeth Andreevna, was a lady-in-waiting at the court, and was married to a Caucasian vicegerent and adjutant-

3

general, Count Illarion Ivanovich Vorontsov-Dashkov, who was also commander-in-chief of the Caucasus military district. His magnificent residence in Tiflis (Tbilisi) has been preserved to this day and is now a recreation center for Young Pioneers and schoolchildren.

The Balashevs were very wealthy and had estates in several provinces. Peter Nicholaevich lived in the province of Podolsk, where he was quite influential. He married Princess Maria Grigorievna Kantakuzen, in whose family's coat of arms there were two imperial crowns. The Kantakuzens were of the highest international nobility.

And so the congress elected Balashev chairman. But it also elected an honorary chairman. Who? Some grand prince? No, the congress elected the son of a country miller, my stepfather, Dmitrii Ivanovich Pikhno, a professor at Kiev University. Why was he elected? Because he was the editor of the *Kievlianin*. Although the landowners did not know each other, they did know of the *Kievlianin*. It was the newspaper that expressed their feelings and molded their consciousness. The *Kievlianin* had been both program and consolation during the difficult days of 1905.

The congress resolved the following: to meet the Polish challenge head-on by doing everything possible to make sure that the Southwestern Region's delegation to the Second State Duma was not dominated by Poles; and to instruct all who attended the congress to hold elections in their districts. Since there were two representatives from Ostrozhsk—Senkevich and I—we were authorized to work there to the best of our ability.

Although I had been brought up in a political family, I had no interest whatsoever in politics. What attracted me was the history of Volyn. This manifested itself in the fact that I had begun to write a historical novel set in the sixteenth century, entitled *Prikliucheniia Kniazia Voronetskogo* ("The Adventures of Prince Voronets"). I have been writing it now for more than sixty years, since 1903. I still haven't finished it, and obviously I never will. And the volumes that were finished, including two that were typed, are now lost. Well, that's adventure for you!

The Two Generals

W E RUSSIAN LANDOWNERS from Ostrozhsk district in Volyn Province had lost the elections to the First Duma. We had not been organized at all, whereas the Poles, numbering roughly fifty-five, if I'm not mistaken, had voted as a body and somewhat ceremoniously slung mud at our candidates. In spite of this, our candidates weren't that bad. They were called "the two generals" and a song popular then was sung about them:

My dva generala,	We are two generals,
sudba nas sviazala,	Fate has united us
na ostrov poslala . . .	Here on an island . . .

General Ivkov really was a general, now retired. The old man lived quietly on his estate, where he had built an observatory. He rested during the day and spent his nights observing the stars through his telescope. He was one of those people who could predict the future. He had a presentiment that in our time, mankind, Russia specifically, would explore the universe. Earthly affairs held little interest for him. A steward managed them.

The other general was of high rank but wore narrow shoulder boards.* His name was George Ermolaevich Rein. Everyone thought his background was German, but as his physical appearance and the pronunciation of his surname as Re-ín attested, he was a pureblooded Russian. Rein was a medical doctor. Since 1874 he had been a professor-obstetrician lecturing at the military-medical academy in Petersburg. From 1880 to 1900 he had been a professor of gynecology and obstetrics at Kiev University, and then had returned to Petersburg, where he moved in the highest social circles. A famous surgeon, he had operated on Grand Duchess Elizabeth Fedorovna, the sister of Empress Alexandra Fedorovna. He had enormous energy and capacity for work, and built a model clinic in Petersburg. His goal in life was to found the ministry of public health that Russia lacked. Eventually he achieved this goal. On September 1 (14), 1916, he was appointed Minister of Public Health, but he was not able to serve even half a

---

*I.e., he was a noncombatant (trans.).

5

year, because on February 22 (March 7), 1917, several days before the fall of the empire, the Central Administration of Public Health was abolished, due to the state of emergency and the impending downfall of the government.

Of course the Poles did not have a candidate like General Rein, but they voted against him anyway. The two generals knew that they would not be elected, but they performed their civic duty and did not consider their defeat a disgrace.

That was the way it was in Ostrozhsk in 1906.

The Campaign Plan

O N THE RETURN TRIP from Kiev to Volyn, Senkevich and I realized that if we were to plan a campaign, we would need a map of the district. I happened to have a very detailed one hanging on a wall in my study in Kurgany. Even more important was the list of voters which had been typed and sent to us along with a copy of the election laws. After we studied these materials, a campaign plan became clear to us.

The Cadets and the parties to the left of them had demanded that the Duma elections be "four-sided," but only one of their four requirements had been implemented: the voting was by secret ballot but was neither universal, equal, nor direct. The elections were not universal because women, lunatics, and criminals were denied the right to vote, although women could transfer their votes to their husbands and other close relatives.* Men on active military service were also unable to take part in the elections. The elections to the Duma were not equal because voting rights were weighted according to the size of one's property. Nor were the elections direct, because they took place in several stages, as will become evident from my account of the election in the Ostrozhsk district.

* * *

Candidates for the Duma were chosen by electors at district assemblies and then sent to provincial assemblies. There were two kinds of district assembly, one consisting of delegates from the volosts (small rural districts) and the other of delegates of the large landlords. The volost form of self-government in the Russian villages had existed since time immemorial. The local volost commune was made up of all the peasant householders in the district. For this purpose anyone who owned any land at all was considered a householder, even if it was only the bit of land allotted in 1861 when the serfs were emancipated.

---

*Women could not vote, but since the franchise was based on land tenure, women who owned land in their own names controlled the vote appertaining to that land and could transfer it to someone else who was eligible to cast a ballot in the election (trans.).

As an ancient form of local self-government, the volost system was familiar to the peasants and formed the basis for the peasant elections to the Duma. The volost communes chose delegates who voted in the run-offs at the district assembly, which in turn chose delegates who voted in the provincial assembly—in our case, in Zhitomir—and it was there, finally, that the members of the Duma were elected.

The second district assembly was made up of landowners, and their voting rights depended on the size of their landholdings. Anyone who owned a plot of land could vote in the district election, but on very unequal terms. The law differentiated between large and small landowners. The word "landowner" did not appear in the law, but in those days people who had full voting rights were commonly known as landowners. Each district had its own law defining the qualifications for voters.

In Ostrozhsk ownership of 2.2 square kilometers (i.e., 540 acres) was required. Since my deed was for 3.3 square kilometers (810 acres), I was fully qualified and had the same voting rights as Germánn, the landlord who, with 109 square kilometers (27,000 acres), had the largest estate in our district. Those who owned less than 2.2 square kilometers were not qualified voters and thus had no voice in the assembly of qualified landlords, but they could "pool" their land. The "pooled" land was divided by 200 to determine how many votes they entitled to. That's how it was in Ostrozhsk.

All this seemed extremely complicated to us at first, but as we studied the elector lists, we realized that the key to victory over the Polish landowners was hidden somewhere in the myriad of regulations.

The delegates chosen by those who pooled their land were called representatives. How many appeared at the Ostrozhsk electoral assembly for the elections to the First Duma? Seven in all. And how many had the right to come, if they had chosen to exercise their rights?

The list of voters stated how much land each one had. After painstakingly calculating the size of the various plots of land, we found that all the "smalls" (this is what we called them for short), taken together, owned more than 175 square kilometers. Dividing this sum by 200, we came to a staggering realization: if the small landowners made full use of the rights to which their lands entitled them, they could send eighty representatives to the Ostrozhsk provincial electoral assembly. Eighty representatives! This meant that the representatives of the small landowners, not the large landowners, would be in control of the elections.

In fact, even if all the fully qualified large landowners, Russian and Polish, worked together, they still would not number eighty. But since a percentage of the Russian landlords would be on our side, it was not crucial for us to have eighty representatives (this is a hypothetical number); fewer then eighty would also outnumber the Poles, since only fifty-five Poles had voted in the elections for the First Duma, the maximum they could muster then or now.

* * *

But how does one get, say, forty electors for the Second Duma out of the seven who turned up for the first?

We carefully studied the list of voters. The properties of the small landowners were quite varied in size. Two or three landowners had about 1.1 square kilometers apiece. There were many with average-sized plots and scores with small plots. How could we reach all these people?

Further study revealed that they fell into three groups. First, there were the rural priests. For many years each church in our country had been allotted a certain amount of land. This had been done since ancient times. Russian landowners, and sometimes Poles also, would allot each church in their domain a plot of land on which the priests would live. The voting laws for the Duma specified that these church lands gave the clergy the right to act as electors at district assemblies on an equal basis with private landowners. There were more than one hundred parishes in the Ostrozhsk district. The size of the landholdings varied, but on the average, each parish owned half a square kilometer. Thus, if the priests exercised their rights to the full, they could send forty representatives.

The second group of small landowners were the Czechs. Empress Catherine II, surmising that actual example would have a favorable influence on the Russian peasants, invited German and Czech peasants, both crowded in their own countries, to move to Russia. The Tsarina thought that the Russian peasants would begin to imitate the foreign settlers; she was convinced that modern agricultural methods gave better results than primitive methods. The settlers were allotted small plots next to those of the natives.

Catherine's plan proved fruitful. By the beginning of the twentieth century we had quite a few people of German and Czech extraction in Volyn. They prospered. It was said that when they owned only sixteen acres they lived like a small landlord, but a percentage of the descendants of the Germans and Czechs became wealthy landlords and bought land.

The most striking example was a man named Faltsfein in Kherson Province. He was very wealthy and founded a huge preserve on the Kherson steppes, with the most varied animals and birds, including ostriches.

In Volyn there were also settlers who became wealthy. I knew one named Arngt, a most pleasant man. His grandfather had been a simple settler, but Ivan Ilianovich already had 11 square kilometers. He lived well but frugally, without unnecessary luxury or waste. His luxuries were his daughters, healthy young ladies who were educated, but had not lost touch with the village or household chores, as had our Russian young ladies. The latter were brought up with the assumption that they would always have maids and cooks, which was not the way it turned out.

In the Ostrozhsk district were mainly the settlers of Czech extraction. Only one of them was wealthy enough to join the ranks of the qualified landlords. The rest were in the category of small landowners; that is, they could send delegates to the electoral assembly only by pooling their lands.

The third group of voters consisted of peasants who owned their own land—that is, who had bought some land apart from their allotments. They had two types of voting rights: in the volost communes because of their allotments, and also as owners of real property. The peasant ranks were quite varied. I knew one old man who was barely literate but owned 6.5 square kilometers of good land and gave all four of his sons a university education. It goes without saying that he was a fully qualified landlord.

There were other fully qualified voters among the peasants. Now I'm talking about peasants with real property, but on a small scale. The majority had small plots, 1 hectare and up, but when their lands were pooled they formed a significant group. The problem was, how to reach them?

The Priests

I N PONDERING THE situation we realized that it was impossible to set up any sort of propaganda machine. We didn't have the people, the money, or the time. I was somewhat experienced. My horse Vaska became involved in the elections for the Second Duma, because in the summer of 1906 I rode him all around the Ostrozhsk district. Like Chichikov,* I raced after dead souls, arousing them for the good of society. Experience taught me that each soul took up at least one day. There were several hundred souls. There were four months left before the election. And what months! Dirty, snowy, rainy, and stormy. It was obvious that Chichikovian methods would not work.

The newspapers? But these people didn't read newspapers. Leaflets? They wouldn't read them or understand them. What was left?

The priests! There were no less than one hundred of them in our district. There was one in every village, and between them they knew almost all of the people in their districts by name. Further, by law they themselves were participants in the elections. The priests were the key to the situation.

Our priest, that is, the priest of our parish, was Father Peter. He was a most worthy man. One day he told me that the local clergy regarded me well, except for one thing.

"What, exactly?"

"Why do you drive a Polish four-in-hand?"

"And what if I told you it was a bishop's four-in-hand?"

"How is that?"

"Didn't you know that the Metropolitan of Kiev and Galicia has ridden in this type of four-in-hand from time immemorial?"

He could not argue because it was the truth. But the important thing was that if a man as worthy as Father Peter declared himself not only a Russian nationalist but also a chauvinist, it meant that the priests would support any action against the Polish landlords.

That is how it turned out. We organized a pre-election committee,

---

*The conniving hero of Gogol's novel *Dead Souls* (1842), who made money buying dead serfs (trans.).

and even the Ostrozhsk protopresbyter joined. It must be said that the clergy was the most disciplined class in Russia. The opinion of the protopresbyter was important, if not the only important thing. We believed that the priests would do as the committee asked. And what did the committee ask of the priests? Nothing contrary to their holy vows. Not propaganda. Our main enemy had showed himself at the First Duma—the absenteeism of the voters. And this is where the priests could help.

I wrote and sent out more than one hundred postcards with the same message: "In your parish, Honorable Father so-and-so, live so-and-so. It is incumbent upon them to participate in the election to the State Duma in such-and-such a place on such-and-such a date. The pre-election committee asks you to remind them of their duty on the Sunday nearest the election, after services."

In essence, these innocent postcards settled the matter.

*   *   *

I now turn to the election.

The decisive day was on us in no time—the election of the representatives of the small landowners.

What would be the result of our tactics and strategy?

On the morning of the decisive day, when I looked at the thermometer, I thought, "What can we expect when there's 30 degrees of frost? Who will come?" A frost of 30 degrees Reaumur, 40 centigrade, is highly unusual for Volyn.

But the frost did not scare them. They all turned up! They came in droves. But the elections almost fell through for a reason that would have been hard to foresee.

At all the polling places in the district there was the same thing: a great majority of small-landowner electors. For the sake of simplicity I will refer to them as "one-hectares." They soon realized how much power they had and decided to elect delegates only from among their own ranks, that is, from among the poor. Then the more prosperous landowners said, "If that's the way it is, why should we stay here and freeze? Let's go home. They can elect themselves without us." At this point our propagandists saved the day. They went to the one-hectares and said, "There are many of you, but you don't have much land."

"Well, so?"

"The fact is, right before the elections they will add up the amount of land. The sum total of land. They will count only the land of those who attended the assembly here. And they will not add the land of those who are already harnessing up their horses to drive home. They will drive away and take their land with them. They will count only the land of you poor people. And you will choose the delegates you want, but how many will you have? Few, because there are many of you but you have little land. And our delegates in Ostrog, at the district assembly, will not be able to outvote the Poles, and no one will get to the Duma."

The one-hectares understood. And they sent a message to the well-to-do landowners: "Don't leave. Don't take your land away. We will come to an agreement somehow."

* * *

"And did you come to an agreement?"
"Yes."
"And—?"
"You won't believe it! All told, in the three polling places sixty delegates were elected. Sixty!!! And there were seven for the First Duma! Who could have guessed?"

* * *

Indeed, this was a victory that was hard to believe. If every single person on the list had come there would have been eighty delegates. Sixty was 78 percent of the highest possible number.

These days, when 99.9 percent of the population takes part in elections, a 78 percent turnout is not impressive. But it was different then. Not long ago, in the city elections in Brussels, the capital of Belgium, the number of people who went up to the ballot box reached 75 percent of the maximum. This was announced everywhere as an excellent example of conscientious citizenship.

But that's Brussels and this is Volyn. The populace was not at all ready. There was a 30-degree frost; besides, we did not have the money, or the people, to agitate among the populace and drum up support.

"This was all done thanks to the priests," I said.

"Thanks to your postcards!" they answered.

"The priests' and your doing. You reconciled the poor and the rich brilliantly. Three cheers for the peacemakers!"

We thus praised each other in our happiness. Then I said, "Let's celebrate, but let's not overdo it. We have sixty delegates. In addition, there are twenty large landowners who will very likely be on our side. The Poles have fifty-five votes at the most. Eighty beats fifty-five handily if—"

"If they don't fight!"

The Landlords

THE DAY OF the district elections arrived. There were misgivings that many of the sixty delegates would not come. But they all did. The twenty Russian landlords also arrived, although they would have numbered sixty if everyone who was listed had attended. But all fifty-five Poles attended as a unified bloc.

They boasted, not without justification, "We forced even those who were in Paris, Nice, and Monte Carlo to come."

As always, some of the Russians were heroes, and some were Oblomovs.* One landlord, who lived in a nearby valley, subsequently became a member of the Third Duma and a friend of mine. The following happened to him. At the time of a certain election in Podolsk Province, he and his wife were in Ceylon. The husband was hunting tigers, and the wife was admiring how the natives fished for pearls. They received a telegram from friends: "Your attendance at the elections is required."

He left his wife to her pearl fishing and returned home alone. At that time there were no airplanes. One had to sail across oceans and seas and race in express trains. He arrived on the day of the election; without saying a word to anyone, because he was a quiet man by nature, he dropped his ballot in the box, and the next day departed for Ceylon, again sailing across the ocean, and shot his tiger.

We in the Ostrozhsk district did not have such Ceylonese heroes, but George Emolaevich Rein arrived from Petersburg, deserting his academy and clinic. And the astonomer, General Ivkov, although he remained in his observatory, sent in his vote with his steward, Lashinsky, as was permitted.

Baron Meller-Zakomelskii came to make jokes, as always. A year before he had sent a telegram to Baron Shtakelberg, who was the governor of Volyn. The telegram read: "If Your Honor does not make an effort to put an end to the anarchy in the province that was entrusted to him, then I will declare myself dictator of the Ostrozhsk

---

*Oblomov, the hero of A. I. Goncharov's novel of the same name (1859), came to signify the chronic physical and spiritual laziness, passivity, and apathy of Russia's landowners (trans.).

14

district and will restore order myself." While in the city of Rovno, having sent the telegram, he had a bite to eat with his son. Returning home to Vitkov, his estate, he decided to test his dictatorial powers on his youthful boon companion, since the boy was daring him to. Ten kilometers from home, he threw his son out of the carriage and into the snow, and told his driver, "After him!"

This incident was related to me by my driver, Andrew, who had previously worked as a driver for Meller-Zakomelskii.

* * *

I want to say a few words about this boy (Meller-Zakomelskii's son). We had hopes for him, and he fulfilled them. A university friend of his, the son of a famous professor, decided to get married in his last semester. Having asked the young baron to be his best man, he had him bring the bride to the church. The clever best man carried out the request and drove the bride to church, but to a different church, where he married her himself. Then the newlyweds ran away, even though no one was after them. But that was more romantic. They ran off into the dense forest, where there were great oaks past which I used to drive. A little away from the road stood a forester's hut. There the young couple spent a relatively quiet honeymoon, because the forest belonged to Baron Meller-Zakomelskii Senior.

When the honeymoon was over, the youthful baroness moved to Vitkovo, became an accomplished horsewoman, and rode dashingly with her husband. And then— Then came the war. The "hero" in quotes became a hero without quotes. He volunteered for the army, received two St. George medals, and was killed.

* * *

And the old baron—this was, of course, before the loss of his son— did his duty; that is, he made jokes.

During the elections to the Second State Duma, upon his arrival in Ostrog, he started in by going to the stable of the Hotel Europa, more simply, Shrier's. We all stayed overnight there. The baron was interested in horses. Seeing my "Polish" team of four silver horses which I had purchased at fairs, and which the driver had fed much too much, in spite of the hard and fast journey, Zakomelskii said to Andrew, "What do you feed them? No doubt the *Kievlianin?*"

After that he went into the hotel. There his wife was scolding Rukhtso Shrier, who was an extremely clever Jewish woman. She kept not only her weak-willed husband well in hand but also Zussman, the chief timber merchant of the district, and through him she was able to have an influence on the entire surrounding area. The baroness was railing against Rukhtso because she had given room no. 1 to Rein and not to her, the baroness. All the rooms in the hotel were rotten, but no. 1 was a tiny bit bigger. But Rukhtso did what she did because she knew everything in the past and everything in the future, and she knew that there was no way the baron was going to be elected. The baron came in, in the middle of the quarrel, and said something to his wife in French. Rukhtso did not speak French, but somehow she understood what he said to his wife. And afterwards she recounted the story: "He said to her, 'Why are you acting like that? Isn't it because you're a baroness? But you're a baroness only because I'm a baron.'"

Breakfast followed. Several of us had breakfast in room no. 1 with Rein. We were having scrambled eggs. Zakomelskii was being witty and, speaking of Ivkov, said, "He's not only an astronomer but a decent person. But he can't be elected. He has scrambled eggs instead of brains." Lashinsky, Ivkov's steward, had been invited to have breakfast with us. He felt uncomfortable hearing this. He said, "Baron, you say those things, but the general likes you very much!"

The baron was a bit embarrassed but recovered right away. "Likes me? He likes me? Well I also—I just adore scrambled eggs!"

*   *   *

In short, everyone acted according to his own nature. But the situation was not that simple. We were faced with having to elect five people from the Ostrozhsk district.

Ostrog

Thus, five would go to Zhitomir and there, along with others, would elect the members of the State Duma. Each one of the five, perhaps, would be a deputy.

Only five! The fact was that the electors, who numbered seventy-nine, included four very different groups of people, although they were split pretty evenly. The representatives of the small landowners presented a curious picture: there were twenty priests, nineteen Czechs, twenty-one peasant-farmers. Then there were nineteen Russian landlords.

All four groups met separately, but all came to the same conclusion: the priests, Czechs, farmers, and landlords should each send one representative, which was four altogether. But what about the fifth? It would have been generous to give the fifth to the minority, the Poles. But there was no magnanimous feeling for the Poles. The generosity appeared in a different form.

The small landowners held long conferences. Afterwards their delegates came to us, the landlords, and said, "There are more of us—twenty-one. Some thought we should rightly have the fifth delegate. But after thinking about it, we all decided that that wouldn't be right. The fifth spot should be given to the Russian landlords; so it turns out that two landlords will be chosen and only one each of the other groups. Why did we decide on this? Because we understand very well what you did, that without you nothing would have been done, and the Poles would have elected only Poles, that's why."

This barrier had seemed to me to be the hardest. Four detachments of troops could start a battle over something as trivial as a fifth place. When now, in my old age, I observe the international quarrels between countries, it sometimes seems to me that certain leaders and rulers have a long way to go before they attain the spirit of concession and the love of peace that the Volynians showed toward one another at the end of April, 1907, in the city of Ostrog.

* * *

Now only personal questions remained. Who would be the unfortunate fortunate ones who would be sent to Zhitomir?

The four groups allowed each other full freedom in this; that is, they would not object to each other's candidates. Thus, all that was left for us, the landlords, to do was to nominate two candidates from among the "landlords." And here the thing I had been afraid of occurred.

* * *

At that time I was twenty-nine. Until then—that is, until the State Duma—I had taken little part in public life, nor had I distinguished myself in any other way. Furthermore, there was another consideration: by law, one had to be twenty-five years of age to be elected to the State Duma. But there was also another law, an unwritten one, by which older people were usually nominated for important public posts. I thought that these two conditions would be sufficient to guarantee that I would be spared any such laborious unpleasantness. That was how I thought of a seat in the Duma. I had absolutely no desire to become a slave to politics. I wanted to live in the country, dabble in the running of the estate, work on my novel, *Prikliucheniia Kniazia Voronetskogo*. I did not object to becoming involved in the zemstvo. I had been appointed marshal of the fire brigade. I liked galloping to the scene of a fire on Vaska and making out reports on the spot, thus speeding up the payment of insurance claims, which was important to the claimants, but I did not aspire to any loftier occupation, and did not plan to put out fires all over Russia. I wasn't born for battle and strife. But fate had different plans for me. I became involved unwillingly in the elections in the Ostrozhsk district.

* * *

"Seven representatives attended the elections for the First Duma. Now there are sixty! Who is responsible for that? Shulgin and Senkevich. Then send them!" Such was the cry of the landowning crowd.

I didn't want to go; I asked to be spared. But they persuaded me with the following reasoning. "So you don't want to go to the Duma? Well, the Duma is a long way off. Preside over the elections in Zhitomir. There will be all sorts of things going on there."

Senkevich was luckier. He was able to get out of it. Besides, we had a most excellent candidate in G. E. Rein, the academician-professor, extremely energetic and efficient, with connections in the capital. Furthermore, he clearly wanted to become part of the Russian Parliament. It suited him. It would be easier for him to create a ministry of public health, the goal of his life, through this route. At the conferences that preceded the elections he was invariably elected chairman, and I, secretary. It was clear: these two would have to go to Zhitomir.

However, the Poles were not sleeping during all this. They came up with a plan to stop the elections, but I realized this too late and they did stop the elections. They used a curious method. The Elovitskiis had owned the Ozhenino estate for a very long time, for centuries. They traced their ancestry to Prince Sviatopol-Chetvertinsky and at one time had lived in Chetvertna. At that time they were Russian and Orthodox, and only later became Polish. At any rate this was a native Volyn aristocracy. The young Witold Gratsianovich Elovitskii had received his law degree with me in Kiev. He also worked for my step-father in the political science department. Elovitskii was about the only Pole who sometimes would visit his professor during the summer. And it was he who cunningly broke off the elections.

In the absence of the Marshal of the Nobility, an arbitrator presided over the district assembly in Ostrog. There was no such duty in western Russia; there they were called "heads of the zemstvo." Ilia Pavlovich Ivashkevich was a most dear man. By the way, while driving around the district, he liked to call on us in Kurgany, and every time he did, he told the same story. He, Ilia Pavlovich, was once for some reason driving in a coach with Bishop Platon, the Metropolitan of Kiev and Galicia. As they drove through a small town, past a Catholic church, the bells chimed, the usual salutation for a high-ranking cleric, but considering the relations between the Catholics and the Orthodox, rather unusual. The bishop stopped the coach, entered the church, blessed the Roman Catholic priest, and listened to a short service. Then he got into his coach and drove on. But this occurrence made an indelible impression on Ilia Pavlovich, and every time he told the story, his eyes filled with tears and his head shook. He was not a senile old man.

If he had wished, he could have functioned as an arbitrator, but instead he merely presided over this assembly so riven by a struggle between nationalities. Ilia Pavlovich was a bit shaken by his task; he was not used to presiding over an assembly of this kind, and that was what Witold Gratsianovich was counting on.

The meeting opened with a reading of the laws for election to the Duma. After the laws were read, Elovitskii asked for the floor and demanded some clarification from the chairman. Ilia Pavlovich became confused as he explained. Afterwards more questions were asked; he became even more confused. It became apparent to me that Elovitskii was making a scene in order to have grounds for invalidating the elections. It was not for nothing that he had become a lawyer. In order to help Ilia Pavlovich I asked to have the floor and explained the law. But I was angry with the Poles, and especially with Elovitski, for engaging in provocation. At this point, several words that should never have been said escaped my lips.

The problem was that the law categorically forbade agitation on election day. Any agitating was to end on the eve of the elections. And my words, which I do not now remember, evidently could be considered agitation. As soon as I began to speak in this vein, the Poles shouted "Listen, Listen!"

I understood and became quiet. But the deed could not be undone.

After this the Poles stopped asking for explanations of the law, and the elections went smoothly.

Five boxes were set up with our names; we received exactly seventy-nine votes for and fifty-five votes against. The only thing left was to go to Zhitomir. The elections of the members of the State Duma were slated for February 6(19).

But Witold Gratsianovich turned out to be more clever than I. His ancestors had been involved in elections and campaign tactics for centuries in the Sejm.* In short, Elovitskii lodged a cessation complaint on the grounds that the elections had taken place in violation of the law. And the governor annulled the elections, scheduling new ones to take place very soon. It was impossible to use the usual formal means, advertisements, to inform the electors that they would have to return to Ostrog. The date could not be moved ahead, because in that case the representatives from Ostrog would not have been able to arrive in Zhitomir in time for the elections to the Duma. This was the basis for Witold Gratsionovich's clever plan, but he had not taken a certain circumstance into consideration.

Back in the days of the Sejm there was no telegraph, but now in 1906 there was such a thing, and it did not work badly. Each telegraph office was attended by a village boy, a youthful herald who delivered telegrams to every village or estate, on foot, in all weather, day or night. The boys were called special messengers, and were paid ten kopecks per kilometer by the sender. The address would read: "To such-and-such a place by special messenger, for so-and-so." If he desired, the recipient could give the boy a tip, but money was dear in those days. A boy who delivered twenty-five telegrams, each distance averaging ten kilometers, could buy himself a nice horse for twenty-five rubles. Witold Gratsionovich had not taken this into consideration. I sent about eighty telegrams, which cost me roughly two hundred rubles. This did not ruin me, and the boys set out on a

---

*Volyn, or Volhynia, had been part of Poland until the end of the eighteenth century, when the country was partitioned by Russia, Prussia, and Austria, hence the presence of a substantial Polish population in the region. The Sejm, independent Poland's parliamentary body, was proverbial for political maneuvering and casuistry, but since all members of the Polish aristocracy and landed gentry (the *szlachta*) were automatically members, Shlugin's implication that the Polish landowners had experience with electoral politics from the era of the Sejm is not really accurate (trans.).

marathon run to all corners of the district. The result? All sixty qualified voters arrived as one. The telegraph is not to be scoffed at! For it was the first telegram they had ever received in their lives, and perhaps the last. The twelve landlords also came. The elections took place again, and the fifty-five Poles went down to defeat again.

* * *

And so, Ostrog was taken by storm for the second time. We had won! Now five people had to go to Zhitomir to elect deputies to the State Duma from Volyn Province. The five were: two Russian landlords (G. E. Rein and myself), one Russian peasant, one Russian priest, and one Czech. Since we lived far away from one another, each of us went to Zhitomir on his own. Election day was February 6 (19). Looking at the snowy fields sparkling beyond the windows of the coach, I could not possibly imagine what awaited me.

* * *

One could live cheaply in the cozy houses in Zhitomir, but there were fine stores on the main street, some of them the pride of the city. Gloves from Zhitomir were famous throughout the land. Well-dressed Polish women, smiling like ballerinas, earrings dancing proudly, sold excellent perfume. High-quality coffee awaited us in the cafes. Polish ladies would say enchantingly, "Prosę pana" and "bardzo dziękuję" ("please," "thank you"), but not without some self-importance. They knew their own worth.

* * *

On the main street there were two hotels opposite each other. The Poles occupied the grander one; I forget its name. We Russians took the more modest one. The Ostrozhsk uprising had ended in victory for us, but what would happen in Zhitomir?

* * *

Neither the Polish gentlemen nor the Russian landlords could get to the heart of the matter. The ratio of power, that is, the number of electors from the various groups, was such that no single group had a majority; consequently an agreement was necessary. The peasants were the most numerous. They were electors sent by the volosts, that is, by the peasants with land allotments, and by the peasants who owned land in addition to the allotments. By nationality they were Russians, or as they were called then, Little Russians, now called Ukrainians.

The Polish landowners formed the second-largest group, and the Russian landowners, the third. The fourth consisted of townspeople, almost all of whom were Jews. Russian priests made up the fifth group, and finally, Czechs and Germans formed the sixth.

On the basis of nationality there were two groups: the first consisting of Russian landowners, priests, and peasants, and Czech and German settlers; the second being the Poles and the Jewish townspeople.

On the basis of class there could be a bloc of all landowners regardless of nationality. If this alliance were joined by the Jewish townspeople, it would have a majority. This could be a serious temptation. The revolution was about to turn the propertied classes into beggars, and it would have been natural for the robbed to combine in a struggle against the robbers. Then the robbers would be men who were promised the landowners' property. According to Marxist theory, that is the way it should have been, but at the time in Volyn this was not the case—the idea of national unity, upheld by the church, prevailed. Under the conditions of 1907, a bloc composed of Russian landowners, Poles, and Jews became impossible. Thus the robbed decided to unite with those who under certain circumstances could become the robbers—could become, but as yet were not. The Volyn farmers were gentle souls; moreover, the restraining hand of the clergy made itself felt.

*   *   *

So the Russian landowners seized Rome, meaning they took over the Rome Hotel in Zhitomir. At meetings in the Rome Hotel, as well as at joint lunches and dinners, it was ascertained that the Russian landowners stood firm: We did not desire an alliance with the Poles and Jews. We must join with the peasants.

Thus we lived in the Rome Hotel. Where did the peasants room? They were offered shelter by the church. Archbishop Anthony, through two assistants, Archimandrite Vitalii and Hieromonk Iliodor, very skillfully fulfilled his Christian duty of saving souls. The electors were simple people completely at a loss when confronted by such a difficult task as choosing from their dark midst people who would help govern the people. Help whom? The Tsar himself! That was how their duty appeared to them. They were quite happy when the gentle monks met them at the train station. In addition to giving them free shelter and sustenance, Archimandrite Vitalii and the monk Iliodor began teaching them how to act properly, that is, how to conduct themselves during the election and later in the State Duma.

The peasants already knew that they would be paid ten rubles per day for their services. Ten rubles! To these people such a sum was beyond their wildest dreams. Those who had completed their schooling knew that if, God willing, the Duma remained in session for the entire five years, as planned, each of them would receive 18,250 rubles. The gray-haired peasant would become not simply a prosperous farmer, like the Czechs and Germans, but a genuine landlord. However, the monks should have explained to them that in order to become a landlord in five years, one must get along with those who were already landlords, with those who were staying at the Hotel Rome, with those would be voting for the State Duma. Without their help not a single peasant would become a landlord. This is what the monks should have said; however, they did not.

I realized this when I met Archimandrite Vitalii for the first time. He was sitting in a corner of a big room in the monastery, not the sacred corner, under the icon, but the opposite corner. An awkward scene ensued. I crossed myself not while facing the icon, as was proper, but while facing the archimandrite. I made it acceptable by approaching him for his blessing. After giving me his blessing, he asked me to sit down on the bench next to him and, with a searching look, said simply, in a low voice, "The people speak well of you."

I was both gladdened and embarrassed, and answered, "I owe that to my stepfather. He sometimes helped others."

"And you yourself?"

He smiled almost imperceptibly, thereby softening the severity of the question, which was more an interrogation. I also smiled and answered easily, "I want to help now."

"In what way?"

"I speak for the Russian landowners. We will not side with the Poles and the Jews."

"Commendable. It would be to your advantage. You would have a majority."

"An advantage is not always advantageous. We want to go with the Russian people, of whom we are a part. But I foresee difficulties."

"Of what sort?"

"Difficulties could arise when the seats are divided."

"How, exactly?"

"There are thirteen seats in all. We must decide how many will go to each group."

"And how do you see it?"

"I'll begin with the easy part. The clergy—one seat, Czechs and Germans together—one seat also."

"I have no objection. That leaves eleven."

"That leaves eleven. Here is what we thought: four seats for the landlords, seven for the peasants. That makes eleven."

I stopped, expecting a reply. But the reply did not come immediately. Evidently the archimandrite was thinking about two things.

Would he be able to persuade the peasants to agree, and could he believe the landlords? Would they be led into temptation? After all, the Poles and the Jews would probably offer them a better deal.

I didn't scrutinize the archimandrite as much as try to understand his inner essence. Lean face, sunken eyes. He fasted strictly and slept on bare boards, perhaps the same wooden boards on which we were sitting. His beard was sparse, not because he shaved, but because it did not grow. At the time it did not occur to me that Christ was portrayed in the same fashion. Something indescribable issued from this man. He spoke softly, asked sensible, grave questions, and followed my simple arithmetic, concealing, however, quite complicated emotional reactions. I was the resultant force of the people who supported me. Was I acting in response to their wishes? It seemed as if the Archimandrite Vitalii knew something that I did not know, that perhaps no one else knew, and this single important something was the essence of this man. Both his appearance and his soft-spoken words were the unimportant things connecting him to the world. In the same way, the silent icon lamp, burning brightly, was the most important thing in the room. The rest—floor, ceiling, benches, the table with a piece of bread lying on it—were unavoidable tributes to a vain world. The simple people felt this ascetic's good "something" and were his followers.

When this instant of mystical thought had passed, the archimandrite said, "We will help you."

He did not express himself precisely, because an "icon lamp" is modest, but I understood. He meant, "God will help you. He will not only help me—the icon lamp radiates light to everyone, prays on behalf of all and for all."

We met in a large hall: peasants, landlords, priests, Germans and Czechs. The peasants were neither primitive nor colorful rustics out of a pastorale. They were pureblooded farmers—as genuine as the black soil of Volyn. Some were dressed in homespun sweaters with homemade buttons and buckles; others were in sheepskins with the wool on the inside. Their faces were familiar, not malicious but friendly. Chroniclers of the seventh century have written that in the sixth century the peasants attacked Tsargrad.* At that time, one must realize, they were not noted for their good nature. Fourteen centuries have passed and people have mellowed. But conceited people, considering themselves cultured, had done everything in their power to return the peaceful farmers to a brutish life.

* * *

---

*Slavic name for Constantinople (trans.).

A grayish-brown blotch of sweaters and sheepskins occupied two-thirds of the room, regarding us expectantly. We in our frockcoats, starched white collars, and ties examined ancient Russia in coarse cloth and tried to guess her thoughts.

Before 1905 we had been able to sense her feelings, but the past two years had rocked the entire country. The general sentiment in the country was revolutionary. Would peaceful Volyn yield to it?

* * *

I do not remember how it started. Leaders singled themselves out from the masses. They spoke the language which our Volynians used after having served in the army—a mixture of standard Russian and local dialect.

No! These people did not want violence. They wanted an agreement with the Russian landowners, but they did not want one with the Polish landowners or the Jews. This showed that we were as one in our feelings, so for that reason talk turned to the distribution of the seats. At this point the ship of harmony struck an iceberg. We quickly dealt with the priests and the settlers, each group receiving one seat in the State Duma. There the talks came to a stop. The landowners wanted four seats, for themselves and seven for the peasants, while the latter offered the landowners three seats and demanded eight for themselves. They took a firm stand on this point. Both sides attempted to give their reasons, but what kind of reasons could there be when people were simply haggling with each other? The peasants said that they did not want to cheat anyone, but that three seats for the landowners would be sufficient. Meanwhile, the landowners maintained that it would be only fair to give them four seats in the Duma. Both positions had their fair and unfair aspects, so neither could be convincingly argued. We parted with sour faces but decided, nevertheless, to meet again the following day.

* * *

The Russian landowners staying at the Hotel Rome reviewed the situation over dinner. One of the Poles had suggested that all the landowners unite; then, with the help of the Jews, they would have a majority. It was resolved to reject a coalition with the Poles and Jews and stand firm with regard to the peasants. We would demand four seats. If this was refused we would leave, that is, not take part in the elections. And I was instructed to announce our unanimous decision.

* * *

We met for the second time. Again we tried to persuade the stubborn ones. But no, they would not give in. Then I rose and with a tremor in my voice said, "The Poles and the Jews have offered to side with us, thereby giving us a majority. And we could have chosen whomever we pleased and however many [seats] we pleased. But we turned them down. We are Russians and did not want to go against our fellow Russians. But it turns out that we cannot side with our own people. You are quite stubborn, brother farmers. Who will we side with? No one. I hereby announce that we Russian landowners will not take part in the elections and are leaving. Farewell!"

And so we left the hall. But no one wanted to travel at night. Where could we go? It goes without saying that we returned to the Hotel Rome for dinner. During dinner some of the landowners drank a bit too much, from sorrow, evidently, and somehow we all began to feel at home with each other. Our spirits rose because we felt like heroes, in the sense of "I will lay down my life for the Tsar, for Russia!"* Many people were smoking; there was a fog in the room. Suddenly the waiter bowed to me and said quietly, "Someone is asking to see you."

"Where?"

"On the porch."

"Who?"

"A peasant."

"Are you sure he's asking for me?"

"Quite sure."

Unnoticed, I slipped out of the embrace of the tobacco smoke and stepped out onto the porch. There were several men waiting there. They were the stubborn ones, a peasant named Garkav at their head, with a Cross of St. George on his chest. I knew him well. He had done most of the talking yesterday and today. And now he turned to me and said, "We came to you, even though you left us. We came to tell you. We need three Russian landowners."

"Why?"

"We're ignorant people. We don't know how to act there at that State Duma. You'll tell us. That's why we need three Russian land-owners. We don't care who; dig up anyone you want! We want you and two others, whoever you name."

I answered, "We want four, as you know. But I'll tell the others exactly what you said."

They bowed and left.

* * *

One other landowner had been present for this discussion. He had, accidentally or not, followed me out to the porch. This made my

---

*A Russian patriotic motto of the period (trans.).

position somewhat easier. Entering the cloud of smoke, I said, "Your attention, please!"

The smoke did not disperse but the talking died down. I related the conversation, omitting only the demand that I "appoint" two others. But the one who had heard our talk from the wings blabbed everything. I added, "I presume that this does not reverse our decision not to go to the election?"

But there was no reply to my question. And then someone said, "I think it does reverse it. We must attend the election but vote for our four candidates. If the peasants change their minds, then they will elect four. If they are obstinate, they will elect three. After all, it's better to have three seats than none at all!"

"If that's how it has to be," said someone, "then we must decide quickly who to send to the Duma. Let us choose four men immediately, and they will cast their votes tomorrow."

This we did.

* * *

In the morning, fourteen ballot boxes with the names of the candidates were lined up in the hall. The peasants ceremoniously came up and dropped their ballots into the boxes. Some thought that they would become confused about how to vote, but no, they voted for a priest, Father Damian of Gershtansk; a Czech, Ivan Fedorovich Drboglav; eight peasants, including Michael Fedoseevich Garkav; and three landowners, George Ermolaevich Rein, Gregory Nicholaevich Beliaev, and myself. They cast nay votes for our fourth candidate. As far as I can remember, the Poles and the Jews did not nominate any candidates but gave nay votes to all of ours.

The end. That vote sounded the death knell for me. I was buried alive forever—a politician who hated politics.

* * *

In church Archbishop Anthony conducted a commemorative service. The choir sang enchantingly, but to me the service seemed a requiem for the dead. On February 6 (19), 1907, I bade farewell to my freedom.

The Duma

F EBRUARY 20 (MARCH 5), 1907, was a gloomy day, one of those days that Dostoevsky described so well. That day an otherwise brilliant St. Petersburg lay before me, gray and dreary. I rode along busy Shpalerna Street, crowded not with people who looked like bureaucrats, as one might expect, but with members of the intelligentsia. And in contrast with the gloomy skies, the crowds looked happy and animated.

In front and in back of me stretched a line of carriages like mine, all carrying deputies like myself. There was nothing unusually grand about them. People greeted the local deputies with shouts and waves; I, of course, was not hailed. Who would know me, a simple country boy? Here and there stood policemen; nobody paid any attention to them.

Finally we arrived at the Tauride Palace, a sprawling, peaceful-looking building with columns in front and a dome perched like a hat on top. It was only a few steps up to the entrance, where a majestic-looking porter took my hat.

I later learned that the porter was a retired soldier whom the sculptor Paulo Trubetskoi had used as the model for his monument to Alexander III.* The porter was roughly a head taller than I and built like a giant.

Then I found myself amid the swirling crowd of deputies in the so-called Round Hall, saw the majestic columns of the Catherine Hall, and finally entered the sanctum—the assembly chamber of the plenum of the State Duma. It reminded me of a university auditorium but on a grand scale. Above the amphitheater on three sides was a gallery with white columns. On the fourth side was the rostrum, and above it, the Chairman's rostrum, carved of heavy oak. Above it hung a full-length portrait of the Tsar by Repin.† All this was quite impressive. To tell the truth, I had never seen such a hall.

---

*Paul (also known as Paulo) Trubetshoi (1867?–1938), Russian impressionist sculptor. In his monument, Alexander III was portrayed as heavy-set man with grotesque features (trans.).

†Ilya Efimovich Repin (1844–1930), Russian naturalist painter (trans.).

Aside from the members of the State Duma whom I had met in the preceding days, I did not know anyone.

The session began after a prayer service. I took a seat on the right with a group of deputies considered either "right-wing" or "moderate." The difference was that the right-wingers tended to be outspoken and excitable, while the moderates, naturally, expressed themselves with restraint.

To our left were the so-called Octobrists, the group that had adopted as their program the manifesto of October 17 (30), the so-called constitution.* However, neither the right nor the Cadets would acknowledge that word, the right because they valued the sovereign's autocracy, and the Cadets because they felt "constitution" meant an English parliament, that is, a government elected by a parliament. Those more to the left, the various socialist groups, did not recognize the autocracy or the constitution. They wanted a revolution.

There was commotion and chatter, then silence. I. Ia. Golubev, member of the Privy Council, approached the Chairman's rostrum. He was wearing a full-dress coat embroidered in gold, with a blue ribbon across the shoulder. He had been commanded by special decree of the Emperor† to open the second convocation of the State Duma.

The first convocation had been dissolved by order of the Emperor before its term was over, "insofar as the representatives of the people, instead of engaging in legislative work, became involved in an area that did not concern them." The First State Duma lasted from April 27 (May 10) to July 8 (21), 1906, or seventy-three days.

What was in store for the Second State Duma? No one could say at the time, but there was some foreboding. The majority of deputies had already taken a position either with the Cadets, who at that time were very fiery, or with the socialists. The latter included thirty-seven Socialist Revolutionaries—in essence, terrorists.

What was the general impression made by the Second State Duma?

I know the opinion of the Chairman, F. A. Golovin, which, of course, was far from impartial, but quite interesting. He says,

> The left-wing faction of the Duma unintentionally shocked the onlooker with its great number of persons who seemed young for the responsible

---

*The "October Manifesto" of Tsar Nicholas II, proclaimed in the aftermath of the Revolution of 1905, promised a series of measures that supposedly ensured the basic civil liberties, a form of representative government, and a legislature with real power (trans.).

†Here and throughout the book, Shulgin uses the terms "Tsar" and "Emperor" interchangeably (trans.).

work of representing the people; moreover, these young people did not even look intelligent. Against the background of this uncultured left-wing youth, here and there one would spot the serious, intelligent faces of some educated socialists, Socialist Revolutionaries, two or three Trudoviks and Social Democrats. But I repeat, in general, the left gave the impression of an uneducated and angry youth, drunk with unexpected, recent success. Nevertheless, their faith in the infallibility of their ideas and their unquestionable unselfishness and readiness to sacrifice themselves in order to advance their principles won the sympathy of the objective and impartial observer.

The right-wing did not arouse such feelings. What caught one's eye first of all were the sly faces of the bishops and priests, the wicked eyes of the extreme reactionaries of the landed gentry, former directors of the zemstvo and their clerks, dreaming of governorships. They hated the Duma, which threatened their material well-being and privileged position in society. From the very beginning they tried to deny its merits and have it dissolved. They interfered with its work and did not hide their joy at its failures.

It was sickening to look at this noisy, cackling bunch, just as it is sickening to look at something deformed; here were representatives of the people who did not recognize, even mocked, the people's parliament!

Steering a course down the middle, squeezed by these two outspoken and powerful factions, were the moderates. The leftists and the rightists were able to achieve majorities in the Duma only by alternately joining with the moderates, who by themselves did not wield any power. The moderates attempted to do their legislative work strictly according to the constitution. At times they were joined by their comrades to the left, who only wanted to exploit the Duma to propagandize their extremist teachings, or by the gentry on the right, who brought the Duma onto a path of scandal and empty declarations. The moderate faction aroused pity and respect in the observer for its fortitude, steadfastness, and political education.

We shall soon see what Golovin meant by "political education."

The deputies sat wherever they chose; there were no fixed places yet. Golubev announced from the rostrum, "Gentlemen! The secretary will now read the signed imperial decree of February 14 (27)."

The secretary began, "The signed imperial decree given to the Governing Senate on the day of February 14 (27), 1907.

"Carrying out our will about the time of the convening of the State Duma, I enjoin Privy Councillor Golubev to open the session of the State Duma on the twentieth of February."

Then Golubev said, "His Majesty the Emperor has enjoined me to welcome the members of the State Duma on his behalf and to wish you God's help as you begin your work for the good of our beloved Russia."

The Emperor's portrait, which hung above the rostrum, seemed to confirm the welcome.

At this point there was an unexpected scene. About one hundred people took part in a planned demonstration; the rest of us were taken by surprise. Krupenskii, the deputy from Bessarabia, rose and shouted, "Long live His Majesty the Emperor! Hurrah!"

Approximately one hundred men stood up, rightists, moderate nationalists, and Octobrists, and answered with shouts of "Hurrah!" The rest of the deputies, about four hundred people, remained seated to show their dissent. Suddenly a man jumped up. He was tall, stooping, with a long beard and red hair.

As he stood up, the others hissed at him, "Sit down! Sit down!" He sat down, but jumped up again, evidently embarrassed. And sat down again, only to get up again. Later it was learned that this was Peter Bernardovich Struve, a university professor who later became an academician.

He is a remarkably interesting man. A staunch supporter of Marxism, he was the author of the manifesto of the First Congress of Social Democrats in 1898 and a participant in the London Congress of the Fifth International. He was a leading representative of "legal Marxism," yet in 1900 he became a liberal. Why?

Struve was a most honest man, and his break with Marxism was a spiritual and intellectual rebirth. At the time he was one of the leaders of the Cadet party. Being well-bred, he knew, of course, that when the monarchy is saluted, constitutionalists rise and join in the salute. But at the time the Cadets were fiercely opposed to the autocracy, and therefore, with this action on opening day, they compromised their constitutionality.

Their leader, F. A. Golovin, member of the central committee of the party and Chairman of the Second Duma, bluntly describes this episode:

> We Cadets, as a group, had made no agreement beforehand to remain seated. . . . As for me personally, I did not see any reason to rise for the salute, since Golubev was not relaying the Tsar's actual words but simply welcoming the members of the Duma, albeit on behalf of the Tsar. I also knew for a fact that the socialists would not rise, of course, and then their feelings toward the Tsar's greeting would be unpleasantly obvious. I did not consider it necessary to cut myself off from the left for no good reason. . . . After all, one can't expect socialists to demonstrate in support of the monarchy when their platform is in opposition to it.

Thus did Golovin demonstrate his "political education."

That day, the Octobrists, uneducated perhaps, but tactful nevertheless, showed themselves to be the only true constitutionalists.

In a letter to his mother, Maria Fedorovna, in London, the Tsar wrote, "Of course you already know how incredibly stupid and disgraceful the left acted in not rising when the right made the salute."

But how could one hundred people collaborate and then manage to keep it secret? I cannot remember exactly who the instigator was. It must have been Paul Nicholaevich Krupenskii. It would be hard to imagine a more energetic and active man. The ancestors of the Krupenskii family were Turks. About a hundred years earlier Bessarabia had become part of Russia. The large Krupenskii family was not only Russianized but also became extremely patriotic. This tendency is noteworthy: the so-called aliens who inhabit the outlying areas of Russia sometimes thought more highly of their adopted country than did native Russians. Bessarabia sent to the Duma P. N. Krupenskii, V. M. Purishkevich, P. A. Krushevan, P. V. Sinadino, and other staunch supporters of the monarchy and believers in the greatness of Russia.

I still remember a crowded meeting that was held, I believe, at Iakunchikov's.* As a simple provincial, I was struck by the beauty of his apartment, particularly by the damask wallpaper, which I had never seen before. The meeting was held in order to nominate a candidate for Chairman to run against the Cadet candidate, Golovin, who was supported by the other parties as well. In short, the group which met at Iakunchikov's was the opposition. We soon rallied around Nicholas Alexevich Khomiakov, a dignified deputy from Smolensk Province. Son of a famous Slavophile writer and poet, and Gogol's godson, Nicholas Alexevich was the personification of charming Russian nobility. There was nothing of the toady in him in regard to his superiors; to his inferiors he was gentle and tactful. He had gained experience in chairing meetings from his work in the zemstvo. The fact that he, like many other leading Slavophiles, was of Tartar descent was of no importance. He spoke with a charming burr, which his children also picked up. Khomiakov was elected, unanimously I believe, to be our spokesman in the Duma. And under his leadership we decided that it would be appropriate to respond in kind to the Sovereign's speech of welcome. This decision was to have serious repercussions.

The leftist and Cadet newspapers vented their spleen upon the honorable Mr. Struve. Describing the scene which took place in the

---

*The electoral campaign for the Second Duma began in December 1906, so although Shulgin does not give the date of this meeting, it must have taken place sometime between December 1906 and February 20, 1907, the day the Second Duma opened (trans.).

Duma when Peter Bernardovich kept getting up and sitting down, the pen-pushers referred to him as *vanka-vstanka*.*

However, it was destined that Golovin would be elected Chairman of the Duma. The final decision was made on the evening of February 19 (March 4), 1907, at Prince P. D. Dolgorukov's, one of the founders and a prominent statesman of the Cadet party. Two hundred and fifty Cadets held a meeting in order to nominate candidates to the presidium of the Second Duma. When Golovin arrived, there was a burst of applause, and he was informed that the group had unanimously decided to award him the Chairmanship of the Duma.

During an earlier conference, on February 18 (March 3), the Social Democratic faction had decided to appear at the Prince's apartment to inform him of their decision. The representatives of the faction, Mensheviks for the most part, announced that they would vote for Golovin. Also supporting him were the representatives of the workers, the SR's, the Poles, the Lithuanians, and the Muslims.

Thus it was guaranteed beforehand not only that Golovin would be elected Chairman but also that a colleague from his town council, M. V. Chelnokov, would be elected secretary. Therefore no one was surprised when Fedor Alexandrovich Golovin was elected Chairman, receiving 356 yea votes and 104 nays. Nicholas Alekseevich Khomiakov, who had received 91 votes, declined to vote, since he was a candidate. Thus ended the first day of the convocation.

* * *

The Tsar wrote to his mother in the aforementioned letter, "Golovin, the Chairman, introduced himself to me the next day. My general impression was that he was a totally worthless character!"

I have written that we were pessimistic about the future of the Second Duma. We could not know then that our forebodings were well-founded, and that the days of the Second Duma were numbered, by the will of the monarch.

Nicholas II wrote to Maria Fedorovna on March 29 (April 11), 1907, "It would be all right if what went on in the Duma remained behind closed doors, but the fact is, every word uttered there appears the next day in all the papers, and is greedily noted by the people. In many places there is more unrest; again people have brought up the business of land and are waiting to see what the Duma has to say

---

*Defined in A. I. Smirnitsky's *Russian-English Dictionary* (New York: Dutton, 1959) as a "doll with weight attached to its base, causing it to always recover its standing position" (trans.).

about it. . . . We will allow the Duma to reach the point of uttering sheer stupidities, and then we will crush it."

The elections of the presidium and secretaries took place during the second and third sessions. The fourth session, on March 2 (15), 1907, began with the usual official words of the Chairman: "I declare this session opened. The minutes of the previous session can be found with the secretary," and so on. Anyone given only the minutes would have no idea what else had occurred between the third and fourth sessions. This was not the only instance where the official reports, although accurate, are not complete. Sherlock Holmes himself would have cause to reflect upon the following:

The minutes of the fourth session continue: "The session opened in the Round Hall of the Tauride Palace at 2:35 P.M."

But why in the Round Hall, when the general session of the Duma always took place in a different hall? This is why.

The grand hall that resembled a Roman amphitheater no longer existed. The seats designated for representatives were filled with plaster and lime dust. Pieces of stucco molding from the ceiling lay everywhere, some of them weighing from fifteen to sixty kilograms.

Many members of the Duma—Purishkevich, Krushevan, Metropolitan Platon, Krupenskii, and I, and many others—would have been killed if this catastrophe had taken place when the Duma was in session. The entire amphitheater was covered with dust, but the right side was especially damaged.

What in the world had happened? The ceiling on the right side of the hall had collapsed. The left side stayed up, hanging crookedly in the air. The quivering beams, boards, and joists also threatened to fall soon.

Of course this event was not included in the minutes. The newly elected Chairman was awakened at 7:00 A.M. in his hotel room by a telephone call from Baron Osten-Saken, chief of the Palace Guard, informing him of the catastrophe. As he dressed, Golovin received another call, this time from the Chairman of the Council of Ministers. The Chairman said that he was already at the palace and requested that Golovin come immediately in order to ascertain where the session, scheduled for 11:00 A.M., could be held.

Golovin found Stolypin in the Ministers' Pavilion. With the secretary, M. V. Chelnokov, and the frightened building manager, the architect Bruni, they went to the damaged hall.

Golovin related later, "The spectacle was staggering. Thick, heavy chunks of plaster had crashed down from a height of twelve meters, mangling the chandeliers. The plaster lay in thick layers on the sides of the semicircle of reading-stands. If this had occurred a few hours later, a large number of representatives would have been killed or maimed. Judging by which reading-stands were smashed, it can be assumed that the representatives nearer the center would have been spared, while those sitting along the wings would have been most seriously injured."

Given the unfriendly attitude toward the government of a considerable number of members, Golovin knew that news of this catastrophe would give rise to such impassioned feelings that it would now be unwise to hear the government's declaration.* Stolypin, however, either did not understand or did not want to understand these feelings. In his opinion, all of Russia and Europe was waiting to hear the government's declaration. Putting off this important action because of some fallen plaster would mean imparting serious meaning to an unfortunate accident.

When Golovin and Stolypin came out into the lobby, they were surrounded by deputies who quite clearly expressed their indignation about the incident. While even-tempered people saw the cave-in as a case of criminal negligence, certain hot-heads saw it as an attempt upon the lives of representatives of the people.

Sensing their bad mood, Stolypin hurriedly left, but first pressed Golovin to arrange the session without fail in the Round Hall.

As it turned out, the session did take place in the Round Hall, but Stolypin was not able to speak. The session, which lasted only forty minutes, focused on premises for future sessions of the Duma and measures to find out what had caused the catastrophe. Tables and chairs were brought from all over the palace and hastily arranged in the Round Hall. Only those who came early were able to find seats. There was even a rostrum—an ordinary chair. I made my first speech in the Duma from this chair. It was one of little significance and was preceded by more colorful speeches.

Gregory Alexevich Aleksinskii, of the Bolshevik wing of the Social Democratic faction, representing the workers of St. Petersburg, made a certain impression. He was short, a bit hunchbacked, with sly eyes and a mocking expression. A satisfaction that he did not try to hide radiated from him apropos the crash. His eyes shone with an unconcealed joy.

Standing beside me was M. M. Nikonchuk, a peasant from Volyn Province, "a self-educated plowman," who whispered to me, indicating Aleksinskii, "Where did it come from?"

---

*At the opening session of each new term of the Duma, an official spokesman read a declaration stating the overall direction of the government's policies (trans.).

"It" spoke in a high, shrill voice, piercing the air monotonously with a pencil stub, as if wanting to implant its words in the brains of its listeners.

"Citizens, deputies."

Aleksinskii used that salutation in order to avoid the phrase "Members of the State Duma."

"I was not in the least surprised to hear that the ceiling had collapsed in the hall where the representatives were to meet. . . . I am convinced that ceilings are sturdier in ministries, police stations, and other government institutions" (Applause, buzzing).

Aleksinskii was hinting too transparently that the cave-in had been arranged by the government in order to do away with the people's representatives. But if this were so, the plan would have backfired. Supporters of the government would have been killed, while its enemies would have gone unscathed.

Next Krupenskii made his way to the "rostrum." He stated that dirty allusions were inadmissible, and he was right. He was booed by the left but not completely drowned out, roaring on so quickly in his bass voice that the stenographers could hardly keep up with him.

I was among those who clambered up on the rostrum, that is, the chair. It reminded me of my student years. My speech was, in general, insipid: "It seems to me, gentlemen, that we are not here as a jury. I propose that we leave off any judgment of the incident. Undoubtedly the guilty parties will be found and punished in a lawful fashion. But at present, since we cannot proceed with our legislative work under these circumstances, I think it would be wise on our part to adjourn until we can find better accommodations."

These were pitiful words. So were those of the other speakers and of Aleksinskii, especially those of Aleksinskii, even though Golovin considered him one of the best orators there.

Everyone pricked up their ears when small, pale Aleksinskii, with the shrill, unpleasant voice punctuated by sharp gestures of his long hands, began his speech with his usual words: "Citizens, deputies!"

This man with the clever eyes and mocking mouth did not foresee his fate.

Aleksinskii was an ardent revolutionary who had served several prison sentences and had participated in the London conference of the Social Democratic party. He was an acquaintance of Lenin, who wrote his speech on the agrarian question for the twenty-second session of the Duma on April 5 (18), 1907. Aleksinskii escaped arrest by chance during the rout of the Social Democratic faction, being abroad at the time. In 1909 he was attending a party school organized by the Vpered ("Forward") group on the island of Capri.

His break with the Bolsheviks began then. With A. A. Bogdanov, he called for a boycott of the State Duma. At the start of World War I, Aleksinskii broke once and for all with his ties of the recent past. He joined the ultra-right-wing Mensheviks and became editor of their newspaper, *Unity*, which called for continuing the war until a victorious end was achieved. Then he apparently stopped supporting the Tsar and began piercing the air with his pencil.

But fate had already spread its evil wings over Russia. The cave-in was a little thing, only an omen of the great downfall yet to come. The imperial crown fell on the State Duma, breaking through the dome of the Tauride Palace, burying both the people's representation and the thousand-year-old empire. All this occurred on that fateful day of March 2, 1917, exactly ten years after the memorable meeting in the Round Hall on March 2, 1907, after the accident.

* * *

Why the ceiling fell in I still don't know. Neither the Duma's commission nor the judicial authorities could find any guilty parties. Golovin thought the accident was caused by old, loose nails. The base of the plaster had been nailed down long ago, during the reign of Catherine II. It could also have been caused by an electrical generator that had been put in the attic for the lighting. The slight but continual vibration of the motor could have loosened the ill-fated nails.

* * *

March 6 (19), 1907, was, in parliamentary jargon, "the big day." The Chairman of the Council of Ministers, Peter Arkadevich Stolypin, was going to speak to the State Duma.

This man had already attracted public attention because of a rather insignificant incident. As governor of Saratov, in 1903, he had displayed courage and resourcefulness in crushing the so-called Saratov riot. Learning that a huge crowd had assembled in the main square of the town, he immediately went there alone, without waiting for a police escort. At the square he got out of his carriage and headed straight for the irate crowd. Realizing that it was the governor, the people rushed toward him, shouting threats, and one hefty fellow brandished a club at him. Russia would never have heard of Stolypin if the governor, fully realizing the danger, had not gone head-on toward the fellow. When they were face to face, Stolypin shrugged off his overcoat, threw it at the man, and barked, "Hold this!"

The hoodlum was taken by surprise and obediently caught the coat, dropping his club. The governor then turned to the crowd and with the same resoluteness ordered them to disperse. They did so.

In itself, this incident merely illustrated how some people have a kind of innate authority. When a man with this trait is destined to hold high office, however, it guarantees sensible and intelligent governing.

I have to add that the former governor of Saratov became head of the government of the Russian Empire in July of 1906 and again displayed exactly the same side of his character on March 6 (19), 1907, in the hall of the nobiliary meeting.

This is how it happened.

F. A. Golovin, Chairman of the Duma, said rather solemnly, "The Chairman of the Council of Ministers has the floor."

Stolypin went up to the rostrum. He was tall, half a head taller than I, with a majestic bearing.

Sometime later, the leftist newspapers compared Stolypin with Boris Godunov: "brown hair, not bad-looking . . . and took the Tsar's throne."*

Stolypin really did have brown hair, but one could not say that he was "not bad-looking." Was he handsome? I suppose so. I would say that Stolypin was the type of man who should be a Prime Minister; impressive-looking, immaculately dressed, but not a dandy by any means. He did not possess Podzianok's resounding bass voice but spoke loudly enough without straining. His manner of speaking was unique in that he did not talk to his audience at all. His voice somehow drifted over his listeners. It seemed to penetrate the walls and resound over a great expanse. He spoke for Russia, which suited a man who, even if he did not "take the Tsar's throne," was worthy of that position. In a word, there was the hint of an all-Russian dictator in both his manner and his appearance.

However, this time he did not make a speech but skillfully read the government's official declaration. Its gist was as follows:

There are periods when a nation lives more or less peacefully and thus is able to introduce new laws made necessary by new demands and add them, painlessly for the most part, to its existing, centuries-old legislation.

But there are also periods when, for one reason or another, public opinion gives rise to discontent. During such eras new laws can conflict with old ones, and great effort is necessary to move forward swiftly, and not let civic life deteriorate into chaos and anarchy. Such was the period now being lived through by Russia, in Stolypin's opinion.

On the one hand, it was necessary for the government to contain the beginnings of anarchy, which threatened to wash away all its historical foundations. On the other hand, it must erect the new structures so urgently needed.

---

*Boris Godunov (1551–1605), as regent, was the real ruler of Russia during the reign of Feodor I, the son of Ivan the Terrible, and made himself Tsar on his death; he was later accused of killing Ivan's other son, Dmitrii, when the latter appeared and claimed the throne (trans.).

In other words, Stolypin put forth a twofold plan of action: fight both the revolutionary forces and stagnation. Reject revolution, endorse evolution—that was his motto.

Since he was in an evolutionary mood, Stolypin did not delve into the complicated program that would be needed to crush the revolution—that is, for the time being he didn't threaten anyone—and instead spoke only of the government's proposed reforms.

* * *

The left responded to this peaceful speech with outrage. Golovin, quite exhausted, dozed in his chair, but was awakened by angry shouts from the right. Rein, the deputy from Volyn, was especially excited and passionately appealed to the Chairman, "Stop them! Threatening an uprising is inadmissible!"

Golovin arose, put his Chairman's bell into motion, and said quietly, "I ask you not to threaten an uprising."

More speeches by the left followed. Tsereteli, in particular, spoke in a passionate and threatening manner.

Finally Stolypin demanded the floor again and said roughly the following: "The government has offered the Duma a number of reforms. They are meant first of all to improve the material well-being of the people and thus give them considerable freedom, for being in comfortable circumstances is a distinct freedom. But certain members of the Duma meet these reforms with threats. To them I say, knowing full well my responsibility, We will not be intimidated!"

These words, carried to all corners of Russia within a few days, restored confidence in the government. The army, the civil servants, the police, and all citizens who did not want revolution, took heart and began to stand their ground. All this was accomplished by the words "We will not be intimidated!"

* * *

Such was my first meeting with Stolypin, a man who would play an enormous role in my life. With the passion of youth I began to battle for his program in the Duma, because I considered his program the only one that could save Russia and enable her evolutionary development to continue. Undoubtedly, as even his enemies admitted, Stolypin was the Russian Empire's most outstanding recent statesman.

I soon became good friends with Peter Arkadevich and began to feel a great deal of respect and affection for him.

* * *

In the four and a half years that passed after that sixth day of March, Stolypin continued to steer the ship of state as he saw fit. Neither leftists nor rightists could intimidate him. And so they killed him. This occurred on September 1 (14), 1911, in Kiev.

The Bomb

O N APRIL 3 (16), 1907, the Duma was considering the question of whether an incident that had taken place in a prison in the city of Riga on March 31 (April 13) was of sufficient urgency as to warrant its immediate inclusion on the agenda ahead of previously scheduled matters.* According to evidence received by the deputy who introduced the question, eighteen prisoners had attempted to escape. Seven of them were killed in a skirmish with prison guards, and seventeen were wounded, of whom two later died. Fifty-six people were being tried before a military court on charges of attempted escape and were sure to receive death sentences.

In reply to a telegram from the Duma, the governor of the Baltic states, Baron A. N. Meller-Zakomelskii, stated that no one had been brought before a military court and thus there was as yet no one to rescue. But the deputy from Riga, the Menshevik Ivan Petrovich Ozol, noting the *as yet* in the telegram, insisted that the incident was being investigated and that the military court, though not in session today, would soon convene.

If Ozol had known then when I learned afterward, he would not have wasted his time speculating about the trial date but would have told the Duma about an altogether different matter. What was it that I learned, although, unfortunately, a bit too late?

During a closed meeting an officer in a Circassian coat had suddenly jumped up.

He said, or rather shouted hysterically, "I am being discharged! Before, I was needed, even indispensable. Who saved Russia in 1906, crushing uprisings in various places? Uprisings of people? No—of animals. I was in the Caucasus. What went on there cannot be described. General Tolmachev was sent there. I was in his command.

---

*Deputies could address unscheduled questions to the government on matters of both foreign and domestic policy, but according to the Duma's procedural rules, a question of this kind, which of course was not on the calendar, could be presented to the house only if it was first decided, by a debate and vote on the floor of the Duma, that it was of sufficient urgency to supersede previously scheduled business. Hence in Duma parlance such questions were referred to as "questions of urgency" (trans.).

Taming the animals, we became animals ourselves. But what else could we do? Tolmachev left no stone unturned. He had only one punishment for revolutionaries: death!

"One day four of them were brought to his headquarters. They sat on the floor in an adjoining room. I, his adjutant, informed him of their presence. And he shouts, 'What do you mean, bringing them here! I gave an order once and for all: People who are arrested always attempt escape—Understand?'

"I answered, 'Yes, Your Excellency.' I went into the adjoining room and shot the four who were sitting on the floor. Am I an animal? Yes! But animals like me saved Russia, and now they are discharging us. It's unjust. If terrible times befall Russia again, we would be useful." With these words he ran into the adjoining room. Luckily there was no one sitting on the floor there.

If he had heard this story, Ozol could have said in front of the Duma, "In the Caucasus, there was General Tolmachev, and in Riga, Baron Meller-Zakomelskii. There is only one difference between them: according to Tolmachev, people under arrest attempt escape, and according to Zakomelskii, prisoners do."

* * *

Listening to these people accusing the authorities of brutality, I became incensed and asked to have the floor. I said, "Gentlemen, very grave, terrible things have been said here, about death, and rescue from death, and so on. Gentlemen, I will not speak for very long and only ask you to truthfully answer one question. The topic under discussion is death, mercy, and so on. Gentlemen, please answer this question: Frankly, with your hands on your hearts, Does anyone here have a bomb in his pocket?"

Immediately an incredible commotion broke out. Ths is what it says in the stenographic record: "*Shouts:* Get out of here! *Pounding on desks.* How dare he! Get out of here! Mr. Chairman, please have him removed!"

N. N. Poznanskii, the Chairman, shook his bell with such fury that one would think I had started a fire. At the same time he shouted down at me that I had insulted the members of the Duma. To this day I do not understand why they were so insulted. The scene was right out of Hans Christian Andersen's fairy tale, "The Emperor's New Clothes." The hypocritical people praise the Emperor's new "clothes" until a child suddenly pipes up, "But the Emperor isn't wearing any clothes!" The insult lay in the spark of truth. I was referring to the SR's, who openly advocated terrorism. Members of their party were known to plant and set off bombs.

If the members of the Duma who belonged to terrorist parties had changed their convictions upon becoming members, then they should have made it known. Not only did they not do this, but when a condemnation of terrorism was proposed, they refused to vote for it. And refused in such a way that the deputy from Kiev, the rector of the Kiev Ecclesiastical Academy, Bishop Platon, said to them in a trembling voice, raising his arms toward heaven, "You act as though you give your blessings to your accomplices for more killing!" Since they would not renounce terrorism, did that mean I must not ask them, as honest men, whether they had bombs? They could easily have thrown a bomb at any one of us: at Bishop Platon, Purishkevich, myself. They could have destroyed the entire government, starting with Stolypin. They had not succeeded in killing him on Aptekarskii Island, where they had set off a bomb a year before. The Prime Minister's house was destroyed, his daughter was seriously wounded, and forty people were killed, but Peter Arkadevich somehow was left unhurt and once again was speaking in the Duma. The dates when he would speak were publicized in advance. What could be better for terrorists? Especially favorable for the killers was the fact that the palace guards had no authority when it came to members of the Duma. Deputies could not be searched for weapons.

Why, then, did they feel insulted? I think it was because I had found them out. They did not want terrorism in the Duma because it would not be to their advantage—the first bomb thrown in the Duma would be the institution's death knell. The Duma would be dissolved forever. And they would loose a vantage point from which they could carry on their revolution with great success.

* * *

Be that as it may, there was quite a furor. The poor stenographers, the only people who did not take part in the indecorous scene, frantically and conscientiously wrote everything down. At the instigation of thirty deputies the Chairman finally proposed a vote to decide whether or not to remove the guilty party (Shulgin) from the chamber until the end of the session. Following the procedural rules, the Chairman gave the accused the floor to explain his actions. At this time one of the Octobrists said to me, "We don't want to vote to expel you, but you have to—not apologize so much as say something conciliatory."

I naively listened to him because he was older and more experienced than I. But respect for one's elders is not always beneficial. Since I did not really want to say something conciliatory, my explanation was clumsy: "The expression I used aroused a storm of protest. I must say that I do not retract the essence of my statement; but my words were inappropriate in the sense that I did not mean to imply that the Socialist Revolutionaries now present would do such a thing; I meant all the members of that party and about their—"

A hue and cry ensued again. I was interrupted by cries of "Not true!" I continued, "So, I did not mean to imply the members now present. Perhaps it sounded that way, but that was not what I meant, because really, it would be strange to suspect such a thing of them. I meant the party in general, and what concerns the party, but no representative of that party can answer my question."

The Octobrists voted in my favor, but that was not important. The important thing was that I should have stood my ground and did not.

* * *

I stood near the rostrum for the vote. I was embarrassed, and instead of looking out into the hall, at the people who were about to expel me from the session, I looked down at my wedding ring. The press noted this, and I later read in the papers, "To show his disdain for the representatives of the people, during the vote Shulgin admired his manicure."

As Pushkin once said,

> A man of sense, I am conceding,
> Can pay attention to his nails;
> Why should one quarrel with good breeding?*

But that did not apply to me. My nails are not manicured at all. Which I came to regret.

---

*The quotation, given here in Babette Deutsch's English version (New York: Random House, 1936), is from Pushkin's *Eugene Onegin*, 1, 25 (trans.).

Crafty Lukashevich

I saw the Tsar for the first time in my life in March of 1907, during the Second State Duma.

The Second Duma, as everyone knows, was the "Duma of the People's Wrath," antimonarchical, revolutionary. To this day how vividly I remember it! The year 1907 filled the chairs of the Tauride Palace with representatives of "democratic Russia."

There were relatively few of us moderates in the Duma. One day a hundred people were honored with an imperial audience. We were received separately in three small groups.

It was a beautiful spring day, and everything about the day was special: the train sent from the Imperial Palace for the members of the Duma, the court escort, the lackeys, grander-looking than the greatest magnates, fellow members of the Duma in evening dress as if going to a ball—all in all, exactly the kind of atmosphere expected and enjoyed by a true-blue monarchist, a provincial no less, when he comes near the person whom after God he obeys most strictly.

* * *

The reception was held in one of the wings of the palace. We were assembled in a semicircle in a small hall. We were asked to stand that way by several court officials, among them Prince Michael Sergievich Putiatin, who said to me, "You are from the Ostrozhsk district? Then we are fellow-townsmen." He meant that his family was descended from Prince Ostrozhskii.

The reception was set for 2:00 P.M. Exactly at 2:00, for as the French say, "punctuality is the politeness of kings," someone came into the hall and announced, "His Majesty, the Emperor."

The room grew hushed. Into the hall walked a middle-aged officer, but we knew it was the Emperor. It could not have been anyone else. He was wearing the uniform of a sharpshooter—a raspberry-colored silk shirt. He was followed by a tall woman dressed all in white, with a large white hat, and leading a charming little boy. We immediately recognized their son from his most recent portrait—he was wearing the same little white shirt and high sheepskin hat. The Empress, on the other hand, did not resemble her portraits at all.

44

The Sovereign began greeting us. I don't remember who was first. Next to me stood Professor Rein, and on his other side stood Purishkevich. I watched the Sovereign greet each person, but he spoke quietly, and the responses were just as quiet and could not be heard. But I was able to hear clearly his conversation with Purishkevich. Twitching nervously as usual, Purishkevich grew more and more emotional.

The Sovereign aproached him, characteristically gliding slowly along the parquet. Someone introduced Vladimir Mitrofanovich Purishkevich. The Sovereign evidently remembered him from somewhere because he had a look of recognition on his face.

We were all keenly interested in knowing whether the Second Duma would soon be dissolved, for we hated the "Duma of the People's Wrath" as passionately as it hated the monarchy. Purishkevich was the most worked up about this.

He said, "Your Majesty, we can hardly wait to know when this disgrace will be finished. This meeting of traitors in the Tauride Palace. They breed revolution throughout the land. We eagerly await Your Imperial Majesty's order dissolving the Duma."

With this Purishkevich's entire body twitched. He made a great effort to control his jerking hands, and succeeded, except for the jangling of his bracelets.

The Emperor smiled slightly. There was a short pause; then he answered quite distinctly, in a quiet but assured deep voice, quite unexpected from a man of his stature: "I thank you for your unwavering loyalty to the throne and to your country, but leave that question to me."

He turned to the next person, Professor Rein, and spoke with him for a short time. George Ermolaevich answered him gallantly and pleasantly. Then the Emperor came up to me.

Meanwhile the little Crown Prince was examining the cap Rein held in his hand. The cap was just at eye level for the boy, who was evidently comparing it to his own white hat. Rein bent down and explained something to him. The Empress beamed and smiled, as mothers do.

The Emperor turned toward me.

I looked at him for the first time in my life. His gaze was pleasant and quiet, but he had a habit of jerking his shoulders, which conveyed his extreme nervousness. There was something feminine and shy about him.

The Emperor held his hand out to me and said, "I believe you are from Volyn Province. All rightists there?"

"Quite so, Your Imperial Majesty."

"How did you manage that?"

He smiled almost happily. I answered, "We are united in our nationalistic feelings, Your Majesty. In our province, landowners, clergy, and peasants all pull in one direction, as Russians. In the outlying districts, Your Majesty, people are more nationalistic than in the center of the country."

The Emperor evidently liked this idea. He astonished me by answering in a conversational tone of voice, as though we were speaking without ceremony. "But that's quite understandable. After all, there are many nationalities here—emotions run hot. We have Poles and Jews here. Because of this people in western Russia are more nationalistic. Let us hope that such sentiments spread to the east."

It is now known that soon after this reception Stolypin sent a telegram to the Kiev group of Russian nationalists. It said, "I strongly believe that the flame of Russian nationalism in western Russia will not go out but will light up all of Russia."

The Emperor asked me one other thing, something personal, and then very graciously excused himself and continued down the receiving line. The Empress also chatted briefly with me.

One of our priests made a shocking scene. As the Emperor approached he got down on his knees and tearfully began to mutter something incoherent.

The Emperor, clearly embarrassed, helped him to his feet, received his blessing, and kissed his hand.

Among those present that day was one Stephen Vladimirovich Lukashevich, a long-time member of the zemstvo of Poltavsk Province and a retired lieutenant. He was over fifty years old, very nice and also very crafty. As I said before, we were all very eager to know when the Duma would be dissolved. The Emperor had indicated by his response to Purishkevich that he did not wish to discuss this, but Lukashevich, with a little maneuvering, was able to get an answer for us.

The Emperor asked Lukashevich where he had served. He answered, "In Your Imperial Majesty's fleet. Then I retired and have been chairman of the zemstvo for a long time. And now I've been elected to the Duma. But I'm uncomfortable; here I am sitting in St. Petersburg and neglecting my duties in the zemstvo. If this goes on much longer I'll have to give up my membership in the zemstvo. I just don't know—"

And he paused, looking innocently at the Emperor.

The Emperor smiled and started toward the next person, but apparently appreciated Lukashevich's cleverness. He turned back to him and said, smiling, "Wait a bit before retiring from the zemstvo."

With this we all realized that the days of the Second Duma were numbered. This made us extraordinarily glad. None of us doubted that the "Duma of the People's Wrath" must be dissolved.

Having greeted everyone, the Emperor stood before us and made a short speech. I clearly remember the end: "I thank you for your courageous defense of the foundations upon which Russia has developed and grown strong."

The Emperor spoke softly but clearly and distinctly. He had a deep, low voice and the trace of an accent, which was the only thing about him that seemed foreign to me, a provincial fellow. Everything else seemed familiar, not grand. His shyness was attractive.

Curiously, the Empress also impressed me as being shy. One felt that even after so many years she still was not used to these receptions. Although we were awed and unsure of ourselves, she seemed even more unsure of herself.

The one person who was quite at ease, displaying a more majestic bearing than either of his royal parents, was the little Crown Prince. He was extraordinarily beautiful in his little white shirt with his white hat in his hand.

After his speech, we shouted, "Long live the Emperor!" He excused himself with a nod and left the hall, which was all lit up that day.

What a grand day it had been! Everyone left in a good mood.

In spite of the Emperor's shyness, we felt that he was in good spirits. He was sure of himelf, and therefore sure of Russia's fate.

As the court carriage rolled gently along the strikingly beautiful paths of the royal palace, we spoke excitedly and happily of the end of the Second Duma. And about two weeks later, on June 2 (15), it was indeed dissolved, and thus the people's wrath was unable to manifest itself in any way. That day an army regiment in full dress paraded down the Nevskii Prospect, and June 3 (16) accomplished a victorious assumption of power.

I spent that day walking around the city, trying to decide, as I told my friends, whether we truly had an autocracy.

That evening, dining at the Donon restaurant,* I clinked glasses with Krupenskii and said, "My dear friend, we truly do have an autocracy in Russia."

* * *

In addition to everything else, I began a peculiar career in the Second State Duma. It could not be termed political or journalistic, although it had to do with both politics and journalism.

The Duma had a so-called press box, located to the left of the

---

*One of the more fashionable restaurants in Petersburg (trans.).

rostrum, for reporters from the various newspapers—leftist, rightist, and moderate. Since the reporters were chiefly Jews, the press box was jokingly referred to as the "Jewish Pale."*

This was mean but witty. After all, it was necessary to respond in kind to the vile terms in which the "Jewish Pale" referred to the elected representatives of the people. Furthermore the slanderous lechers provided me with an enormously successful career.

* * *

When I first stepped up to the rostrum and called the attention of the "Jewish Pale" to myself, they described me thus: "A certain Shulgin is speaking. Haggard face, hoarse voice, lackluster little eyes, and a badly made suit. . . . He reminds one of a line in a departmental order of the old regime."

Upon reading this, my stepfather said, smiling, "You don't drink, so where do they get this 'haggard face' from? Your voice isn't strong, but it isn't hoarse either. But this 'badly made suit' is entirely beside the point. Why insult Vilchkovskii? He's the best tailor in Kiev!"

Speaking with him made me feel better. But actually there was some truth in their description. I wasn't so much haggard-looking as exhausted. Also, I've had a weak voice from birth, but in the Duma it completely gave out. As for the suit, even though Vilchkovskii was a good tailor, I was a country boy, and did not know how to wear a suit properly.

However, I progressed rapidly. In the course of a month the "Jewish Pale" was calling me, among other things, a thug and a psychopath. They wrote, "Shulgin is again at the rostrum. Cherubic eyes flashing slyly, this four-eyed snake says incredible garbage."

From lackluster eyes to cherubic eyes; from a departmental line to a four-eyed snake. That's quite a difference. Not a word about the suit anymore.

Three months later the press wrote, "Speaking is the Alphonse-like Shulgin, known to all."

"Known to all"! Hadn't they scornfully used the term "a certain Shulgin" not so long before?

Of course, "Alphonse" is an insulting expression, meaning a man who lives on the means of a woman to whom he is not married. It was accepted, even in the highest circles, to spend the money of one's rich but lawfully wedded wife, but I wasn't able to take advantage of this

---

*Jewish rights of residence in Russia were restricted to a region in the western and southern part of the country (mainly in the Ukraine and the former Polish territories) known as the Pale of Settlement, instituted by Catherine the Great in 1791 (trans.).

deception. Katia, my wife, was from an ancient noble family that had long been impoverished.

Under the circumstances it did not pay to challenge any of the reporters to a duel. On the contrary, since the term "Alphonse" means, first of all, an elegant man, the press had given me my revenge for the insult of the "badly made suit."

* * *

When the Second Duma was dissolved, I hoped that I was through with it forever. I hated politics, and the drudgery of the past 102 days had not altered my feelings. But man proposes and God disposes. For a variety of reasons that I won't go into here, I ended up taking part in the elections again. I purposely use the term "take part in," not "stand for election."*

On June 3 (16), 1907, the day after the Duma was dissolved, a law was passed changing the voting system. The elections this time were peaceful, even boring. Thirteen people were elected from Volyn Province: five peasants, three priests, three landowners, one doctor, and one teacher. All were rightists.

* * *

And so here I am in the Tauride Palace once again, but the atmosphere was completely different. The stenographic record describes the change better than I could:

> *State Secretary:* The royal decree of October 28 (November 11), 1907. *(reading)* "In carrying out our will about the time of the convocation of the newly elected State Duma, I hereby command Privy Councillor Golubev to open the term of the State Duma on the first (fourteenth) of next month." Underneath is written in His Royal Majesty's hand, "Nicholas."
>
> *Golubev:* His Majesty the Tsar *(all members rise)* has conferred a great honor upon me; he has commanded me to extend a welcome on his behalf, at the opening session of the third convocation of the State Duma, to the elected members of the State Duma.
>
> *Krupenski (from his seat):* Long Live His Majesty the Tsar! Hurrah!
>
> *Members:* Long live His Majesty the Tsar! Hurrah! Hurrah! Hurrah!
>
> *Golubev:* His Majesty the Tsar has commanded me to extend a warm welcome on his behalf, here at the opening session of the third convocation of the State Duma, to all the elected members.
>
> His Highness asks for the blessing of the Almighty and for peace and

---

*As is indicated in the next sentence of the text, the voting procedure was changed before the election of the Third Duma. Shulgin is trying to say, tactfully, that the franchise now became so restricted that deputies were virtually appointed rather than elected (trans.).

order in the beloved motherland as the State Duma undertakes its impending tasks devoted to the enlightenment and well-being of the people, to the strengthening of the state system, and to enhancing the greatness of the united, indivisible Russian government.

The members cheered the Tsar again. Golubev and Baron Iulii Alexandrovich Ikskul von Hildenbrandt read the corresponding paragraphs of the laws, after which the members rose to listen to the text of a solemn oath:

> We, the undersigned, vow before Almighty God to fulfill our obligations as members of the State Duma to the best of our ability and powers, to preserve the faith of his Imperial Highness the Tsar and the all-Russian autocracy, and to think only of bringing good to Russia and benefiting her, in witness of which we sign our names.

Upon which follows the process of signing the solemn oath. Golubev warns that only those signing the oath can take part in the election of the Chairman. The election was conducted first by nominating candidates on paper, then voting for the desired candidate.

Nicholas Alexevich Khomiakov received 371 yea and 9 nay votes. Fedor Alexandrovich Golovin, the former Chairman, was nominated only once, evidently by some ill-wisher who wanted to confuse things. But the votes were indicative of the great change of mood in the Tauride Palace. In the second Duma, Golovin had been elected by a majority, receiving 356 yea votes and 102 nays.

Thus opened the Third State Duma, which lasted until June 9 (22), 1912, that is, the entire slated five-year term. Nicholas Alexevich Khomiakov served as Chairman only until March 6 (19), 1910, when he was succeeded by A. I. Guchkov.

*   *   *

The Presidium of the Duma consisted of the Chairman, two vice-chairmen, the secretary, and five undersecretaries. These were all elective positions.

During the election of the Presidium, certain parties wanted to observe some covenants regarding the distribution of offices among the various factions. The Octobrists received the Chairmanship and one vice-chairmanship. The other vice-chairmanship was granted to us, the faction of right-wingers and moderates. This faction did not last long. The moderates, unable to endure the crudeness of the right, separated and on October 25 (November 5) founded a new faction, the Russian Nationalists, with approximately one hundred members.

I remained with the right. Although I felt I was a moderate, my place seemed to be with the right. Who else but us moderates could stem the fury of the immoderates on the right? However, after a while I also fled to the Russian Nationalist camp. The All-Russian National Union, with P. N. Balashev as chairman, was founded on January 31 (February 13), 1910. But I did not permanently join this party either. At the beginning of 1915, during the Fourth Duma, I helped form the Progressive Russian Nationalist faction. Much later, when I was abroad, I saw the bad side of nationalism. The world entered a period in which nationalism ceased being a constructive force. Adolf Hitler, among others, taught me a valuable lesson in that respect.

* * *

Thus the faction of moderates and right-wingers had to chose a vice-chairman. A group consisting of Krupenskii, Polotskii, and myself took the initiative and quickly agreed upon Prince Vladimir Mikhailevich Volkonskii. But we ran into a block—he absolutely refused.

This occurred one evening in the dining room of the Duma. Krupenskii, still believing he could wear Volkonskii down, invited him, Alexander Alexandrovich Polotskii, and me to his apartment for coffee.

* * *

Paul Nicholaevich had a cosy apartment. There were several carpets and, I believe, a polar-bear skin on the floor in the living room. There was also an easel with an unfinished painting.

I asked, "Do you paint?"

He answered, "I'm only an amateur. But the Duma—the Duma this, the Duma that—can drive you out of your mind. I don't have any children, I can't drink, so I have to do something or I'll scream. I had never even held a crayon in my hand. Then one day I bought paints, brushes, easel, and a maulstick. Look at this!"

He had a rumbling bass voice and spoke so quickly that the dismayed stenograpers in the Duma couldn't keep up with him. He pointed to a painting on the wall. A landscape. I glanced back at the easel. His unfinished copy was excellent. He continued, "We had a daughter who died. Since then, my wife—you'll see her, poor thing, she—"

A lady came into the room. She was still a young woman. She had a deep olive complexion, black eyes and hair, and must have been Turkish or Romanian. She was in mourning. Her languid eyes were beautiful but filled with the utter sadness of a mother whose child had died.

She smiled at us, but her eyes became even sadder and she passed through the door like a shadow. Krupenskii explained, "She doesn't hear anything. She's not herself at all. Meanwhile I go to the Duma, day in and day out, the Duma, always the Duma, and I paint and paint and paint so I won't go out of my mind."

* * *

We drank many cups of coffee that night. By 5:00 A.M. Polotskii had exhausted all his arguments and was dozing in his chair. Krupenskii continued trying to persuade Volkonskii to accept the Chairmanship.

The Prince stood his ground.

"What kind of Chairman would I be? My education? I'm an officer in the Guards. They don't teach Marx in the military schools."

"Thank God!"

"But I don't even know our laws. I barely made it as a member of the Duma. What kind of Chairman would I be?"

"The Chairman needs to have the following qualities: First, a strong voice, which you have. Second, he shouldn't doze during the sitting, as Golovin does—the Chairman needs to pay attention. Third, he has to be independent, not bow and scrape before the government or the revolution, and he must be fair."

"Fair?"

"Yes. If the left-wingers make a row, you throw them out. If the right-wingers do, they go too."

"And you think I can do that? Why? You don't even know me."

"I know you. I've seen you in action."

Water wears down rock. At 6:00 A.M. Volkonskii said, "All right! I'll assume this damned mandate. And—"

"What?"

"You won't be sorry."

He kept his word. He took to the Chairmanship like a fish to water. Where did he get the ability to do so?

At the time I was of the opinion that the whole reason for the aristocracy was their hereditary aptitude for governing. But when the elite meddle with things that are not their affair, and counts and princes become writers and poets, they lose their innate authority, that is, they become inept at ruling. Then they should willingly and promptly give up their positions of authority, because if they don't, their inferiors will bump them on the way up, and will rule in their place until they too degenerate. Stolypin did not degenerate, however. He was not an aristocrat who began writing poems and romances; he devoted himself to work—he ruled. And was killed.

Volkonskii was not born to rule in terms of government rule. This was revealed when he was appointed Deputy Minister of Internal Affairs. But he had enough authoritativeness to keep the Duma in order.

Sometimes there would be incredible chaos in the Duma. When it became impossible to reach an agreement, both left and right would demand, "Get Volkonskii!" To the sound of applause, the Prince would advance to the rostrum. Throwing out some troublemakers from the left and from the right, he would calm everybody down. Once, when someone made a scene, he barred the man, a leftist, from the meeting. Then he also barred Purishkevich. Gathering his papers, the latter cheerfully went to the door, then stopped on the threshold and said with a defiant look, "Good night!"

Volkonskii quickly retorted, "For his disrespectful outburst I move that Deputy Purishkevich be barred from five sessions of the Duma. Those opposed are asked to rise. Motion carried!"

No sooner did Purishkevich close the door than he was informed of this additional penalty.

* * *

Volkonskii came up for election on November 5 (18), 1907. The balloting was preceded by much wrangling about the sequence of voting. Finally Prince Vladimir Mikhailovich Volkonskii was elected vice-chairman by a majority of 262 to 140.

* * *

"The fleet will ruin Russia." This prediction was made a few years before the Russo-Japanese War, therefore long before Tsushima. It was a flash of clairvoyance as sharp as lightning, but I realized this only much later, when the fateful prediction came true.

The man with such foresight had a shrewd mind. He said quite logically, "What right have we, with our backward industry, to challenge those who are so advanced? We would need years and years to build warships equal to those of England and the other world powers.

"Furthermore, what need do we have of huge ocean-going ships? We are cut off from the ocean by easily-mined, narrow straits, such as the Great Belt and the Little Belt.* And even if we could get through them, we would have to pass through the English Channel and the Straits of Dover. We would be lucky if England remains neutral, but if she doesn't, we will never be able to sail through those straits. Therefore I predict that we will be ruined if we continue to build huge battleships." Pacing back and forth, he talked as we drank our nightly cup of coffee. This tirade had been provoked by a telegram from the Petersburg Telegraph Agency.

The telegram informed him that the government had decided to appropriate 90 million rubles for the construction of new warships. At the time I was still very young and understood little about political matters, especially the kind of high politics that looks far into the

---

*The two routes through the Kattegat Strait, near Denmark, from the Baltic to the Atlantic (trans.).

future, but I long remembered what Dmitrii Ivanovich, my step-father, said that night.

All his predictions came true. On January 27 (February 9), 1904, war broke out with Japan. The warships of the Second Pacific Ocean Squadron, under the command of Vice Admiral Z. I. Rozhdestven-skii, were sent around the world to strike the decisive blow at the Japanese fleet.

*　*　*

At the same time that our doomed ships were sailing around Asia, I happened to be in Petersburg. I visited a certain lady, Maria Vsevolodovna Krestovskii, who was trembling over the fate of her son, Ensign Kartavtsev, assigned to the *Aurora,* I believe.

While his ship was moored off the island of Ceylon, he sent letters to his mother through the diplomatic pouch, that is, secretly. If the information his mother received from him had been made public, it could have done Russia great harm; nevertheless, she read me one of his letters, which said, "Mother, prepare yourself for the worst. The sailors don't know the truth, of course. It is carefully kept from them. But we officers know everything. We are going to our doom!"

After explaining about the barnacles that covered the underside of the ships and slowed them down, he continued, "Speed in battle is very important. By the time we get to Japan we will be going slower by several knots. But that is not all. Our guns are not as long-range as those of the Japanese. We will not be able to reach their ships, but they will be able to hit ours."

As everyone knows, that was exactly what happened.

On May 15 (28), 1905, near the island of Tsushima in the Korean Strait, the Russian fleet met with complete and utter defeat because of the stupid mistakes of its commander, Admiral Rozhdestvenskii, who was taken prisoner by the Japanese. The main reasons for their victory were their long-range guns and fast ships.

Kartavtsev survived the battle but was stranded in the water for several hours and rescued by the Japanese.

Why is the sentence "The fleet will ruin Russia" true? Because Tsushima was the beginning of the end for the autocracy. The humiliating defeat could not be forgotten, and it reflected upon the Tsar. In Lenin's words, Tsushima signified "the complete military defeat of the aristocracy,"* and thus helped cause the Russian Revolution.

Grand Duke Alexander Mikhailovich, who was himself a sailor and

---

*V. I. Lenin, *Works,* 4th ed., vol. 8, p. 449 (trans.).

understood naval matters, wrote in his memoirs,* "If I had been in the Tsar's place, I would have renounced the throne the day of the defeat at Tsushima. He was responsible for sending Vice Admiral Rozhdestvenskii's squadron. The Tsar had a weak character, but in that instance he displayed not only weakness but obstinacy."

The Grand Duke had been present at the meeting where the decision about the battle was made. Everyone except the vice admiral had opposed the plan to sail around Asia and give battle in Japanese waters. Only Rozhdestvenskii supported the idea, and as a result he ended up leading the Russian ships to a battle that was already lost.

The Grand Duke wrote this after he emigrated, but all St. Petersburg knew of the Tsar's role in the decision. Although I greatly regret having to say this, the defeat at Tsushima was considered the Sovereign's fault. The memory of Tsushima was the main stimulus to his much later decision to renounce the throne, which he made after conferring with his five commanders.

My uncle's prophecy, "The fleet will ruin Russia," proved to be a spark of clairvoyance which flashed like lightning for a second and then was gone.

* * *

I had to speak about the question of the Russian fleet on May 23, (June 5), 1908, at the first session of the third convocation, in connection with the budget commission's report estimating the expenses of the Naval Ministry for the year 1908. The commission's speaker, the Octobrist and zemstvo member Alexander Ivanovich Zverintsev, told the members of the Duma about the necessity for serious reforms in the Naval Ministry in order to ferret out the evil which prevailed there and had brought Russia to defeat at Tsushima. After his report, the issue came under debate. Taking part in the debate were Prince I. V. Bariatinskii, P. N. Krupenskii, and Prince A. P. Urusov from the Russian Nationalist party, A. F. Babianskii of the Cadets, and N. N. Lvov and A. A. Fedorov, both of the Progressive party. All of them criticized the Naval Ministry from one standpoint or another and proposed measures to improve the strength and fighting efficiency of the Russian fleet.

The man who most sharply denounced the ministry was the deputy from Kubansk and Tersk Province and Chernomorsk Province, Ivan Petrovich Pokrovskii, a doctor who had been in battle in Manchuria. Ivan Petrovich Pokrovskii was a Social Democrat who leaned toward

---

*Alexander, Grand Duke of Russia, *Once a Grand Duke* (Garden City, N.Y., 1932) (trans.).

Bolshevism. He did not concern himself with appropriating money to improve the fleet but said,

> In the three years since Tsushima, we have seen a battle between the old order and the new order in Russia. . . . The majority in the Duma, capitalizing on their control over matters of defense, have presented us, through their commission, with a huge report that begins with, and is completely imbued with, criticism of the Naval Ministry and all our naval policies. Now, criticism can be a good thing, but there are two kinds of criticism. There is the kind that tears down the old, cleanses, and then indicates new paths. And there is the kind of criticism, seeking to shore up the old, that admits to insignificant defects and proposes measures to remedy them. In troubled times the ruling classes are especially inclined to the latter kind of criticism. Before any revolution the ruling classes are always ready to institute reforms, simply to preserve the essentials of the old order. . . . Everything was fine before the war with Japan, and we were proud of ourselves, weren't we? The gilding on the Russian giant shone like gold. But then the pygmy Japan pushed Russia with its iron fist, and the giant fell to ashes, because under the gilding the giant was rotten. Isn't the Duma's majority leading the country to rebuild the same kind of fraudulent might?
>
> . . . But the people do not want to relive the shame that was forced upon them against their will. The humiliating defeats at Tsushima and Mukden, which were brought upon us by the old order, the order that thrives on feudalism, the order that squanders the people's money on political adventures—this shame awakened the Russian people from their centuries-old sleep, and aroused in them a frenzied desire to build the new order that alone can save Russia from destruction, save the government from bankruptcy, and save the people from poverty and ruination. . . .
>
> But the heroic Russian people, whose hands and feet had been tied for centuries, only had strength enough for a short, violent outburst. The old order had outlived its time, and its facade was falling apart, but unfortunately it still had a foundation of iron, the so-called internal defense, and it turned this against the country, choking the Russia that was aborning. *(Commotion on the right.)* The old order rose again, the old crow sat on the roof again and crowed over the bloody field. *(Hissing from the right. Applause from the left. Chairman rings bell for order.)*
>
> The ancient past fell upon us again, the old birds flew back and sang the same old songs, again inviting the people to drop their pennies into the bottomless treasury, inviting them to forge their own shackles and build a billion-ruble fleet. *(Shouts of "Enough" from the right.)*
>
> The Duma's majority dares invite the country to spend billions to build a fleet to satisfy the fancy of the government and the babbling Russian bourgeoisie. No, this must not be!

After Pokrovskii it was my turn to speak. Remembering my step-father's fateful words, I wanted to get right into my views on the naval reform and therefore did not engage in polemics with Pokrovskii. But I had to respond to his speech somehow, and thus I began as follows:

> Gentlemen, members of the State Duma, before my speech I have to say a few words to Deputy Pokrovskii.
>
> I do not understand why Deputy Pokrovskii is so up in arms about the Naval Ministry. When the proletariat arms itself and musters its troops, it will have to deal with the army, not the navy, so there's no point in the left worrying about it. *(Noise from the left. From the right, "Socialists, be quiet!")*
>
> . . . One has to look at the root of the problem, which is this: Russia exists but has no plan of defense. . . .
>
> You are living without a plan for the defense of the country. In my estimation, we must begin by working out a defense plan, then we can decide what kind of navy we need.
>
> If you will permit me, I will say that although I cannot definitely say what kind of navy I would like, I am inclined toward a defensive navy, a mine-laying and submarine navy. However regrettable it may be, one must admit that we are technologically very backward.
>
> That is all I have the honor of saying, gentlemen, and since speeches usually end with a reference to the Andreevskii navy,* please allow me to say that it is a pretty picture, now that our ships have all been destroyed, to imagine those proud battleships again in our seas, but it seems to me that we can paint an even more attractive picture: Take the Andreevskii flag and quietly fold it up and put it on a submarine, and after it has done its duty, when the foe is demolished, unfurl the Andreevskii flag in all its glory.

* * *

Late one evening, late parties being the style then, we were invited to Stolypin's, we being A. I. Guchkov, P. N. Balashev, myself, and perhaps someone else. That night Peter Arkadevich frankly explained his views on the so-called naval program. He said that proponents of a large program—a navy made up of battleships—had convinced the Sovereign that the Russian shipbuilding industry could only go in this direction. Stolypin asserted that the matter was settled, in the sense that if the Duma openly rejected the government's proposal, then the Duma would be dissolved on the grounds that it had refused to appropriate funds for defense.

"Knowing this, I did all that I could," continued Peter Arkadevich. "The large program initially called for 3 billion rubles. I was able to knock this incredibly wasteful sum down to 1.5 billion. A compromise. I am entirely in favor of a so-called small navy, made up of light

---

*The navy of Tsar Peter the Great, so-named because it flew the flag of St. Andrew as its ensign (trans.).

cruisers and submarines. But there's nothing I can do. The Duma will be dissolved and then I will retire.

"That is why I have to accept this compromise, and I ask you to reflect upon the consequences."

* * *

The government's announcement made a very painful impression on some of us. We had to compromise only because those sailors, who in our opinion were wrong, had presented the matter to the Sovereign in such a way that he agreed with them.

This is supported by his own words in a letter to his mother on March 27 (April 9), 1908: "The other day that idiot said in the State Council that the Duma showed its patriotism by wanting to refuse money for a navy. I find this more dangerous than what the revolutionaries say. Don't you agree?"

We thought about it for a long time and finally decided that our faction of Russian Nationalists would vote for the appropriation, but several of us—P. N. Balashev, A. A. Pototskii, myself, and someone else—would demonstratively decline to vote. How do I mean demonstratively? If people decline to vote, this is usually not noticed, since first one group rises, than the other group. No one notices if a few people do not rise to vote. By demonstratively I mean leaving our seats and going to the passageway which separated the seats of the members of the Duma from the so-called governmental benches. That is the ignominious way in which this page about the navy ended for us.

* * *

January 28 (February 10), 1909, was a hard day for me. A bill to do away with the death penalty was introduced, with 103 signatures. The text was just a few lines long. The 103 thought to abolish the age-old merciless conflict between Good and Evil with one scrap of paper. People of all kinds had signed. For many of them the attempt to abolish the death penalty was simply a gesture to make themselves look good, but it turned out to be an awkward gesture, because it did not succeed.

If we had known then what we know now, the 103 legislators would not have introduced this childish bill and would have agreed with the Octobrist Nicholas Ivanovich Antonov, who said that abolishing the death penalty was an extraordinarily complex problem. The bill was naive and insidiously hypocritical. I could see that, or rather, could sense it. but at the time people were frightened by current trends. I was a greenhorn, only thirty years old, and it was hard to cut a furrow through hard-packed virgin soil.

And to add to the difficulty, a host of formalistic complications cut off any possibility of honorably retreating from the field. The authors of the bill themselves blocked its passage by demanding that it be rushed through, hardly giving a thought to the fact that it would do away with a means of defense against murder that humanity had used for the past three thousand years. To abolish the death penalty under such conditions, and hurriedly to boot, was just impossible. Naturally the majority in the Duma wished to send the bill to a judicial commission. The members of the commission, lawyers for the most part, would thoroughly discuss this complex problem, after which it would again come before the plenum of the Duma.

This is clear to me now, but at the time I too demanded an immediate discussion of the bill by a plenum. Why? Because the right as well as the left had decided not to avoid the tragic question of the death penalty but to state their opinions.

Debates on matters of urgency had certain rules. Only two speeches in favor of urgency were allowed. If urgency was admitted, then the Duma immediately brought the bill under consideration.

The rule obviously assumed that one of the two speeches would be for urgency and the other against. However, in this case there were unending altercations among the deputies and between the deputies and Chairman N. A. Khomiakov.

During this chaos speeches were made, although technically that was not allowed. The Chairman was unable to make the members restrain their passions within the limits set by the rules. In the end, however, it all turned out well. A deputy from Suvalsk Province, a Lithuanian Trudovik named Andrew Andreevich Bulat, repeated all the fundamental arguments that opponents of the death penalty all over the world have used since time immemorial. A lawyer who had served as counsel for the defense in many notorious political cases, Bulat was secretary to the procurator of the district court in the city of Revel. After organizing the strike of postal, telegraph, and railroad workers, he had served time in prison and was released on 10,000 rubles bail. I note here only the most characteristic parts of his speech.

Gentlemen, members of the State Duma! . . . For those of us who staunchly oppose the death penalty, speaking against it is like breaking down a door that is already open. . . . Gentlemen, before the Manifesto of October 17, the death penalty was rarely used. In the course of the three years since the manifesto, until October 17 (30), 1908, 2,835 people have been executed in Russia. These 2,835 people did not lose their lives in the heat of passion, or at the hands of thieves or terrorists, but at the hands of the government, which is supposed to be the champion of humanity, the champion of culture. Russia, the country which is striving toward culture, and which has promised us the free development of this striving for culture, has permitted 2,835 people to be legally murdered in the three years since the manifesto. And more than 5,000 death sentences have been issued.

The death penalty does not deter anyone. On the contrary, in the element of humanity that is inclined toward crime, it evokes a desire to become a hero of sorts by risking one's life, and thus increases the number of crimes which it is supposed to deter.

Gentlemen, perhaps you will allude to the Bible. Unfortunately, the Russian press right now is filled with sickening articles that treat the death penalty almost as if it were holy. Some of these articles were once distributed to the members of the Duma so that we could all learn how the death penalty has existed since ancient times—since the Old Testament—and how it is a form of retribution, and so on. But gentlemen, you don't need to be theologians to deal with this question; you only need to know this: "Love your neighbor as you love yourself." This, gentlemen, is what the New Testament is based on, and it says so quite clearly, regardless of whether the death penalty is permitted from a moral and religious standpoint. . . . Is it possible that the members of the State Duma need any further guidance on the question of whether hanging is permissible?

Restitution of one kind or another is always possible when a punishment is imposed mistakenly. A person who is falsely convicted can always be compensated. The only exception is the death penalty.

I do not think that any of you would deny that the courts make mistakes. I am convinced . . . that you will admit that there have been cases where a death penalty is imposed and it is subsequently discovered that an innocent person was put to death.

Tell me, how would you overturn such a sentence, how would you give life back to an innocent person who was put to death? Gentlemen, remember this, and if there is the slightest bit of morality in you . . . you will have to say that the courts are not perfect, because man is not perfect, and therefore the death penalty cannot be allowed, in order that no innocent person be killed.

Undoubtedly Bulat's speech was of some value. The main argument against the death penalty is its irreversibility, and he argued it well and was sincere. But his hypocrisy showed when he called upon us to follow the Bible and obey the commandment to "love your neighbor."

Who were Bulat's neighbors? Probably the organizers of the postal, telegraph, and railroad strikes—the people he defended in court and before the State Duma. However, in regard to us, the deputies sitting near him, his hatred was totally evident.

* * *

It finally turned out that two ballots were cast in favor of immediate discussion of the question of the death penalty, although for totally different reasons. Handing in the ballots were the chairman of the

Social Democratic faction, assistant barrister Evgenii Petrovich Gegechkori, and myself.

Gegechkori wanted the bill to be up for discussion immediately so that the death penalty could be eliminated once and for all. Shulgin also wanted it up for discussion immediately, not to do away with the death penalty but to establish the fact that the death penalty cannot be abolished.

The destiny of the State Duma compelled me to give a speech on the death penalty on January 28 (February 10), 1909. Undoubtedly in giving it I overstepped the law, because my speech was only formally in favor of urgency, but actually was on the essence of the death penalty. This was obvious both to the members of the Duma and to the Chairman. Then why did Khomiakov not stop me? Because under the pressure of the uncontrollable emotion in the Duma he had also allowed Bulat to speak on its essence.

I will give the stenographer's record word for word, avoiding repetitions and parts that would not be of interest now, and inserting explanations where necessary.

Gentlemen, members of the State Duma, the faction of the right is in favor of rejecting this bill without passing it on to the commission, for the following reason. We know—after all, everyone knows—that much has been written about the death penalty and that there has been much legislation and judicial activity. It follows that to discuss it here would not be at all horrifying, would not be impossible; on the contrary, it would be a normal task for the State Duma. But, gentlemen, all this would be so only if that suggestion did not include, if you will allow me to use the expression, a hidden motivation, and even, if you will excuse me, a lack of clarity, and, I humbly beg your pardon, a certain mockery of the Duma. In order to avoid saying unpleasant things without substantiating them, allow me to refresh your memories on certain points.

We all remember perfectly the reign of the late Emperor Alexander III and the first few years of the reign of His Highness our current Sovereign. We remember perfectly well that at that time we had forgotten about the death penalty, and any of us would have great difficulty remembering an instance when it was used.

It is true that I can remember the execution of some robbers in the Caucasus, of whom it was said that on Monday they kill a little, on Tuesday they kill a lot, and on Sunday they murder here and there. They were executed, but there were only a few of them. Also imprinted in my memory is the execution of the ringleader of a gang of gypsies. This gang killed forty people while pillaging in a certain rural area. The newspapers wrote about the incident for two weeks. I can recall no other instances of execution during this period.

I have already said that during that time Russia forgot what the death penalty was, and this is quite understandable, for the Russian people have an instinctive aversion to the death penalty, and to judicial cruelty in general. This is not just something carried down from the time of Elizabeth Petrovna.* This aversion is noted by our scholars: it has been so since ancient times, and it is a source of national pride and consolation, strengthening our faith, when we say that the Russian people have to be the masters in our enormous empire, because we believe that only they will be humble and gracious rulers. *(Applause from the right. S. N. Maksydov asks from his seat, "And who are the Russian people?")*

The Russian people—*(Chairman: "Please, no questions. And please do not respond to questions.")*

Sadretdin Nazmutdinovich Maksydov was a pure-blooded Tartar, an educated man who had received his law degree in Paris in 1906. He must have meant that the Russian people included so many "aliens" that the whole population of Russia was made up of "aliens," including Tartars. The Chairman was justified in not allowing us to quibble over this statement, which was beside the point, and I continued:

I will not spend much time on this question. But I do want to remind you that during the Dark Ages, when in the West the Holy Inquisition burned witches and sorcerers at the stake by the tens of thousands, in Russia, in the Orthodox Church, the church that only atheists can speak of with disdain, do you know how sorcerers were punished? They were forced to bow to the floor before icons or lie like a cross in church. There, gentlemen, is an example from earlier times.

Now recall the educated society of the period before the revolution. I remember this perfectly. Among my family and friends I knew Russian women who actually would fall ill, physically ill, when they read descriptions of executions.

Now I ask you to shift to a slightly different epoch. The action takes place in Kiev in 1908. The murderers of the Ostrovskii family are on trial.

Who were the Ostrovskiis? A poor Jewish family, all the members of which were butchered, for a few pitiful rubles, by thieves who assumed that they had a large amount of money hidden someplace.

This murder horrified all of Kiev. For two weeks it seemed as if a dark cloud were hanging over the city. Crowds of people stood for hours before the Ostrovskii house, grim, upset, staring at the walls in superstitious horror. Finally the day of the trial arrived. The sentence was harsh: death for the four murderers. Two female accomplices, who were only guilty of not complying with the law, were sentenced to fifteen to twenty years at hard labor, while on the street in front of the courthouse a crowd of people shouted, "Give us the murderers! Don't protect that scum!" Only with great effort did the police protect the murderers from the mob.

---

*Tsarina Elizabeth Petrovna, the daughter of Peter the Great, reigned from 1741 to 1762 and attempted to codify Russia's laws (trans.).

And here is another example: Vilno, December 1907. The murder of Justice of the Peace Rusetskii by a certain Avdotia is being investigated. Avdotia had been taken on as a servant by Rusetskii, and then murdered and robbed the justice and his wife. Rusetskii was Polish, and the court-room was filled with representatives of Polish society, among them people of the highest rank. And then, when the public prosecutor demanded the death penalty for the murderer, the hall rang with applause, which was taken up by the crowd outside. *(The Cadet A. I. Shin-garev calls out from his seat: "He's getting carried away!")* The crowd shouted, "If you don't execute him, we'll tear him limb from limb with our own hands!"

(The Cadet P. N. Miliukov, from his seat: "Savages!" Commotion.)

Addressing the left, I continued, "We did not interrupt you. Gentlemen, here is the difference between these two incidents, between that era and the present one." By "that era" I was referring to the time about which Bulat had said, "Before the Manifesto of October 17, 1905, there was very, very little use of the death penalty in Russia."

I daresay that it would be misleading at this time to maintain that the government is responsible for the endless executions we have seen. If the government were to stop executing criminals, there would be such an outbreak of mob law that the lynching of Negroes in America would pale in comparison. *("True," heard from the right.)*

Now, gentlemen, let us turn to the history of this bill. It was introduced in the First Duma, which unanimously voted against the death penalty on June 19 (July 2), 1906. I cannot think of anything more hypocritical. We know that the National Convention in France voted to sentence its king to death. That was horrible, but at least it was not hypocritical. But as for the First Duma, an assemblage which would have put a guillotine in every house if it had not been dissolved, an assemblage which stood on heaps of corpses, an assemblage which was drenched in blood, an assemblage which began by demanding complete amnesty for all fighters for freedom—in other words, murderers—an assemblage which stated, "Thousands killed by the revolution is too few!"— *(M. S. Adzhemov, from his seat: "That's a lie!")* —that assemblage is the one that voted to do away with the death penalty. People are saying "That's a lie!" It is not a lie— *(Chairman: "Would you be so kind as to argue about what is and is not a lie during the recess?" Clamor, voices from the right, "Don't interrupt, don't interrupt!" Chairman: "I ask that you not interrupt the speaker. The issue is too grave to aggravate further.")*

At this point I will leave the stenographer's transcript of my speech, since the rest is not clear. The incident to which I alluded took place not in the Third but in the First Duma, in about this way:

The deputy from Ekaterinoslav Province, a Trudovik sailor from the Black Sea fleet named Leo Fedorovich Babenko, went up to the rostrum and said, "You know what is happening in Sevastopol. I have to tell you: let our ministers resign. From their responses—"

Babenko hesitated, and Chairman Muromtsev interrupted, "Are you reading your own opinion? If the reading is difficult for you, then we will add it as an appendix."

Babenko proceeded, "Let them resign, otherwise the same fate will befall them as befell the officers on the battleship *Potemkin*."

Relating this incident from the First Duma, I asked the deputies, "Gentlemen, do you know to whom this was said? It was said to the chief naval procurator, Lieutenant General Vladimir Petrovich Pavlov, who was killed afterwards."

The following is my speech:

> This bill was passed on to the Second Duma, but was not discussed there because other bills had already been introduced but we—and members of the Second Duma who are present remember, of course— we had a marvelous rehearsal apropos the courts of the left, and we witnessed a remarkable scene. As you know, in the Second Duma there was a party which openly called itself the Socialist Revolutionary party; there were thirty-four of them. And these gentlemen, at the very time that their comrades were issuing death sentences and carrying them out,* these gentlemen quite calmly voted against the death penalty. *(Voices from the right: "Bravo!")*
>
> And then, finally, your obedient servant, almost in a frenzy, was obliged to ask them if anyone among them was in possession of a bomb, and was immediately expelled. *(E. P. Gegechkori, from his seat: "Flung out of the hall.")* Flung out of the hall, because this question seemed extremely tactless to certain members. *(Voices from the right, "Bravo!" Laughter and thunderous applause from right and center.)*
>
> No less voluble were the Social Democrats, the same people who advocated mutiny, a mutiny for which many of them, Tsereteli included, were sentenced to penal servitude. All these Aleksinskiis talked of mutiny, and if it had occurred, it would have cost Russia rivers of blood. These same gentlemen proved just as colorfully, almost as colorfully as Deputy Bulat is proving now, that the death penalty is absolutely unthinkable.
>
> The Cadets also spoke very well. The same Cadets whom we could not persuade, by appeals, prayers, or threats, to condemn terrorism. We could not pin them down. They explained themselves by saying, "We too believe that killing should not be allowed, but if you kill, we do not blame you." This was the plan, the basis for an agreement between the Cadets and the more leftist factions. *(Applause from the right. Count V. A. Bobrinskii from his seat: "Quite correct, quite so, lackeys of the revolution.")*

---

*Shulgin is alluding to their acts of terrorism (trans.).

Finally, gentlemen, hobbling along on one foot, I wearily put this question before the Third Duma. . . . They want to make a political gesture. I have to say that some of the 103 signatures are undoubtedly those of people who did not compromise themselves, and I will allow that they are genuinely opposed to the death penalty.

But the majority of the opposition? I don't think so, because just recently the opposition announced here, through the words of a deputy who spoke for the entire opposition, that the bayonet is the highest court. . . .

Gentlemen, we call ourselves obedient servants of the Russian Emperor, and our hands must be as clean as the diamonds in his crown! *(Applause from the right.)*

I feel that the bill we have examined is nothing but a political gesture. There is no reason to spend any more time on it or to pass it on to any committee. Let us simply allow certain people to have their political gesture, and let those who oppose it make a counter-gesture, and then we will vote this bill down, and let us do so on the basis that since the opposition, through its speaker, has announced that the bayonet is the highest court, the State Duma hopes that in the future the opposition will change its tactics, because only then will it be possible to speak seriously about the abolition of the death penalty, when people cease to instigate political terrorism *(Voices from the right: "Bravo!")*

. . . But there is still another danger: as soon as we open the debate, such a flood will be set loose that it will probably occupy every session until the very end of this term. There is only one possible alternative: to put an end to debate, while guaranteeing freedom of speech as stated in article 92 of the mandate.

I would like to add something. The issue of the urgency of the abolition of capital punishment is weakened somewhat at the present time by the decision of the Ekaterinoslav court, which sentenced a score of people to death for organizing the railroad strike and several other strikes.

And if you refer to the book *Nashi deputaty* ("Our Deputies"), on page 415, under "Duma member Bulat, A. A.," you will find the description, "Served time in prison during the Octobrist movement. Released on 10,000 rubles bail." But the important thing is, "Organizer of the postal, telegraph, and railroad strikes."

In these circumstances it is no wonder that Duma member Bulat is in such a hurry to abolish the death penalty, since its existence puts him in danger.

Chairman: Deputy Shulgin, I perceive an insult in your words.

Voices from the right: Nothing of the sort.

Chairman: I stated what I felt, and do not take my words back.

N. E. Markov, from his seat: Mistakenly.

Chairman: And ask you to remain silent.

Voices from the right: We are silent, it's you who are making noise.

Clamor; Chairman rings bell for silence.

The rest of my speech was devoted to uninteresting details about the law. There was no decisive outcome; nonetheless, the right and center praised me noisily and exclaimed, "Well done!"

Having given Bulat and Shulgin the opportunity to speak on the essence of the death penalty, the Chairman also had to allow the Cadet V. A. Maklakov and the Social Democrat E. P. Gegechkori to speak.

Chairman N. A. Khomiakov attempted to conduct the debates as much according to the law as he could. He was a charming man and a distinguished Chairman, but was too weak to hold in check the passions that burst forth that day. Since I do not have the ability to give an accurate picture of the chaos that day, I will quote from the stenographic record, which is the only way to give a clear picture.

I ask the reader to read it in one sitting, because it holds the key to many important questions. The State Duma, whatever its defects may have been, was a natural environment for political freedom. Maximum freedom of speech was guaranteed within its walls. It was the framework of the Russian Parliament, but there was one hitch—an assembly of five hundred can work effectively only if the participants have been schooled in self-discipline. But it takes decades to learn this, as is reflected by the English Parliament.

In London, only recently, at the end of the nineteenth century, the famous filibuster by Charles Stewart Parnell took place. A group of Irishmen purposely made a scene, giving long speeches and making noise to hold up the work of the Parliament, with the aim of obtaining ratification of a bill on Home Rule, that is, Ireland's autonomy within the British Empire. The troublemakers had to be literally carried out of the hall, one at a time, because of the inviolability of Parliament. This problem took up so much time and energy that the paralyzed Parliament could not go on with its work.*

Our indiscipline led to a much more grave consequence—the State Duma conflicted with the crown during a time of war. As a result, both the dynasty and the parliament perished.

---

*Shulgin is referring to Parnell's "obstruction" policy, a tactic that intefered with the normal business of the House of Commons by exploiting that body's antiquated procedural rules, in particular the right of any member to speak to a given motion as long and as often as he pleased. As Giovanni Costigan notes in *A History of Modern Ireland* (New York: Pegasus, 1969), "the Irish members were ready to oppose everything that was proposed—even the customary motion 'that candles be now brought,' which was the prelude to turning on the gas—so that the House continued to sit through a dusk that deepened into darkness" (trans.).

Here is the tragicomedy which was played out in the Duma when I left the rostrum.

Chairman: Two motions have been received—one to send the existing bill on— *(Noise from the right. Voices: "Recess.")* If you continue to interrupt, I will declare a recess. *(Markov, from his seat: "Please do.")* I ask again for silence. Two motions have been received: one, to pass the bill on to a commission on court reform according to paragraph 56 of the mandate; the other, to suspend debate on this issue. *(Bulat, from his seat: "I wish to object to the second motion.")* Excuse me, I have something to add. Another motion has been brought up, on the order of the voting, and still another by Duma member Bulat on a personal question. A deputy may have the floor for a personal question upon the completion of the debate on the issue at hand. The debate is finished today; now we come to the voting. Duma member Bulat has the floor on a personal matter.

Bulat: Duma member Shulgin announced that the bill to abolish capital punishment, which I signed, is insincere. Also he suggested that both the First and Second State Dumas acted insincerely; he characterized— *(Clamor from the right. Chairman rings bell for silence.)* —he crudely stated— *(From the right: "Get out of here!")*

Chairman: Silence please. *(From the right: "This is not a personal matter.")*

Bulat: Now they are telling me what is and isn't a personal matter. I repeat, I was the first to sign this bill, which Mr. Shulgin—I will not refer to him as a deputy, a member of the State Duma—called insincere. *(Clamor from the right. Voices: "What is this! It's an insult!")* In order for Mr. Shulgin to talk about my sincerity or insincerity, he must have proof, otherwise it is nothing but an unsubstantiated, deliberate lie (I myself will use the right expression). That's one thing, but Deputy Shulgin, personally speaking, is always excused— *(Noise. From the right: "And you aren't?!")* —he has so little understanding— *(Laughter. Noise from the right. Purishkevich from his seat: "Ass!")* —of what is sincere and what is not that he has trouble discriminating between what is sincere and what is not. He took a document and read— *(Noise from the right. Purishkevich from his seat: "Idiot!")*

The speaker, turning to the Chairman: I would ask you, Mr. Chairman, to protect me from such outbursts.

Chairman: Allow me to ask you not to interrupt, and if you do interrupt, then do it so that the Chairman can hear you. *(Purishkevich shouts from his seat: "I told him that he is an idiot!" Laughter from the right. From the left: "Throw him out!")* Duma member Purishkevich not only makes remarks that are inappropriate in a properly conducted session but also repeats them. I move that he be removed until the end of the session.

(Noise. Voices from the right: "That's not fair!" Purishkevich from his seat: "Allow me to explain. Deputy Shulgin will give an explanation for me.")

Chairman: Deputy Purishkevich has the right to express himself on this issue. *(Purishkevich, from his seat: "Shulgin will speak for me." Voices from the right: "He can do that.")*

Chairman: Duma member Shulgin has the floor. *(Noise.)*

Shulgin: I cannot totally justify my colleague's remark, but I must say that it was brought on by the words of Duma member Bulat, who took it upon himself, firstly, to say that he will not refer to me as a member of the State Duma, that's one thing, and secondly, took it upon himself to say that I personally am completely lacking in understanding, that's the second. It is not my habit to respond to such comments, but Vladimir Mitrofanovich Purishkevich, who has a quicker temper, said what I should have said myself.

(Applause from the right. Voices: "Bravo!" A professor of general history, the rightist A. S. Viazigin, from his seat: "I ask to have the floor in regard to a violation of the mandate.")

Chairman: Duma member Viazigin has the floor in regard to a violation of the mandate.

Viazigin: On the basis of paragraph 106 of the mandate, explanations on a personal question are not given in sequence, but are held back until the business at hand is concluded. At this session opinions on the matter at hand were not concluded. *(Voices from the left: "They were.")* No, they were not, and Duma member Bulat was given the floor. *(Applause from the right.)*

Chairman: The debate on the given issue was completely concluded. Duma member Krupenskii has the floor in regard to a violation of the mandate.

Krupenskii: In the mandate it is stated: "If speeches from the rostrum are disorderly, the Chairman will stop the speaker." In this case the Chairman did not hear the charges that were hurled at Deputy Shulgin, and he did not stop the speaker and call the session to order. Therefore I ask the Chairman to first look at the shorthand record of what Mr. Bulat said, and then move that Deputy Purishkevich be removed. *(Applause from the right.)*

Chairman: The debate is now over— *(Bulat from his seat: "I have not finished on a personal matter.")* The debate is over in view of the fact that we must have the balloting, and that is why I let Deputy Bulat have the floor on a personal matter. And since Deputy Bulat has the floor, I suggest that the State Duma hear his explanation through to the end, and then I will put the proposed question to a vote. *(Exclamations from the left: "And Purishkevich?")* Would you be so kind as to allow me to chair this meeting as I see fit!

Bulat: Mr. Shulgin said that in Ekaterinoslav people were sentenced to death by hanging for organizing railroad strikes. Then he said that according to the document in his hand, I, Bulat, was the organizer of the railroad, postal, and telegraph strike. If this were so, then I would have been sentenced to death, of course, and would not be attending this session. *(Noise.)* Obviously Mr. Shulgin has so little imagination that he does not realize this. *(Noise. Exclamations from the right: "Again!")*

Chairman: Gentlemen, members of the State Duma, please take your seats. *(Noise.)* Duma member Bulat, I ask that you not use this rostrum for wrangling. When there is quarreling, both parties are guilty. *(Applause from the center and the right.)* I hope the parties involved will bear this in mind. Pardon me, gentlemen, but lack of self-control is unacceptable. It is impossible to tell when the line between acceptable conduct and unacceptable conduct has been crossed; I, at least, cannot do it. I implore you to have some regard for the dignity of this assembly, which you are obligated to respect. *(Loud applause from all sides.)* On the one hand, the speaker is told, "You are a striker." The response is, "You are brainless; you are an idiot." *(Bulat: "I did not say that.")*

Gentlemen, who can tell what is acceptable and what is not? It is all up to you. The Chairman cannot do everything. It would be a disgrace to have to remove some of you from the session each and every day, a terrible predicament for the Chairman to be in. It is easy to say, "I move that Duma member so-and-so be removed from the session," but what a time-consuming and terrible way to chair a session! If you have any pity for your Chairman, spare him from this. *(Applause from the center and right.)* *(Turning to Bulat)* I warn you: stay within the aceptable limits of personal explanation and do not aggravate the issue.

Bulat: Gentlemen, I will do my best to follow the Chairman's orders and will try to remember what is respectful. Since it is unacceptable to tell someone from the rostrum that he has revealed a lack of understanding, I will not do so again, but I have to clear myself. The comment just made implied that I used the expressions "brainless" and "idiot." I said no such thing. And now, in regard to my personal question: Deputy Shulgin, knowing the facts, said that people are given the death sentence for organizing railroad strikes. Obviously he also knows that people who are given such sentences cannot be sitting here in the Duma, on these very chairs. Nevertheless he took it upon himself to allege that I was the organizer of the postal, telegraph, and railroad strikes— *(People on the right point to the book* Nashi deputaty *["Our Deputies"].)* I will not point to such things in *Russkoe znamia* ["The Russian Banner"]. Is it really permitted to accuse someone from this august rostrum, to say "You are guilty of this, which is written here"? Of course, I am not allowed to speak of Deputy Shulgin's lack of comprehension, since that is unacceptable, but gentlemen, try to understand, what else would you call Deputy Shulgin's lack of understanding of his own words and ideas?

Chairman: Now we will have the voting. Since the quarrel has been resolved, allow me to withdraw my motion to have Duma member Purishkevich removed from the hall. *(Exclamations: "Bravo!" Applause from center and right.)* Duma member Maklakov has the floor in regard to the voting order.

Maklakov: Gentlemen! Since the debate is ended, I have the right to speak only on my proposal about dividing the question into two parts and adding one correction. For this reason, and this reason alone, I have to allow Deputy Shulgin's speech to pass without comment. Unfortunately, I have to refrain from responding to the surprising accusations which we heard from him. *(Noise from the right.)*

Chairman, ringing his bell for order: I ask that you speak only on the voting order. *(Voice from the right: "We ask that you speak about the voting order, not about Shulgin. Shulgin has nothing to do with it.")*

Maklakov: But Deputy Shulgin should know— *(Count Bobrinskii from his seat: "Speak about the voting! This is not allowed! You are taking advantage!")* —All right, I will speak only about the voting order, since you are too noisy for me to answer Shulgin.

(Voices from the right: "This is not allowed!" Noise. Shulgin from his seat: "Please . . ." Voices: "No, you can't ask them.")

V. A. Maklakov speaks further about the voting order, and sometimes, unbeknownst to the Chairman, expresses his indignation at Shulgin's speech. P. N. Miliukov, speaking about the basis for the vote, does the same thing. E. P. Gegechkori was especially stubborn in his arguments with the Chairman, who interrupted him seven times with the admonition, "Please speak only about the order of voting."

Nevertheless, Gegechkori managed to insult Shulgin several times, which is entirely understandable. Crafty Shulgin, with luck, infringing upon the mandate, was somehow able to give his entire speech on the merits of the death penalty. Therefore it is understandable that his political opponents were likewise determined to reply on the merits of the question.

Finally, after no end of trouble, the question about the transfer of the bill was put up to a vote, and was passed by a vote of 170 to 133. The Duma decided to transfer the bill to a commission on court reform.

At which point V. M. Purishkevich exclaimed in his ringing tenor, "A first-class funeral for the bill."

Purishkevich was correct. The State Duma, as far as I can remember, never returned to the question of the death penalty. The war started, and in wartime the death penalty is used even in countries that don't use it in peacetime.

However, there is an exception to every rule. In 1917 the Provisional Government abolished the death penalty during the war. By that time I was not speaking in the Duma about its abolition.

* * *

Fate decided that the next day there would be an imperial audience at the Tsar's palace.

The peasants of Volyn sent a delegation of twelve men, one from each district, to St. Petersburg, headed by Archbishop Anthony of Volyn and Archimandrite Vitalii, a monk from the Pochaevskii monastery.

The Duma members from Volyn Province—peasants, landowners, priests, and intellectuals—joined the deputation, and thus it increased to twenty-seven—thirteen Duma members and twelve peasants headed by two clergymen.

It was notable that all of them, servants of the church, uneducated peasants, educated townsmen and landowners, representatives of the highest class, wore pins indicating their nationality and their political and social views.

They presented the Sovereign with a petition bearing one million signatures. What did the million loyal subjects ask, or rather beg, their Tsar to do? The petition was directed against the Duma. The church, the peasants, and the upper classes, speaking as one, informed the Tsar that they set all their hopes on the monarchy that God had ordered them to obey. Citizens aching for their country, they asked the Tsar to preserve the centuries-old power of the autocracy and not allow the Duma to infringe upon its rights.

The First and Second Dumas were seditious both in makeup and in action. Both trespassed on rights that historically belonged to Russia's Tsars. But in no way could this be said about the Third Duma. The majority of the deputies were loyal subjects—monarchists—and thus the tone of the petition was inappropriate with regard to the Third Duma. In this respect the request of the people of Volyn was a bit overdue and thus put the Sovereign in a difficult position. If he had not wanted a Duma at all, then there would have been no reason for him to allow elections for a Third Duma. With the Manifesto of October 17, 1905, he had created a people's representation. If he later became convinced that Russia was not mature enough for representative institutions, he could have discontinued the attempt and returned to the former autocratic order. But the Emperor did not do this. He recognized that Stolypin was right—the monarch and the State Duma must rule Russia jointly. As it happened, however, the following circumstances made it possible for the Sovereign to get out of this difficult position.

It had been decided that only one speech would be given before the Tsar, and that Archbishop Anthony would give it. The archbishop was a man of imposing appearance. Some said, in fact, that he looked like the renderings of the Lord as imagined, in their simplicity, by folk icon-painters.

He stood before the Tsar in his majestic purple cloak, leaning on his crosier with both hands. Speaking intelligently and feelingly about the relationship between the monarch and the State Duma, he asked the Tsar to retain his autocratic powers.

In his secular life, Archbishop Anthony was a member of the prominent Khrapovitskii family, which owned a large estate in Vladimir Province, roughly halfway between the cities of Vladimir and Murom. Now, in 1965, his estate and its buildings are a school of forestry.

In his youth he had been a cavalry officer. Taking monastic orders in 1885, he attained a high position in the course of time, becoming bishop of Volyn in 1902. On May 6 (19), 1906, he was made an archbishop, and not long before the start of the war, on May 14 (27), 1914, he was appointed archbishop of Karkov and Akhtyrsk.

After the February Revolution, on May 1 (14), 1917, the fifty-four-year-old archbishop was retired and sent to the Valaamskii monastery. On August 19 (September 1) of the same year he was reinstated by a decision of the Holy Synod and nominated for Patriarch by the regular clergy. In the election of October 1 (November 13), 1917, he received 150 votes, and Archbishop Tikhon received 162. Archbishop Anthony was elevated to the rank of Metropolitan on November 28 (December 11), 1917, and on May 19 (June 1), 1918, he became Metropolitan of the Ukraine. Metropolitan Anthony later emigrated to Yugoslavia, which at the time was called the Kingdom of the Serbs, Croats, and Slovenians. The Serbian Patriarch, Dimitrii, lived on a large and beautiful country estate in the town of Sremski Karlovtsi, and it was there that Metropolitan Anthony took up residence.

In 1921 a general meeting of representatives of the Russian church in exile, calling themselves a "synod," was convened in Sremski Karlovtsi. This so-called Karlovatskii Synod, which was concerned more with politics than church business, founded the Synod of Russian Churches in Exile. Metropolitan Anthony was appointed Patriarch, replacing Patriarch Tikhon, without the latter's consent. This caused a schism in the Russian Orthodox Church. The Moscow patriarchate resolutely disavowed the political actions taken by the clergy in exile, proclaiming that Metropolitan Anthony had no right whatsoever to speak in the name of the Russian Orthodox Church and the Russian people.

In a testament before his death, Patriarch Tikhon wrote, "The so-called Karlovatskii Synod did not bring about any good for the church and the people. We denounce it again and consider it necessary to declare clearly and strongly that any such attempt in the future will call forth strong reprisals."

After Patriarch Tikhon's death on April 7, 1925, the new Patriarch, Sergei, issued a decree repudiating the Karlovatskii Synod and declaring its actions illegal. It goes without saying that this had no effect on the priests in exile, who continued to bless the Russian people in "the battle with communism."

Thus Metropolitan Anthony's name is connected with one of the most tragic pages in the history of the Orthodox Church. As a staunch monarchist, he could not accept the revolution, but in the last years of his life he was not involved in politics. In his old age he was gentle and quiet, readying himself to leave the earthly world for the place where the righteous rest in eternal peace. The Metropolitan died in 1936 in the pastoral peace of the city of Sremski Karlovtsi, where the Serbian Patriarch, Dmitrii, had given him shelter.

I had deep ties with Anthony when he was the archbishop of Volyn. It was he who sent me to the State Duma three times. For a long time I wore three crosses that symbolized his pastoral blessing, but later lost them in the vicissitudes of life.

I continue my story of the royal audience in the palace.

On the other side of the petitioners stood Archimandrite Vitalii in black monastic attire, with the face of an ascetic. The archimandrite could have spoken more harshly but had decided to restrain himself. Suddenly one of the peasants spoke up. He and the other district representatives all held huge ledgers filled with signatures. Laying his ledger down, he began to speak in a loud voice, totally uncalled for since he was only a few steps away from the Sovereign. His surname was Bugai, which in Russian has two meanings, "bull," and "bittern," a type of bird. He lived up to his name, really roaring like a bull and wailing like a bittern. He reviled the State Duma in crude terms.

Not at all embarrassed, the Tsar listened to his indecent speech and responded with a totally unexpected question, which startled every-one, especially me. He asked, "Which one of you is Shulgin?" I was thunderstruck. Responding to some inner reflex and despite being dressed in tails, I took a giant step forward like a soldier and said, "I am, Your Imperial Majesty!"

His next words were, in essence, a reply to Bugai. The Tsar said, "At breakfast today the Empress and I read the speech you made yester-day in the State Duma. You spoke like a real Russian."

Somehow I managed to mumble, "I place the opinion of Your Imperial Majesty above everything else."

I'm afraid it came out as though I could not care less about the Empress' opinion, but I do not think that the Tsar took my words in that light. At any rate, the audience ended on this note. The Tsar bowed and left.

* * *

This incident showed one important thing—the Tsar clearly indi-cated that there are Dumas and then there are Dumas. In this case, through me, the Third Duma had expressed total respect for the monarchy. The Emperor specifically noted this and asserted that it was the true national path for Russia, a path which proclaimed itself a Union of the Russian People.

The founder of this union and of its organ, the newspaper *Russkoe znamia* ("The Russian Banner"), was a physician from St. Petersburg, Alexander Ivanovich Dubrovin. The union was ultra-right-wing, hostile to all other nationalities, especially Jews. If it had stayed within the bounds of good sense, it would have defended exclusively Russian interests. However, since the best defense is a good offense, Dubrovin switched to the offensive. And certain words were said and certain actions were taken that could indeed be construed as offensive. Among the masses, these slogans aroused pogromist feelings, and as a result the Union of the Russian People was justifiably blamed for starting pogroms.

The Volyn branch of the Union of the Russian People was not founded by Dr. Dubrovin but by Archimandrite Vitalii, the editor and publisher of the *Pochaevskii list* ("Pochaevskii Leaf") and the *Volynskii eparkhialskie izvestii* ("Volyn Diocesan News"). Vitalii never crossed the fateful line that would have permitted the masses of defenders of the faith who followed him to join the black camp of the aggressors. The movement he led, energetic but nonviolent, found its public expression in mass processions through towns and villages where the populace was mainly Jewish and Polish, the marchers carrying gonfalons, icons, and portraits of the Sovereign and loudly proclaiming, "Rus is coming!" So far as I know, pogroms against the Jews were unheard of in Volyn. There may have been some isolated outbreaks of hooliganism, but if so, they broke out under the dying hand of Archimandrite Vitalii.

*   *   *

Here it is appropriate to refer again to Archbishop Anthony. He was a leading statesman of the right wing, but because he was always mindful of his holy vows, he never allowed himself to cross certain lines.

In April 1903 the horrible pogrom in Kishinev took place. It was notorious for its bloody cruelty. After the pogrom, Archbishop Anthony, cross in hand, made a speech from the pulpit. This is what he said: "The people responsible for the massacre of the Jews in Kishinev dare not call themselves Christians. They gave themselves up to the Devil's prompting. Christians dare not forget that our Lord Jesus Christ was a Jew, as were his holy apostles. The Mother of Jesus was a Jew. She had relatives among her native people. Their descendants perhaps even now live among the Jews. It is horrible to think that among those who were killed in Kishinev, there may have been people whose veins pulsed with blood related to the blood of the Virgin Mary."

Undoubtedly Bishop Anthony's views made an impression on his subordinates, Archimandrite Vitalii and the monk Iliodor. The latter was a very colorful figure of that time. By birth he was a Don Cossack, and his Cossack vigor and boldness were always evident. Iliodor had a violent nature, but he did not overstep the ruling hand of Bishop Anthony, his superior. Iliodor had a singular talent for oratory; he was at his best speaking to groups and could captivate people into following him, but this gift turned his head.

Iliodor was a demagogue of the most unusual kind. I began to understand him one day in 1907 at a so-called Russian meeting in St. Petersburg, the first convocation of a group set up specifically for the purpose of bringing the capital's intelligentsia together. Many of those who attended were rather far from being Russians. Purishkevich, who was by no means a full-blooded Russian, played a major role in organizing the meeting, as did the barrister Paul Fedorovich Bulatsel, a Romanian from Bessarabia. As far as I can remember, the chairman did not have a Russian surname either.

On the evening I have in mind, it was the organization's governing council, rather than its full membership, that had assembled. It was not a large group. The deputies from Volyn, peasants and nonpeasants whom Iliodor had brought to St. Petersburg and tutored, had been invited. The chairman and the monk Iliodor were sitting at opposite ends of a long table covered by a green cloth with gold fringes.

The current situation was the subject of the discussion, and the government's weakness was being sharply criticized. Iliodor listened to the caustic comments about what should be done and suddenly, without even asking the chairman for the floor, said, "I hear and I see. None of you is proposing what is really needed. Our ancestors told us, 'For our sins the Lord sent us Tsar Ivan the Terrible.' And I say unto you, 'For our sins God gave us a weak Tsar.' And here is what should be done. When I raise the people of black Volyn and bring them here, to the capital, to our 'noble' St. Petersburg, and when we take steps to restore order, then we'll have what we need!"

Iliodor stopped speaking, but his raised arms threateningly finished what had been left unsaid. The wide sleeves of his monk's robe hung in the air like a blackbird's wings.

This bird had to rise from the fields of Volyn. And since I was no less responsible for the deeds of Volyn than the monk, I conquered my fear and said, in the guarded silence that fell after Iliodor's ringing words,

> I really don't know what side to be on, Father Iliodor. On one hand, I should go with Volyn. You called her "black." Two months ago, along with these peasants, the farmers of Volyn, who truly are black, because they toil in our black earth, and because our enemies call us the Black Hundreds, even though there are a million of us, two months ago I along with them won the election to the State Duma. Against whom?

Against the enemies of the Russian people. And you, Father Iliodor, in no small way assisted in that victory. Therefore, in truth I should go with you when you march on St. Petersburg.

But there is another side to the matter. A march on St. Petersburg! Why, that would be declaring war on the Tsar's capital, from which the Tsar rules Russia. For this reason, dear Father Iliodor, I am very much afraid that the Tsar, our Little Father, will see your attempt to restore order as a most real disorder, or, in other words, as riot and mutiny against the powers that support his autocratic rule, which God Himself orders us to obey, as is written in our Fundamental Laws. And I fear, honorable Father Iliodor, that His Imperial Majesty will see fit to order the Russian army, of which he is the commander, to put down the mutiny of which you, Father Iliodor, will be the head, using appropriate measures.

You said—perhaps succumbing to the temptation of your own eloquence—you said words that rang out like the Tsar's Great Bell.* But as we all know, the Tsar's Bell never rang. It fell from its height without ever making a sound. And for that reason you are not correct, Father Iliodor, when you say, "For our sins God gave us a weak Tsar." No! I say, "For our sins the Lord sent us a violent mutineer, if that is what the Don Cossack and monk from Volyn will be."

That was my speech in the spring of 1907 at a Russian meeting in the capital city of St. Petersburg. Perhaps I did not specifically mention the Tsar's Bell. I thought that up just now, carried away by my pen-pushing, as Iliodor once was by his eloquence. But all the rest I relate as it happened, and probably exactly as it was, if my memory does not fool me.

* * *

The day after this meeting, I came across Iliodor again in the richly furnished apartment of an acquaintance. Iliodor, in his black robe, was sitting in state in a beautiful silk-upholstered armchair. I went up to receive his blessing, as is proper. Making the sign of the cross over me, he asked, "Why did you attack me yesterday?" I answered, "Father Iliodor, is it permissible, no matter what happens, to so disrespectfully, one might say, take the Emperor by his collar and shake him?"

He answered, "And why not, if it's necessary?"

At that point we were interrupted. But it made me understand Iliodor.

---

*The Tsar's Great Bell is one of the most striking sights in the Kremlin. Weighing 193 tons and standing 6 meters high, it is the largest bell in the world. It was cast in 1733 but fell from its scaffolding during the Kremlin fire of 1737 and subsequently was set on a granite base. It has never been rung (trans.).

A year later, in 1908, Iliodor was transferred to Tsaritsin, where he expanded his activities, arousing both dismay and laughter throughout Russia. Under the sympathetic patronage of Bishop Germogen of Saratov, Iliodor built a church with a hall for meetings of the local chapter of the Union of the Russian People. No longer limiting his demagogic sermons to the Jews and the intelligentsia, he now attacked the privileged classes in general—merchants, civil sevants, the police. From the pulpit, with Germogen's support, he openly denounced Count S. S. Tatischev, the governor of Saratov, and as a result, in 1910, the governor was forced into retirement.

In January 1911 the Holy Synod transferred Iliodor to the Novosilskii monastery in the Tula eparchy. Refusing to obey the order, he locked himself up in his church with his followers, who numbered several thousand, and proclaimed a hunger strike, prostrating himself on the floor with his arms extended in the form of a cross and vowing not to get up until the unfair decision was changed. Whether he got up by himself or was picked up I cannot now remember, but in an effort to persuade the rebellious priests to obey the Synod, Bishop Parfenii of Tula was sent from St. Petersburg to Tsaritsin and then to Germogen in Saratov, and in addition, an aide-de-camp, Colonel A. N. Mandrika, was dispatched by royal order. All these exhortations failed, however, and Iliodor remained in Tsaritsin, while Germogen, in December of 1911, went to St. Petersburg for the winter session of the Holy Synod.

On January 3 (16), 1912, by royal command, Bishop Germogen was banished from the capital to his eparchy and was dismissed from the Holy Synod, whose decision he had refused to sign. The bishop, however, did not submit to the imperial will and, remaining in St. Petersburg, sent for Iliodor. Together they demanded that Rasputin break off all relations with the imperial family. In interviews with reporters the refractory priests, who considered themselves loyal subjects of the monarchy, sharply denounced the Holy Synod and Public Procurator V. K. Sabler. I remember reading a little poem in one of the leftist newspapers,

Nadoeli, nadoeli	I am sick of
Germogen, Iliodor,	Germogen and Iliodor.
Vot uzh skoro dve nedeli	Soon it will be two weeks
ikh poet gazetnyi khor.	That the papers have been singing their praises.

On January 17 (30), 1912, as a result of these seditious activities, Germogen was retired, and his cohort Iliodor, by a decree of the Holy Synod, was incarcerated in a monastery, the Florishchev Hermitage, about twenty-five kilometers from the city of Goro. Despite his imprisonment in the forest on the banks of the river Lukh, Iliodor still refused to submit to the will of his superiors. In October 1912, after unsuccessfully trying to escape from the hermitage, he sent them an accusatory message in which he addressed them as "worshippers of the holy devil, the dirty *Khlyst** Gregory Rasputin," demanding that the latter be defrocked and excommunicated, and condemning him as "this blasphemy masked under the name of God." When this missive went unanswered, Iliodor, on November 20 (December 3), sent the Synod a "renunciation" of God, faith, and the Church, slitting his wrist with a razor and signing the letter with his own blood. Only after this did a trial finally take place, and on December 17 (30), 1912, Iliodor was defrocked. Later he was released from the monastery and went home to the Don area, where he married under the secular name of Serge Trufanov. But soon after he was summoned in an inquest dealing with insults to the Tsar's family. The rebellious former monk did not tarry to learn the outcome of the inquest but disguised himself as a woman and fled abroad on July 2 (15), 1914. He settled in Oslo, Norway, where he wrote a book about Rasputin entitled *Sviatoi chert* ("The Holy Devil"). When the revolution began, Iliodor was living in America, pining for his former glory. In 1920 the former "loyal servant of the monarchy" again turned up in Tsaritsin, and under the title of "Russian pope" he founded the Living Church.† Proclaiming himself "Patriarch of all Russia" he came out against the head of the Orthodox Church, Tikhon. I do not know what happened to Iliodor.‡

* * *

---

*The Khlysty ("flagellants"), an orgiastic religious sect with gnostic overtones, maintained that immersion in sin, especially sexual sin, was an essential step in attaining holiness (trans.).

†Finding the established Orthodox Church insufficiently subservient for its purposes, the Communist government "adopted" the nascent Living Church, which enacted a sweeping series of liberal religious reforms and cooperated with the government in various spheres. Patriarch Tikhon, while in prison, was persuaded to endorse the new body but withdrew his support, after his release, when he became aware of what Timothy Ware, in *The Orthodox Church* (Baltimore: Pelican Books, 1963), calls "its crypto-communist character." For the same reason it was soon totally discredited among Orthodox believers both inside and outside Russia and by 1926 fell into a state of desuetude (trans.).

‡According to Robert K. Massie, in *Nicholas and Alexandra* (New York: Atheneum, 1967), Iliodor eventually found his way to New York City, where he became a Baptist and worked as a janitor in the Metropolitan Life Insurance Company building on Madison Square. He died in Bellevue Hospital in 1952 (trans.).

Among those at the Russian meeting that portentous night was another "loyal subject," an ultra-rightist. Later he said to me, "When I heard you speak at the Russian meeting, I thought you were an Octobrist." Coming from him, this was almost an insult, in spite of the fact that the Octobrists had accepted the October Manifesto in good faith and were loyal monarchists. Like Iliodor, this right-winger was only a monarchist for show. In essence he was a revolutionary. For this reason, in retrospect, the following thought occurs unwillingly.

The Bolsheviks, heading the revolutionary movement, had to come to power, because, leaning on the people, they chipped away at the monarchy from the left. And the right? The right virtually aided them by attacking the monarchy from the right. This became clear when Purishkevich stood up against Stolypin in 1911, and even clearer when he killed Rasputin in 1916. No matter how corrupt Rasputin may have been, he was, after all, the closest "friend" of the imperial family. By killing him, the monarchist Purishkevich lifted his hand against the monarchy.

When the news of Rasputin's murder was announced in Moscow, a play was being performed in the Imperial Theater. The audience welcomed the news with applause and demanded that the national anthem be sung. This event throws a bright light on the confused views of the Russian monarchists of the time.

These contradictory feelings had begun much earlier, and the loyal subject to whom I referred above was an outstanding example of these "heroes of our time." Undoubtedly, he shared Iliodor's psychology, and, to boot, he had developed a persecution mania.

One day we attended a large political banquet, put on after some charity performance with the aim of supporting a recently formed group of academy students. Its members were supposedly defending the universities against political intrusions, but since everything was topsy-turvy at the time, they themselves formed a political party, and a very active one at that. Upon finishing the university in 1899, I too, with revolver in hand, had defended my right to attend lectures.

It was only natural that the "loyal subject" and I would attend the academy dinner together. It happened that I was seated next to his wife, a very pretty German woman. Suddenly she said to me, "Lean over a bit and block me from my husband's view."

Since he was very jealous, I naturally asked, "He isn't really jealous of me, is he? There is no reason for it."

She wisely answered, "Jealousy needs no reason. But I just want to eat some caviar."

"He won't let you?"

"He won't let me eat caviar, because he says it is easiest to poison someone that way."

Without him noticing, I put some caviar on her plate. A few days later I observed another example of his paranoia.

One morning we were having coffee together in the Andreev Cafe. In the evening this cafe was filled to capacity with ladies of easy morals, but during the day it served excellent coffee. The waitress stopped at our table with a large tray of pastries. I indicated the apple pastry closest to me, but my companion interfered.

"Allow me to choose one for you," he said, pointing to an identical pastry at the opposite end of the tray. She put it on my plate, and when she had left, he said to me, "You are not at all careful. Never accept what they thrust upon you."

"Why not?"

"Because you might be poisoned."

This was unlikely, but I did not waste time arguing. I preferred to steer the conversation back to general politics. I already valued P. A. Stolypin. I liked his healthy common sense in the face of Iliodor and the like, but he was attacked by both the left and the right.

Further conversation with the man who feared pastries revealed to me the deep-rooted, wild fanaticism that lay hidden in him. He made up all sorts of things about Stolypin, and related the following anecdote.

"When Stolypin was still governor of Saratov, a certain old general paid him a visit. The conversation turned to the vicissitudes of life. And Stolypin said, 'Your Excellency, today you paid me a visit. I am grateful for the honor you have shown me, but you really shouldn't have done it. Even though I am governor, I cannot guarantee that you will not be attacked as you leave.'

"Stolypin's fear was realized. A bomb was thrown at the general's escort. It is true that he lived, but you can't convince me"—here the maniac's eyes shone triumphantly—"that Stolypin did not know of the planned murder."

I thought he was crazy but nonetheless asked, "But why would Governor Stolypin want to kill a retired general?"

"Why? You are so naive! Why, the general was a true rightist."

"And Stolypin?"

"Stolypin is a leftist, a secret revolutionary, and the rightist general, even though retired, was in his way!"

After this I decided to keep my distance from this intriguer, but it was not always possible.

* * *

South of Berlin, in Germany, lies a town named Wittenau. Perhaps the ancestors of the renowned Russian statesman were Wittenauers, that is, inhabitants of the town of Wittenau. I am going by analogy— the surname of the former federal Chancellor, Adenauer, means "inhabitant of Adenau."

Sergei Iulevich Witte, as he himself said one day in the State Council, was a school friend of Dmitrii Ivanovich Pikhno, another member of the upper house. The former school chums met again, although not on school benches but in the smoking lounge of the legislature.

The two friends maintained a warm personal relationship, although they often differed on political matters. D. I. Pikhno greatly respected Peter Stolypin, while Count Witte opposed Stolypin's programs.

Witte was born June 17 (29), 1849, in Tiflis to the family of a high-ranking official. Upon graduating from the Novorossiiskii University in Odessa with a degree in physics, the future Minister of Communications and Finance studied railroad transportation. In 1883 he wrote a book entitled *Printsipy zbeleznogorozhnykh tarifov po perevozke gruzov* ("Principles of Railroad Tariffs in the Transportation of Goods") which brought him widespread fame.

Involved in this, he again ran into D. I. Pikhno, whose dissertation also was on railroad tariffs. Pikhno at that time held a chair in the University of St. Vladimir in Kiev. He became a professor very young, when he was twenty-four years old, in 1877. Students attending his lectures were often older than their professor. However, he had to interrupt his teaching at the Kiev university when he was invited to move to the capital by the Minister of Finance, Nicholas Christianovich Bunge, who from 1887 to 1895, the year of his death, served as Chairman of the Council of Ministers—what would now be called Prime Minister. Bunge was born in Kiev on November 11 (23), 1823, on the shores of the Dnieper River, and at age twenty-seven, in 1850, occupied a chair in the economics department at the University of Kiev, and from 1865 served as director of the Kiev branch of the State Bank.

Nicholas Christianovich was one of those Germans about whom Prince A. D. Obolenskii said that they could not simply be called Germans, but "Russian Germans." Formerly a Lutheran, Bunge asked in his will that a Russian service be recited at his funeral. I don't know if it could be considered proof of his "Russianness" that he was godfather to whom? Sinful me.

I met him only once, 1886, after we had moved to St. Petersburg. I was then eight years old. Suddenly I was summoned into the living room.

"Come here, your godfather has arrived!"

Being a young boy, I had only a vague idea of what a godfather was. All of a sudden I saw a tall man in a black coat trimmed with gold and—oh, horrors!—white pants! The little boy thought his godfather was in his underpants, and wanted to run away. The fact of the matter was that Bunge was paying a visit to Dmitrii Ivanovich straight from the palace, where he had been presented, in court dress, to the

Sovereign. And white trousers were a necessary part of the uniform.

I was side-tracked. D. I. Pikhno did not serve very long. Disagreeing with the minister to whom he reported, he handed in his resignation. However, he had already been promoted to Councillor of State and thus, as an official of the fourth class, was addressed as "Your Excellency."* Along with the title he was admitted to the hereditary nobility—in other words, his children would also be members of the nobility.

As is well known, to a large extent the Russian nobility consisted of persons who had distinguished themselves in service to the state and thus were called the "service nobility." Members of the ancient nobility accepted them, but only to a certain point. The line of demarcation often seemed to go unnoticed, but in actuality it was uncrossable. Some were painfully aware of this.

Fortunately, it did not bother me, but only because I always expected to find barbed wire among the beautiful flowers of graciousness, even where it did not exist.

I have digressed again. Why, I was talking about Sergei Iulevich Witte! He, of course, had to struggle through barbed wire, for St. Petersburg was hostile to his career advances. Very much so. Empress Maria Fedorovna ordinarily did not meddle in her husband's affairs, but about Witte she said, "They say that he's a real character."

And how did the Emperor respond to the gossip in the capital?

In a kingly fashion. He summoned Witte and told him, "They say the devil knows what about you. Pay no attention to it. Remember one thing—the Tsar is behind you!"

How did Witte achieve such a great, even brilliant, career? After the railroad tariffs he continued working on the railroad; that is, he continued to be involved in railroad matters, even though he was not an engineer but a mathematician. His successful railroad career was no less headspinning than his later political career. He served as district manager of the state-owned railroad in Odessa and soon moved to St. Petersburg as traffic superintendent of the Southwestern Railroad, and later, to Kiev, as general manager. The Southwestern Railroad belonged to an extremely wealthy and modern-minded private company. The salary of a railroad director was 40,000 rubles a year, while the salary of a minister was 17,000. In time, a man of Witte's ability would have attained that post and thus would have been earning twice a minister's salary. But fate decided differently.

*   *   *

In 1888 I was ten years old, but I remember well the oh's and ah's

---

*In the Table of Civil Ranks, a Privy Councillor was equivalent in grade to a Major General (trans.).

and the talk and lamentation in connection with the derailment of the imperial train not far from the Borki station. The royal family was spared, but the youngest daughter, Olga, received a sharp blow in her back and the poor girl became hunchbacked for life.

People began to view the accident as a miraculous saving of the imperial family. God-fearing old women called it "the sacred catastrophe." Many years later I learned that the "sacred catastrophe" could have been avoided if the Tsar had heeded Witte's warning. He had stated that the huge imperial train was very heavy. Passenger-train locomotives could not pull it alone, so two freight locomotives were attached. These monsters, if driven too fast, begin to sway so hard that they can rip up the ties and then the rails, causing a train to derail.

The memoirs of Witte and A. F. Koni cover this incident more thoroughly, although the two memoirists differ somewhat in their explanations. But undoubtedly, when the accident occurred as Witte had predicted, Alexander III remembered the Southwestern Railroad man's warning. That circumstance could well have been the reason for Witte's meteoric and brilliant rise.

The next year, on Alexander's wishes, he was appointed director of the railroad department of the Ministry of Finance, and on February 15 (27), 1892, he was appointed Minister of Communications. Then, on August 30 (September 11), of that year, Witte assumed the post of Minister of Finance. From that time on he worked in two directions: correcting the state of Russia's finances, and building railroads. Furthermore, he assumed two other duties, becoming the patron of technological enlightenment, and exerting pressure on the government to build schools of higher education, including the polytechnic in Kiev named after Alexander II. There he again met up with his old friend D. I. Pikhno, who was involved in the construction of the polytechnic.

Witte's fourth act was less respectable, or at any rate was controversial. Witte established a state monopoly on vodka, and thus the treasury began to trade in this poison. The more hostile opponents of the policy said outright that the treasury was helping to create drunkards.

Foreseeing such criticisms, Witte established temperance societies at the same time that he set up the vodka monopoly. The St. Petersburg temperance society spared no expense, building a recreation center for 10,000 people, with theaters and various other forms of entertainment. But the work of the societies had no noticeable effect on drunkenness. It had been assumed that entertainment would distract the people from vodka, but this happy thought was never fulfilled. Even when the cinema was introduced, people did not stop drinking. After an interesting show, they would cap the evening in the society of the even more enticing green snake.

In comparison with the past, the treasury's profits from the monopoly increased significantly, and the quality of vodka improved. To prevent theft, employees of the monopoly were paid relatively high wages, thereby attracting a better class of salespeople. However, there were revolting sights in front of the government liquor stores. Before the monopoly people would go to drinking houses and taverns, sit at tables, and perhaps have something to eat. The drinking house was a sort of club, albeit of low standards. After the reforms, the drinking houses closed. People who needed vodka guzzled it right out of the bottle, and drunks would collapse in the street.

Also under Witte's initiative the Siberian railroad was started, an event of great significance. On Alexander III's monument was written, "Builder of the Trans-Siberian Railroad."

In 1897 Witte instituted a monetary reform based on the gold standard, for which a gold reserve of half a billion rubles was started. He attracted 3 billion rubles of foreign capital to Russia. This in turn helped develop industry and various businesses, for example, tramway construction. Witte raised the issue of voluntary liquidation of peasant land communes.* Economists at Kiev University, starting with Professor N. C. Bunge, had long called for a solution to this question.

On January 22 (February 4), 1902, a special council, with Witte as chairman, was formed to study the country's agricultural needs. The council, given a wide mandate, established 536 district committees. In general, the central and provincial committees passed resolutions on the desirability of transferring allotted land to the peasants as personal property. Keeping in mind that there were 1.6 million square kilometers of allotted land, the reform was grandiose. Because of the opposition of Minister of the Interior Plehve, Witte was not able to begin the reform. However, with the Manifesto of November 9 (22), 1906, Stolypin was later able to accomplish what Witte could not. It seems to me that this was the true reason for Witte's intense hatred of Stolypin.

Witte's Far Eastern policy was two-sided. For economic reasons he sought to obtain the port of Dairen as an outlet to the Pacific Ocean, but he opposed the construction of the fortress at Port Arthur, fearing an untimely war with Japan. Thanks to the treaty he negotiated with China in 1896, the Sino-Western Railroad was built between 1897 and 1903, a matter of great importance in view of the developing economic ties between Russia and Korea. In opposition to State Secretary

---

*The agrarian reform proposed by Witte, subsequently implemented in many respects by Stolypin, was intended to increase agricultural productivity and provide a new social prop for the regime by fostering the development of a class of independent peasant freeholders unimpeded by the traditional authority of the communes (trans.).

A. M. Bezobrazov and his group, Witte condemned the proposed seizure of Korea, which had the aim of exploiting her natural resources and would have been carried out by the Russian Forest Industry Company, founded by the State Secretary's group in 1901. On this Witte was again in agreement with Pikhno, who considered further involvements in Korea a dangerous game.

However, on August 16 (29), 1903, the opponent of expansion in Manchuria and Korea was dismissed from the post of Minister of Finance and appointed Chairman of the Council of Ministers.

Undoubtedly, Witte's greatest accomplishment was the peace treaty with Japan, signed on August 23 (September 5), 1905, in Portsmouth, New Hampshire. Although in Russian the name Portsmouth sounds like "port of disturbances," there was no discord in Portsmouth that day. On the contrary, an agreement favorable to both sides was reached. After her unsuccessful war with Japan, Russia expected to be required to pay a large indemnity and suffer a significant territorial loss. Witte managed to spare Russia from paying any indemnity, and in territory Russia only had to return to Japan half of the island of Sakhalin, which was not a significant loss. In return for negotiating this treaty, the title of count was quite deservedly bestowed upon him. Nonetheless, certain wits immediately began to make fun, calling Witte the "half-Sakhalin count." But the Portsmouth treaty could probably be considered Witte's swan song.

* * *

On October 17, 1905, the imperial manifesto was signed, granting various freedoms and establishing a representative assembly in the form of the State Duma. It was hoped that this would appease the country, which had been greatly affected by the defeat in the Far East. It is now known that the plan backfired. The liberal reforms only incensed the revolutionary elements in the nation and pushed them to greater activism.

Meanwhile, Witte was one of the three men who had extorted the manifesto from Nicholas II.

The first of them was a nonpartisan lawyer, G. S. Khrustalev-Nosar, who in 1905, as chairman of the St. Petersburg Soviet of Workers' Deputies, managed to organize a nationwide general strike. Everything stopped: mail, telegraph, railroads. Stores, newspapers, and theaters closed. Life stood still. Even Tsarskoe Selo was cut off from St. Petersburg, its private railroad also shut down.

The second man involved was Grand Duke Nicholas Nicholaevich, commander of the St. Petersburg military district. Begging the Tsar to grant the manifesto, he further thickened the painful atmosphere by threatening to shoot himself if Nicholas refused. He maintained that he could not vouch for the troops, who were ready to mutiny. This seems to have been the truth.

Finally Serge Iulevich Witte also insisted upon the manifesto. In connection with the establishment of a representative system, the Committee of Ministers was abolished in April of 1906. Its administrative functions were divided between the State Council and the Council of Ministers, with Witte appointed Chairman of the latter. But since the manifesto did not accomplish its goal, and Serge Iulevich had compromised himself in the eyes of the Sovereign, he was obliged to resign as Chairman on April 16 (29), 1906, though he remained a member of the upper house and became the leader of the opposition. Witte died on February 28 (March 13), 1915, during the war, leaving his valuable *Memoirs*.*

* * *

When the Emperor was informed that the plan to reform the zemstvos in the western provinces was Stolypin's idea and did not have anyone else's support, the Tsar supposedly said, "Then I was fooled again," and the plan was killed. Learning that the Emperor believed that he "had been fooled again," Stolypin had no alternative but to resign. But the Tsar did not accept Stolypin's resignation.

The Tsar had no one to replace Stolypin. St. Petersburg gossips made much of the fact that Empress Alexandra Fedorovna did not like Stolypin. For example, Stolypin's wife once put on a dinner party, inviting various dignitaries, both military and civil service. It was the custom for men to remove their weapons for dinner parties and leave them in the antechamber.

Military men dined in possession of their weapons only with the Tsar at the imperial palace, but during the dinner at Olga Borisovna Stolypin's, the military men did not remove their weapons, and dined with sabers and dirks on their belts. When this breach of etiquette was brought to the Empress' attention, she supposedly let drop a comment, "Well, before there were two Empresses, and now there will be three: Maria Fedorovna, Alexandra Fedorovna, and Olga Borisovna."

This anecdote, if it is an anecdote, throws some light on the atmosphere around the throne. Empress Alexandra Fedorovna did not like the widowed mother of the Emperor, Maria Fedorovna. Antipathy between wife and mother-in-law is not unusual, but in this case there was another reason. The dowager valued and supported Stolypin. She understood that he was a prominent statesman fully capable of replacing Witte, but that there was no replacement for Stolypin.

---

*Count Sergius Witte, *Memoirs,* trans. and ed. by Abraham Yarmolinsky (New York: Doubleday, Page, 1921) (trans.).

The reigning Empress did not like Stolypin for the very reason that he was a dignitary of high caliber. It was as though he overshadowed the Tsar, her husband.

Perhaps she was right. Stolypin possessed qualities indispensable in an autocrat, and Nicholas lacked them, as was manifested even in his relations with his wife. Empress Alexandra not only displayed caustic humor but also drew good caricatures. And it was said that the Tsar would sometimes find the following type of drawing on his desk:

He, the Emperor, with crown and scepter, would be portrayed as an infant at the breast of his mother. This was directed at the dowager.

In another caricature Nicholas was dressed in the style of the seventeenth century, with the face of the spineless Tsar Fedor Ioannovich. The caption reads, "Well, am I a Tsar, or am I not?"

It was said that Nicholas would laugh good-naturedly at his wife's caricatures.

But the fact is, Tsars live in glass houses. Everything that goes on in the palace immediately becomes known. And the whole capital laughed at the autocratic Tsar, but far from good-naturedly. They vilified him. Grumbling St. Petersburg called the Tsar "the Colonel" because after the death of Alexander III there was no one to promote Nicholas to a general's rank.

When Stolypin submitted his resignation, the capital suddenly grew fearful and gloomy. A black cloud hung over the city for three days. The Tsar insisted that Stolypin stay, while the insulted Prime Minister held his ground.

The newspapers did not pass up this opportunity to strike another blow at the already shaky government. A poem appeared about Boris Godunov, and the way he was described made it obvious that the author was describing Stolypin. Even the leader of the Cadet party, Professor Paul Nicholaevich Miliukov, announced from the rostrum of the Duma on March 15 (28), 1911, to the sound of applause from the left, "We have the new Boris Godunov to thank for these measures!"

Many people did not like Stolypin, most of all the Tsarina, then Count Witte. It seems to me that this important dignitary envied his successor and could not reconcile himself to the fact that after his dismissal from the post of Prime Minister, he was appointed to the State Council, which was called a warehouse for discharged ministers.

In short, St. Petersburg was worried and waited impatiently to learn the outcome of all this.

And the outcome was—

* * *

Ordinarily I go to bed late, and in those days even more so. My solicitous valet, Nazar, would bring me my morning tea and wake me.

One morning, as I was having breakfast in bed, my stepfather, Dmitrii Ivanovich, came to see me. He was in his robe, holding a newspaper, and said, "What heavy hands Peter Arkadevich [Stolypin] has!" The tone of his voice was both complimentary and critical.

This is what had happened. The State Council and the State Duma had been adjourned for three days, from March 12 to 15. On Saturday, March 12 (25), 1911, when the deputies of the Duma assembled in the Tauride Palace, A. I. Guchkov had opened the session with the following announcement: "Your attention, please. I will now read the signed imperial decree to the Senate: 'On the basis of article 99 of the Fundamental State Laws, I command that the work of the State Duma cease on the twelfth (twenty-fifth) of this month, to be resumed on March 15 (28), 1911.' The next session will take place on Tuesday, March 15 (28), 1911, at 11:00 A.M. I declare this session of the State Duma adjourned." And everyone left.

On March 14 (27), 1911, by a royal mandate secured by Stolypin, the law on the formation of zemstvos in the western provinces was passed on the basis of article 87 of the Fundamental Laws.

On the same day that the Emperor signed the decree adjourning the Duma, a royal command was put into effect banishing Trepov and Durnov abroad until January 1 (14), 1912, for agitation and strong opposition to Stolypin's bill in the State Council.

This royal attention to the health of V. F. Trepov and P. N. Durnov was, of course, only a gesture to satisfy Stolypin. It turned out that it was two half-crazy old men who said that he had "fooled the Tsar." Accusations by crazy people mean nothing, but one of them, Trepov, did not obey the royal command and submitted his resignation. He was removed from his post on April 29 (May 12), 1911, and found work in the private sector.

Thus the law on the zemstvos was passed under article 87 of the Fundamental Laws, which is why both houses were dismissed for three days, after which time they resumed their work.

Already at the first evening sitting of the Duma after work was resumed, that is, on March 15 (28), 1911, four inquiries against Stolypin were submitted—"four pillars, or mainstays," as I said, from the following parties: Octobrists, People's Freedom, Progressives, and Social Democrats. The inquiries were about the irregularity of the royal edicts of March 11 (24) and 14 (27) suspending the legislative institution and the passing into law of article 87 on the zemstvos in six western provinces.

Even the Octobrists were upset by this "pressure on the law." Only part of the right and we Russian Nationalists were loyal to Stolypin in trouble.

I defended Stolypin as well as possible, not out of fear but out of conscience. However, I defended him badly, that is, with poor results. At the end of my speech I said,

> Today there was a prolonged attack on P. A. Stolypin. I was not called upon to defend him, and so I put before you one question.
>
> This man undertook a great burden. On his shoulders lies the dissolution of the First Duma, the dissolution of the Second Duma, the law of June 3, the law of November 9, the fight, a hard battle, against disorder in the universities. This man is overburdened— *(Laughter from the left)* —perhaps he can be pushed, perhaps you will shake him, perhaps he will fall. But answer this: who then will undertake the burden?

There was applause only from the nationalists. The right was silent. But there was a violent reaction to my words from the others.

My sharpest critic was an Armenian deputy from the Don province, a doctor and lawyer, the Cadet Moisei Sergievich Adzhemov, who said:

> Gentlemen, a fashionable group is speaking as if it were a government group. Its newly chosen leader, Deputy Shulgin, is speaking, and what do we hear?
>
> According to Deputy Shulgin the important thing that was said was that everything was directed against P. A. Stolypin. In the words of Deputy Shulgin, he is "overburdened." He is overburdened, says Deputy Shulgin, with the dissolution of two Dumas; he is overburdened with the law of June 3, which is an act of revolution; he is overburdened with the act of November 9, which, it seems, from the point of view of Deputy Shulgin, was unlawfully passed by article 87, since he places it on the same level as the law of June 3; he is overburdened, finally, with the events of today, and we hope that this load is such that it will sink him.

Not a few rebukes were directed at me by Count Alexei Alexevich Uvarov, the spokesman of the Progressive faction, who had served as clerk of special commissions to the governor of Warsaw, Gurko, and to Minister of the Interior Plehve, and as councillor of the city duma in Saratov and member of the Saratov district zemstvo.

> Since the government is not represented here at the present time, I feel that Mr. Shulgin is serving as its spokesman. . . . I must say to Shulgin that I personally have always opposed the law on western zemstvos.
>
> I think, gentlemen, that you *(addressing the right)* have absolutely nothing to do with the western zemstvos and have nothing to do with article 87. You just meekly and blindly obey the orders of whoever is in power.
>
> In this regard, I remind you of the following: The motto of Count Arakcheev, who lived at the beginning of the last century, was: "devoted without flattery." Yes, he was as devoted to Alexander I as you gentlemen are to Stolypin; but you cannot include the words "without flattery" in your motto.
>
> . . . if you continue to support Stolypin, you will destroy yourselves.

Why are you here? No one needs you. We could just as well have wooden dummies in your place that would respond with a yes whenever Stolypin says anything.

The deepest impression, however, was made by V. M. Purish-kevich's speech. So long as Russian history is recorded, I do not doubt that the name of this deluded, mutinous, impassioned statesman of the final, stormy, and tragic years of the fall of the empire will never be forgotten. This particular speech of his reveals the extent to which the act of March 14 (27), 1911, shook the foundations of the already unsteady government.

Furthermore, it explains psychologically why Purishkevich, an ardent monarchist, participated in the murder of Rasputin, who was idolized by the Tsar's family.

Purishkevich received loud applause from the left, but this did not embarrass him or stop him. His speech was so unexpected and out of character that even Iu. K. Ermolaev, an Old Believer peasant from the village of Melnitsa who was the deputy from Vitebsk Province, said in bewilderment, "When Mr. Purishkevich stepped up to the rostrum, I didn't know who was speaking, Purishkevich or Gegechkori. I think they exchanged tongues!"

I will include the more characteristic parts of Purishkevich's speech, as a document which reflects the confusion and shaking of minds during the government's crisis.

   . . . Apart from the law passed by the Sovereign, which we cannot discuss, there are the actions of the Chairman of the Council of Ministers, and it is precisely about these actions that I want to speak, because at the present moment only a groveler would be able to remain silent after what has been done to us, and specifically, I will say, as a member of this house, after what has been done to me. The Chairman of the Council of Ministers has trampled on the authority and meaning of the State Council.
   . . . Chairman of the Council of Ministers Stolypin, stung at the very moment when he was unsuccessfully speaking about the law to introduce zemstvos, decided to even his personal accounts with members of the State Council, one by one. Taking advantage of his influence, he distorted the spirit and meaning of their speeches and allowed himself to deal an indirect blow to the State Council, discrediting for many years to come the authority of this high imperial institution.
   At a time when the most strenuous use of the legitimate powers of the empire is needed, at a time when the empire is on the eve of great internal and external upheavals, the Chairman of the Council of Ministers, out of personal feelings, not governmental need but personal vengeance, allows himself to square accounts, all the while crying about legality, with the chairman of the rightists in the State Council, P. N. Durnov. The nationalists of the party of the right cry, "Oh my!" but the

nationalists hid in their burrows during the years of disturbance, when P. N. Durnov, to whom Russia virtually owes its peace, worked like a slave to crush the revolutionary powers and achieved brilliant results.

An authentic nationalist is not he who shouts that he is a nationalist, but he who works in a spirit of nationalism to preserve the age-old traditions of Russia's origins.

Does the Chairman of the Council of Ministers want to turn the State Council into his personal office? He will never be able to achieve this, because any desire to work is lost when one is under the whip, under the rod, of the Chairman of the Council of Ministers, and if the Chairman is not pleased, then out you go, take yourself abroad.

Yes, gentlemen, today, while we were in session, I learned that P. A. Stolypin has deigned to send P. N. Durnov a letter in which he wrote, "You may go abroad, since you are unwell." The response was, "I am fine and will remain in Russia." Gentlemen, P. A. Stolypin, who has re- peatedly spoken here about conformity with the law, now brings us back to an era that did not taste of the freedom of October 17, not to the time of Bühren* but to far worse times, when certain people would betray those whom they considered objectionable. And P. A. Stolypin, feeling powerless to fight P. N. Durnov with the strength of his convictions, although he has more authority than Durnov, demanded that his polit- ical opponent, one of the most outstanding, powerful, strong, and tal- ented people in Russia, be betrayed.

That is what Stolypin has done. The spokesman of the nationalist faction, V. V. Shulgin, appealed to us, defending P. A. Stolypin's actions by saying, "You will drive him away, you will overthrow him, but with whom will you replace him?"

To this I reply to the nationalists: We have no right to drive him away; we do not encroach upon imperial rights, nor do we have the right to replace him, but I daresay that poor is the country, poor, the people, that rest all their hopes for the salvation and regeneration of Russia on one man.

* * *

In the Ministers' Pavilion of the Tauride Palace there was an ever-present official who in the jargon of the Duma was called "manager of the ministers." Members of the Duma went to him on all matters. This was Councillor of State Leo Constantinovich Kumanin, Clerk of Spe-cial Commissions to the Chairman of the Council of Ministers.

A glassed-in veranda led away from the so-called Half-Circle Hall. When darkness fell, a green velvet drape would be drawn so that the

---

*Ernst Johann Bühren (1690–1772), a German, was one of the favorites of Empress Anna, who reigned from 1730 to 1740. He had great influence at court and is said to have utilized an extensive network of informers and spies (trans.).

ministers, walking to the meeting hall, could not be seen from outside. There had already been enough attempts upon the life of Stolypin. Since it would have been possible to shoot at the glassed-in veranda from the yard, a drape covering the entire length of the veranda was put up.

In his office Kumanin kept all manner of books on Russian and foreign laws, encyclopedias, dictionaries, and other reference books. This highly placed official was distinguished by his extraordinary politeness; in spite of this he held himself coolly aloof from everyone. I never saw a smile on his face. As the saying goes, he was buttoned all the way up, though in reality he did not button a single button, because it was not proper to button the long black frockcoat which he unfailingly wore. The lapels of his frockcoat were sewn with black lace, his vest trimmed with a snow-white braid. He wore starched collars, and a tie with a plain gold tie pin. If he had not been somewhat stooped, he could have been called a tailor's delight. Like Stolypin, he dressed elegantly but not foppishly.

Kumanin worked far beyond his strength but hid this fact. One's health is an intimate thing, and to be on intimate relations with anyone at work was not proper.

He came up to me and said, "Peter Arkadevich asks that you come see him." P. N. Balashev and someone else, I can't remember who, were also invited on this occasion. Peter Nicholaevich Balashev was the spokesman of our faction, the Russian Nationalists. After the Octobrists, we were the strongest party, numerically. The constellation of Stolypin, Guchkov, and Balashev formed the "belt of Orion" in the Duma. Everything that Stolypin introduced, if agreed to by Guchkov and Balashev, would pass the Duma.

The meeting took place late at night, as was usual at that time. He went to bed at 4:00 A.M., having started work at nine. For this reason he would receive people late at night.

When we entered, Peter Arkadevich turned first to me. He held out his hand, which was crippled, I do not know how, but still usable for a firm handshake. At the moment I reflected that this was the very hand about which my stepfather, Dmitrii Ivanovich, had said, "What heavy hands Peter Arkadevich has!" Peter Arkadevich addressed me: "I am grateful that you defended me today. But I cannot be defended." He continued, now addressing all of us. "It can be said, of course, that I applied pressure on the law. Article 87 of the Fundamental Laws was intended for a longer time period, but that is not indicated in the article. Therefore, formally I am right; I did not violate the Fundamental Laws. But technically, if one honestly interprets the intentions of the legislators, my interpretation definitely presses the letter of the law to the limit. And you may try to defend me, but you cannot." The last sentence was directed at me again, softened with a grateful smile.

He continued, speaking to us all. This was a defensive speech, not directed at us but over our shoulders. After all, we were not judging him—we defended him.

"But what else could I do? You remember, of course, that not so long ago the Sovereign received a delegation which consisted solely of peasants. And addressing the peasants in western Russia, the Tsar said, 'You will have zemstvos.'

"These words were given full circulation, and all of Russia soon learned what he had said. But can the Tsar's words be treated in this fashion? If the Tsar makes a promise and his officials break it, the throne itself is shaken. I had to repulse any such action, otherwise I would be joining those who are undermining the monarchy with 'authority and ignorance.'"

The western peasants, whom the Tsar had promised zemstvos, evidently anticipated that they would thereby strengthen their position in the Duma, where they had seventeen deputies out of a total of sixty-one. The reform which Stolypin put into effect did not have the desired effect, however. The six western provinces were able to send only fourteen peasants to the Fourth Duma.

My memory fails me on what happened next. Probably nothing very important. After all, Peter Arkadevich had asked to see us in order to bare his soul, so to speak, before friends who had not deserted him in his hour of need.

However, it must be said that Peter Arkadevich overplayed his hand. Very likely it would have been better to have given Trepov and Durnov a warning after they gave wrong information to the Tsar, and not to have rushed through the matter of the western zemstvos. The government had the right to reintroduce a law in the State Duma after a period of time. This was not as effective but was more constitutional, and if Stolypin had done so, his authority would not have suffered—and this was important. Very important.

The Chairman of the Council of Ministers waited for the raging passions within the walls of the Tauride Palace to subside, and it was not until April 27 (May 10), 1911, that he made a response to the four inquiries in connection with the adoption of article 87 and the dismissal of the legislative houses for three days. Stolypin assured the Duma that his actions had strengthened, not reduced, the rights of the people's government.

However, the people's representatives did not agree, and at this session, by an overwhelming majority of 203 to 82, they passed a resolution to turn their attention to the usual matters, acknowledging a violation of article 87. The Duma called the government's action unlawful and its explanation unsatisfactory.

It was not only in Russia that hereditary monarchies were losing their authority. Certain "leaders"—in other words, the newly risen fascism—came to their aid. In Italy, Mussolini saved the Savoy dynasty for a time. But I daresay that Stolypin was his predecessor. He attempted to save the Romanov dynasty with the help of reforms. He preserved the State Duma, but by hastening the slow-moving five hundred-voice behemoth, he attempted to quickly heal Russia's foremost weak point—the disgraceful land situation.

And force did not speed up legislative procedure in the matter of the western zemstvos. Although the zemstvo question was again introduced in the Duma, the Third Duma did not come to a decision, and the fate of the bill was left to the Fourth Duma.

Gunshot in Kiev

O N SEPTEMBER 1 (15), 1911, I was somewhere in the Crimea, or perhaps on a steamship. That day, actually that evening, at the Kiev Theater, an agent of the Kiev secret police, G. D. Bogrov, shot Chairman of the Council of Ministers Stolypin and fatally wounded him. I did not witness this catastrophe, but my stepfather did and told me about it.

Why did this occur in Kiev, a city that was not only the most pro-monarchy but also the most pro-Stolypin? Stolypin's famous telegram, "I believe that the light of nationalism which has been burning in the western part of Russia will in a short time light up the entire country," was addressed to Kiev, to the Kiev Nationalist Club. Perhaps it was to be expected that Stolypin would be killed in Kiev, so that he could be buried in the Pecherskii Monastery, a thousand-year-old Russian sacred place. And to this day, although the Uspenskii Cathedral has collapsed, there is a big black marble cross near the ruins with the words, "Peter Arkadevich Stolypin."

I do not know what opera was being performed in the theater that evening. Perhaps it was *Zhizn za tsaria* ("My Life for the Tsar"). If it was not being performed on the stage, it was certainly being performed in the orchestra. And Stolypin, just before he fell, fatally wounded, made the sign of the cross in the air, in the direction of the Tsar's box.

Dmitrii Ivanovich Pikhno was sitting in the fourth row of the orchestra. In front of him sat ministers and other government dignitaries. Sitting on the aisle that led from the stage to the theater entrance, Pikhno saw someone walk past quickly, then heard a shot. Peter Arkadevich was standing, leaning on the orchestra rail but facing the auditorium, that is, the royal box, as was proper during intermission. He was wearing a white tunic, which immediately became covered with a bloody spot. Having done his job, the man in the dress-coat began to run back up the aisle.

It goes without saying that the audience was confused and shocked, and the killer nearly escaped because only those near Stolypin, such as my stepfather, had seen what happened. Some thought that the Tsar had been shot, but he was not in the theater at the time. Nevertheless,

Bogrov did not escape, because someone in the dress-circle also saw the killing. He saw Bogrov running up the aisle. And just as he reached the exit, the man in the dress-circle jumped down on him and knocked him to the floor. Thus the killer was caught.

A letter of another witness has survived, the witness being Emperor Nicholas II himself. This is what he wrote on September 10 (23), 1911, from Sevastopol to his mother, Maria Fedorovna:

We had just left our box during the second intermission, since it was very hot in the theater. Suddenly we heard two noises, as if something had fallen on the floor. I thought that someone had been hit on the head by opera glasses dropped from above, and ran back into the box.

To the right I saw a group of officers and other people dragging someone. Some ladies screamed, and opposite me in the orchestra stood Stolypin. He slowly turned to face me and with his left hand blessed the air.

Only then did I notice that he was pale and that there was blood on his hand and tunic. He quietly sat down in his chair and began to unbutton his tunic. Fredericks and Professor Rein were helping him.

Olga and Tatiana had entered the box after me and saw everything. While Stolypin was being helped from the theater, there was a commotion in the corridor outside our box—some people wanted to do away with the killer. Unfortunately, the police pulled him away from the crowd and led him to a separate building for questioning. Still, he was badly beaten and had two teeth knocked out. Then people began to come back into the theater, the anthem was sung, and I left with my two daughters at eleven o'clock. You can well imagine my state of mind.

Poor Stolypin suffered greatly that night, and was given morphine often. The next day, September 2 (15), there was a magnificent parade of the troops. . . .

I returned to Kiev on September 3 (16), in the evening, and stopped by the hospital to see Stolypin. I saw his wife, who would not let me in to see him. On September 4 (17), I went to the First Kiev Gymnasium, which was celebrating its hundred-year-jubilee anniversary. With my daughters I saw the Military and Arts Museum, and that evening, on the steamer *Golovachev,* I went to Chernigov. . . . I reviewed an infantry regiment and the two-thousand-man Poteshnii Regiment, attended a meeting of noblemen, then went to a museum. . . .

On September 6 (19), at 9:00 A.M., I returned to Kiev. While still on the pier I learned of Stolypin's death. I went to the hospital immediately, and a requiem was held in my presence. The poor widow stood as though carved out of stone, and could not cry. . . . At 11:00 A.M. we—that is, Alex, the children, and I—left Kiev, crowds accompanying us in a touching display of farewell. Orderly crowds filled the streets. In the cabin I was able to rest fully. We arrived here in Sevastopol on September 7 (20) in time for tea. It was a marvelous, warm day. What an enormous pleasure it is to be on the yacht again!

The following day, September 8 (21), I reviewed the Black Sea

Fleet. . . . The shiny ships and cheerful, valiant faces of the crews were truly delightful. What a difference from the recent past! Thank God!

Thus, in the midst of noisy, brilliant parades and celebrations, ended the suffering of the fatally wounded Prime Minister of the Russian state.

Very likely Olga Borisovna knew what she was doing when she did not allow the man he had blessed after the shooting to see her dying husband. Not without reason did V. N. Kokovtsev say, "If Stolypin had not been killed by Bogrov, he would have been removed in October."

Who did Stolypin's killer turn out to be? The killer's father was a rich Jew, owner of a multistoried building on Bibikovskii Boulevard. The young Bogrov was not only one of Kiev's golden youth but a secret agent of the Kiev branch of the Okhrana, in other words, a Kiev gendarme.*

This fact is surprising. This was already the tenth attempt on Stolypin's life. He had survived unscathed the bombing of his summer home on Aptekarskii Island in Petersburg, on August 13 (26), 1907, when forty people died. He had survived a plane trip with a pilot who was given the duty of killing him. I will not relate the other incidents, but I will add one shocking note. Stolypin kept reiterating his belief: "I will be killed by my Okhrana."

In any case, I must add one more fact. This incident greatly upset the gendarmes in Kiev, for they knew that they would be blamed for the murder of the government leader, and thus it was essential that Bogrov be convicted hastily. He was hung within five days so that all traces of the crime could be covered up. This was certainly a disservice, for as a consequence of the haste with which everything was done, no one could learn the whole truth. But the truth had to be known.

The Okhrana's collaboration with the Socialist Revolutionaries was revealed in part during an inquiry by the Social Democratic faction of the State Duma in connection with the murder of the Chairman of the

---

*The names and functions of the Russian police agencies mentioned here and in the account of the Beilis case can be confusing to the uninitiated. The Okhrana—more formally, the Third Section of the Ministry of the Interior— was the secret political police. Its functions were primarily investigative, including surveillance of suspects, infiltration of revolutionary organizations, etc. Its undercover agents were often accused of provoking or actually perpetrating the acts of terrorism they were supposed to be investigating. The Corps of Gendarmes, or security police, a uniformed force that was technically subordinate to the Third Section, served as the enforcement arm of the Okhrana and in addition had special guard and anti-riot duties. The "secret police," referred to in the translation simply as the "police," was what Westerners might designate the "criminal police" and had no political responsibilities (trans.).

Council of Ministers, announced by the Secretary of the Duma at the
first sitting of the fifth session, October 15 (28), 1911, forty days after
Stolypin's death. The first inquiry was signed by a man affiliated with
the Bolsheviks, the Social Democrat I. P. Pokrovskii.

On September 1 of this year the Chairman of the Council of Ministers,
P. A. Stolypin, was murdered in Kiev. The shocking and unprecedented
murder, and the circumstances connected with it, which clearly indicate
the involvement of members of the Okhrana, rivet the public's attention.

Without digging very far into history it can be shown that in the past
decade we have had a whole series of similar murders of high Russian
dignitaries in which members of the political Okhrana were involved. No
one doubts that the assassinations of Minister of the Interior and Chief
of Police V. K. von Plehve, Governor Bogdanovich of the city of Ufa,
Grand Duke Sergei Alexandrovich, commander of the troops in the
Moscow military district, and Major-General V. F. von der Launits, the
governor of Petersburg, were organized by an agent of the Okhrana, the
famous Azef. . . .*

. . . These are the known facts about the activities of the political
Okhrana with its well-developed and far-reaching system of provocation. But if this system demands sacrifices at the top from among its
founders and defenders, in the rest of the country it has taken thousands
of victims, a bloody nightmare hanging over society. The system of
provocation, cultivated from above, has bloomed with luxuriant colors
throughout the entire Okhrana, down to the lowest level. It is drama-
tized everywhere: the publishing of illegal literature, bomb factories, the
smuggling of illegal literature and weapons, the planning of acts of
terrorism, assassination attempts on the lives of government leaders, and
so forth.

Thanks to these widespread activities thousands of victims have fallen
prey to this hellish machine and have been sent into exile, prison, hard
labor, or the gallows. People from all levels of society have fallen victim to
the hammer of the Russian police state. The Okhrana has become a state
within a state, a government within a government, a ministry within a
ministry. The Chief of Police has become master of the situation; even
the Minister of the Interior trembles before him.

In this fashion, the Okhrana, created by the government as a weapon
of brute force against a populace that was becoming increasingly
politicized, has intensified the corruption, demoralization, and anarchy
in the higher organs of government. Indeed, it has become an instru-

---

*Yevno Azef, the most famous double-agent of the period, joined the Okh-
rana in 1893 and subsequently infiltrated the Socialist Revolutionary party,
becoming head of its terrorist arm, the Battle Organization, in 1903, and a
member of its Central Committee in 1905. Working for both sides simulta-
neously, he successfully engineered numerous acts of terrorism, including the
assassinations mentioned in the text, and also provided the authorities with
information leading to the arrest of important SR leaders, among them some
of his personal enemies (trans.).

ment for internecine warfare between various persons and groups within the government.

The most striking example of the anarchy in the organs of government administration is the murder of Chairman of the Council of Ministers Stolypin. Stolypin, who openly, before the whole country, defended the present government's need for a system of political surveillance and protection; Stolypin, who said, according to Prince Meshcherskii (*Grazhdanin* ["Citizen"], no. 37), "I will be killed by a member of the Okhrana"; Stolypin, who founded the cult of the Okhrana—Stolypin died by the hand of a member of the Okhrana, with the cooperation of high officials of the Okhrana. The circumstances under which he was killed are known.

He was killed by Bogrov, an undercover agent of the Okhrana. Bogrov was summoned to Kiev by the commander of the Kiev Okhrana, Colonel N. N. Kuliabko, in order to guard Stolypin. He was given a ticket to the theater where the killing took place by the commander of the Okhrana himself, and with the knowledge of other high-ranking officials: M. N. Verigin, Clerk of Special Commissions in the Ministry of Internal Affairs and Senior Assistant Director of the Police Department; Major-General A. I. Spiridovich, commander of the Palace Okhrana;* and Deputy Minister of Internal Affairs P. G. Kurlov, the head of the Okhrana. Bogrov was admitted to the theater to expose terrorists who, so he had told the Okhrana, were going to attempt to murder Stolypin.

In the light of all this, it can be surmised that officials of the Okhrana knowingly and purposely allowed terrorists into the theater, since the Okhrana was in charge of tickets and, of course, distributed them carefully. Presumably this was done in order to ensure that the Okhrana would achieve the greatest possible glory whenever it prevented a murder at the last possible moment. Note that one of the entrances to the theater was not well guarded, because it was in that very direction that Bogrov fled after firing the shots.

On the basis of these facts, which are common knowledge, most people, even ultrarightists, have concluded that the Okhrana was undoubtedly involved in the assassination of Stolypin.

And so, with all our resources devoted to the Okhrana; with the government treasury spending as much as a million rubles on the Okhrana; with the Deputy Minister of Internal Affairs and Chief of Police himself directing the Okhrana; with Okhrana officers, presumably under the supervision of the highest officials of the Okhrana, supposedly devoting all their attention to protecting Stolypin—and so, Stolypin is assassinated!

The following inquiry to the Chairman of the Council of Ministers

---

*The imperial bodyguard, a mixed force of gendarmes, cossacks, and troops from the various Guard regiments, officially designated "His Majesty's Imperial Combined Infantry Regiment" and commanded by a high-ranking Okhrana officer (trans.).

and the Minister of Internal Affairs was submitted on behalf of those whose names were appended to the statement.

> Do they realize that the assassination of the former Chairman of the Council of Ministers, P. A. Stolypin, like the similar assassinations of other high dignitaries, was the inevitable, logical result of the existence of a political-police organization that utilizes an extensive system of collaboration, a system that inevitably corrupts its leaders, besmirches the organization itself with the scandal of collaborating with hired assassins, imposes the yoke of unconcealed brute force on society, and paralyzes the vitality of the people? Do they intend to do anything to destroy the political Okhrana and its system of provocation?

* * *

As I have already mentioned, many people in Petersburg did not like Stolypin and worked to undermine him. Of course it cannot be said that Count Witte, State Council members Durnov and Trepov, and many others wished for or were pleased by Stolypin's death, but they all publicly reviled him to such an extent that it was possible for a clique of unethical underlings to spring up.

But that's not all. Empress Alexandra Fedorovna did not conceal her dislike for the Chairman of the Council of Ministers. All this being so, who am I to say that there were no careerists who thought that they would be able to climb higher if Peter Arkadevich was removed from the picture?

The painful impression made by this event was heightened by the fact that the people responsible for the death of the head of the government were not punished by due process of law. On September 9 (22), 1911, by a royal decree, the investigation of the actions taken by the Kiev Okhrana was assigned to Maxim Ivanovich Trusevich, a Privy Councillor, Senator, and member of the State Council. The conclusions which this dignitary arrived at on the basis of the investigation were passed on to a Privy Councillor whose surname was the same as mine, Senator Nicholas Zakharovich Shulgin, who, also by royal decree, had begun a preliminary investigation.

But when Shulgin began looking into the actions of the chiefs of the Okhrana, Colonel Kuliabko, Attorney Verigin, and Generals Kurlov and Spiridovich, who were guilty of inaction, of not taking proper measures to guard the Prime Minister, and of exceeding their authority, the investigation was stopped by order of the Emperor. Only Kuliabko was punished, and he was brought to trial not for assassinating Stolypin but because it was revealed during the investigation that he had embezzled a large sum of treasury money. Verigin and Kurlov were removed from their posts, but by the Tsar's personal request, the commander of the Palace Okhrana, Major-General Spiridovich, who was directly responsible for safety in the theater, since the Tsar himself was there, was not suspended from his post even for the duration of the investigation.

* * *

After the assassination of Stolypin, the State Duma was not summoned for a special session. The fifth term convened as scheduled on October 15 (28), 1911. It was not announced that the first sitting, which fell exactly on the fortieth day after the government leader's tragic death, would be held in his memory.

After the session was opened, the Duma was informed, not of the assassination of Stolypin, but of the loss of one of its members, S. N. Mezentsev, a retired lieutenant-general from Minsk Province and the former director of the police departments in several provinces.

The Beilis Case

W HAT WERE THE FACTS on which a court trial of Mendel Beilis could be based?

On Verkhneiurkovskii Street, on the outskirts of Kiev, there was a two-story wooden house, on the second floor of which lived the landlady of a den of thieves, Vera Vladimirovna Cheberiak. Her husband was a lowly postal clerk. They had three children, two girls, Valia and Liudmilla, and a boy, Zhenia, who was a friend and schoolmate of a boy named Andrew Iushchinskii. The police in Kiev were aware that professional thieves often visited the Cheberiak apartment. Vera Vladimirovna had been arrested several times for possession of stolen goods, and made the rounds of police stations.

On the morning of March 12 (25), 1911, the day of his disappearance, Andrew Iushchinskii had stopped at Zhenia's so that they could go to the property of a certain Berner, where they liked to play. The property consisted of a wooded, vacant lot situated on the wide slope of the hill which led to Kirillovskii Street. At the bottom of the hill, stretching out to the horizon, could be seen a brick factory with the same pipes and smokestacks that were found in the factory of the neighboring property of the merchant Mark Ionovich Zaitsev, for whom Mendel Beilis worked as a steward.

The "crumbler" was a structure which crumbled, that is, kneaded, clay for bricks. When the workers were not around, the children would turn it into a merry-go-round, riding around on the rotating poles that were fastened to a stake. After playing on the Berner property, Zhenia and his friend Andrew went home. In itself this fact is an indication of wrongdoing. How?

After Iushchinskii's disappearance, Zhenia Cheberiak told Vladimir Golubiev, the president of the Double-Headed Eagle youth organization,* that he had returned home with Andrew. However, in later talks with Golubev he denied this, although witnesses Kazimir and Uliana Shakhovskii, who lived near the Cheberiak apartment, attested to the fact that they had seen the boys together at Zhenia's house.

---

*A local anti-Semitic group similar to the Black Hundreds (trans.).

But why was the student Golubiev interested in this matter? What did he, personally, want? A single circumstance can explain everything. This student's motto was: "Scratch a Jew and you'll find a devil." For this reason, Zhenia Cheberiak's denial of his previous testimony indicates that the persons who were able to instill such a denial were interested in hiding the fact that Andrew had returned from the Berner property to Vera Cheberiak's house. And the fact that Zhenia obeyed these persons indicates that they must have had a certain amount of authority over him.

Beilis was first blamed for Andrew's death in the testimony of Kazimir Shakhovskii, a lamplighter in that section of Kiev. According to Shakhovskii, three days after Andrew's disappearance, he, Shakhovskii, met Zhenia Cheberiak on the street and asked, "Well, did you and Andrew have a good time that day I saw you?"

Zhenia answered that they had not played very long because on Zaitsev's property, not far from the brick-making oven, they had been frightened by a man with a black beard.

"In the testimony he gave to an investigating magistrate," it states in the accusation, "Shakhovskii announced that in his opinion, the man with the black beard was Mendel, the steward of the factory, and concluded that Beilis had been involved in the killing of Iushchinskii and that Zhenia Cheberiak had lured Andrew to the property."

This is how the "Beilis affair" began—with Kazimir Shakhovskii's supposition that the man Zhenia Cheberiak called "the man with a black beard" was Mendel Beilis, who, in the opinion of the perspicacious lamplighter, had been involved in the Iushchinskii killing!

But why was Shakhovskii, whose neighbors maintained that he could rarely walk a straight line, suddenly interested in whether or not Zhenia Cheberiak had had a "good time" three days before with Andrew Iushchinskii?

How could Zhenia not know the surname or even the first name of the steward who had lived for twelve years on the same factory grounds where the boys played almost every day? And if he did know the steward's name, why did he not state it?

All these circumstances testify to the fact that Beilis could not have been guilty. This is not evidence against him, as the prosecution maintained, but, on the contrary, in support of him. But later, from this "factual" groundwork a fantasy was played out involving a growing number of "witnesses."

Thus, Kazimir Shakhovskii's wife, Uliana, stated that a certain beggar-woman, Anna Volkina, supposedly told her that when Zhenia Cheberiak, Iushchinskii, and a third boy were playing on the Zaitsev property, a man with a black beard who lived there had grabbed Andrew right before her eyes and dragged him away, in front of everyone, in broad daylight, to a burning oven. However, Volkina, whose surname turned out to be Zakharov, declared under questioning that she had never had any such conversation with Uliana.

In spite of this, under pressure from someone, Uliana continued to insist it was true, and as the documents prove, in a drunken state she informed Agent Polishchuk, who carried out the search, that on March 12 (25), her husband Kazimir personally saw Beilis drag Iushchinskii away to an oven.

Beilis was brought to trial on the basis of such senseless evidence from the Shakhovskiis, although, as the interrogator himself admitted, they changed their statements several times and contradicted themselves.

Some even more unbelievable documents were also connected with this case. For example, there was an alleged note from Beilis to his wife, but the note was written not by him but supposedly in his name by some prisoner, and was handed not to the prisoner's wife but to another prisoner, by a prison guard.

A statement by a certain Kozachenko testified that Beilis had offered him a certain sum of money to poison two witnesses, including Nakonechnyi, who was interrogated several times and continuously testified in favor of the accused.

Vera Cheberiak's husband informed the court that Zhenia supposedly told him about two Jews dressed in strange-looking suits who visited Beilis, and whom he had seen praying.

But the culmination of the accusations was the testimony of Vera Cheberiak's nine-year-old daughter Liudmilla, that she, Zhenia, Iushchinskii, Evdokiia Nakonechnaia, and other children were playing on the "merry-go-round" and suddenly Beilis and two other Jews came running at them. The other children all were able to run away and hide, but the Jews grabbed Andrew and dragged him away to an oven. Unfortunately, the accusation did not explain how the Jews could kidnap Iushchinskii in public, outside the factory, and not be caught that very day or even that very moment.

These were the charges in a case that had all Russia worked up and attracted the attention of the whole world.

*　*　*

On September 28 (November 11), 1913, in issue no. 267 of the *Kievlianin,* I published a critical analysis of the work of the Kiev procurator's office in the Beilis case. One can imagine the reaction from the right. The editor received a flood of the most vile abuse, including not a few charges that the *Kievlianin* had been bought by Jews.

But not one of the people who damned me to hell and back wrote one word refuting my assertion of the total groundlessness of the Beilis indictment. And even after that, when the lexicon of foul language was exhausted and the time had seemingly come to turn to the heart of my argument, the lawyers remained silent.

Why? Weren't any of Russia's conservative elements educated in the law or connected to a judicial department? Why was it that only abuse made the newspaper columns? Why did no one venture to refute the essence of my criticism?

The fact was that the *Kievlianin* only published a definitive statement that the indictment was groundless because it had knowledge of the impartial viewpoint of certain incorruptible lawyers. Dmitrii Ivanovich Pikhno initiated a true explanation of this matter on the pages of the *Kievlianin*. In 1912, a year before his death, in issue no. 148 of the newspaper, he published the disclosures about the Iushchinskii murder by the head of the Kiev criminal investigation department, Nicholas Alexandrovich Krasovskii, who paid dearly for his action.

He was an experienced detective who had succeeded in solving a whole slew of major crimes after the local police had dropped the investigations because of a lack of evidence. When members of the criminal investigation department turned up nothing in the Iushchinskii murder, Krasovskii was called in to solve the case. He determined beyond any question that the boy had been killed in Vera Cheberiak's apartment by a gang of thieves who wanted to get rid of him because he knew what they were up to. And the ritual manner of his murder was simply a pretext to start a pogrom and cover up traces of the crime.

However, as Dmitrii Ivanovich wrote in the *Kievlianin*, instead of being thanked for solving the crime, Krasovskii was for some reason removed from the case. Later he was transferred to a provincial administrative board, and finally, on December 31, 1911 (January 13, 1912), he was permanently dismissed.

V. G. Korolenko, who was present at the Beilis trial, relates the following: "I saw Mr. Krasovskii, in civilian clothes, in a very ticklish situation: the prosecutors persistently, stubbornly, and not especially subtly tried to convince the jury that he wasn't simply a former policeman but a dark evildoer who used a pastry to poison Cheberiak's children."

The prosecutors tried to convince the jury of this because soon after Andrei's tortured body was found in a cave on the side of the hill on Berner's property, Vera Cheberiak's children, Zhenia and Valia, with whom Andrew had played there, died of dysentery. On this subject there were also not a few rumors and innuendos in the papers.

* * *

The *Kievlianin*'s published reports on Krasovskii's investigation of the puzzling Iushchinskii murder aroused a storm of protests in the

Duma. A week before the dissolution of the fifth and final session of the Third Duma, at the 145th sitting, June 2 (15), 1912, Chairman M. V. Rodzianko made the following announcement: "The undersigned members of the State Duma propose that the statement about the inquest given to the Minister of the Interior by the right-wing faction of the Duma on the unlawful activities of members of the Kiev police in the investigation of the murder of Andrew Iushchinskii be brought up for discussion at one of the forthcoming sittings."

Rodzianko understood this announcement to mean that these members of the Duma were asking that a special evening sitting be scheduled to examine the question. But this would have been very hard to arrange in view of the many matters still left to be decided before the dissolution of the Third Duma.

The leader of the Social Democratic faction (the Mensheviks), E. P. Gegechkori, told the members of the Duma about Krasovskii's disclosures in the *Kievlianin* and then appealed to them to vote for the following declaration:

"I believe that all Russian society, all honest Russian society has to say: enough of this ignominy, enough of these lies, enough of the misanthropy which has been promoted by these people. I believe that everyone who does not fear the truth, everyone who wants the truth in this horrible affair, has to vote in favor of our proposal."

All this time G. G. Zamyslovskii, who a half-year before had conducted an investigation of irregularities in the Kiev police department and had reported his findings to the ministers, sat silently. Quite naturally, now that Dmitrii Ivanovich's articles had been published, it was not to Zamyslovskii's advantage to allow the matter to be investigated. Beilis was already under arrest, all the police officials who wanted to unearth the truth had been removed, and as far as he was concerned the inquest was proceeding favorably. His careful planning has paid off. That is why he kept silent.

During the debate on whether or not to schedule an evening sitting to look into Zamyslovskii's inquiry, Count Alexei Alexevich Uvarov maliciously asked me a provocative question that was intended to compromise the right even more. The fact was that at the time I had not yet made a public statement, either from the rostrum or in the press, in defense of Beilis. Uvarov said, "I personally would like to know what the honorable Vasilii Vitalevich Shulgin has to say about the explanations that were given in the *Kievlianin*, the organ of the equally honorable Mr. Pikhno. The blood ties between these honorable members of the chamber are known to you; for this reason it would be extremely interesting for us, when we discuss this question, to know Vasilii Vitalevich's view of Mr. Pikhno's opinion."

To this I replied: "Duma member Count Uvarov has done me the honor of asking what I think about the subject at hand. . . . I believe that the *Kievlianin,* by opening its pages to the views of a veteran detective, has provided the court of public opinion with an understanding of this case that is just as authoritative and worthy of just as much attention as the understanding of those who see the case differently. But how can you ask that I, or even the State Duma, settle this question? Wait and see what the court decides."

After my speech there was a vote, and with a majority of 104 to 58 it was decided to convene an evening sitting on this matter.

But as I have already said, for practical reasons this was impossible. Every evening until the closing of the Duma was already engaged. As a result, on the eve of the last day of sittings, at ten o'clock at night on June 8 (12), 1912, the leader of the Cadets, Paul Nicholaevich Miliukov, of the People's Freedom faction, unexpectedly raised the question of Zamyslovskii's inquiry again. In the face of shouts of indignation from the right, he said that the agitation in support of pogroms was continuing over the corpse of the unfortunate boy, and the horrible legend of the ritual murder, created, as it turned out, by a person close to the supposed murderer, had been snatched up again and was being voiced from the Duma's rostrum.

> In view of the fact that our work is coming to an end, the People's Freedom faction demands the immediate implementation of the Duma's recent resolution. Let the shameless agitators who never pass up any chance to defile the tribune of the State Duma with impudent, lying— *(Noise and voices from the right, "What is this?")* —words of bloody slander— *(Noise and voices from the right: "What is this? Get out of here! Unscrupulous agitator! Out!" Applause from the left. Chairman Kapustin rings his bell for quiet.)* —receive their just retribution. Otherwise the Third Duma will carry with it into history the stamp of moral sympathy for a barbarous legend— *(Noise and voices from the right: "Disgraceful!")* —circulated by professional criminals— *(Voices from the right: "Unscrupulous lout!")* —and supported by professional pogromists.

Noise, cries, and oaths drowned out Miliukov's last words. His unexpected sharp statement agitated many people's passions. Of course the faction of the right had been convinced that this question would not be brought up in the Third Duma when only one day of work remained.

Zamyslovskii answered Miliukov. Calling his speech a "garish outburst for publicity," he said, "With this speech, filled with oaths, there can be no peace in the Duma, and we were informed today from the throne that where there is no peace there can be no genuine government business."

Invoking the protection of the throne, and trying to cover up the conviction of the innocent Beilis by referring to "genuine government business," Zamyslovskii brushed aside the need for any disclosures, stating that no matter how much "the Jews and their yes-men" yelled about the importance of such disclosures, they were not worth a cent. They were just plain rubbish, the usual publicity ballyhoo.

"So far as the Iushchinskii case is concerned, nothing has changed. The duly constituted judicial authorities indicted Mendel Beilis, stating that he, along with several accomplices, tortured a Christian child, that they injected forty-three needles into his body and drew out his blood. The crime was quite clearly a ritual murder. . . . Unraveling the puzzle of that ritual murder from the rostrum of the Duma is our goal. . . . Let us now consider how to proceed with the inquiry," cried Zamyslovskii, applauded by the right. Stepping down from the rostrum, he added, "However, now, at ten minutes to eleven, we can hardly take up this question."

That was exactly what he was counting on. A stormy debate marked by reciprocal insults and accusations followed, but the hands of the clock relentlessly moved on to 11:00 P.M., at which time the meeting would adjourn. V. M. Purishkevich forfeited his right to speak by referring to the left as "lousy vagrants." E. P. Gegechkori, over the noise and the Chairman's bell, was able to say to the knights of ritual murder, "Your cannibalistic howling will not make things any better. . . . Now you are trying to hide in the bushes. . . . Nothing is left for you to do but insult us. . . . Deputy Zamyslovskii tried to discredit Krasovskii, but he forgot that the testimony of all the witnesses mentioned in Krasovskii's investigation was confirmed by Police Colonel P. A. Ivanov, of the procurator's office. Thus, gentlemen, you are no longer able to discredit Krasovskii's investigation!"

And A. A. Bulat, a Trudovik, cried out last, "I maintain that Iushchinskii's murderers, the perpetrators of the Iushchinskii murder, were not Jews, but Cheberiak and the gentlemen on the right who are now so concerned about this murder!"

Chairman M. V. Rodzianko called for a vote on the proposal that the discussion on the inquiry into the Iushchinskii case be continued at the next day's sitting, but for the reasons cited above, it was voted down by a majority of 111 to 87. The meeting was adjourned at 11:13 P.M.

And the following day, June 9 (22), 1912, at 3:53 P.M., by a royal decree to the governing senate, the Third Duma was dissolved until a new election could take place.

* * *

Everything is quite clear. To convict a Jew of ritual murder in the face of such paltry evidence was not only unethical but stupid. And it is useless to plead stupidity and say it was not we who disgraced ourselves before the world, but the Jewish newspapers that publicized the Beilis affair to the four corners of the earth. There is no point in pretending to be innocents. Is anyone really so naive as to think that the Jewish press could have remained silent about a matter of such importance to Jews?

Well, then, will this vicious, evil deed, this death of a child by torture, go unpunished? Doesn't the blood of Andrew Iushchinskii clamor for justice?

When people who were horrified by the crime maintained that there must be retribution, they aroused sympathy. But when others took the same stand, others who had nothing in their hearts but political spite, whose cold, calculating, cruel minds had long ago learned to crush any feelings of pity and sympathy, then such reasoning sounded repulsively hypocritical.

Will the dead boy be happy if a man who never lifted a finger to harm him was sentenced to twenty years hard labor? The boy's blood will stop clamoring for divine justice only when the people who actually murdered him are convicted.

And as reported in the *Kievlianin*, our Kievan youth, members of the Double-Headed Eagle, encouraged by the example set by the coryphaei of the Duma and the press, ended up by maintaining that even if Beilis was not guilty, it would not matter. Why? Because even if Beilis did not kill Iushchinskii, he deserved to be sentenced to hard labor because he was one of those who had greeted our military defeats with joyful laughter and celebrated when more of our soldiers were killed than the enemy's, one of those who had killed Russians or lured them to their deaths, who killed our best people and filled the ranks of the revolutionary underground.

This is what the denial of justice brings us to! But one must admit that the brainless, cold-hearted members of the Double-Headed Eagle were simply formulating conclusions that were based on the premises whispered by their elders. And what exactly did their teachers preach, those coryphaei whom they endeavored to imitate? Here is what was written in issue 177 of the newspaper *Russkoe plamia* ("Russian Banner") in 1913, before the Beilis trial:

> The government is obliged to acknowledge that the Jews as a people are as dangerous to humanity as wolves, scorpions, adders, poisonous spiders, and other creatures subject to extermination for their predatoriness, a people whose destruction is encouraged by law. . . . The Jews must be forcibly put into such conditions that they will continually die off. This, then, is the obligation of the government and of the best people of the country.

Thus it turns out that Hitler's ideas were fostered in brilliant St. Petersburg many years before they were fostered in Germany, in a newspaper bearing the name *Russkoe plamia.*

After such lessons it would have been bolder and more logical of the members of the Kiev Double-Headed Eagle Association to preach that Jews simply are not subject to trial by jury and could be sent to hard labor at the order of their leader, the student Golubiev of the motto, "Scratch a Jew and you'll find a devil."

If such a law had been passed by the State Duma, then proof of ritual murder would have been superfluous.

* * *

The day of reckoning approached. The Beilis affair was drawing to a close amidst the greatest tension and excitement. For two and a half years the heretofore unknown steward had been languishing behind bars, steadfastly proclaiming his innocence.

Stephen Petrovich Beletskii, the Chief of Police, spared no effort to establish Beilis's guilt. Under Zamyslovskii's instructions, at great expense, the police sent to Italy for ancient books containing evidence of the ritual use of blood by Jews. Every case that showed the slightest indication of ritual murder was extracted from the government archives. The Minister of Justice appointed the assistant public procurator of the St. Petersburg judiciary, O. Iu. Vipper, to serve as prosecutor. Zamyslovskii himself went to Kiev to assist him as a civil plaintiff.*

All in all, 219 witnesses and 14 experts were called. Among them the most notable were the priest Iustin Pranaitis, Master of Theology, Professor I. A. Sikorskii, Doctor of Medicine D. P. Kosorotov, and the well-known anti-Semitic lawyer A. S. Shmakov. They all confirmed the ritual character of the murder. Witnesses who would not aid the prosecution were unceremoniously kept away. Beilis's defense was organized by the St. Petersburg Committee for the Rebuff of Bloody Slander. The best lawyers of the time participated: O. O. Gruzenberg, A. S. Zarudnyi, N. P. Karabchevskii, and Duma member and Cadet V. A. Maklakov.

Not only Russia but also the West closely followed the progress of this grandiose case, in which medical luminaries and history profes-

---

*There is no suitable English term for Zamyslovskii's status at the trial. Under Russian law in this period, the heirs of the victim of a crime could make a claim for civil damages against the perpetrator of the crime and could be represented at the trial for this purpose by a private attorney. The private attorney—in this instance, Zamyslovskii—and the state prosecutor worked independently but tended to cooperate because it was in their mutual interest to obtain a conviction (trans.).

sors debated with the crooks and thugs who were the chief witnesses
for the prosecution.

Twelve jurors had to defend the honor of Russia before the world
and save the man who had suffered so needlessly. The jury was
selected in the same fashion as the witnesses for the prosecution. In
Kiev there was much confusion and gossip about the situation. Even
in minor criminal cases the court ordinarily had at its disposal among
the jurors three professors, ten intellectuals, and only two peasants,
but in the Beilis case ten of the twelve jurors had only attended village
schools, and some of the peasants were almost illiterate. It was obvious
to everyone that the jurors were of too low an intellectual level for
such a complicated case, but that was exactly what the organizers of
the trial were counting on. They were sure of success.

*   *   *

The day of judgment finally arrived. V. G. Korolenko describes the
atmosphere of anticipation and tension in Kiev that day:*

All movement in front of the courthouse ceased. Even the trams were
not allowed past. There were police details, both mounted and on foot,
in the streets. In the Sophia Cathedral there was going to be a requiem
for the dead child Andrei Iushchinskii at 4:00 P.M., conducted by the
archbishop. On the street where the courthouse was located, the blotch
of people at the walls of the Sophia Cathedral darkens and increases.
Here and there torches flame up above the crowd. Dusk falls on an
atmosphere of painful worry.

It becomes known that the chief judge's summation is definitely accusatory. When the defense protests, the chief judge decides to add to his
summation, but Zamyslovskii objects and the chief judge declines to add
anything after all. The jurors leave under the influence of a one-sided
speech. The mood in the court becomes even more strained, and this is
communicated to the rest of the city.

At approximately six o'clock reporters rush out. The news that Beilis
has been acquitted spreads like wildfire. Instantly the crowd's mood is
transformed. Many groups of people are seen congratulating each other.
Russians and Jews come together in mutual happiness. The pogrom
stain near the cathedral loses its ominous significance. The nightmares
fade away. The exclusivity of the makeup of the jury even more emphatically underlines the significance of the acquittal.

*   *   *

Happiness and exultation suffused the editorial staff of the *Kievlianin,* which in common with many like-minded persons had suffered

---

*Vladimir Galaktionovich Korolenko (1853–1921) was a well-known journal-
ist and writer of the period; his account of the trial is found in his *Collected
Works* (Moscow, 1955) (trans.).

not a little during this time. On October 29 (November 11), 1913, I wrote in issue no. 298,

> In spite of the fact that everything possible and impossible was done, in spite of the fact that the most cunning temptations were used, the simple Russian people took the right path.
>
> When we think about this, we become both happy and distressed. Distressed because we have clearly seen how those at the top, those who should have set an example for everyone below them, veered off the proper course and took the crooked path, blinded by political ambition. It is distressing to see the leaders of the people in the role of tempters and seducers.
>
> But our heart swells with happiness and pride when we consider how ordinary Russian common people, lacking the knowledge and intellectual sophistication to extricate themselves from the horrible thicket into which they had been led, and with only their purity of heart to guide them, were able to find the true path out of a forest so haunted by terrifying apparitions.
>
> Bow low to these simple Kievan folk! Their names will soon be drowned again in the faceless sea of humanity, but these poor unknowns, however rough and untutored, remained faithful to the good and the true, and thus rectified the evil perpetrated by those for whom the courts are just an instrument, for whom there is no good and evil, but only political advantage or disadvantage.
>
> These gray citizens of the Kievan earth had to defend the purity of Russian justice and the honor of the Russian name before the whole world. We thank them, we thank the earth that nurtured them, we thank ancient Kiev, from whose heights light has once again began to sparkle throughout the entire land of Russia.

* * *

How did the heroes of this tragedy end up? Mendel Beilis emigrated to America, where he died in 1937. Vera Cheberiak? Did she take a seat in the dock? Of course not.

The prosecution had to find a way out of the compromising situation in which it found itself thanks to the ignorant peasants who had acquitted Belis. What a predicament! Could they really get away with locking up an innocent man for more than two years, doing everything they could to convict him, and at the same time protecting the real murderers by every means possible? Consider how many high officials of the criminal investigation department had ended up in trouble when they got on the right track. After all this, how could they take action against Vera Cheberiak? Rumor has it that the students of Kiev dealt with her during the revolution.*

---

*According to Maurice Samuel, in his *Blood Accusation: The Strange History of the Beilis Case* (New York: Knopf, 1967), Cheberiak was shot in the Cheka prison in Kiev sometime before 1920 (trans.).

And as for me—I was put in the dock instead of Vera Cheberiak, of which more anon.

* * *

It was during World War I, on January 20 (February 2), 1915, in the city of Tukhov, not far from Tarnov. The entire populace had fled the city, which was a heap of ruins, its streets full of pieces of broken glass.

In the middle of a park of dark-green evergreens, however, a manor house was still standing. Billeted in the house was the unit I commanded, the Second Advanced First Aid and Commissary Detachment of IUZOZO.*

Once I had the detachment's work in hand, on this significant day, I allowed myself to indulge in some unhappy reminiscences. But since I am a frustrated musician at heart, the thoughts and memories in my ill-balanced brain, even today, are usually interlaced with a melody of some kind. As I looked through the window at the dark-green evergreens, they seemed to sway to the tune of an old waltz and the following song came to mind.

Ia pomniu valsa zvuk prelestnyi	I remember the lovely sound of a waltz
Vesennei nochiu v pozdn chas.	On a spring night at a late hour.
Ego pel golos neizvestnyi,	It was sung I know not by whom,
I pesnia chudnaia lilas.	And the wonderful song filled the air.
Da, to byl vals prekrasn, tomnyi	Yes, it was a beautiful, languid waltz;
Da, to byl divnyi vals . . .	Yes, it was a marvelous waltz . . .

There was no waltz, only memories. It was exactly a year before, on January 20 (February 2), 1914, that I had been tried in Kiev and sentenced to prison. And for what?

"For deliberately disseminating false information about certain high-ranking officials . . ."

How did this happen?

On the third day of the Beilis trial, September 27 (October 9), 1913, I wrote an editorial in the *Kievlianin* in defense of the accused. But

---

*The zemstvos organized noncombatant civilian units, roughly comparable to the YMCA units that accompanied the U.S. Army in World War I and to the USO of World War II, to provide various kinds of supportive services to the field army, such as warm food and clothing and first aid. Shulgin's IUZOZO (Iugo-Zapadnaia oblastnaia zemskaia organizatsia = Southwestern Region Zemstvo Organization) was a unit of this kind. Unlike Shulgin, however, many of the men who volunteered for such units, pejoratively referred to as "zemstvo hussars," were merely seeking to avoid combat duty at the front (trans.).

that issue was never published; it was confiscated by the police. And I had to stand trial because of the editorial.

Since the editorial is of some interest as an historical document, I will cite it almost in full, despite its length.

As is well known, the indictment in the Beilis case has attracted the attention of the whole world. Not since the Dreyfus case has a trial so excited public opinion. The reason is obvious. The Beilis indictment is not simply an indictment of one man, but an indictment of an entire people for one of the most heinous of crimes, the indictment of an entire religion for one of the most infamous of superstitions.

Under such circumstances, and with millions of minds scrutinizing us, Russian justice should have guided itself throughout with prudence, and should have done everything in its power to protect its august reputation. The Kiev procurator's office, taking upon itself a task that no other court in the world has ever been able to resolve, should have understood that it must come up with a decisive indictment, one that was so strongly forged that it would be able to withstand the colossal force of the tidal wave that was rising to confront it.

One doesn't have to be a lawyer, but need only have some common sense, to understand that the Beilis indictment is mere prattle which any defense attorney could break down without even trying. And understanding this, one involuntarily begins to pity the Kiev procurator's office, and Russian justice itself, for venturing to be tried before the court of the whole world on such pitiful grounds.

But the purpose of this article is not to analyze the indictment. At the moment we have another duty, a duty that is painful but unavoidable.

We have to discuss the circumstances in which Mendel Beilis was indicted.

The murder of Iushchinskii, puzzling and brutal, brought to life a centuries-old legend that Jews, for ritual purposes, sometimes torture Christian children. This version of the murder, naturally, alarmed the Jewish population. And in certain elements of the Russian population and in certain political circles, a fear arose that the Jews would try to sidetrack the police and the investigation.

The inquiry of the rightists in the State Duma began as an extreme expression of these fears, accusing the Kiev police of concealing the true character of the murder under Jewish pressure. During the discussion of this inquiry, State Duma member Zamyslovskii maintained that Jews commit ritual murder only in districts where they can bribe the police, and thus the very fact that a ritual murder has taken place in a district is proof that the police in that district have been bribed. . . .

Of course, the Jews would not be so foolish as to depend only on the police in such a dangerous matter. If they were trying to conceal a crime so evil that its discovery would threaten, at the very least, a repetition of Kishinev, they would certainly not stop at the police station but would go much higher. And thus it was inconsistent for Zamyslovskii to stop where he did. He too should have gone higher, placing the blame for the concealment of the ritual crime on the investigating magistrate, the procurator of the district court, and the procurator of the judicial chamber.

Zamyslovskii did not do so. But apparently this thought, though suppressed, implanted itself and took root. The fear of being suspected of making deals with the Jews proved too great a burden on the soul for many people. And we knew courageous people who laughed at bombs and guns but could not bear the weight of such suspicions. Thus, however strange it may seem, Zamyslovskii's declaration brought the decisive pressure to bear on the Kiev procurator.

At any rate, the procurator of the Kiev judicial chamber, G. G. Chaplinskii, began to act as though his only goal was to convince Zamyslovskii that he, the procurator, was as clean as glass in this respect.

The notion that Iushchinskii had been ritually murdered was not easy to substantiate on any grounds. The chief of the Kiev criminal investigation department, E. F. Mishchuk, refused to see any ritual characteristics in the barbarities committed upon the boy.

Removing Mishchuk from office on May 7 (20), 1911, under suspicion of bribery by Jews, the judicial authorities turned to a gendarme lieutenant-colonel, P. A. Ivanov, for help, and Ivanov called in the famous detective N. A. Krasovskii.

But Krasovskii, like his predecessor, Mishchuk, also decisively rejected the idea of a ritual murder and blamed the crime on a gang of professional scoundrels grouped around Vera Cheberiak. Krasovskii began a serious investigation along these lines, and his findings were reported to the procurator's office.

When Krasovskii's views became apparent, he, like Mishchuk, was removed from the case, charges were brought against him, again as with Mishchuk, and he was prosecuted. Once the two chiefs of the detective department had been removed in this fashion, the case began. . . .

The entire police force, terrorized by the actions of the judicial chamber's procurator, realized that anyone who uttered a word—that is, who said anything other than what the authorities wanted to hear—would immediately lose his post and be thrown into prison. Naturally, under such circumstances, everyone was silent, and a version of the Beilis case began to prevail that was "contrary to common sense, in defiance of the elements, but the joy of the chamber's procurator."

However, we are convinced that among the masses there are honest people who can speak the truth even in the face of a threatening procurator. We assert that the procurator of the Kiev judicial chamber, Privy Councillor George Gavrilovich Chaplinskii, intimidated his subordinates and choked off all attempts to cast light on the case.

We have weighed the meaning of the words uttered here. They must be said; we have a right to say them and will say them.

* * *

It was for this article, which "deliberately disseminated false information," that I was brought to trial. The jurors knew, of course, no less than I, that I was not lying. I could be wrong, but I was not a liar.

And this was the venom with which they wanted to poison me. Like an angry yellow hornet, they stung me painfully but not fatally.

Misfortune, they say, never comes alone. When I arrived in court, my strength was already exhausted. The night before there had been the heartbreaking funeral of a certain young man who had committed suicide. I did not sleep a wink the entire night, but spent it consoling a person who was inconsolable. For this reason I could have avoided the trial, but I did not do so.

When I took my place in the dock, I saw that the spectators' stand was filled to capacity. Everyone in Kiev with the title of lawyer was there, almost to a man. In the crowd I spotted the very familiar face of Vasilii Ivanovich Fenenko. If he told the jurors what he knew, they would not be able to convict me of "deliberately disseminating false information."

What was the substance of my condemnation of Chaplinskii, the senior procurator of the Kiev judiciary, in the article in the *Kievlianin?* That he had pressured an investigating magistrate, something a procurator has no right to do, since investigating magistrates, like judges, are inviolable in this respect.

And what kind of man was the magistrate who did not succumb to pressure? He was the same Fenenko who was sitting in the stand not far from the jurors who were trying me. At the time, serving as investigating magistrate in particularly important cases before the Kiev district court, he had been entrusted with carrying out the preliminary investigation to determine the truth in the case of the murder in Kiev of the boy Iushchinskii.

I knew Fenenko from childhood, knew that he was an irreproachable man who dared to have his own opinion.

When I visited him in his modest little house, he said to me, "I am not a rich man, but I have a place to lay my head. I am not married; I live with my old nurse, and my needs are few. The only luxury I allow myself is to serve honestly.

"I was assigned to conduct the investigation in the case of Mendel Beilis, the suspect in the murder of the boy Andrew Iushchinskii. I examined the evidence and declared it totally untrustworthy.

"The only evidence came from the ten-year-old girl Luidmila. She said she had seen, right before her eyes and the eyes of the other children romping across from the building where Beilis worked, how he grabbed Andrew by the hand and dragged him away somewhere.

"If Beilis did intend to commit a horrifying, evil act with a ritual purpose and indeed had grabbed Andrew in the presence of the children and other people present in the building, then he was a downright fool, hence not responsible for his actions. That was why I used my authority to call off the investigation, as I had the right to do.

"But Chaplinskii threatened me, saying that much unpleasantness could befall me for closing the investigation, and promised me some sort of reward or decoration if I reopened the case. To this I answered, 'Your Excellency, there are other magistrates besides Fenenko. Fenenko is not suited for this kind of case.' "

* * *

Naturally, when they brought a suit against me for disseminating false information, I called several witnesses. Vasilii Ivanovich by himself would have been sufficient, but the court refused to allow me to call him as a witness on my behalf. And so now he sat next to the jurors as a witness to the unlawful proceedings of the court, but a mute witness.

If I had not been so upset, perhaps I would have acted as I should have. I would have proclaimed loud and clear, "Since the court finds it necessary to deny me my most important and comprehensive witness, I consider the court unjust and do not wish to remain here. Try and sentence this empty seat. I am leaving the courtroom."

I should have but I didn't, I thought sadly, as I gazed through the glass of the window at the swaying evergreens.

Teper' zima, no te zhe eli,	Now it is winter, and those few evergreens,
toskuia, v symrake stoiat.	now grieving, stand in the twilight.
A za oknom shumiat meteli	And outside is the noise of a snowstorm,
i zvuki val'sa ne zvuchat.	and the waltz is heard no more.

The road leading toward me, that is, toward the wing of the manor house spared by the bombardment, really was covered with snowdrifts, because of the blizzard.

Suddenly I saw an automobile making its way with difficulty through the drifts. During the war not everyone had a car, so the driver had to be a "somebody." And in this weather! Evidently, it was an important matter, and it could only concern us, since aside from ourselves, there was no one here. I ordered the primus stove, which in wartime had replaced the samovar, turned on, and had a bottle of red wine and some cookies served, as was always done in the field. Meanwhile the visitor was escorted in by the soldier on duty. From his shoulder-boards I saw that he was a colonel, and from his face I saw that he was thoroughly chilled.

At that time automobiles were open, with rare exceptions, so I greeted him with the words, "Colonel, a mug of hot tea?"

"Oh, yes! Yes! What weather!"

When he had warmed up, he said, "I came to see you. You personally."

"Oh?"

"I am an army lawyer. All lawsuits against military personnel are
officially transferred to the military judicial department. I have been
given two cases that involve you. Which one would you prefer to
begin with?"

"If possible, with whichever is simpler."

"Fine. The assessor of the city of Kiev has brought charges against
you, as editor of the *Kievlianin,* for running an advertisement for
Valda's Lozenges in your paper without his authorization."

"Valda's? Allow me to offer you one. I always carry some with me,
and it seems to me that you're a bit hoarse—damn this weather!"

"Ah, thank you very much. . . . They're very good. I have heard of
them. But by law I must ask this question: Do you admit your guilt in
this awful deed?"

"Yes. I ran the ad and hope to go on running it. However, allow me
to inform you—"

"Please."

"Colonel, you are a lawyer, and a high-ranking one at that. I'm a
lawyer too, although nonpracticing, and for that reason will allow
myself to ask you a question: Do the actions of the higher agencies of
government have to be taken into consideration and carried out by
the lower agencies?"

"Yes."

"Well then, I ran an advertisement for Valda's Lozenges in the
Kievlianin without authorization by the Kiev assessor, but the same
advertisement appeared in the Petersburg newspaper *Pravitelstvennyi
vestnik* ("Government Herald"), which presumably was given its authorization by the highest medical authorities."

"That's obvious. Case closed."

"I thank you."

"Now we will turn to the important case. Please read this."

I read, "Announce to Shulgin, V. V., editor of the *Kievlianin,* that
His Majesty the Tsar wrote on the report of the Minister of Justice:
'Consider the case nonexistent.'"

*   *   *

"Consider the case nonexistent." There is a Greek proverb, "The
gods themselves cannot make the existing nonexistent." But that
which was not possible for Greek gods was possible for Russian Tsars.

"Consider the case nonexistent" was a judicial term similar in meaning to a Roman law. To consider a case nonexistent was a prerogative
of the Russian Tsar as the highest judicial authority in the state. Every

sentence handed down in the empire began with the words, "By order of His Imperial Majesty."

With this the judge would put a chain around his neck as a sign that he was passing sentence by order of the Tsar.

To consider a case nonexistent means more than amnesty. Amnesty is pardon, oblivion, but "consider the case nonexistent" was a judicial term meaning that there had never been any charges against Shulgin—he was never tried, he was never sentenced.

There is one curious circumstance: the Sovereign did this on the basis of a report by the Minister of Justice, I. G. Shcheglovitov. The Minister of Justice is considered the Supreme Procurator, the highest representative of the prosecuting authority. From this it follows that the prosecution had renounced its unlawful case and was eager to correct it at the first suitable opportunity.

Such an opportunity occurred when I enlisted in the regiment and was wounded, for it would have been awkward to send me to prison. Furthermore, as a member of the State Duma, I could not be sent to prison without the Duma's consent. And it would not have consented to my arrest. Certain formalities were observed.

All this came back to me on that day of celebration, January 20 (February 2), 1915, when the mysterious colonel delivered the command of the supreme court: "Consider the case nonexistent."

* * *

And four months before this anniversary, at the very beginning of September 1914, an astounding thing happened to me. I set off from Kiev to the front, since I had been assigned to the 166th Rovnenskii Infantry Regiment as an ensign.

The train's last stop was in Radzivilov, at the time a small town with a customhouse, in the Kremenets district of Volyn Province, on the Austrian border. There I hired a light carriage to go to Brody. Halfway there I crossed the border, overtaking a hundred Cossacks.

They were singing, probably out of boredom. Oh, how they sang! Perhaps some of them were the ones who several years later would become internationally famous singers, performing throughout Europe and the Americas.

In one hour, having traveled twelve kilometers, I arrived in Brody, a small Austrian town on the Russian border. The first impression was shocking. There were no houses—the wooden walls had been burned. Stove pipes poked high into the sky, the tin roofs had slipped down and lay at their feet like wrinkled black mushrooms.

It was said that the houses had been burned by Cossacks. What! The same Cossacks who had been singing so sweetly on the Austrian border? No, not them, some others, who had come earlier. Then I believed it and was horrified. But later I learned that in wartime, abandoned houses acquire a talent for spontaneous combustion from neglect.

Not everything had burned. There was a house that had been saved, thanks to the fact that it sheltered the Red Cross within its walls. This was a detachment sponsored by the State Duma and funded from the personal means of its members. Each deputy contributed fifty rubles a month, one-seventh of his salary.

Here I became acquainted with Countess Sofia Alexeevna Bobrinskii, head of the detachment. Near her, on some wooden steps, sat a nurse in a white scarf, with beautiful eyes. But in the approaching officer she recognized a "representative of the people" who stood on a "high rostrum" and gave speeches with which she did not always sympathize.

* * *

At the station the train was taken by storm by a crowd of soldiers' greatcoats. Among them, with the courage born of despair, a small handful of people in civilian dress, undoubtedly Jews, tried to get through. My officer's shoulder boards cleared the way, and I ended up in a car before the soldiers and the Jews. Noting with surprise that the car was almost empty, I found myself a place in one of the unoccupied compartments.

The train started. After a while I discovered that the adjoining car was full, and that the Jews I had seen on the platform were walking along the corridor. After standing there for half an hour they asked permission to enter my sleeping compartment, which had become "mine" by right of war and by the Roman law that a thing which does not have an owner belongs to whoever first takes possession of it.

I granted permission and they took seats in the compartment. After a while they procured a teapot filled with boiling water and began to drink tea. Finally, although quite timidly, they offered me a glass. I accepted with pleasure. Then they began to feel more at ease with me and even began to ask me some questions. I answered evasively, but it turned out that they too were Kievans, going to Lvov on business.

And they, I don't know how, they found out that I was the editor of the *Kievlianin* who had interceded for Mendel Beilis. From that moment on I became the object of their most intense solicitude. At 2:00 A.M. we arrived in Lvov, which the Russian army had taken not long before, on September 6 (19), 1914. Making my way through the crowd milling around the barely lit station, I ended up on the street. Black night, rain, no porters, no wagons. The darkness was occasionally torn by stabs of light from automobiles. And then the endless transport cars could be seen. And again endless night on earth, and rain from the heavens. What was I to do?

Suddenly the same Jews appeared from out of the darkness.

"Well, are we going to stand here in the rain?! We can't offer you the comforts you're accustomed to, but at least there will be a roof over your head!"

It was very late when they led me to a hotel. Immediately the room was lit up with candlelight: the electricity did not work. Magically, quickly, a samovar, the unfailing comforter of those times, appeared on the table. The room was cosy but strange: one was unused to candles. I drank tea alone, my patrons having disappeared. It was probably three or four in the morning; night—black as the grave—peered into the windows. Rain knocked quietly at the glass.

All of a sudden the door opened. There were enough candles to see. An old man with a white beard came in. He came up to the table, and leaning on the back of an armchair covered with red velvet, gazed at me. He was extraordinarily handsome, with the beauty of a patriarch. His black eyes, framed by equally black brows, made a biblical contrast to the whiteness of his hair and beard. It's not that his eyes burned—they shone.

He gazed at me, and I at him. Finally he said, "So it's you."

This was not a question. And for that reason, I answered, indicating the armchair, "Please sit down."

But he did not sit down. He began thus: "And how did those swine dare to say that you had taken our money?"

I smiled and asked, "Would you like some tea?"

He did not answer, and continued, "Well, we know where our money went!"

His shining eyes flashed as if with a threat. But what he said next was not a threat.

"I want you to know that we Jews have someone, just as you have your Metropolitan. No, greater! He is for the entire world. He ordered—"

He paused for a minute and said, "He ordered—he set a day and a time—throughout the world! And throughout the world, wherever there are Jews who believe in God, at that day and time they prayed for you!"*

---

*Since Judaism has no ecclesiastical official comparable in formal standing to the Patriarch of the Russian Orthodox Church, the old man was probably referring to the Rebbe of one of the Hasidic sects that proliferated in Russia at this time. The Rebbes exercised total authority over their followers, and a Hasidic pietist might well have regarded his personal Rebbe as holding sway throughout world Jewry (trans.).

I felt a deep emotion. I was touched. There was something sublime in this. In some way I felt the ecumenical prayer of people whom I did not know but who had learned about me and directed their spiritual strength at me.

The patriarch added, "God hears such prayers!"

I remember to this day the tone of his voice and the expression in his eyes as he pronounced these words. His eyes seemed to be lined with blue around the lashes.

They seemed to be imbued with spiritual radiance. After a short time he said, "I came to tell you this. Farewell!"

*   *   *

Sometimes, when I am very poor, I tell myself, "You are rich. People all over the world prayed for you."

And I feel better.

Part II

THE WAR

War

I LEARNED ABOUT the event that was to determine the fate of the whole world in surroundings that were totally out of character for me.

I have committed one hundred thousand sins, but as God is my witness, debauchery was never one of them. However, fate saw fit to acquaint me with a way of life that was on the verge of disappearing forever. And this, at first glance, was the inner meaning of the experience.

* * *

At the beginning of June, before the second session of the Fourth State Duma adjourned on the eve of June 14 (27), 1914, I went straight from the Tauride Palace to Kiev and lowered myself into the editor's chair. I found it rather hard, for I did not have the necessary staff to help me, and there was much, probably too much, work.

On June 15 (28), 1914, in the evening, my nephew Efim came to see me. He was only eight years younger than I, and as a result he sometimes took a few liberties. On this occasion he said, "If the State Duma hasn't permanently mashed your brains, it will happen now. You have to churn out an editorial every day and face a swarm of visitors, three-quarters of whom talk too much. In the end they will totally wear you out. You need to have some fun, at least for one night."

"What do you have in mind?"

"Let's go to the Apollo."

"What's that?"

"A cabaret on Nicholaevskii Street."

"Are there saloons on the best streets now?"

"Why, do you need a university or a polytechnic?"

I laughed and said, "Let's go!"

* * *

The Apollo was not a university, but it wasn't a tavern either. We saw an amazing juggler, a master of the miraculous art of the boomerang, who sent twelve big plates spinning off with his right hand in such a way that they flew around the entire theater and then came back, to be caught in his left hand. They fluttered in the air like a flock of white birds. It was well worth watching.

125

Then we listened to a line of so-called lyrical singers who sang "Khrizantemy," "Molchi, grust', molchi," "Pozhalei ty menia, dorogaia," and other romantic songs. The singers were dressed in long gowns. Then we listened to a pleiad of music-hall singers in short dresses. But their dresses were no shorter than those worn now not by music-hall singers but by young girls.

Finally the gypsies came on stage. The men, with guitars, stood in the back, while the women sat in a row in the front. They sang, sometimes individually, sometimes in a chorus. Then a young gypsy girl in a black dress arose. She came out to the center of the stage and began to dance, not with her feet but with her arms—actually, with her shoulders. She had a very dark complexion, cheekbones like the Sphinx in the desert, and huge eyes that sparkled like black diamonds.

Niura, who sat in the middle and had the face of a matron, was the soloist. She had taken voice lessons from Varia Panina, a very famous singer of the time. She had a low voice that emanated from her mouth and her nose at the same time, and thus her voice had a somewhat nasal twang. Her pearly teeth added silver to this low, chesty, somewhat nasal voice, and it became both toneless and ringing at the same time, and all in all it was marvelous.

Nezhnaia rosa	A gentle rose
rozu laskala,	Caressed another rose,
fialka k fialke	a violet stretched her petals
listki prostirala,	out to another violet,
siren' sladostrastno	a lilac voluptuously
siren' tselovala	kissed another violet.
liliia lilii	a lily whispered something
chto-to sheptala . . .	to another lily . . .
Uvy!Uvy! Eto byli tsvety,	Alas! Alas. They were flowers,
No ne ia i ne ty!	And not you and not me!

Either Niura, or the Sphinx in the desert, or the devil-tempter forced us to do something we had not intended to do.

The devil, in the form of a waiter, whispered to us, "Your excellency, wouldn't you like to invite them to a private room, to listen to them. Not expensive. Only one hundred rubles—"

Many writers have described gypsies, but N. S. Leskov best of all. Since I cannot match him, I refer the reader to his story "Ocharovannyi strannik" ("The Enchanted Wanderer").* Whoever reads it will

---

*The text of the story will be found in *Nikolai Leskov: Selected Tales,* trans. David Magarshack (New York: Farrar, Straus & Cudahy, 1961), pp. 51–211 (trans.).

not regret it. Coming from me it would sound cold and hard. In that private room I learned a few things about gypsy customs, and about gypsies too.

When they left the stage, the gypsy men did not change a bit. As they had on the stage, they stood in a row along the wall. The gypsy women, on the other hand, were totally transformed. On the stage they had seemed like singing dolls, but off-stage they became living beings—cheerful, happy. They acted as though we had always been friends, and they were gentle in the Moscow fashion. They had the beautiful pronunciation typical of the city of white stone,* but with an Egyptian accent. One of them happened to say to me, "A gypsy woman? What is a gypsy woman? A gypsy woman must be obeyed—and showered with gifts.

"In Moscow everyone knows that. But here they"—by "they" she meant the Kievans—think that a gypsy is a music-hall singer. A gypsy will go off with you wherever you want!"

Later on she taught me this: "A gypsy woman can't live without her gypsy camp"—by "gypsy camp" she meant "chorus"—"but if a gypsy woman falls in love, it's a different story. She'll go with you to the end of the earth. But not for long. For a year or two. Then she'll return to the camp. And no one will upbraid her. She was in love—that's all. She left—she returned. And that is by no means a music-hall singer!"

* * *

Efim and I immersed ourselves in the company of the Egyptian Muscovites with the black diamond eyes. They sang and drank. Champagne, of course. They drank, but they made us drink more. I protested as much as I could, but they knew how to deal with protests. Under the hum of the guitars continuously strummed by the row of men along the wall, Niura struck up a song in her almost sepulchral voice:

Kak tsvetok dushistai	As a flower disperses
aromat raznosit,	Its aroma,
tak bokal nalitai	The full goblet asks
(kogo-to) vypit' procit.	Someone to drink it.

All this, whether good or bad, was possible. But at that instant the impossible came down upon our heads. The men played as if 100,000 bottles were breaking on thousand-year-old pyramids, and the gypsies' wail (it could no longer be called singing) became the Niagara Falls, with myriads of black diamonds sparkling in the churning water.

---

*Moscow (trans.).

"Vyp'em my za Vasiu—" (how in the world had they managed to learn my name?) "Vasiu daragovo."*

It was impossible not to drink to Vasia, to Filia, to my nephew, to Ducia and all the other gypsies, especially since they were now wailing: "A poka ne vup'iut, ne nal'em grugova."†

The devil take them! In Gogol's book the madman cries, "They're pouring cold water on my head!" They brought the entire Nile River down upon us from the top of the pyramid.

There were short breathing spells. Then the gypsy with the high cheekbones, who was awfully nice, a stranger, but already a close friend, would smile broadly and repeat something over and over again in the gypsy language.

Ah, in the gypsy language? I'm no worse than she. And I answered her in the gypsy language with the only phrase I knew, "Tu nadzhinəs someə takə norakirava. A mə takə ser-so səu mussel."

The first words mean: "You, dear friend, do not understand anything."

The rest is in such an old dialect that many gypsies nowadays do not understand it. And it is better that the reader not understand it. But Ducia, the gypsy with the high cheekbones, understood it, and Niura also. And they, and the others after them, began to carry on so, that I decided I must put an end to it. But how?

My savior turned out to be the devil-waiter, who this time played a good role. He bent over to me, right down to my ear. Through the gypsies' wails I heard, "Sir, there is a telephone call for you."

I knew what it was. Before going into the private room, I had called the newspaper and told them where to call if anything happened. Taking the receiver, I heard, "Vasilii Vitalevich, come to the office. The heir to the Austrian throne has just been killed in Sarajevo."

I answered, "Throw out the editorial I gave you. Leave room for another one."

In twenty minutes, having poured cold water from the faucet on my head, I was writing a new editorial.

* * *

What had happened? On June 28, 1914, the anniversary of Serbia's defeat on the field of Kosovo—a day of national mourning in Serbia—the Austrian command planned to hold maneuvers near the

---

*Russian drinking song with diminutive of Shulgin's first name inserted: "Let us drink to Vasia, dearest Vasia" (trans.).
†Part of the same song: words to the effect that until the glass is emptied, another one will not be poured (trans.).

Serbian border.* The heir to the Austro-Hungarian throne, Archduke Francis Ferdinand, and his wife were to observe the maneuvers, and that was why he had come with his entourage to Sarajevo, the capital of Bosnia.

The organizers of the assassination took advantage of this circumstance. As was learned later, they belonged to an organization of nationalistic Serbian officers called Unity or Death, better known as the Black Hand. The organization was headed by the chief of intelligence of the Serbian General Staff, Colonel Dragutin Dmitrievich, who had devised the plan of attack.

Afterwards it was said that the Serbian government, headed by Prime Minister N. Pashich, knew of the impending murder but did not take any measures to thwart the plan. In addition it was said that the Prince-Regent of Serbia, Alexander I Karageorgievich, was close to the Black Hand.

The attack was executed by members of the Young Bosnia organization, which advocated the freeing of Bosnia and Herzegovina from the Austro-Hungarian yoke and the formation of a single Yugoslavian state. This organization was closely connected to the officers of the Black Hand, and they incited one of its members, a secondary-school boy who by a strange coincidence was named Princip, to kill the prince of the Hapsburg dynasty.

With the help of Nedelko Chabrinovich, Trifko Grabezh, and other conspirators, all of them members of Young Bosnia, Gavrilo Princip killed the Austrian heir, Francis Ferdinand, and his wife. The Austro-Hungarian government, urged on by Kaiser Wilhelm II of Germany, used the murder as grounds for presenting Serbia with an ultimatum on July 23, 1914. In this way, Princip's shot at the prince served as a signal for the start of the First World War.

What was the fate of this unfortunate youth? As a minor, he was not executed, but sentenced to twenty years of penal servitude. On April 28, 1918, he died in prison of tuberculosis.

After the liberation of Serbia from Austrian domination, a memorial plaque was erected in Sarajevo on the spot where the attack took place.

In April of 1941 the last conqueror marched into Sarajevo—Adolf Hitler. He immediately ordered the memorial plaque removed, as a warning to the "mutinous" city. He was certain that the city's role in history was finished. The ending is known to all. Soon the entire

---

*As a result of the defeat at Kosovo in 1389, Serbia came under Turkish domination, a status that continued until the nineteenth century (trans.).

country rose to fight the conquerors. And now the people of Yugoslavia revere Gavrilo Princip as a national hero.

* * *

And so, war was declared—declared by Germany on Russia, not the
reverse. Russia, in the person of her sovereign, sought a peaceful
outcome. The Tsar suggested a meeting of the three emperors,
Wilhelm II, Francis Joseph, and Nicholas II, to settle the conflict by
negotiation. The aged Austrian emperor was ready to agree, but
Wilhelm II's mustaches were curled upward and he refused. Alexander I Karageorgievich, having become the Serbian Prince-Regent in
June 1914, during the reign of his aged father, sent a touching telegram to our Tsar in which he asked for aid on the grounds that Russia
had always been the protector of the Slavic peoples.

The Tsar wrote back in this vein: "What a lovely telegram. How can
we help?"

At this time two opposing currents were raging in Petersburg, the
capital. Some people felt that Russian tradition demanded that Russia
step in on behalf of violated Serbia. Others said that we did not have
the right to sacrifice hundreds of thousands, perhaps millions, of
Russians in the name of Serbian sovereignty.

Both the former and the latter were right—the former because
Russia always had defended the Balkan Slavs, the latter, because when
a government responds to a question of war with an answer that
means death, not life, it is essential that the masses and the rulers be in
agreement on the subject. After all, the Serbs, having murdered the
heir to the Austro-Hungarian throne, Francis Ferdinand, were regi-
cides, and the Russian Tsar was not obligated to intercede for them.

However, the Tsar took the position of the former group: "We must
help." But how? If they did not want to negotiate there would be war.
But war with whom? With Austria alone, or with Germany? The Tsar
thought that the war would only involve Austria, and the intelligence
available to us indicated that we could defeat the Austrians. For this a
partial mobilization would suffice, mainly of the Southern Corps. But
quite obviously the Tsar was mistaken. Wilhelm II would undoubtedly
interfere, and the German army presented a most serious threat to
Russia.

Here it is appropriate to mention that Kaiser Wilhelm II apparently
felt a personal enmity to Nicholas II. They say that he expressed his
irritation more than once in these words: "After the Japanese war,
which was unsuccessful for Russia, the Revolution of 1905 broke out.
At this time Russia was so weak that I could have reached my hand
out and taken Petersburg and Moscow. But I did not. The Russians

responded with black ingratitude, concluding an alliance with England and France against me." I will not take it upon myself to judge whether this was so or not, but I know that his own mother, the English Princess Victoria, called her son Wilhelm II a "monster."

And so another battle raged in Petersburg about what kind of mobilization should be ordered, partial or general. This matter is discussed in detail in Colonel Sergievskii's very interesting book, published in Belgrade. The author very vividly describes the entire drama of this question. In his opinion, conducting a partial mobilization first, followed by a general one, would have threatened anarchy. In the end the Tsar was persuaded to declare a general mobilization. He did so, but this still did not mean war. The troops were mobilized as a precaution. Kaiser Wilhelm II seized upon his decision, however, and the following day, July 19 (August 1), 1914, declared war on Russia. The Rubicon was crossed and the Great War began.

*   *   *

I learned of this under the following circumstances. For reasons that would be of no interest to the reader, I had traveled a considerable distance in my four-in-hand, with Andrei, the coachman, and planned to send the horses back by rail, which at that time did not present any difficulties. Andrei bustled off to speak to the stationmaster, but soon returned and announced, "The stationmaster will not assign you a car." He paused and added, "And they're saying at the station that mobilization has begun."

I immediately set off for Kiev by train, and for a few hours I was able to get some sleep in a private sleeping compartment. But around dawn I jumped out of bed. For an instant I thought the train was being fired upon by heavy guns, but it turned out that someone was knocking at the door. And then I saw who was knocking. It was some members of the beautiful weaker sex, also known as "heavenly creatures," transformed into furies. They were milling about the corridor with countless suitcases, baskets, children, even cages with parrots, and kicking the door. Naturally, I opened the compartment door and asked with all possible politeness, "What can I do for you?"

Roars and squeals answered me.

"What can you do for us? You can give us seats!"

For an instant I was dumbfounded, but then an evil thought occurred to me. I opened the door noisily and with an exaggerated gesture invited them in. And I walked out, that is, squeezed out, into the corridor. What I had thought would happen actually did happen. In their rage at me, they tore into the sleeping compartment and filled it to overflowing. Then, directing their rage at one another, they began to scuffle. Trying to hold my ground in the corridor so as not to get trampled, I exulted and cried, "No seats? There's plenty! Come in, come in!"

However, those few minutes were enough for me. I totally understood the situation, remembering Marcus Tullius Cicero's saying, "Law stands mute in the midst of arms."* I had a lawful right to my sleeping compartment but had been thrown out. That meant war.

And in reality, those unfortunate women, the wives and daughters of various officers, clerks, and officials, had been ordered to evacuate because the enemy was approaching.

* * *

In Kiev I learned that the State Duma was hastily convening in Petersburg for an unscheduled emergency session on July 26 (August 8), 1914, and that an express train was being sent from Kiev with cars reserved for the deputies from the provinces closest to Kiev. A similar train left Odessa. It was supposed to connect with the Kiev train at Kazatin, and then together we would force our way to the capital.

I say "force our way" because we were moving against the current. All the other trains were heading for the front, and we were going toward Moscow. That was also something new. Before, in peacetime, express trains from Kiev to Petersburg would pass through Vilna, but now Vilna was also under attack.

In Kazatin we joined other members of the State Duma from the more southerly provinces, including the Bessarabians. Among them was Purishkevich.

For a long time there had been a serious disagreement between us, and thus we were not speaking to each other. The reason does not matter, but it was a serious disagreement. When I saw him at the end of the car, I didn't know what to expect, but I began to understand everything when he suddenly ran up to me, hand outstretched, and said, "Shulgin, war washes things away. Let's forget the past!" We shook hands and even kissed as a sign of reconciliation.

Yes, war washes things away. It washes away laws, as Cicero said, but it also washes away petty discords. War is a great teacher and tester. Within the next twenty-four hours I saw this proven in the Winter Palace.

* * *

In the meantime, from a different perspective, I observed all the new things that war had brought. In our car was Vsevolod Iakovlevich Demchenko, a member of the State Duma from Kiev Province, chair-

---

*Cicero, *Pro Milone* 4, 11 (trans.).

man of the Kiev district zemstvo council, and a communications engineer building the Kiev-Poltavsk Railroad. He was an extremely energetic man, and thanks to that he had connections among many classes and subdivisions of the people, specifically among the railroad men.

I have said already that we were moving against the tide. And for that reason we all worried that we would not arrive in time for the opening of the Duma, especially since we would have to force our way into Moscow, which was especially swamped. Demchenko disappeared at every stop. He pestered stationmasters and sent countless telegrams to Petersburg, Moscow, M. V. Rodzianko, Chairman of the State Duma, and various ministers—well, in a word, to everyone. Finally, with a satisfied look he calmed down, announcing triumphantly, "The mobilization is proceeding ahead of schedule, but we will still arrive in Petersburg on time."

In order to understand the significance of the mobilization proceeding two days ahead of schedule, one must know that Germany was banking on the likelihood that Russia would be a whole month late in mobilizing its troops, while Germany would carry out its mobilization to a tee, which in fact did happen. And Germany then would have a significant numerical superiority over Russia, since many of the Russian troops would not have arrived at the front.

Why did the German General Staff think this way? Because the Germans remembered the Russian general strike of 1905, remembered the revolutionary enthusiasm of the workers and the intelligentsia, and hoped that it would be repeated during the mobilization, but it was not.

The railroads were caught up in a storm of patriotism which could in no way have been anticipated. All Russia was caught up in a patriotic fervor. Reservists from the provinces arrived in formed units and did not even mutiny when the sale of vodka throughout Russia was discontinued in single drastic step. It was a miracle. Absolutely unbelievable.

I observed all this but could not explain it to myself. I was as cold as ice, not believing my eyes, and in the depths of my soul I felt that this universal fervor was a mirage. But, of course, I locked my lips and acted as though I shared the feelings of these impassioned people.

* * *

The train successfully forced its way through to Moscow. At the Moscow station there was a dinner prepared especially for us, and refreshed, we left Moscow in hopes of reaching Petersburg on time. There was very little time left, however. The others arrived on time, but I was late, for an absurd reason. Since the reception was to take place in the Winter Palace, I assumed that evening dress would be required. But dressing in the cramped compartment was difficult, my cufflinks and white tie got lost, and by the time I found them, all the other Duma members had run off. I was unable to find a taxi at the station, but managed to flag the last wagon. Standing in the wagon, I persistently hurried the driver and begged him to go faster, repeating over and over, "The Tsar is waiting for me."

This worked, and we flew from the Nicholaevskii Station to the Winter Palace at a gallop.

The square was completely empty. There was the palace, stately, beautiful, with numerous windows and several entrances! And no one, not a single sentry or even a person whom I could ask which entrance to rush into. I ran at random into the first one. The doors were wide open. The white marble staircase with the red carpet lay before me. I hurried up the stairs at a speed allowed only by youthful lungs. Again a majestic door, behind it a hall, shining with parqueted floor. But where to run? Suddenly I heard cries, loud human wails. I realized what they were and ran in the direction of the noise. I ran into a hall filled by a huge crowd. And it was all the members of the State Duma. It was they who were yelling so. The crowd was milling around someone; at first, I did not know who. But then, pushing others aside, I made my way forward a bit and saw.

So crowded that he could have reached out and touched the men in the front row as they dashed around in an emotional frenzy, there stood the Sovereign. This was the only time that I ever saw worry on his bright face.

And who would not worry? The crowd, composed not of youths but of middle-aged and even old men, was shouting, "Lead us, Sire!"

It was perhaps the most significant thing that I have ever seen in my life. This was what all real monarchists dream of: unfabricated, authentic, sincere patriotism.

This united meeting of the State Duma and the State Council, opened with a speech by Emperor Nicholas II, took place in the Winter Palace on July 26 (August 9), 1914.

* * *

I returned to Kiev. Soon after my arrival a general in the infantry, Michael Vasilevich Alekseev, asked to see me. Later, as one of the main organizers of the counterrevolutionary movement in the southern Caucasus, he would join with Generals L. G. Kornilov and A. I. Denikin to found the "Volunteer Army," and in March 1918 he was elected its Supreme Commander and leader of the special conference. But his early death, on October 8 (21), 1918, in Ekaterinodar, interfered with his projected campaign against Soviet Russia.

At this time he was chief of staff on the southwestern front.

It was our first meeting. By birth Alekseev was a commoner, born in 1857. Although his father was only a common soldier, that did not prevent Alekseev from finishing the course at the General Staff Academy in 1890, and thanks to his exceptional capacity for work, he acquired such wide knowledge as a staff officer that in 1898 he was appointed a professor of military history at the Military Academy. All this was expressed in his face. When I spoke with him I sometimes felt as if I were speaking to an intelligent sergeant major, and at other times his eyes sparkled through his glasses like those of a serious, thoughtful professor. His voice was squeaky and slow, like an ox cart, but pleasant to listen to. He spoke eloquently and impressively.

He had called on me about an insignificant matter which I could not take care of immediately, but that was only an excuse. His words made such an impact that I have remembered them all my life.

"Certain frivolous people and officers, even high-ranking officers, think, and even say, that the war will be over in three months. That's nonsense, harmful nonsense. The enemy is tough. We won't be able to finish him off with one great charge. The war will go on to the point of exhaustion, and our people will be fighting with each other. This being so, what is our most important problem?

"The most important thing is to maintain the spirit of the people. Victory will be ensured only by their steadfastness, or, as we officers say, by the endurance factor. Generally speaking, the Russian army has a high endurance factor, but the army is one thing, and the people as a whole are something else. The army derives from the people, and therefore, in the final analysis, everything will be determined by the people's will to endure.

"I repeat: the most important thing is to maintain the people's spirit. And so I turn to you, as a representative of the people, and it is indisputable that you are, because the people elected you to the State Duma three times. Furthermore, you are the editor of an influential newspaper. And therefore you have an obligation to do what you can to keep the people's spirit from sagging when hard times befall us, as they will."

* * *

I was deep in thought when I left General Alekseev. He was right, but what could I do? There was an icy cold in my soul, even when I heard the cries, "Lead us, Sire!"

In such a frame of mind, how was I to maintain the people's spirit? I considered the war a mistake and foresaw disaster, yet I had to write uplifting patriotic articles in the *Kievlianin* every day, and I did not have the strength to wring them out of myself. There is such a thing as white lies, of course, but in this case it would be an attempt with worthless resources. My inner coldness would force its way in between the lines no matter how many exclamation points I provided.

What was I to do? Suddenly, quick as lightning, I came to a decision.

To the front! Everything worth having must be paid for with blood. If a man who was legally excused from serving in the field forces were to do so anyway, this in itself would be an example of patriotism that would in some small measure maintain the people's spirit.*

But only if one was really serious about it, going into combat and exposing himself as a target. I had a lowly commission as an ensign in the reserve field engineers—in other words, as a sapper—but that would not do. I had to share the manly fate of my peasants from Volyn. After all, it was they who had sent me to the State Duma, and I should be with them, shoulder to shoulder at the front, in the trenches, if I was really to be their representative.

Thus, I had to join the infantry, the holy infantry, the "ignorant beasts," to use the words of Michael Ivanovich Dragomirov, commander of the Kiev military district and governor-general of Kiev, Podolsk, and Volyn.

In the years 1873 to 1877, when he was the commander of fourteen infantry divisions, he had expounded his method of training the "ignorant masses" in a series of articles under the heading "Army Notes." He successfully applied his experience during the Russo-Turkish war of 1877–1878, leading the crossing of the Danube River at Zimnicea and participating in the defense of Shipka in August of 1877.

But he did not live to see the day when his beloved "ignorant masses" were no longer willing to obey their teachers and, throwing down their rifles, scattered and ran home. Michael Ivanovich Dragomirov, distinguished military theoretician and pedagogue, did not live to see the December armed uprising. He died in Kiev on October 15 (28), 1905, two days before the manifesto was published.

*   *   *

Having made up my mind, I sent a telegram to the headquarters of Nicholas Iudovich Ivanov, commander of the southwestern front: "Request assignment to the 166th Rovnenskii Infantry Regiment. State Duma member Shulgin."

The next day I received an answer, "You are assigned to the 166th Rovnenskii Infantry Regiment. General Alekseev, Chief of Staff, southwestern front."

I must say that it was easy for me personally to make the decision to go to war, but it was extremely cruel to my nearest and dearest. Some

---

*Duma members were exempt from military service (trans.).

men enlist because they are unlucky in love, but I was lucky in love. As a result, I started tears flowing before I ever caused any blood to flow. But when the flood subsided somewhat, my loved ones sewed me six silk shirts; this was a comfort both to those whose tears were flowing and to me, the cruel hangman.

However, somewhere in the depths of my heart I must have known my fate. The happiest time of my life was during the war. For me personally the war had a happy ending.

However, that is not something that should be included in these memoirs. There are two kinds of memoirists. Some, on the model of Jean-Jacques Rousseau, write "confessions." Here the author represents himself as a whole—as a political figure, as a thinker, and as an ordinary mortal. Such people are rare, and I cannot follow in the footsteps of this genre of thinkers. At the present time I have worked my way into the company of those memoirists who are concerned with only one aspect of the person, surgically dividing themselves into two parts. Like them, I speak only of my modest political activities. When one is writing memoirs in this fashion, his personal qualities become something of an irrelevancy.

I am guilty of doing this, but it was Gaius Julius Caesar, not I, who invented the genre. His classical memoirs about the war in Gaul, written in the purest Latin, are the best remedy I know for sleeplessness, but I cannot help admiring them, and so I write as circumspectly as possible about my personal affairs.

Battle

I WROTE SEVERAL VOLUMES about the war. Goodness knows where they are. Whether they were lost during my various moves, both voluntary and involuntary, or whether they still exist, hidden somewhere, I don't know. But perhaps it is better this way. I wrote those volumes without dividing things into two parts; they treat my personal life as well as my political life, and in such intimate detail that the following is written on the first page of the first volume: "These memoirs are not to be published during my lifetime."

The curious reader if he is interested, may wait until these memoirs appear in published form. When this will be I don't know.

And now I will attempt to recall some events of the war.

* * *

Since this was in September 1914, I had to catch up with my regiment, which took six full days. It would be very amusing for me to describe my wanderings. I saw how the other half lives, and at the time it lived poorly. In general I saw many interesting things, but I cannot allow myself the luxury of telling about them all. I will only say that during my travels the thought never left me that in the end I would reach the Peremyshl fortress.

There, I fancied, I would see the terrible, so-called wolf-pits with their sharp stakes protruding upward to the sky.

I knew from previous accounts that sometimes such fortresses were taken only after the wolf-pits were fulled to the brim, even above the protruding stakes, with the bodies of the dead and the seriously wounded. New attacks went on over the bodies, and the fortress would be taken. It seemed to me that my fate was a wolf-pit with its sharpened stake piercing my back.

The 166th Rovnenskii Regiment actually was south of Peremyshl, but there were neither wolf-pits nor sharp stakes. The regiment was still fighting at the frontier fortifications. The citadel was about thirty-five kilometers away. The regiment's headquarters was in the middle of a beautiful wood. The autumn was golden that year. The oaks and birches were decorated in warm yellows and reds. I presented myself to the regimental commander. The colonel shook my hand and, since we were in the presence of other officers, said very politely, "We are flattered that you chose the 166th Infantry Regiment. For us you are not an ensign but a famous member of the State Duma. You are extraordinarily punctual; we received the order about your assignment only today. I am assigning you to the First Company to assist Captain Golosov. Please report to him."

I presented myself to Golosov and we spoke most cordially. I liked Golosov very much; he had a fine voice, soft and ringing, with a charming burr. After our talk, I fell asleep as he was telling the following story to the some other officers:

"Never in my life have I struck a soldier. But this time I had to, and he was a noncommissioned officer."

Another voice asked, "Well, why did you do it?"

"I gave him some money and sent him to get meat for the regiment, but he didn't bring any meat and stole the money—"

I fell asleep at this point, and when I woke up it must have been an hour or two later. Something was quietly, not very melodiously, droning—singing, actually. I realized that it was field telephones. Nearby, in another room, telephone operators, lying on the ground, were speaking to men in the trenches. It was cosy, mysterious, and a bit eerie. I fell asleep again.

* * *

Since the First Company was in reserve, I went for a walk in the morning with the regimental doctor. All around were forest-covered mountains. What was called an "artillery duel" began, and shells droned continuously all around us.

I was surprised at the seemingly peaceful sound of this music. The shells droned on in a very businesslike way, calling to mind a moving tram. We couldn't hear either the reports of the guns or the explosions. Both sides were firing, but it was impossible to determine what they were firing at. The shells flew high above our heads, hitting unknown targets.

Suddenly the nervous stutter of machine-gun fire interrupted this peaceful music. The doctor said, "Well, something is starting. Let's go home."

"Home" meant the regimental headquarters. On our way there we came across several soldiers, under the command of an officer, leading pack horses laden with machine-guns and ammunition.

The doctor asked, "Going to work?"

A lieutenant, I believe it was Makovskii, answered, "Yes, it looks like they've begun an attack."

Going a bit farther we met up with Captin Golosov. I turned to him and in a friendly manner asked, "Can I go with you?"

Sizing me up at a glance, he barked, "You're out of uniform! Sling your coat over your shoulder. Get your rifle."

Then he strode off quickly, with the regiment stretching in a line behind him.

The doctor said to me, "Well, let's get dressed."

The new overcoat was slid off me and slung over my head onto my shoulder. Then they adjusted a pouch with sixty cartridges and put a rifle in my hands. One of the officers said sympathetically, "How are you going to fight, you beanpole?"

I was insulted, not understanding that it was my build that had evoked this comment. I was tall and skinny. I snapped, "Where is the 1st Company? Where did they go? How can I find them?"

Someone responded, "The wounded will be coming in soon. You can go meet them."

This I did. I went up a road that led me into the woods and hills. The bursting shells and the crackling of gunfire gave no sign of which direction to go. It seemed that they were bursting on all sides. But suddenly some wounded actually did appear. Their hands were bandaged and bloody in places. One of them walked toward me rather briskly, but with a gloomy expression. His hand must have been broken, since it was in a splint.

I was in a stupid mood and asked him, "Did you get your share?" He gave me a vicious look and answered, "There's enough for everybody."

Lermontov's poem ran through my mind:

Chto? Ranen?	What? You're wounded?
Pustiaki, bezdelka!	That's nothing!
I zaviazalas perestrelka . . .	And the wound was bandaged.

Probably that's how it was in the deadly Caucasus about a hundred years ago, when there were no shells and no grazing fire. It was child's play in comparison to modern warfare. In 1914 war was not a "trifle," as Lermontov wrote; for as General M. V. Alekseev had told me, "The enemy is tough."

I saw many soldiers, some of them wounded, but the First Company of the 166th Rovnenskii Infantry Regiment was nowhere around in the hills and woods. I only knew one man in the company, Captain Golosov, and I despaired of ever finding them. No one could help me. I found myself in a ridiculous position. My happiness depended on finding the company that promised me death or maiming. Finally, I was lucky enough to find it. Some soldiers started moving up the road, with Captain Golosov at their head. I dashed toward him, as happy as if he were my own father. He gave a rather critical glance, saying, "There you are. Well, let's go."

I followed him, beside myself with happiness. Everything was fine now.

We wandered through the hills and woods for a long time, but Golosov seemed to know exactly where to go. Bullets began to pierce the treetops, whistling rather pleasantly. But there were unpleasant ones also. Some bullets ricocheted off the birches, which had very hard wood. When they did, they began to twist and turn and shriek unbearably. Ricocheting bullets are the most dangerous of all and can inflict horrible wounds.

My stupid frame of mind continued. I did not feel the slightest fear. Nor did the others show any sign of horror, as though the bullets were of no concern to them. To tell the truth, the bullets were flying high above us, but soon a grazing fire began, and the bullets began flying lower. We reached a grassy area. We had been walking in single file, close together, but now, at Golosov's order, we strung out. I realized that we were face to face with the foe, but he was still far away, somewhere beyond the woods. Since the bullets were flying low, Golosov gave the order to take cover.

The regiment took cover, holding their rifles with bayonets at the ready. Then came another command. "Get up! Make a run for it! Quickly!"

We ran across the field and again took cover on the other side, in the woods.

At this point I again lost my only happiness—Golosov. This occurred because the strung-out line of a hundred or so men had ended up in the woods, and one could see only the men on one's right and one's left.

But again a command was heard, "Forward! March!"

We went on. I never saw Golosov again.

In this way the part of the regiment that could see me fell naturally under my command. I already had a certain amount of command experience, for in the same way I had found myself at the head of a group of soldiers deserted by their officer during the pogrom against the Jews in Kiev. We were seeing each other for the first time in our lives, but after a short while they began not only to obey my orders but also to anticipate my every move. A soldier likes to be led.

Now I had a rough idea where the enemy was and concluded that we had to do close battle with him.

Only much later did I realize that this was absurd, and that we did not have to advance. But Golosov's last order had been "forward," and at the time he was for me both law and prophet. I led the men in small dashes wherever the terrain permitted.

"Get up! Run for it! Take cover!"

Besides myself there were still two noncommissioned officers. And they surprised me.

They did not take cover, despite my order. They struck out in plain view. And then, in a silence that fell for an instant, I suddenly heard, "In case of my death, I appoint Ivanenko."

This meant, "If I am killed or wounded, Ivanenko will take command. Obey him."

This order, strictly according to regulations, was given with complete composure during peacetime training, when the words "in case of my death" sounded totally unreal, but now my death could actually happen at any minute.

I shouted at them again, "Down!" I thought, "The hell with you." It seemed as if the fear of death was totally unknown to them.

We were moving through a beautiful wood filled with hornbeams and oaks, with wild hazelnuts growing below them.

Meanwhile the bullets began to fly lower and lower. Once I saw a kneeling soldier suddenly start and begin to swear. Right above his head a bullet had pierced a leaf, which shone like gold in the setting sun.

But I had taken on a totally stupid role and led the men farther and farther forward. I did it without knowing why, but was convinced that I was right. Meanwhile, a much louder sound was added to the whistle and drone of the bullets. Shells began to explode above the trees, and the hazelnuts were peppered with shrapnel, as though with an invisible hail.

I sensed that just about here, right in front of us, was our goal. Urging my men on again, I found myself at the edge of a wood, the very kind of spot that, as a rule, is regularly fired upon, but at the time I did not know this. An unceasing thunder of shells was exploding precisely on the spot, but it was nothing in comparison to what would come later.

The wood was encircled by a ditch. It was not a trench dug by troops but simply a shallow ditch, indicating the border of the wood. Beyond the ditch stretched an open field, gently sloping downward. At the bottom, about six hundred paces off, was another ditch. Behind the ditch the field rose, and beyond it was another wood, just as beautifully crimson-gold, about a thousand paces from our wood.

There were men lying in our ditch, leaning against its side as if it were a breastwork. They lay shoulder to shoulder. Thinking at first that it was our company, I ran from one to the other and, lying down, asked a question of the nearest soldier. I said "asked," but I mean that I yelled in his ear with all my strength, so that he could hear me over the din of the artillery.

"First Company?"

Also straining his voice, he answered, "Not at all, Your Excellency, it's the Sixth."

I ran over to the next group. Again they mentioned some absurd company, but not the First.

Finally I left off searching for it and diverted my attention to what these men, my fellow-countrymen, were doing. There were both young men and old men, reservists. One of them, about forty years old, imperturbably shooting five times, put in another five cartridges and fired again.

When I was leading my men through the woods, I had seen how hard it was to bring up additional cartridges. The sixty cartridges a private carries are used up quickly, so new ones are constantly brought to the firing line, but with great difficulty because of the distance and the firing. A horse pulling a cart loaded with cartridges was killed before my very eyes.

So I yelled into the fellow's ear, "What are you shooting at?" He pointed at the ditch at the bottom of the field, about six hundred paces away. At that time my eyesight was very sharp—20/20, I might add—and I yelled into his ear, "There's nobody there!" Looking closely, he answered, "Nobody there?"

I shouted, "Stop! Don't waste cartridges!"

He replied, "Well, where do I shoot?" He pointed to the left, along the length of our ditch. I said, "You can't, those are our machine-gunners, understand?"

I realized that Lieutenant Makovskii was there. We did not have many machine-guns at the time, but our guns sang more cheerfully than those of the Austrians, so I could distinguish them. The fellow asked again, "Where do I shoot?"

Realizing that it was vital for him to shoot somewhere, anywhere, I indicated the ditch opposite us, a thousand paces away. The Austrians would be there if they were as stupid as we, that is, lying along the edge of a regularly fired-upon wood. My countryman nodded, pulled a new clip out of his pouch, and dropped it into the magazine. I yelled, "Set it for one thousand paces!" Setting the sights at one thousand paces, he got to work, much as a conscientious peasant works, thriftily.

Seeing that everything was under control, I ran to the next place. I squeezed between two young soldiers, one of whom was laughing at the top of his lungs, revealing snow-white teeth.

"Why are you laughing?" I shouted into his ear. His response was: "It's fun, sir!" But I was unable to hold a discussion in regard to such a happy philosophy in the middle of this hell. Something hit me in the back, actually in the right shoulder-blade, in such a way that, starting from the unbearable pain, I fainted.

When I regained consciousness, I found myself a few feet away from the ditch, under some large trees that were brightly lit by the setting sun. Medics from one of the companies were bandaging my right arm. I said, still feeling a hellish pain, "Forget it, I'm going to die anyway." The medic answered, "Not at all, sir." I asked, "Why are you bothering with this arm? Isn't the wound over here?"

"No sir. This is where you are bleeding."

I didn't argue with him. The pain in the shoulder-blade became bearable; at any rate, I was able to breathe, and was very happy when they finished. "Lift me up," I asked. They set me on my feet, and I said, feeling well enough to walk, "I'm going."

"No sir, you can't get there on your own." One of them took me by my left arm and led me through the woods. The farther we went from the place where it was so much fun, in the opinion of that young soldier, the better I felt. At the same time I thought to myself that these heroic medics, who so calmly bandaged the wounded only a few steps from a fired-upon ditch, were more needed back there than with me. I would get there.

| Chto? Ranen? | What? You're wounded? |
| Pustiaki, bezdelka! | That's nothing! |

This meant that the stupid frame of mind was returning. I said to the medic, "Go back." However, he did not obey immediately. Spotting a gray overcoat and white bandages in the distance, he shouted ringingly, "Hey! Hey, you!" But the soldier did not turn around, perhaps not hearing the medic. Then he said to me, "Sir, he's walking too fast; you won't be able to catch up, but look over there. They're carrying someone on a stretcher. They'll walk slowly and you can go with them."

Truly, I overtook them. An army overcoat, fastened to rifles somehow, served as a stretcher. Then four men could carry someone who was too heavy for two to carry. They walked slowly, while I wanted to get home, that is, to headquarters.

Again coming under the power of the stupid frame of mind, I left them. It's nothing, I'll make it! But I was punished. I got lost and again came under fire. There I realized that the psychology of a well man is very different from that of a wounded man. I hid behind a knoll and, resting, thought about how nice it would be if somebody's hands would help me get there so that I could drink a cup of strong hot tea in total safety. The stupid frame of mind went away completely.

Meanwhile, the sun was setting, and it was getting darker by the minute. I didn't know the roads, and had no idea whatsoever where regimental headquarters was located. Furthermore, I was so disoriented that I didn't know which was the enemy and which was my side. Sitting down beneath a tree, I tried to decide what to do.

The fighting stopped. No bullets, no shrapnel. But with the last round either we or the Austrians set fire to a building with a straw roof. The fire burned brightly and I went toward it. Finally, climbing several ditches, I reached a main road. Whitish-crimson, it went in two directions. The fire did not say which way the enemy was and which way our troops were. I went to the right and guessed correctly, because after a short time I reached the little house that served as our headquarters. I recognized it in the light of the fire. A few steps farther was the grassy area where the wounded were being treated. Some, already dead, were lying under the trees, while the doctor who had gone for a walk with me earlier was working on some others. I went up to him.

"Ah, here already?" he asked. No longer under the influence of inspiring martial poetry, I answered, "Take a look at this." They removed my bloody field shirt, which was very painful, then they pulled off my heavy camel's-hair jersey. As I later learned, the jersey had saved me from serious misfortune. The fact was that the first hit, from which I lost consciousness, was from a long-range shell, that is, from a copper-tipped shell. That thing alone would have been enough; falling from above, it hit me at the same time that a shrapnel shell was exploding over my head. The camel's-hair jersey was pulled off, full of holes. Under that was a silk shirt, turned into a bloody rag. After that the doctor was able to examine me. He said, "They really got you. Four wounds, and shrapnel fragments are embedded in the flesh over here. I can't remove them here—you will have to be evacuated."

However, he made a mistake. When they brought me to Lvov, a certain famous professor commented to his younger colleagues, "Take a look at this nice clean wound. There are no shrapnel fragments; otherwise there would have been inflammation long before now. A single bullet made four holes. First it entered the arm above the elbow from the outer side. This is the first point of entry. Then it went out of the arm on the inner side, which is the first exit, severing a nerve, which will make the arm useless for a while. Then it again entered the body, which is the second point of entry, and making its way through the flesh on the back, it again left the body. This second exit is two centimeters from the spinal column. Four in all. You are to be congratulated. Then you received a strong blow from something heavy, most likely from the head of the shrapnel—this will resolve itself."

* * *

In spite of the doctor's orders to evacuate, I did not leave immediately. That evening I ran a high fever, which occurs from loss of blood. The other officers hovered around me, brought me tea with red wine, and spoke very kindly to me. Not for nothing had I ended up in the 166th Rovnenskii Infantry Regiment. But I will not recount any of that. Well, in a word, I felt as if I were among family. What I had dreamed about, while taking cover from the second shelling, had finally come about—friendship and hot tea. I suddenly realized how war turns friends into family. Toward morning my fever subsided and, hiding from the regimental commander, who had ordered me to evacuate, I strolled through the oak and hornbeam woods, which had become even more beautiful. However, I accidentally ran across the commander, and he gave a strict order which I could not disobey.

Since I had lost my rolled greatcoat after being shot, I was given a blue Austrian overcoat belonging to a prisoner who had died. I was brought to Lvov in it, and at the entrance of the Saxony Hotel the following scene occurred.

Nicholas Nicholaevich Lvov, a Progressive and one of the founders of the Union of Liberation, who knew me well, was standing there, but he did not recognize me because of the blue overcoat draped over my shoulders. Notwithstanding the costume, someone else did recognize me, however, and began to kiss me, happy that I was safe. Later Lvov told me, "How indignant I was when I saw him welcome an Austrian officer so warmly!"

What happened next? See the following section.

*   *   *

Donning a white armband with a red cross but keeping my officer's shoulder boards, I arrived in Lvov and went straight to the IUZOZO base. It was on Sheptitskii Street, named after the well-known Polish patron of the arts who had founded an enormous library in Cracow. Anyone with a university degree could use the library. The base was located on a large, very disorganized farmstead, with some houses, storehouses, barracks; it had everything we needed. I was stationed at this farmstead and there began to equip my detachment.

Besides the detachment, the base itself was also under my command. People the army did not know what to do with were stationed there. They all had some influence. Some found themselves there because they were actually unsuited to serve at the front; others because they did not want to go to the front. Their reasons were not my concern. In the meantime I gave them food and a cot, and tried to train them. I was assigned several students as aides (but what it was they were supposed to do was a mystery), and also two young nurses from Polish Galicia—I will tell you about them later. One might think it would not be much trouble to equip a small detachment, but it was a bother. I will spare the reader the details.

Finally we were ready to march and I even acquired a map. We set off in the direction of the Austrian city of Sambor on the left bank of the Dnestr River. There was a huge house there, actually a castle or palace, which served as headquarters for the Eighth Army, commanded by General A. A. Brusilov. In the meantime we were overtaken by P. N. Balashev and N. N. Mozhaiskii in a car. They dragged me off to Brusilov.

Alexis Alekseevich Brusilov was a cavalry general, refined and young-looking despite his sixty years. He was born on August 19 (31), 1853. We spoke about this and that, but I did not foresee the role Brusilov would play in the future. The fact that the troops under his command broke through the Austro-German front in 1916, as well as his highly developed leadership ability, were to make him one of the best military commanders of the First World War.

Of course, at the time, I could not foresee that the general speaking to us would be named Supreme Commander-in-Chief on May 22 (June 4), 1917. I probably would not have believed it, thinking it nonsense, if I had been told that Brusilov, during Lenin's lifetime, would join the Red Army in 1920, serve in the high command of the People's Commissariat for Military Affairs, inspect the Red Cavalry, and carry out the most important commissions under the Revolutionary War Council.

When we passed the city of Sambor, the country became more and more wild and unexplored. In a word, we were in the Carpatho-Ukraine, where huts without chimneys still existed.* We had all sorts of little adventures.

For example, we had two field kitchens, but not the usual type. Field kitchens, if I may say so, are ordinarily very mobile, and meals are cooked while they are in motion, with the cook walking directly behind. As a result, when the company halts for a meal, soup is ready.

Our kitchens could not be used when moving, being huge and unsteady. While we were crossing a hillside, they toppled over into a river. My several student aides displayed the typical uselessness of the intelligentsia with pious ardor. They got soaked to the skin but were unable to drag the kitchens out of the river. The old men calmly pulled the kitchens out, and those majestic unwieldy carriages rolled on once again.

However, the road became worse by the hour, until finally I left the kitchens and students and sped off in an automobile to make sure that we would not be threatened with completely impassable roads. I ended up in a traffic jam. All the transport vehicles had stopped;

---

*Shulgin actually says "Carpathian Rus," using the ancient term for Russia, to emphasize how primitive the region was (trans.).

there was no way through, because there was impassable mud on both sides of the road, and in places it was simply a bog. I was stuck in the traffic for thirteen hours, with transport vehicles standing stock-still in front of us and behind us. Driving around them was impossible. One could only get past them on foot, and for thirteen hours the infantry slogged by through the mud.

Naturally, their mood corresponded to the situation. The most grandiloquent and variegated display of cursing rang out—our only consolation. In this regard my driver, young Gorbach, was every bit as good as the infantrymen. In Kiev he had been a taxi driver, and even the taxi drivers regarded themselves as the lowest of the low. One of Gorbach's priceless qualities was his stout-heartedness.

The long line of infantry stretched out along both sides of the road. Plodding through the mud, they naturally hated us for having an automobile. They cursed away at us, and Gorbach, defending our honor, left none of their yells unanswered.

It was devilishly cold—a strong wind was blowing, and our car was open, so in order to calm Gorbach and also to warm up, I ordered him to make some tea. He was delighted to do so. Making his way through the mud, he set up the primus stove on a small hillock so that we would not be injured if it exploded when the gasoline was lit. But the primus stove did not explode—on the contrary, it began to shine in the closing dusk like one of the brightest stars. It warmed our souls and bodies several times in the course of that endless night.

Finally, the dawn came, and with it our freedom. The vehicles began to move forward. At first, we followed them, but when the road improved, we passed them and went on to the village where the corps headquarters was stationed. The corps medical officer, the object of our visit, was a very likeable old man. He offered me some superb coffee and cookies, and we were joined by two middle-aged doctors, his assistants. They had narrow shoulder boards but were equivalent in rank to a colonel.

I tried to explain to the medical officer, that is, the old man, who I was and why I was there. He understood that I was a Duma member but not what I wanted from him, but he did manage to tell me all about his family. He was awaiting his wife, who would be arriving in the guise of a nurse. Then he complained, "She's sick, poor thing. Horrible rheumatism. I massage her as best I can, but, you know, it's difficult. I don't have to worry about her front legs, but even though she's gentle as a lamb, she kicks with her back legs."

I was shocked. The other doctors bit their lips, and then I finally realized that he was a horse fancier, as were many other doctors. My confusion had arisen when he switched the subject from his wife to his horse without transition.

Finally, I made him realize that we were a detachment of the corps and, to begin with, needed quarters—in other words, a hut, since that was all we could expect. The doctor said, "Yes, truly, we are short on quarters. I've taken this small house, and there's nothing else. Ivan Ivanovich will show you, though." I went out with one of the doctor colonels.

"Are you angry?" he asked. "You'll cool off."

I did not reply. We walked along the dirty street until we came to a building similar to a barracks. We entered. It was a rather large building, filled to overflowing with sick and wounded men lying on straw. He gestured and said, "These are the wounded. And over there are the cholera cases."

Unable to contain myself, I exclaimed, "Wounded and cholera cases in one room!" He replied, "There's no place else—what can we do?"

If you can't do anything, you can't do anything. At any rate, we found a rather spacious, empty hut. There was even some straw strewn over the dirt floor. The straw was plentiful, although dirty. I said, "For want of anything better, I'll take this hut."

My kitchens and students did not arrive immediately, so I decided to follow the advice of the corps medical officer and visit General N. A. Orlov himself, the corps commander, whose headquarters was located beyond the hills and woods. A plank road led to his headquarters.

The ancient Romans had a saying: "Germans love to sing, but when they sing, their voices sound like the rumbling of wheels along a plank road." We called such roads *klavishy* ("keys"). I drove along the "keys" to the general, and learned that it is possible to drive on planks if one can bear it.

* * *

Nicholas Alexandrovich Orlov gave me a very warm welcome. Evidently he was as lonely as the corps medical officer. He invited me to have dinner with him and his staff, and after dinner the two of us sat and talked for three hours. It was obvious that he had plenty of time on his hands. What did we discuss?

With a member of the State Duma one may speak freely about politics, important military questions, the condition of the army, and finally, since I was attached to the medical corps, about its affairs also. As far as the latter were concerned, the general said that the corps medical officer took care of them. I had wanted Orlov to use his power to move my detachment closer to the front, because it was obvious that I would have nothing to do while I was with the corps medical officer.

Well, then, what did we discuss for three full hours? Believe it or not—the cultivation of fodder in Siberia! Orlov had been stationed there at one time and was interested in Siberia. I could not care less about it, especially about the cultivation of fodder, but I listened patiently and attentively. On my return trip along the thundering "keys" I thought, "There's going to be trouble here."

I was right. In a short time, when I was already gone, the enemy broke through our front, making a gap thirty versts wide. It was a catastrophe. Everyone fled; those who didn't were taken prisoner. My detachment almost fell into the latter category.

Then I remembered that this was not Nicholas Orlov's first adventure. Back in 1904, during the battle of Liaotung, the defeat of the general's division had brought about the mopping up of the Russians in Liaotung and the retreat of General A. N. Kuropatkin's entire army. Such things happen. At the same time, Orlov was an educated general and a professor at the General Staff Academy. Once again I realized that education alone does not assure a talented military leader.

* * *

Let us return to the time when the detachment was still under my command. We somehow made ourselves at home in that hut and settled down to work. We prepared gauze, bandages, splints, and so forth. The students worked willingly, while the others merely did their duty.

Also doing their duty were two young men about sixteen years of age, from aristocratic families, who served as messengers. They were the sons of Peter Nicholaevich Balashev and Professor Chubinskii. Young Chubinskii was called "Poopsie." He was baby-faced but spoke in a deep bass voice. I was heartily sick of him, as he would repeat continuously, "Vasilii Vitalievich, when will we carry the wounded out of the trenches?" That was what they had come for, having plagued their parents until they sent the boys to my detachment. They simply would not understand that as part of the corps staff, we were light years away from the trenches.

However, one fine night the wounded from the trenches came to us. Every night we kept a bright lantern, lighting up a red cross, at the door of our hut. A guard was assigned the duty of making sure the light did not go out. It was a freezing night. At three o'clock in the morning there was a knock at the door, and a soldier entered. He was absolutely frozen and his arm was bandaged. Everyone jumped up; the hut was bathed in candlelight. The primus stove was lit, and in ten minutes the exhausted man was given hot tea with wine. He began to warm up and answer our questions.

"Where did you come from?"

"The front."

"How far is it?"

"About thirty kilometers."

"How long were you walking?"

"About ten hours, I'm not sure."

"Your dressing is soaked. When was it put on?"

"Back there, near the trenches, a medic put it on."

"And you didn't get a fresh dressing anywhere else?"

"No. I didn't see a single light anywhere."

Meanwhile, I knew for sure that there was an aid station about fifteen versts away from us in the direction of the front. We redressed his wound. His dressing was saturated with blood, even though his arm had been put in a sling. The bullet had broken the bone.

After this first soldier, other wounded started dribbling in. Like the first one, they all were able to walk; only their arms had been wounded. Aside from everything else, they were all deathly cold, so a mug of hot tea was like a gift from God. Some willingly explained what was happening at the front:

"There's a huge hill, dammit! The antillery is God-awful. Our dead are lying there by the truckload." And repeated, "The antillery is God-awful."

The Hungarians had taken this "huge" hill. Some Austrian prince had visited them, and they had made a solemn vow not to give up the hill. And they did not, until the "antillery" came to our aid.

With the greatest difficulty we had manhandled some cannons up another hill from which we could see the "huge" hill and could reach it with our shells. Once the "antillery" began hitting them in earnest, the Hungarians fled, and we took the "huge" hill.

Behind the "huge" hill, on an even higher hill, stood a border sign in the shape of an obelisk. On one side the word "Poland" was engraved, on the other, "Hungary."

* * *

There was a certain member of the State Duma who understood something about finance and thus was very useful in the Tauride Palace. At the front he was very fidgety. One day he swooped down on me and cried, "Let's go!" "Where?" "To Hungary. The corps commander is there."

My detachment had its work under control and I was able to absent myself for a time. We went. Passing the border sign, we entered Hungary, a very pleasant place. Here the southern slope began. We had come from the northern slope, where there was snow and frost, but here it was spring. We descended rapidly, and it became progressively warmer. After we had driven several kilometers, the road suddenly disappeared, washed away by the steams of melting snow running down the mountains.

"We'll go on foot." He was mulishly set on going. Leaving the automobile, we set off. We came to a deserted village with straw-roofed huts. Suddenly we heard droning and a passing shell tore the straw off the roof of the hut closest to us. He said, "My God, that's nasty!"

We continued on, since he wanted to see the corps commander at all costs, although we had absolutely nothing to say to him. We arrived safely at a larger village and came to a main road that led straight to the enemy. Suddenly, thinking at first that I was imagining it, I saw light blue Austrian overcoats heading straight at us, in formation, four abreast, stretching off into the distance. What was it? This:

An entire regiment was coming over to our side. It turned out that these men were Slavic mutineers from the Austrian army. The war with Russia was extremely unpopular among the Austrian Slavs. The Austrians generally mixed them with other nationalities but failed to notice that Slavs formed the majority in this regiment, and they— Poles, Czechs, Serbs, and Slovaks—went over to their fellow Slavs. Since they were an overwhelming majority, they had taken a small group of Hungarians with them. And so they came along the road, in spite of the Austrian artillery raining down upon them.

The village in which we ended up was called Mezalaborche. I mention it because I was to meet up with the same regiment one more time that day. In volume I of his memoirs, which were published in Prague in 1971, L. Svoboda, former President of the Czechoslovakian Soviet Socialist Republic and general of the army, describes how he was drafted into the imperial Austro-Hungarian army in 1915. When his infantry regiment arrived at the front, twenty-year-old Ludwig Svoboda went over to the Russian side at the first opportunity, as did many thousands of other Czechs and Slovaks. This occurred on September 8, 1915, near the city of Ternopol, now in the U.S.S.R. Evidently I was one of the first witnesses of this great movement of the Slavs to their brothers in Russia. The signs of disintegration began to show in the ragged Hapsburg monarchy from the very beginning of the war.

Allowing the Slavs to pass us, we went on to headquarters, a rather large house whose inhabitants were preparing to leave, since shells were constantly falling on the roof and in the yard. A cart, actually a large wagon, filled with all sorts of belongings, stood in the yard. At the very top of the cart, on an armchair, sat a large white goose, evidently tied down. He fearfully watched the sky, which thundered and rained shells.

Since I had already been under this salute and had been wounded, I must honestly say that I was not at ease either. I was very happy when my companion came out and said, "Time to go." We decamped at once and were able to find our car. In the meantime the regiment of Slavic turncoats had started to ascend the hill. As we passed them, we saw that some of them were drunk and all were hungry to the point of bestiality. My sympathetic companion threw them a round loaf of bread and a piece of suet. What a scene ensued! One soldier caught the bread and ran toward a field with it, while the others rushed after him. He was knocked off his feet, but managed to keep the bread under his stomach. They rolled him over, grabbed the unfortunate loaf of bread, and began to tear it away from one another. The same thing happened with the suet. We sped away from this horrible sight.

I arrived home, that is, to my detachment. Several hours later I received a telegram which said, "Prepare to feed two thousand men." I felt feverish, realizing that those soldiers who were so crazed with hunger were going to fall upon me. Two thousand men! Allowing one loaf of bread for four men, five hundred loaves would be needed. I rushed an assistant to the nearest army bakery. They brought the bread, but we still had to prepare a dinner. My enormous kitchens came in handy here. I calculated that the "blues" would not be able to reach us today but would arrive in the morning, even more hungry. We were at the top of a hill, so I ordered a guard to be on the lookout. Finally, I was informed that they were coming.

I ran out onto the road and saw the "blues" appearing over the ridge. Our kitchens started working, and since there was no wind, the smoke triumphantly climbed upward to the clear sky. However, the smell of food spread even without wind, and the hungry soldiers would become even more ferocious from the smell, so I went out to meet them, hoping that one of our detachments was escorting them. I was right—there was an escort, and its commander, a sensible non-commissioned officer, immediately ran over to me.

I came straight to the point and asked, "Has the escort eaten yet?"

"No, sir."

"How many in the escort?"

"About eighty."

"Divide them in half. Forty men are to march to the mess to eat. Forty stay here."

"Yes, sir."

The Russians headed toward the kitchens at a run. When they returned I dispatched the other half. When the escort had its fill, I said, "Surround the kitchens," and ordered, "Let them in." They descended upon us in a frenzy. It was lucky that we had taken precautions, because they would have overturned the kitchens and ruined their dinner. It would have been the end for them also. However, the escort had the upper hand, so when the blues rushed the kitchens, the escort turned its rifles and bayonets on them. The crazed soldiers retreated. Russian bayonets were feared to the point of panic.

At this point I came out and began to speak with them in three languages—German, Russian, and Polish—but I best made myself understood by using sign language. I made a sign with my fingers: 4, 4, 4. This they easily understood. Then I repeated over and over that they must count off by fours, which they also understood. Hunger is a great teacher. When they had assembled into columns of four, I ordered that a loaf of bread be given to each four-man rank. In an instant knives of all sorts appeared among them, and they began to cut the bread.

When they had eaten, the beasts again became human. I could see by their eyes that they had changed completely. Fury disappeared and reason showed. Then they were allowed in groups to the kitchens. All had mess kits, and five hundred grams of rich, delicious soup was ladled out to each man. The meal took a long time but finally ended. Thanking us in several languages, and with gestures also, they set off once again, escorted by the convoy. The fate of the Slavs in Russia was not bad. They settled on farms, both in villages and on large estates, where they worked willingly.

Later an army division was formed from these Slavs and Czechs. On June 2, 1917, Ludwig Svoboda fought shoulder to shoulder with Russian soldiers against the Austrians and Hungarians at the city of Zborov, in what is now Czechoslovakia.

* * *

Somewhere in Galicia there is a little church of the sort that can only be found there, made of logs of unimaginable thickness. No one knew how old the trees were when they were summoned for the exalted assignment of becoming the walls of a church. The church was tiny, the size of a room.

Steps a quarter-meter wide led up to the little church. Its single cupola was a fraction of the size of the great Tsar Bell. The church stood in the midst of a green glade, where flowers grew during the summer. Inside was an altar, with everything as necessary. Several people could pray in the church at the same time. Galician women in their long, white skirts sometimes prayed here before the war. Now a Russian nurse in a white kerchief, similar to a wedding veil, would come and pray for everyone.

At night this nurse sat at a small desk in a huge tent. A kerosene lamp would light up only her white kerchief and her notebook, which held information about which medicine to give to whom, and so forth. The nurse was surrounded by cots with seriously wounded soldiers.

The ones closest to her were discernible, especially their white pillows and bandages, while those farther away could hardly be seen in the darkness.

There was silence, sometimes interrupted by a quite groan.

All this I saw when I entered the tent. The nurse waved to me and indicated a chair near the desk. She finished reading her notes, got up, and wandered in the semidarkness, performing her duties. Then she returned and poured me a mug of hot tea with red wine, the unchanging custom in that war. We whispered about this and that—her work, my adventures, our near and dear ones in Kiev.

Pro krai rodnoi, pro gulkie meteli,	About my native land, driving snowstorms
pro radosti i skorbi iunykh dnei,	About the joys and sorrows of youth,
pro tikhie napevy kolybeli,	About peaceful lullabies,
pro otchii dom, pro krovnykh i druzei.	About my father's home, my kin, my friends.

However, all the while she listened in case anyone called. Someone did. She went to him, and did not return for a long time. With difficulty I could make out the white kerchief bending over someone as she attentively listened to a long speech. I listened to the silence and thought, "What is this unknown, seriously wounded man telling the nurse? Probably about his illness, his wound, the suffering it has caused, or perhaps about the children he has at home."

Finally the nurse returned. I could tell from her familiar face that something had happened. Her gray eyes, flooded and with widening pupils, seemed black. After a while she said, "He told me a horrible story. He was given leave. His train arrived at night. He set off for his village on foot through the woods. Everyone was sleeping. Only one hut had a light on. He walked in and saw two people sleeping together in a bed—his wife and his father. There was an ax in the corner. He picked it up, went over to the bed, and killed them both. They didn't even wake up. He closed the door, walked back through the woods, and took a train back to his regiment. The following day he was seriously wounded. I don't know if he will live. He thinks he will die. He is tormented by guilt, and asks that I call the commander of the regiment. He wants to confess and be tried. He's asking me. What should I do?"

I did not reply for a long time. She gazed at me unwaveringly with those gray eyes that had become black. I thought and listened. Somewhere in the distance, above the tent, somewhere in the darkness I could hear the words:

Pro tikhie napevy kolybeli,	About peaceful lullabies,
pro otchii dom, pro krovnykh i	About my father's home, my
druzei	kin, my friends.

And then my thoughts traveled to the little church with its immense walls, where this nurse in her wedding kerchief, with gray eyes that had become black, prayed on her knees for everyone and everything. After a long silence, I said, "He can see me. Go and tell him that the officer says it is not necessary to tell the commander of the regiment, only the priest at confession."

*   *   *

Maria Nicholaevna Khomiakov did not stay there long, in the wilds of Galicia, near the ancient, ramshackle little church. She was transferred with part of the State Duma detachment to Tarnov (Poland), while we, that is, P. N. Balashev, N. N. Mozhaiskii, and I, advanced along the main road to Lvov. Then Balashev took one car and set off directly for the city, while Mozhaiskii, in another car, grabbed me and wanted to go somewhere, but drove into a dead end, one might say.

We found ourselves in front of a blown-up bridge which one could barely cross on foot, let alone by car. The river was rather wide, but the slope leading down to it was easy and sandy. Since we imagined ourselves masters of the river, we gunned the car into the water without hesitation—and immediately became stuck. The river proved to be not only wide but deep. Water began to fill the car to the seats. We jumped onto the back but the engine had stopped, of course. What was to be done?

Gorbach, not thinking, jumped into the water, which was more than waist-deep. Mozhaiskii would not let me do the same, although he too jumped in, saying, "Guard the car."

"Who do I guard it from in the middle of the river?" However, I obeyed, and furthermore, did something sensible. For example, I was able to pull the sleeping bags out to the back of the car before they got wet. They were useful later.

Mozhaiskii and Gorbach set off for a nearby village, where they kicked up a row, found the village elder, and brought the entire village running to the riverbank. They were the local peasants, very polite and bustling. There was no vulgarity, only courtesy and lamentation, but they did not help us. In vain did Gorbach bawl that they must go into the water and pull out the car—"salvage it," as he said. The peasants ran along the shore but would not enter the water. I sat in the middle of the river on the back of the car, observing all this and thinking, of course, that they must salvage it.

Gorbach changed his tactics and shouted, "We need horses, understand?" They understood and brought two small horses and a rope. Gorbach tied the rope to the springs of the car. The horses were urged on.

Frightened by the shouts, they began to pull. Everyone shouted again, they strained again, and the rope broke. The car remained in the same spot. Gorbach's despair and obscenity were indescribable. "They don't even have a decent rope!"

We heard the unexpected sound of a motor. A truck came down the hillside and the driver announced, "Headquarters sent us to pull the car out."

We were overjoyed and said, "Right, right, there it is, in the river."

Next came the usual swearing without which nothing can be accomplished. They threw Gorbach a chain, saying, "Tie it on, stupid, you got it there!" Gorbach tied it on, the truck started, and the chain was pulled taut, but the car remained in the same place. Then they decided that the horses should be harnessed to the truck.

The chain broke. The driver began to swear indescribably, gunned the engine, and drove away. Later we learned that there had been a slight misunderstanding. Headquarters had not sent him to help us but to rescue another car, a staff car which had also been planted in the river.

Darkness was falling. Mozhaiskii decided we would sleep on the opposite shore in our sleeping bags. They lifted me off the car without getting me wet, and Mozhaiskii and I crossed the bridge. I told Gorbach, "Go the village and warm up. Dry your clothes."

"What about the car?"

"Nothing will happen to the car."

We climbed into our sleeping bags. Not surprisingly, I warmed up quickly, but the soaking Mozhaiskii, after removing his boots and clothes, was also able to get warm. We fell asleep. There was a pleasant smell of grapevines in the air, and the river gurgled almost inaudibly. At dawn a brilliant idea occurred to Mozhaiskii. He said, "Let's see the transport commandant." He turned out to be a Czech from Kiev, with the surname Pospeshil ("Hurried"). Czechs sometimes have rather strange surnames, for example, Nevyderzha ("Lacking self-control"), Vyskochil ("Jumped out"), well, and Pospeshil. This Czech was a Russian officer and the son of a Latin teacher in Kiev, which meant that we were fellow-townsmen. Pospeshil hurried up and said to us,* "I will give you twenty-five of my scoundrels—my transport command. Do with them what you will. These good-for-nothings could take the devil himself by the horns and pull him out of the river."

---

*There is an untranslatable pun here. Shulgin says, in effect, that "'Hurried' hurried up and said . . ." (trans.).

We marched back to the beach at the head of the transport command. When we arrived, nothing had changed. Gorbach was still swearing. With the senior noncommissioned officer at their head, the squad stood in formation and waited. I thought for a while and finally formed a plan. Calling the senior noncom aside, I had a little talk with him.

"The water is cold."

"Yes, sir, it is."

"I can't order men to climb into cold water."

"Yes, sir, you can."

"I can, but I don't want to. Only if they're willing."

"Yes, sir, voluntarily."

"Tell them there's twenty-five rubles in it for them, a ruble for a drink for each one, if they can pull the car out."

"Yes, sir, a ruble apiece."

"He went up to the motionless soldiers and said something to them. They became extremely excited and began to swear violently at each other.

"What are you waiting for? Stop staring! Take off your pants!"

After having shouted and removed their pants and boots, they climbed into the icy water, still swearing. All twenty-five grabbed hold of the car, amidst cries of, "Rock her free, come on, rock!"

At first the car would not give in, but finally it obeyed and began to rock. Then there were cries of, "Don't let her fall back, come on! Heave-ho!"

The car yielded to these persuasions and swayed harder and harder, and the tops of the tires came out of the water. Then the cries of "Don't let her fall!" became mixed with shouts of "Get some boards; Put boards under her!" The peasants milling about on the riverbank understood and threw them some boards, which were set in place. Now she could not get stuck again. Dragging the car onto the boards, they were able to pull the damned thing out and onto shore.

As I watched all this, I simply got a lump in my throat from delight and from something else. The "scoundrels" and "good-for-nothings" hurriedly dressed, swearing all the while, then got into formation. I gave the money to their sergeant, who said, "Thank you very much, sir."

My voice cracked as I shouted to the men, "Thank you, fellow countrymen!" They answered amicably, "Glad to give it a try!"

Some "scoundrels"!

* * *

We all know that man is a political animal, but not solely. Everyone has a private life. Among the ancient Greeks, people who did not become involved in politics, that is, in the work of running their society, were called idiots. This was not a term of abuse; it became one only much later, when people became more stupid. I do not suffer from self-importance, but I am a complete idiot, in the Greek sense. Even before I understood what the word meant, I hated politics. For example, when I learned to read as a boy and came across newspaper articles telling of parliamentary battles in such-and-such a country, I simply could not comprehend such a thing. In the imagination of a little boy, a battle meant a fight with Indians on the Great Plains.

In a word, I was an amateur when it came to politics, but fate, that merciless Moira, compelled me to become a member of the State Duma, with all its consequences. Therefore in war I was a parliamentarian, practically speaking—that is, I perceived war from the point of view of politics because I am, after all, a political animal. However, I also experienced the inexplicable mystery of war on a purely personal plane, which I cannot write about here. In view of the fact that I am a memoirist of the conventional type, one-half of my brain has been removed, and nothing can be done about it.

It was the same with Leo Tolstoy. His great work has a double name—*War and Peace.* War is the political part; peace is deeply personal. Tolstoy could allow himself to reveal the bewitching personal part only because he called his masterpiece a novel. For example, he called his mother "Princess Volkonsky," and this innocent lie allowed him to tell the whole truth about a plain woman better than about a beautiful one. I cannot allow myself this, so I will continue my story from a political point of view.

This is what will come of it. I was sent to Kiev for medical treatment because my wound had left me unable to use my right arm. After recuperation and treatment, when I was able to lift it high enough to touch my right ear, I felt I had to return to the front.

* * *

I was again in Lvov. Before leaving for the front, I went to the theater. The audience was composed solely of Russian officers. Something very unusual occurred. I came across acquaintances from the State Duma: Peter Nicholaevich Balashev and Nicholas Nicholaevich Mozhaiskii, gentleman-in-waiting at the royal court and chairman of the Bratslav district zemstvo council. Many members of the State Duma found themselves at the front. Some, as I had, joined the active army, violating the law that prevented Duma members from serving in the army, while others established themselves in the army by other means. Count Vladimir Alexevich Bobrinskii, Marshal of Nobility of Bogorovits and member of the last three Dumas, was General Radko Dmitriev's adjutant. The nationalist Alexander Dmitrievich Zarin,

Duma secretary and Marshal of Nobility of the Porkhov district, was middle-aged and, one could say, built like a barrel. He simply joined the infantry, endured many hardships, and consequently became embittered. The Octobrist Alexander Ivanovich Zverintsev, zemstvo member and deputy from Voronezh Province, was also connected to some staff or other, but later died in the crash of the plane *Ilia Moromets.*

Some Duma members donned the badge of the Red Cross and worked in the humanitarian field. For example, V. M. Purishkevich organized a splendid train for the wounded, which brought them straight to Moscow or Petersburg. To get on this train was the dream of every wounded soldier. P. N. Balashev and N. N. Mozhaiskii took the same route. They did not want to work with the already established All-Russian Zemstvo Organization for aid to sick and wounded soldiers, so they set up their own organization under the name of IUZOZO. They had a car, which was extremely important. Instead of having to track down my regiment on foot, as I did the first time, Balashev and Mozhaiskii offered me a ride to the headquarters of General Radko Dmitriev. There I would learn the exact location of my regiment. In the meantime I harbored an idea which subsequently came to fruition.

* * *

I must say a few words about Radko Dmitriev. He was Bulgarian by birth and was considered one of our most outstanding generals. Furthermore, he had a gift, something like clairvoyancy, as Bobrinskii told me:

"The soldiers were convinced that he had a sixth sense. I remember one occasion when the general, with his entire staff, was walking along the edge of a wood, which, as you know, is almost always fired upon. Shrapnel fire was exploding above the trees on our left and right. Without a doubt, the Germans could see us, so movement was dangerous. But since the general was on the move, we had to go with him. It was a gorgeous day. Radko Dmitriev was very happy, joking and offering us chocolate. He had us make a somewhat long, drawn-out stop under an enormous oak which stuck out along the wood's edge. He examined our position while white puffs of shrapnel were exploding on each side of us. Then, walking on about one hundred paces, Radko turned around and looked at the oak, and saw that for some unknown reason, a young officer was standing under it. The general ordered in a loud voice, 'Lieutenant, over here! On the double!'

"The officer ran away from the oak. No sooner had he left than a shell struck the trunk of the tree exactly where he had been standing. This made an impression on the soldiers, who without any hesitation said, 'He has a sixth sense.'"

Radko won a tough battle south of Lvov, on August 13 (26), 1914, on the banks of the river Zolotaia Lipa. He had two divisions, as opposed to the Austrians' three, and he won the battle only because he personally led an attack with his last reserve battalion, that is, his headquarters staff and personal detachment. The Austrians, unable to withstand this paltry assault, retreated.

* * *

That day and night there was a very fierce battle south of Iaroslav, a city south of Lvov. The cannonade was so powerful that we could hear it at the corps headquarters. The officers were somber, but the general immediately ushered us in and asked us to dinner. Before we sat down to eat, Radko Dmitriev had a talk with us. He spoke energetically and with a slight Bulgarian accent. He said, "I am Bulgarian, as you know. I am proud of the fact that I am a Russian general. I am proud that I command the Russian soldier. There is not a better soldier in the entire world. I love him. But I do not dare love him. Don't dare. If I allow myself to feel love, then I will not be able to fight. How can I love him when I send companies, regiments, entire divisions, to their deaths! Do you hear me?"

While he was speaking I could clearly hear the thunder of artillery through the open door. Radko continued, "I cannot love him. I don't dare—" It sounded like a command—curt and sharp. Then his voice softened. He continued, "But someone must love him. Pity him. Take care of him. Someone must. Who? You, the Red Cross. It is your obligation." Then he suddenly turned to me personally and said, "Take yourself, for instance. At the front, what are you? Nothing. A lousy ensign. That's not for you. Well, now you've seen a battle, you've been wounded. You set an example. Everyone knows that. Enough. Join the Red Cross. As your commanding officer I order you." He then asked Balashev, "What unit are you in?" Balashev answered, "The Southwestern District Zemstvo Organization—IUZOZO." Then Radko called over his chief of staff and said, "Assign Ensign Shulgin to the Southwestern—well, in a word, to IUZOZO."

* * *

Thus they decided my fate. I honestly wanted to return to my regiment, but—

We had dinner. The night was hellish; there was rain with snow and wind. First the chief of staff, then the general's adjutant would get up and leave, to listen to the thunder of artillery. Then they would return and say something quietly to the general. He also spoke softly, but we could hear the following:

"Getting the better of us? Nonsense! They'll retreat."

The officers would nod their heads and their faces would cheer up immediately. Radko continued talking with us about various things, and only his short fingers drumming on the table revealed that he was worried.

We were given cutlets, cooked medium rare. I couldn't eat them and drank only tea. I put a lump of sugar in my tea and thought. "By the time it melts, how many people will be killed? One hundred, two hundred?" The most horrible thing was that I could see them in the rain and snow, which had turned into mud. They lay there, losing blood, while the artillery continued to strike. The officers would go listen to the thunder. The chief of staff said that he had heard on the telephone that the enemy was fierce, but Radko, drumming his fingers, maintained, "They'll retreat." He added, "They'll retreat at dawn. They always put on the pressure before a retreat." At about 10:00 P.M. he bade us farewell and went to bed, saying that he was to be awakened if anything out of the ordinary happened. But nothing did. By dawn the enemy had retreated.

Radko actually did have a "sixth sense." It was as though he were clairvoyant. How did he know they would retreat when all the reports pointed to the contrary? An ordinary mortal cannot know such things. Neither military science nor experience can teach it. That night I learned that the true essence of a general's talent consists of two elements—personal courage and a secret gift of clairvoyance. I only don't know whether Radko Dmitriev could divine his own tragic fate.

* * *

Six months after this worrisome, rainy, snowy, windy, artillery-filled night, during which the courageous general had been so quiet, there was another, even more frightening night. There were several such nights in a row, and the general's brave attacks could no longer bring victory. This occurred on April 19 (May 2), 1915. Radko Dmitriev, who at the time was commanding the Third Army, had to take upon himself the main blow of the mighty ram of General Mackensen, who headed the German Eleventh Army. By order of German Chief of Staff Falkenhayn, Mackensen had been brought from the Western European military theater. The sides were unequal. According to the statistical information, the Russian Third Army had, at the beginning of the operation, 219,000 bayonets and sabers, 600 machine-guns, 675 light guns, and 4 heavy guns, while the Austro-German troops had 375,400 bayonets and sabers, 660 machine-guns, 1,272 light guns, and 334 heavy guns!

In a telegram dated April 22 (May 5), 1915, Radko Dmitriev reported to General N. I. Ivanov, the commander of the southwestern front, "The enemy almost exclusively uses heavy artillery, against which our light artillery is powerless. The assigned supplies of artillery shells are insufficient for even routine needs. We urgently need a fresh supply of field artillery . . ."

Furthermore, this was the first battle in which the Germans used heavy trench mortars, something we did not have. Also, while the Austro-German artillery had reserves of twelve hundred shells per light gun, our army had a daily ammunition allowance of ten rounds per howitzer battery, in other words, one or two rounds per gun per day. The lack of ammunition caused uncertainty and unrest among the soldiers. Even our defensive positions were insufficiently secured, since we did not have concrete bunkers. In view of the imbalance of strength, it was clear that Radko Dmitriev's Third Army could not win, or even resist, but even in this extremely difficult situation the general's courage did not fail him, and his authority among the soldiers did not waver.

The German high command assigned General Mackensen the task of breaking through the front between Gorlits and Gromnik, south of Peremyshl. Having accomplished that, his army was to begin an offensive on Iaslo and Fryshtak, which lay to the east, in order to force the Russian Third Army to retreat along the entire front. At 10:00 A.M. on April 19 (May 2), 1915, after almost twenty-four hours of continuous artillery fire, the Austro-German troops attacked Radko Dmitriev's army along the entire thirty-five-kilometer front. This was the beginning of the "Gorlits breakthrough"—General Mackensen's first blow at the Russians. The Germans broke through our first line of defense, taking 17,000 prisoners and eight guns.

However, despite the enormous superiority in strength of the German forces, the Russians, inspired by their leader, revealed great courage and steadfastness, forcing General Mackensen to call upon his reserves by the second day of the attack. That same day, April 20 (May 3), Radko Dmitriev telegraphed General Ivanov, the Supreme Commander of the front: "I cannot report the exact amount of cartridges available, but I am informed that the stocks of the columns in battle are almost exhausted."

Although it resisted manfully, the Third Army continued to roll back eastward under the onslaught of Mackensen's iron fist. One can judge what was on Radko Dmitriev's mind from the following telegram he sent to headquarters: "Three divisions of the Tenth Corps sustained an especially ferocious blow which literally caused the men to bleed profusely. Not meeting resistance in kind, their fifty heavy guns quickly and easily silenced our light guns, blasting trenches off the face of the earth in a half-hour and downing ten men with a single hit. Many were wounded from exploding shells also. As a result, parts of the Tenth Corps have no more than four or five thousand men."

Between the lines of this telegram I could hear the words he said at headquarters on that memorable, violent, November night: "Do you hear me? I am proud to command the Russian soldier. There is no better soldier in the whole world. I love him. But I don't dare love him. I don't dare. If I allow myself to love him, I will not be able to fight. How can I love him, when I send entire companies, regiments, divisions to their deaths?"

But headquarters was deaf to such outpourings. Quartermaster General Danilov, the Deputy Chief of Staff, informed General Dragomirov, then chief of staff of the southwestern front, "I feel that at the present time, on the eve of possible support from neutral countries, it is not to our advantage to undertake such radical measures to change our strategic position as you have outlined, unless there is an emergency, which I personally do not perceive at present."

Evidently headquarters did not consider the enemy's enormous numerical and technological superiority on the southwestern front enough of an emergency to settle the question of saving the Third Army. What was Dragomirov's plan? It was unanimously decided, in view of the German breakthrough, that the only expedient decision would be to withdraw our army beyond the river San, thereby preventing loss of lives and buying time. Then the plan was to concentrate a strong body of troops near the river in order to launch a counterattack along the flank of Mackensen's advancing army. However, headquarters would not agree to a withdrawal, even though it would win the army more time, and demanded that the army hold its positions, no matter what losses it sustained.

Although General Ivanov, commander of the southwestern front, was well aware of the difficult situation of the troops, he avoided any conflict with headquarters and agreed with it about everything, sending fresh reinforcements into battle in order to hold back the advancing Germans. By this time, though, it was impossible to stop them. The Russian army began to retreat before the ever-increasing onslaught of Mackensen's army. The disagreement between the commander of the Third Army and the commander-in-chief of the front helped ruin the situation.

After a fierce battle for the city of Iaroslav on May 3 (16), the Russian troops retreated to the right bank of the river San, leaving the city to the Germans. By May 11 (24), Austro-German troops had control of the entire right bank of the river. Thus Dragomirov's and Radko Dmitriev's prediction came true—the Third Army withdrew beyond the river, notwithstanding the orders from headquarters, but only after a grave delay and at what a cost! However, Radko Dmitriev was no longer there, for on May 7 (20), 1915, he had been removed from command of the Third Army. Did he predict this also? His was a sad fate. I am told that, as a tsarist general, he was shot in 1918 in Piatigorsk.

* * *

At that time, that is, in 1914, M. A. Stakhovich, one of the founders of the Union of October Seventeenth, was commissioner of the Red Cross in the Third Army. During the Russo-Japanese War he had been commissioner of the medical corps.

And I? I was the head of an advanced first aid station. Since I wore a red cross on my sleeve, Stakhovich was my superior. In other matters we were acquaintances. He had been a member of the First State Duma. The official announcement of his election to the Duma as Marshal of Nobility of Orlov Province was made on December 12 (25), 1907. At the beginning of December 1914, we were both in Lvov, and I asked Stakhovich to sign some official papers. Among them were a significant number of documents, actually passports, which stated that so-and-so worked for the red cross, certified by an official stamp. These passports were intended for people working in my advanced detachment. They were important because they would provide us with some protection against any unpleasantness if we were taken prisoner. A person wearing a red cross, which anyone could put on under false pretenses, might easily be suspected of espionage.

When we finished our business, Stakhovich said, "It is now the beginning of December. I am leaving for the front, to the headquarters of the Third Army."

"Where is that?"

"In Radomysl."

"What? Radomysl in Kiev Province?"

"No, the other Radomysl, in Polish Galicia. Do you have a map?"

"Yes."

"Well, you go along the main road toward Lvov and Cracow. Before Tarnov you turn. Here it is, Radomysl! Do you have a car?"

"Yes."

"Then I'll expect you in Radomysl on December 17. It's important. I want to introduce you to someone. Will you be there?"

"Yes, on December 17."

* * *

That year, instead of frost, we had slush for Christmas. The road conditions were horrible. We had to put chains on the tires, but they did not always help. In Galicia the roads are paved with soft stone, and the unceasing movement of the transports turned the road into just so many ruts. The car drove through the pits and bumps like a ship's boat on a choppy sea. The chassis would "belly-flop," the motor would whine in first gear, but the wheels would only spin in the air, more accurately, in the slippery dirt, with nothing to grip.

There wasn't even time to swear. Looking both ways, I saw a hut and a yard with open gates. I shouted, "Over there!"

The motor gave one final sigh, inched through the gate, and died. By accident I had made a good decision, but actually there had been no decision whatsoever. It was the closest hut; we surrendered ourselves to its protection. The master of the house—the mistress, rather—and a passel of children gave us a most warm welcome.

To use Igor Severianin's expression, my Gorbach was a "God-fearing Russian hooligan." This became clear when, seeing a litter of kittens playing on the floor, he caught them in his gasoline-stained hands and started to pet them and scratch them behind the ear, showing his knowledge of cats. With this he won the children's hearts. But I bought them away from him. My pockets were always filled with suckers—in the line of duty, one might say. At the same time I charmed the mother, but she would have been happy even without the candy.

An automobile! That meant an officer and his driver. They not only would not demand anything but would actually contribute something themselves. When he was done playing with the kittens and children, Gorbach lit the primus stove. That day, in that half-dark hut, our primus stove lit up like a star. Hot tea was ready in ten minutes, bringing us back to life after our luckless night.

While we sat around the table I did some calculations. Around me the primus stove, the children, and the kittens were playing noisily. According to the map, Radomysl was thirty kilometers away. There was no gasoline in the little village. It was absolutely necessary for me to get to Stakhovich, and on foot I might be able to do fifteen kilometers today, sleep somewhere, get up early, walk another fifteen, and arrive on time, at noon on the seventeenth.

Ordering Gorbach to wait for me there, even if it was for several days, I set off, leaving him wrapped up in kittens and children. He itched to go with me but realized that we could not both leave the car. Uneasiness appeared on his face, the face of a fallen angel. After all, he was a driver through and through. The last thing he said to me, in a pleading tone but gritting his teeth, was, "Get some gasoline!"

Walking along the road in the rain I saw no one, absolutely no one—no people, no cars, no carts. All movement was paralyzed because of the impassable roads. I walked on, holding onto the fences. It was possible to walk near the fences, but the road itself was drowned in a sea of black muck. I came out onto a town square of some sort, surrounded by one-story cottages and shops, Jewish-owned, of course, as in all the villages in that area. But the houses were silent, the square empty, and the shops closed.

Several of our soldiers were milling near the one open shop. I went over. They were bartering sugar for tobacco. Russian sugar was much in demand in Galicia, being harder and sweeter than Austrian sugar. Several pathetic-looking local women, all bundled up, were also standing there. Some of the soldiers, being nice, gave them a bit of sugar. The women thanked them; our fellow-countrymen nodded their heads, muttering, "Just look at them—" The shop-owner, a Jew in a long coat, with a long beard and a yarmulke—in a word, looking as if he had stepped out of the Middle Ages—was bartering a few things that were much in demand. I asked him, "How far to Rado-mysl?"

I spoke Polish as well as he spoke Russian, but we managed to understand one another. He answered, "Thirty kilometers, Your Excellency."

In his knowing eyes I could read the words, "It *was* thirty kilometers, but now that the transports have passed through, who knows?"

When I walked on a bit farther, I saw the transports, motionless, bogged down in mud. Evidently they had been there a long time already. They showed white against the black "jam," white because they had been carrying bags of flour. The horses, powerless against the terrible elements, had already been unharnessed. Where were they? The same place the soldiers were—in the evergreen wood. A field kitchen had somehow had been pulled out of the mud and was now cosily working in the midst of the reddish trees. However, I could not take a break.

I walked and walked, sometimes not without the help of my arms holding the tops of my boots, otherwise the mire would have pulled them off my feet. This ordeal occurred whenever the woods fell back from the road, which was not actually a road, but a beaten path across the field. Otherwise I walked along the edge of the fields, through the pine trees, on top of the moist needles. It was sheer bliss. I was alone, completely alone. Such happiness rarely occurs during war. Aside from everything else, war torments such misanthropes as myself by its ever-present people. Meanwhile, here were only gentle forest noises. Damn war, with its violence and bullets amidst streams of blood! I was not afraid of losing my way. I was led by the black road, at times as wide as the Black Sea, and at other times as narrow as the Darial Gorge. Furthermore, I was guided by telegraph poles and wires trembling with electrical life. At times, resting, I would lean on one of the oak poles and could hear a weak noise—not the electrical current, of course, since it is soundless, but the wire itself, producing a sound like that of an aeolian harp from the wind. Putting my ear to the pole I could hear a strong, low, pleasant noise, saturated with beautiful overtones. One would think it would bring comfort to a lonely wanderer, but it could not, and so the pole hummed on, grandly but sadly. There was a sense of doom in its grandness.

Having rested a bit, I continued on. Just before setting, the sun broke through the clouds, and the trunks of the pines turned crimson. I stood in that lonely spot, again leaning on the telegraph pole, but no longer listening to its hum. I felt extreme exhaustion. The sunset, signifying nightfall, scared me. I had walked far, probably the entire fifteen kilometers, without seeing a single soul. I would have to sleep in the forest, on the pine needles, which were soft but cold and wet. What was I to do?

At that instant came salvation in the form of a young girl. She was making her way through the pines along the edge of the field.

No sooner had I called to her than she came over to the telegraph pole, which I was embracing so as not to fall. Approaching a bit closer, but not completely, she said, "Panie ranny?" ("Are you wounded?")

The music of sympathy sounded in her voice. I replied, "Nie. Tylko bardzo zmęczony" ("No, only very tired").

She asked, "Gdzie pan tak idzie? To jest daleko?" ("Where are you going? Is it far?") She smiled. Then I noticed that she was pretty, with gray eyes framed by dark lashes, light hair, dark brows, and a sweet smile. All Polish women, regardless of class, know how to smile like that. She said, "Daleko, prosze pana" ("Far, sir"). Then she added, in a strict tone, "Tak nie może być, proszę pana, noc zachodzi" ("You should not do this, sir, night is falling").

"A co mam dzielat?" ("And what am I to do?").

She began to think. "Tutaj jest jedna chałupa. Tutaj zaraz. Niech pan idzie tak" ("There is a hut nearby. Go there").

She motioned, "Nie daleko" ("It's not far"). Smiling charmingly, she shook her head. She was wearing a kerchief, otherwise her earrings would have shook proudly. From this gesture alone, I could tell that she had Polish blood in her.

I thanked her, "Bardzo dziękuję, proszę panienki!" Then I added, unexpectedly even for myself, "Niech panienka idzie do domy, I to prędko! Noc zachodzi" ("Thank you, Miss! You should go home, and quickly. It's almost night"). That instant the dying sun threw a crimson glow on the girl. She gazed at me with the kind of smile that a mother gives a playful child.

In fifteen minutes I could make out a faint red light through the trees, and in another five minutes I could see a hut with a straw roof, dark with moss. I knocked on the low door, heard a cry of "proshe" ("come in"), bent over, and entered the hut. A stove lit up the room. An old man was sitting at a table, and two girls were hiding behind their mother, who was standing at the stove.

"Good evening!"

"Good evening!"

I sat down heavily on a bed and groped in my pocket for a candy, which I held out to the girls. "Candy?"

The older one, who was about five years old, let go of her mother's skirt and came over.

During dinner we talked, and I learned that the old man was the woman's father-in-law. Her husband had been drafted, and she did not know what had happened to him. Perhaps the girls were already orphans. As she said this a tear rolled down into her plate. Seeing their mother cry, the girls began to cry also. The old man said, "Stop!"

They quieted down, and he added, "Ianek is alive!" They believed him, and began to question me about where I was going. I was told that Radomysl was fifteen kilometers away through the woods. Then the woman served soup with mushrooms as proof that this was a forest kingdom.

Finally they put the guest and the girls to bed. I slept on some hay. The girls? They were put into a basket serving as a cradle, hung from the ceiling not far from my bed. They were sitting on their knees. The older one gently rocked the cradle, evidently hoping to rock her sister to sleep, but she put me to sleep instead. The sound of the basket rocking was soothing, and I closed my eyes blissfully. Then I heard singing. The older sister was softly singing a lullaby, while the younger one repeated the word, "Maria, Maria." I fell asleep, envisioning two angels singing and rocking in heaven. I don't remember what I dreamed about, but most probably it was of the heavenly paradise! I soon learned that this paradise was located in hell. I want to tell about the war.

* * *

It was drizzling when I awoke. It was easy for me to get up, since I didn't have to dress, not having undressed that night. I needed a cup of tea, but my hosts were fast asleep. I laid some money on the table as thanks for their hospitality, and left, trying to close the door softly.

Through the pines I could see Venus, the morning star. During the night there had been a frost, and now it was easy to walk along the firm earth, but when the sun came out the ground again became boggy. Keeping along the woods, I was able to move ahead. When the forest ended, however, I again ended up in the power of the dreadful, dirty, elements.

Finally, having endured fate's harsh blows, I entered the city of

Radomysl. Asking directions from passers-by, I found a private residence with a sign in Russian letters. In four hours I had gone fifteen kilometers, and at about 11:30 A.M. I reached Stakhovich. Catching sight of me, he exclaimed, "To bed!" Evidently, my appearance corresponded to my mood. He put me in a real bed and said, "I'll wake you for lunch." I again fell asleep like a log. The ability to fall asleep instantly is a gift from above.

*　*　*

Two hours later I woke up and was given what I had been longing for all morning—tea. Furthermore, I was given it in bed, a forbidden indulgence. Sitting in an armchair alongside my bed, Michael Alexandrovich patiently waited for me to feel myself again. He finally said, "Now you look like a human being again. When you came in, you scared me. Where is your automobile?"

"Thirty kilometers away."

"Did it break down?"

"No, we ran out of gas."

"When?"

"Yesterday morning."

"And you had to walk?"

"The transports are stuck."

He smiled and said, "Holy Russia, I recognize you. I'm happy to see you, but tell me, to what do I owe this good fortune?"

I searched his handsome, clever, slightly mocking face. He couldn't have forgotten, could he? I said, "Today is December 17, Michael Alexandrovich."

It was then his turn to attentively examine me, and finally, evidently convinced that I was still sane, he asked, "Excuse me, but what is December 17?"

He did forget!

"When we met in Lvov, you said, 'I will expect you in Radomysl on December 17,' and you added, 'It's important.' Remember?"

In his face I could read vexation, pity, and happiness all at the same time. He exclaimed, "My God! For that you traveled thirty kilometers by car on crazy roads and twenty on foot! My dear boy! How I adore you!"

All decent people are terribly muddle-headed. I could have been more specific about who was confused in this case and who wasn't, but I preferred to keep silent. He continued, "Yes, I thought that it was important. We have to shake up these young people. They stew in their own juices and don't know anything. That's why I wanted to introduce you two, so that you could speak with him."

"With whom?"

"Oldenburg."

"Prince Oldenburg?"

"Yes, not the elder, but the younger one. It's important, of course, but to accomplish such a feat for that! Let's go have lunch!"

* * *

Lunch was good, bearing in mind that we were at war. But I ruined it, because I do not drink vodka, and not only out of principle. My frail body simply cannot tolerate alcohol. During the war, vodka was banned for the army at the beginning of the mobilization, but the ban was only observed in relation to enlisted men, and the officers could obtain alcohol from the doctors, who were issued it for medicinal purposes. The doctors themselves drank and shared their vodka with the officers.

I found that this disgraceful practice undermined discipline and further widened the already large gap between officers and men. In a word, the practice meant trouble. However, it was easy for me to have such high principles. After all, Mother Nature was on my side; she had gifted me with an aversion to alcohol. To others, Nature was an evil stepmother who endowed them with a natural bent for the green snake. I did not lecture Stakhovich, but I disappointed him by forcing him to drink alone, which is dull.

We had lunch alone. Stakhovich was an engaging conversationalist. We spoke about everything, but primarily about the Red Cross, in which Michael Alexandrovich held an important post. All Red Cross establishments connected to the Third Army were subordinate to him. He said, "In resources, the Red Cross is weaker than the army medical units, which are much better equipped. They have plenty of doctors, medics, hospitals. Their means of transportation, that is, ambulances, for the sick and wounded cannot be compared to those of the Red Cross, but—" He drank another shot of vodka. "But the importance of the Red Cross does not correspond at all to its material resources. Its importance is much greater. I tell my workers over and over, 'Remember, you are the doctors' conscience!' Yes, conscience, because, I must admit, the army doctors often have no conscience at all."

I thought back to all I had seen when I was working with the first detachment of IUZOZO and said, "Quite right, Michael Alexandrovich. The regimental doctors are better, but the farther they are from the front, the more they become, as you say, unconscionable."

"So you've noticed also? It's difficult to explain what causes it. Red tape? The whole army is caught up in red tape, but the soldiers can be heroes. They not only kill but die themselves—but not the doctors; their primary duty is to stay healthy, and that gives rise to a different, more vile psychology. On the other hand, perhaps it is not so. In any case, the Red Cross preserves a certain lofty tradition of humanity, and it can and must be an example to the degraded army doctors. This is its significance!"

He had another drink. His eyes shone and his speech became somehow inspired, almost prophetic. I realized that it was not in vain that I had come to Radomysl on December 17 (30), 1914, however unreasonable and in defiance of the elements. I heard prophetic words, ideas that were later realized.

"I am going to tell you something that I would not tell anyone else. This war has no genuine psychological foundation. Our poor forgetful Ivans simply cannot understand the reason for the war. Tell me, do you think this war will end the same way as other wars—wars that were unquestionably just?"

"What do you mean, Michael Alexandrovich?"

"This. For better or for worse, at other times our peasants went off to die for their faith, their Tsar, and their motherland. But now? Who is threatening our Orthodox faith? No one, it seems. Well, perhaps Russia's autocratic Tsar is threatened? Again, it doesn't seem that way. The motherland? Could we truly call this a patriotic war? It's a patriotic war for those who were attacked, the Serbs. And why did Austria attack Serbia? Because some Serb assassinated the future Austrian Tsar."

"My dear Michael Alexandrovich! What you are saying is both true and not true."

"How so?"

"Superficially what you are saying is true; it's easy enough to see that—but wars have more deep-rooted causes."

"Exactly what do you mean?"

"The truth is that the assassination of the heir to the Austrian throne was only a pretext for the war. The real reason was that Germany is infected with a psychological sickness, also known as the *Drang nach Osten.*

"This mental derangement had two spearheads. One variant was to go through the Balkans to the Persian Gulf, with Russia's tacit agreement. In this case Germany would not touch Russia. The second variant would be put into effect if Russia revived her long-standing tradition of serving as the defender of her fellow-Slavs. In that case Germany would not have to reach the Persian Gulf; it would be sufficient at first to take the Balkans, the black soil of southern Russia, the Caucasus with its oil, and the territory beyond the Caucasus. Since Russia did intercede for Serbia, the second variation was put into effect, and now this war is a war for the motherland. We southerners especially feel this way."

"You in IUZOZO!"

"Yes. For us, southern Russia, in other words, Kiev, is what Moscow is to you Russians, the motherland."

Stakhovich poured himself another shot of vodka and raised his glass.

"I am happy to welcome you here. But I'm going to tell you something, only don't feel insulted. You Ukrainians don't make the decisions. We Russians do."

"That's true."

"If that's true, it's bad."

"Why?"

"Because this is how the war will end: both our peasants and yours will thrust their bayonets into the ground and leave. Mark my words!"

Our conversation continued, but on a lower level. That's how it is with alcohol. Taken in moderation it liberates hidden abilities that are normally reserved for moments of danger or inspiration. Alcohol artificially sets them free. A few shots of vodka elevated Michael Alexandrovich to the heights of prophecy: "They'll thrust their bayonets into the ground and leave." A few more drinks, however, and the quality of his thinking deteriorated. Since what he had to say was not very interesting, I no longer remember it.

After lunch Michael Alexandrovich was cheerful and solicitous. He said, "I'll give you a light carriage and three horses that run like the wind. Ivan, who has all the qualities of a good coachman, will drive them. Most important, I'll give you two cans of gasoline. Finally—I'll give you Pares!"

"Bernard Ivanovich Pares!"

"Exactly. Three men, three horses, a carriage, and gasoline. What more could you want?"

On December 18 (31) 1914, we set off, after drinking some tea, according to custom. A Russian without his morning tea is reduced to despair. The horses did not run like the wind, of course, but they were good horses, and depending on the road conditions, they either trotted along easily or went at a walk. By midday, the sun shining above the pines warmed the ground, turning it into mud blacker than night. We were forced to plod along slowly. Suddenly something cracked; the carriage swayed to one side, and the horses stopped. Ivan jumped down into the dirt, then announced, "The axle is broken."

I said to Bernard Ivanovich: "Man proposes, God disposes." Then I asked Ivan, "How far have we come?" He replied, "About fifteen kilometers." In other words, only halfway to Gorbach, where the automobile was. What were we to do? Return to Radomysl? Continue on our way? We couldn't drive, although we could unharness the horses and lead them, but what would we do with the carriage?

Pondering the possibilities, I sorrowfully cast my eyes down the road and along the outline of the woods. Suddenly I recognized the pines and the turn in the road. I jumped down. Beyond the clump of trees I should be able to see the hut with the straw roof blackened by moss. I went a few steps. There it was!

Sir Bernard Pares, whom we called Bernard Ivanovich, was a correspondent for a London newspaper. From the opening of the State Duma he had been informing British readers about events in the Tauride Palace. When the war began, he transferred to the Russian front as a war correspondent. That was how I met him at Stakhovich's.

His interest in the young Russian parliament never flagging, he now was going with me to Tarnov, where a unit of the State Duma was working, headed by Maria Nicholaevna Khomiakov. Pares was very friendly with the Khomiakov family. Maria Nicholaevna's father, Nicholas Alexevich, former Chairman of the State Duma, headed the Red Cross in the Eighth Army, as did Stakhovich in the Third Army. Now an axle had broken under Bernard Ivanovich, and he was forced to share our adventures of December 18 and 19, 1914 (December 31, 1914, and January 1, 1915). And even longer. He was in Russia during the Revolution of 1917, and described it in his book entitled *The Fall of the Russian Monarchy.**

*   *   *

In the meantime Ivan had dragged the carriage to the hut and unharnessed the horses. Our ill-starred carriage was left in a small coachhouse until better times, and our lightning-fast steeds were turned into pack animals. Ivan loaded the precious gasoline onto the first horse. He put the cans into two sacks, tied them, and threw them over the back of the horse that had served as the wheel horse in our troika. He adjusted the two bags of oats onto the right trace horse in the same fashion. And the third horse? It was given the honorable assignment of carrying Sir Bernard Pares's baggage, which consisted of a small suitcase and a rubber tub. Ivan entrusted the tub-owner himself with leading the horse, which delighted the correspondent. Ivan took the horse carrying the oats, while I led the one with the gasoline. Thus we set forth—three men and three horses, followed by all sorts of parting words of good wishes.

For a foreigner, Pares spoke Russian well. After an hour, when we stopped to rest, entrusting Ivan with all three horses for a while, Bernard Ivanovich said, "While Ivan takes care of the horses, allow to ask you a question. Do you think this war is being waged under the banner of nationalism?"

---

*New York: Vintage Books, 1961 (trans.).

"Without a doubt."

"Could you be a bit more concrete?"

"I think that Germany's extremely virulent nationalism awakened Russia's much more passive nationalism. That is the reason for the war."

"In general, that's true, but there is also British nationalism—"

"Of course. What do you think of it?"

"This. You probably remember Kaiser Wilhelm's visit with Tsar Nicholas II. The two crowned kings were very informal with each other, calling each other 'Willy' and 'Nicky.' Willy said, 'Forget the treaties; we'll divide the world between us!' As you said, Willy was very virulent, and Nicky was too passive. Thus Willy convinced Nicky that Germany's and Russia's futures depended on their mutual friendship. Nicky forgot former treaties and signed a treaty of friendship with Willy, who then went back to Germany. Along the way he sent the Tsar a telegram which said, 'The Admiral of the Atlantic Ocean salutes the Admiral of the Pacific Ocean,' to which Nicky carefully replied, 'Have a good trip!' "

"I remember, but now, my dear Bernard Ivanovich, I will tell you what I think of you Englishmen."

"What exactly?"

"I think that when it was learned in London that Willy had divided the oceans, England immediately decided to go to war with Germany, on principle."

"You think so?"

"I am sure of it. Willy underestimated the nationalism of the Englishman. The latter does not cry to the entire world 'England über alles,' but his nationalism is deeper than the German's. The Englishman upholds his mother country above all else. Could the 'Empress of the Seas,' as England was called, yield her hegemony in the Atlantic Ocean? For this reason it was decided that impudent Willy must receive a dressing-down. As for Nicky, since he did not accept the title of Admiral of the Pacific Ocean, which Willy offered, he was still considered a friend. Isn't this so?"

"You are not far from the truth."

"I am very glad that the British-Russian axis, unlike the axle of our carriage, did not break. Thus, with your permission, let us continue."

"Let's go!"

This occurred on December 18 (31), 1914. The three of us proceeded in a file, each leading his assigned horse properly, on a short rein. In other words, the horse's head almost touched the back of the man leading him. Bernard Ivanovich did the same, perhaps knowing why, while Ivan probably had been taught by an older coachman to lead a horse on a short rein. As for me, a horse had taught me that a long time ago. My horse, Zbyshka, was at the time six years old, in the prime of life, but at times still frolicked like a colt, so I would lead him on a long rein. One day Zbyshka suddenly began to prance back and forth, which I found amusing, but he concluded by whirling about and kicking me with both hindlegs. He did not mean to kick me; we were the best of friends. It was simply an accident. I escaped with only having to stay off my feet for a week. Since then I led horses on a short rein, but there is an exception to every rule.

The horse carrying the rubber tub was a gentle horse that was unlikely to frolic under any circumstances. He walked so closely behind his temporary leader—on his heels, in other words—that he actually stepped on Sir Bernard's heel. Bernard Ivanovich, who was in front of me, abruptly stopped, as did his horse. I called out, "What happened?"

"Nothing, nothing. She pulled off one of my galoshes."

"Did she hurt you?"

"Oh no, but she trampled it."

Since Bernard Ivanovich was wearing high boots under his galoshes, no harm was done. We had a good laugh. This incident occurred not too far from the place where two days before I had struggled to hold my high boots by their flaps so that the mud would not pull off my galoshes or the Wellingtons under them. This meant that we were not far from Gorbach, the automobile, the girls, and the kittens.

Thus it was. We could just barely see the hut through the trees. There was the car in the yard. Yes, it was the same hut. I opened the door and saw exactly what I had expected. Gorbach, the driver with the face of a fallen angel, was sitting on a bench, with kittens playing on his lap and girls surrounding him. Everything was as usual. Spotting me, he jumped up, the kittens falling to the floor like leaves in a storm, the children recoiling in fright. In a voice mixed with hope and despair, he shouted, "Did you get the gasoline?!"

*　*　*

We set forth immediately, because there had been a slight frost. At first everything went well. The sticky jam had thickened somewhat, giving the chains something to grip. By the time the early red moon became silvery, there was an even more severe frost. The road became hard and would have been perfect if not for the pits and bumps. The quiet, impassive moon threw a light on our misfortunes. Near midnight, at the birth of the new year, 1915, the wheels of our car lodged in a deep pothole, which should have been covered. At this point the road went past some little gardens with bare trees. Here and there were fences, not completely broken down, which could have served as suitable material to fill the abyss, but we needed an ax. I berated Gorbach for leaving the ax at the base in Lvov, but since verbal abuse did not help matters, I set forth in search of one.

Where there were gardens, even bare ones, there must also be huts and people. By the light of the moon, I did eventually find a hut, moreover with a girl standing in front of it. She had gray eyes, dark lashes, light hair, and black eyebrows. I went up to her, she glanced at me, and we recognized each other. Either from the moonlight or for some other reason she was very pale and sad. My watch said exactly twelve midnight, and hoping to cheer her up, I said in Polish, "Happy New Year!"

She understood, and whispered, "Boże!" ("God!") Then she burst into tears but managed to thank me.

What did the new year 1915 promise for her and for me?

* * *

Overcoming all difficulties, we finally moored at dawn at a hotel in Tarnov. The hotel corresponded to wartime—the rooms were unheated, and lighted by a single kerosene lamp. The beds had on them only dirty mattresses without sheets or blankets. We threw our sleeping bags on the mattresses. Before crawling into his sleeping bag, Bernard Ivanovich did something that was normal for him but seemed heroic to me. He set his inseparable companion, the rubber tub, on the floor. I assumed he wanted to wash his feet, but he undressed completely, stepped into the tub, and in that freezing-cold room, poured icy water from a pail on himself! Then he rubbed himself dry, crawled into his sleeping bag, and bade me good night. I felt humbled, because I could never accomplish such a feat.

Several hours later we had to part. I had to hurry to Lvov to outfit the third detachment of IUZOZO for the road, while Bernard Ivanovich set off to Tarnov to visit the State Duma, represented there by the extraordinarily hard-working infirmary headed by Maria Nicholaevna Khomiakov.

The March on Tarnov

JANUARY 1 (14), 1915, was a beautiful, sunny day. The sun shone; the snow shone. I again set forth for Tarnov from Lvov with a newly formed advanced food and first aid detachment of IUZOZO. The detachment consisted of a commander, that is, myself, a doctor, a fifth-year medical student, twenty medical orderlies/coachmen from the reserves who were unfit for active duty, and two lower-division medical students. Our animate inventory was forty horses; inanimate—twenty carts loaded with equipment. Most important of all were our automobiles.

When it comes to moving together, horses and automobiles are not compatible. The latter in one hour can cover the same distance it takes horses an entire day to travel. I would send the students off in a car as a billeting party, charged with finding and preparing lodgings for the entire detachment. The students had to get up early, and to keep their spirits up, I composed a short song to a motif popular at the time.

Kvartirery, kvartirery,	Members of the billeting party,
Ne dano vam dolgo snat,	You are not allowed to sleep late.
Vmeste s utrennei Veneroi	With Venus of the morning
Pokidaete krovat.	Your beds you must forsake.

They bravely sang the song and raced off in the cold dawn. When we arrived much later, having covered forty kilometers, we would find quarters ready for us.

Twenty carts stretched along the road, the first and last of them bearing large white flags with red crosses. I ordered once and for all that the line was not to break up, that is, that they were to stay together in order. It was hard not to get separated when there were obstacles like other transports and cars on the road also, but since all our drivers were soldiers, they were disciplined and obedient; after all, I was wearing an officer's uniform.

I had bought the horses along the way from some transport drivers who were desperate to sell them. They had said, "Sir, we're not in the army, we're free men, but they grabbed us back in Russia and said, 'Just drive to such-and-such and then you'll be let go,' but there we

178

were chased still further. And now we're here, four hundred kilometers from home. Then they said, 'Well, go home now,' so we will, but who knows, they might catch us again. We're better off selling the horses and carts and going on foot. That way we'll get home." So I bought their equipment, since we needed carts. I can't remember now how much I paid, but it was reasonable. They thanked us very much. The horses did not look presentable, but my soldiers—peasants, of course—weighing them at a glance, said, "Its O.K., sir, we'll wash them. They're strong little horses."

We had several very interesting adventures on the road, but I do not have the time to tell about them. I will only tell the following story.

Two of my soldiers had curious surnames—Vovtornik ("On Tuesday") and Sreda ("Wednesday"). Furthermore, they walked one behind the other in formation. We reached the city of Ianov on Saturday, and stayed at the home of a Polish woman named Subota ("Saturday"). Everyone found this amusing, because on Saturday, Tuesday and Wednesday stayed at Mrs. Saturday's. This woman was kind to a fault. At dinner she told a sad story. Although she spoke in Polish, we were able to understand her, and our doctor, Vatslav, who was also Polish, translated what we could not understand. Mrs. Subota was the wife of a burgomaster, but her husband had fled from the Russians, because the Germans had reported that we would kill all the men. She said, "They said that the women would not be killed, so I, my daughter, and our cook stayed. So here we are, and our house is still standing. But we were very frightened. The first Russian I saw asked for water. We gave him some, and he went on. Then others came, but no one touched us. And they all continued on, hurrying somewhere." The doctor asked, "But wasn't there a fierce battle here? The whole city is in ruins." She waved her hands energetically and said, "I didn't see any battle, and the city is in ruins from a fire. The fire broke out when our Austrian troops were still here. The square was covered with them. Wounded took up the entire square, lying on straw. And smoking. The straw caught fire; some escaped, some didn't. Then the wooden shops and houses caught fire. And there was such a fire that even the stone houses started to burn inside. And now everything is in ruins. But since we are on the edge of town, we were spared. Also, our house is in a yard and the wind was in our favor."

After a pause, she continued, "Well, we are still alive. Nothing is wrong, the Russians are kind, and I hope my husband will return."

We left at dawn, but I still remember the town of Ianov, because in November of 1914, when I was in another detachment of IUZOZO, the following occurred: I was driving along a main road and saw a red cross, a bright signal that help could be found here. However, recalling that I had helped some wounded soldiers who had passed by this

Red Cross station without seeing it, I stopped and asked the nurses, "Why don't you have a light at night?"

They answered, "We never thought of it."

Perhaps they hadn't, or perhaps they were lazy, but I didn't say so. Then they asked me, "Do you speak German?"

"Yes, I can make myself understood. Why?"

"Well, there are two Hungarian officers here who keep pestering us, asking for something, but we can't understand them. Talk to them."

I entered the tent. The two young Hungarian officers were lying on cots. When I asked them in broken German what was the matter, they immediately brightened up and said, "We want to write to our relatives, because we now know that we were not told the truth."

"And what were you told?"

"We were told that the Russians kill all enemy wounded, and we believed it. When we were shot and couldn't walk any farther, we decided not to be taken alive. We lay there waiting with our revolvers in our hands. Then Russian medics came with stretchers, picking up all the wounded and carrying them off somewhere. We thought they were only picking up their own soldiers, but then we saw that after they had picked up their soldiers, they picked up our wounded also. And so we thought, we won't shoot yet. Let them come closer.

"They came and put us on stretchers. And so here we are, and the nurses are taking good care of us."

I asked, "The medics didn't take anything away from you?"

"No, no, nothing. We gave them our things."

I did not try to ascertain whether this was so or not, but asked, "What do you want?"

"We want to write to our families and tell them that what was said about the Russians is not true. Can we?"

"Yes, write to them. I will give your letters to headquarters."

This I did. I think our side sent the letters through the Red Cross, as was done then. It was to our advantage to see that those letters got through, but whether or not they reached the Austrian field mail, I don't know, of course. After all, to a significant extent, war is based on false propaganda.

* * *

Now we go to Tarnov. At times there was sunshine, at times, snow, then again blue skies. In a word, it was beautiful, and I forgot about Ianov. However, we were still far from Tarnov, probably thirty kilometers, when we began to hear from time to time what seemed to be heavy firing. We could tell it was heavy firing, judging by the distance. Then we saw dots in the blue sky—undoubtedly planes. We decided that the planes must be bombing Tarnov. This continued the entire day. Then the dots disappeared, but the firing continued and became louder, making the ground shake. That day we counted approximately thirty explosions.

It was almost sunset when we came to a hill from which we could see Tarnov. Slanting sunbeams lit up a cupola, not a Catholic church but a majestic Jewish synagogue, as I learned later. One hit, preceded by the roar, whistle, and grinding characteristic of the flight of a large shell, indicated that it was not planes bombing Tarnov.

I made some psychological observations. We were going toward the bombardment, under the shelling, and I looked at the men's faces. The older men were totally quiet, not even particularly curious—the officers had not given the order to stop, so everything was all right. The students' faces were alert, but nothing more than that. I thought it would be senseless to expose people to danger needlessly, so, about two kilometers from Tarnov, in a small village, I gave the order to stop and make camp for the night. I told the doctor, "You will be in command. Wait for me here."

"Where are you going?"

"I have to go to Tarnov."

"Why?"

I did not tell him. I set off for Tarnov, calculating that I would reach it before sunset. Along the way, I saw carts and carriages—inhabitants of the city, fleeing, unable to withstand the artillery fire. However, there were not many people fleeing. In Tarnov there were quite a few Jews, and they fled, fearing the Cossacks. The Poles were not as frightened, so a number of them remained in the city. The Russians were also leaving. I saw a priest go by, his cassock flying. An officer was walking next to him, and I heard the officer, who was scared out of his wits, say, "Father, they can shoot me, but I can't stand it!"

To tell the truth, I had not yet seen any horrors. Only the setting sun seemed ominous. Entering the city, I walked up a street which went up a slight hill. It was an ordinary street, with long purple shadows cast by the red sun. I overtook a draft horse pulling a cart, good-heartedly trying to make the hill, the driver walking alongside. Suddenly I heard a hollow sound in the distance, then a blood-curdling howl. In ancient times, the dragons probably roared like that. The howl turned into a grinding sound directly overhead. I calculated later that such shells fly for fifty-five seconds, but at the time my nerves were on edge, and those seconds seemed like a dream. Everything stopped as if by magic. The horse froze in midstep, the driver froze with one hand in the air. A boy selling papers stood stock-still, holding a paper in the air. Through an open door I could see a Polish woman in a cafe standing motionless, tray in hand. They all stood this way for only a few seconds, but it seemed longer. Then the whine abruptly ceased, and the shell hit the ground, shaking the entire city. In five seconds everyone began to move again—horse, driver, boy, woman.

I thought about how incredibly adaptable man is. After all, the bombardment had started only that morning. Thirty shells had fallen on the city, but the people, seeing that nothing extraordinary happened, were already taking the shelling in stride. A bit later I learned what had happened. When I was there, only the train station was being shelled, and the guns were hitting right on target. The real danger began when the machine-guns opened fire, because they were not as accurate. Then the monstrous shells began falling at random. The machine-guns were able to fire probably one hundred shots at one time.

I continued walking, and even though I did not know the road, I found what I was seeking, a detachment of the State Duma that was working here. Making certain that no one was hurt, I had a talk with Maria Nicholaevna Khomiakov and the other nurses. These women were completely fearless. The hospital was located in a Catholic monastery, and at the moment was completely filled with seriously wounded men. Our nurses took care of them, and the Catholic nuns fed them.

In the meantime night fell. There was no electricity, only kerosene lamps and candles. In the candlelight I continued my talk with one of the nurses from Kiev. Both her brothers, like her father before them, were serving in the 166th Rovnenskii Regiment. Her father, a colonel, had died before the war, and she feared for her brothers. She was a young woman, a volunteer, of course, and did not receive any pay. Maria Nicholaevna Khomiakov called her a first-class nurse.

Suddenly a young man tore into the tent. How he was able to find me in the absolute darkness reigning over the city I don't know, but he gravitated toward me like a drowning man grasping at a straw. Waving his thin arms, he shouted in French, "Des soeurs, elles pleurent!" ("The nuns, they're weeping!").

His story about the weeping nuns was so funny that even the nurse I was talking to almost burst into laughter. Seeing a medal pinned to her breast, the young man began to bow and scrape before her, saying, "Oh, madame, madame est titulaire de l'ordre de saint George!" ("Oh, Madam has received the Cross of St. George!").

I asked in Russian, "Tell me what happened. How are the nuns, you pathetic Father Superior!"

"They're weeping."

"I already know that. Now, where are they?"

"Here somewhere, I came from there."

I have to explain about this young fellow, who was wearing a soldier's uniform but with the insignia of a volunteer. He was a Jew, about twenty years old. He had already shown great courage several times in the past. When I commented on this, he responded, "Why should I be afraid? I was born at seven months. They kept me wrapped in cotton wool for two months. I don't have any kidneys, and I have tuberculosis. What is there to be afraid of? Things can't get any worse!"

He couldn't stop babbling. "My sister took all my courage. She drives an automobile in Paris. So far she hasn't run over anybody, but she will! Actually, I am a depraved child of Paris, nothing else, and now I am a Father Superior. The nuns are weeping. What do I do with them?"

"Let them weep. Where are our cars?"

"At the station."

"But wasn't the station leveled?"

"Right. There's nothing left but our two cars."

"How do you know?"

"How do I know? I was there and saw everything."

"Tell me quickly, when did you arrive?"

"When did we arrive? This morning, before the attack."

* * *

We had left Lvov in marching formation on December 26, 1914 (January 8, 1915), and he had left the same day by train, in two cars, with all our baggage and five nuns. And it turned out that we arrived on horseback the same time as he did by train.

He managed to hide the weeping nuns somewhere. Actually they were not nuns, but novices who wanted to serve God.

Then he gave me a bit of news which flabbergasted me. "Shpakovskii and Shunko are with the nuns."

"That can't be. I left them in the village."

"They ran off and brought the carts—five of them."

"What for?"

"My God, for the nuns and the baggage! The station has been leveled; we have to get them out!" He said something else, but a shell crashed nearby and I couldn't hear him. Then in comes Shpakovskii wearing only one boot. He ran over to us and said, "Vasilii Vitalevich, the nuns are wailing bitterly, what should I do?"

I answered, "Find your boot."

"Goddammit! I lost a boot!"

Quite evidently this was no ordinary evening. I had no sooner asked where Shunko was, although I knew that he was consoling the nuns, than in runs another man. I had no idea what was going on. He thrust a box of candy into my hands and shouted hysterically, "From your wife! From your wife!—I was a prison warden. I ran away. They wanted to kill me. I ran to the front. But I can't fight. I can't join a regiment. Take me into your detachment."

I asked, "What does my wife have to do with it?"

"I visited her in Kiev."

"And where are you from?"

"From Siberia."

"How did you get to Kiev?"

"I don't even know. I ran. In Kiev they told me about the *Kievlianin.* They said, go to the *Kievlianin.* She told me, your wife did, where you were."

How she knew where I was, considering the situation, I don't know to this day. She had sent him here and hastily gave him a box of candy for me. Everything was clear now, including the fact that a former prison warden had gone crazy. I said to him, "I'll look into this matter tomorrow, but now, go back to the village." I realized that the doctor, who had stayed with the detachment, had sent him to me.

I should explain a few things. I had designated Levenberg, the "depraved child of Paris," as my adjutant. The nuns were under his care. He took his duty very seriously and brought the baggage untouched from Lvov to Tarnov, to the station, which had now been leveled by one-ton shells. "Let's go back to the nuns," Levenberg said. We set off in total darkness. Luckily he knew the road. The street was completely covered with broken glass from windowpanes. Along the way, Shpakovskii luckily found his boot and rejoiced. Now we were armed for battle.

The nuns were overjoyed to see us and again began to weep, this time from relief. Levenberg pestered me unceasingly, wanting us to go save the wagons also. I said, "First of all we need sleep. Then we'll see." Everyone fell asleep, totally exhausted. Levenberg slept on the floor next to me. There was only one couch in the room. I slept like a dead man, immediately falling into a deep sleep. A flash and a dull, faraway sound woke me, but I immediately fell asleep again. I even had a dream. Then I awoke again. There was a howl, a grinding noise, then a crash which shook the walls of the house. Levenberg jumped up. The nuns began to weep. Shpakovskii and Shunko began bustling about in the darkness. I said to Levenberg, "To the station!"

With the help of Shpakovskii's and Shunko's flashlights we found our men and our five carts. The men were indifferent, as before, as if none of this had anything to do with them. We conducted our search in total darkness. Some time had passed since the last salvo, which had occurred around midnight. Now it was 2:00 A.M. We found the railroad tracks and followed them until we found the train, that is, the remains of the train. Everything had been destroyed, and enormous shell-holes, big enough to hold a horse and rider, gaped at us. Our cars had survived unscathed, however; only the doors had been blown off, and this was handy enough, since it spared us the trouble of trying to open them.

We worked for quite a while. We had to drag the carts to the cars. Surprisingly, the horses were as quiet as the drivers. Five men and two soldiers transferred the things, supervised by Levenberg, the depraved child of Paris, whom no one would obey. Meanwhile I took a flashlight and examined the station platform. Everything was indescribably mangled. The roof had been blown off, the windows broken, but the clock, the clock!

The large station clock had been torn off the wall and now stood importantly on the platform between two ruined columns. Its face was undamaged, and showed several minutes past eleven, evidently in the morning. Of course the clock was not working; it preserved the time when it had been thrown from its place and put neatly onto the platform. To me the clock was a mysterious witness, mutely saying something.

I went back to hurry the men. It was not wise to gamble with fate by waiting for another shell to fall and destroy the miraculously undamaged cars and us with them. We got away without a scratch, but at 3:00 A.M., when the carts set off toward the village, there was another shell. "Depraved" Levenberg shouted with joy, "Nous l'avons echappés belle!" ("We've managed to escape!")

The following day, N. N. Mozhaiskii arrived from Lvov with my ladies. The senior nurse was Mozhaiskii's wife, Matilda Alexevna. She began giving orders to the nuns, who came from Podolsk Province, where Mozhaiskii was the patron of a monastery. Arriving with them was Maria Konstantinovna, Balashev's cousin—a saintly soul! And finally, Kira, a tall, beautiful young woman who knew a little about medicine, and eighteen-year-old Mura Zabugina. Finally, with all present and accounted for, the third detachment began its very useful work to the glory of IUZOZO.

* * *

We were assigned to a town with the unpleasant name of Tukhov,* twenty kilometers from the city of Tarnov. The town had been almost totally demolished, not by artillery but by fire, that is, by spontaneous combustion. There were no inhabitants, only broken glass and brick. By the way, it was during our stay there that I observed how even stone houses can disappear from the face of the earth. On a hillside

---

*The name Tukhov brings to mind the Russian word *tuklyĭ*, "rotten" (trans.).

there was a stone house which I passed every day. When I saw it for the first time, even the windows were unbroken, although the owners were no longer there. Then one fine day not only the windows but also the window frames and doors disappeared, which was convenient for those passing to and fro. One day I went in. The wooden floors were also gone; the stove had been overturned but was still usable, though it too eventually disappeared. At the time people would kindle fires right in the houses. Who would do this? you ask. The transport drivers.

During the war, the transport drivers were utterly uncontrollable, a state within a state. They had their own "laws" and ran their own affairs. There were transport officers, of course, but the Lord has created things both visible and invisible, and they were among the "invisible."

And so, our entire detachment moved into this manor house, which served as what was called a divisional station. Wounded and sick soldiers from four regiments of the division would trickle into our station. This was where they were classified more strictly. Those who were not seriously ill were sent to Field Hospital No. 1, while contagious cases were sent to Hospital No. 2. Still others were evacuated by rail. The railroad station was nearby, but we could only move men there at night because it was regularly fired upon in the daytime. Our role was to aid the divisional station. Since this meant that I would be reporting to its commander, I began by going to introduce myself to him. The commander of the divisional station was a surgeon named Bushuev, from the Alexandrov Hospital in Kiev. On my way I had to pass through a building where the sick and wounded were housed. They were lying right on the floor, not even on straw. That day there was a frost of $-4°$ Celsius; snow was coming into the room through the broken windows and accumulating in drifts on the floor. I saw more broken glass when I passed through the former conservatory. Knocking on a door, I was ushered into a large room where a pleasant warmth enveloped me. I immediately noticed a piano, soft couches, armchairs, and even a carpet. Several men sat drinking tea at a table covered with a tablecloth, I went over and presented myself, "Such-and-such. I have been assigned to your divisional station."

Bushuev rose, held out his hand, and said, "Please sit down; we'll have some tea with jam." Then he added, indicating the two younger doctors, evidently his subordinates, "These young fellows are bored because they have nothing to do. The divisional station doesn't need any help, but since the powers that be have issued an order, so be it. Please make yourself at home."

Restraining myself, I did not insolently remark on the contrast between this warm room and the sick and wounded soldiers freezing in the next building. Stakhovich, chief commissioner of the Red Cross in the Third Army, had written a directive: "Not by words but by deeds; Don't criticize—shame."

When I finished my tea, I went to get settled, but I had to settle the others first, not myself. I called one of my men, Buian ("Ruffian"). That was his surname, and when he was drinking he lived up to it, but when sober he was an excellent right-hand man. I said, "Did you see the broken windows where the wounded were lying?"

"Yes, sir, There was snow under them."

"Can you replace the windows?"

"Yes sir, I can. We have glass coming out of our ears."

That same day he put new glass into every window in the building. It did not warm up, but at least the snow melted, and when the stoves were lit it became very pleasant. I said to Matilda Alexevna, "Did you know that the divisional station is not feeding the sick and wounded?"

"I know. We are going to feed them."

"Will you be able to handle all of them?"

"Why do you think I brought the nuns?"

Several days later we learned that Bushuev loved music. Mura played piano well and sang like a nightingale. I said to her, "Your mission is to get Bushuev to let you play his piano, so you can charm him with your singing."

She asked, "Why?"

"Because I don't have any cots, and furthermore, I can't give orders to his orderlies and medical aides. He has plenty of supplies. You must get cots from him and have his people bring them here, and somehow we'll come to an understanding with them."

She left, played like Orpheus, and sang like a nightingale. From the top floor we could hear her warbling in Bushuev's lair. The next day, cots appeared. I said to Mura, "You thieving little nightingale, rob him some more!"

Thus we robbed him. Mura became friendly with the homesick young doctors, and they gave her all the medications we needed from the divisional stores. I relieved Mura of all her other duties; she had a more important job now—obtaining supplies.

In the history of Kiev there were two famous women named Zabugin. One was the daughter of my secondary-school friend Platon Zabugin. She was a famous beauty, and half the young men in Kiev were in love with her. She broke hearts as though they were eggs and tossed away the shells.

My Zabugin, Mura, that is, was more plain, but one could not say that she was not pretty. At eighteen years old, she was pleasant-looking and very healthy, which is not surprising, since she was a child of Kronshtadt. Let skeptics think what they will about Father John of

Kronshtadt; I know that he was a genuine miracle-worker.* Mura's parents wanted a child very much, but infertility inhabited their home. Finally, thanks to Father John's prayers, a daughter was born to them. They named her Mura, and here she was, working miracles in turn on Bushuev.

In a short while Buian had fixed the broken windows in the former conservatory. It became a good, well-lit operating room where my Dr. Vatslav and Bushuev's two homesick doctors worked diligently, but Bushuev stubbornly refused to work. Short, neckless, and fat, he sulked in his warm room. I was not worried that Mura would fall in love with him. For the time being she was in command.

One day Bushuev finally made an appearance in the operating room. After all, he was a surgeon, and a good one, and there was a tracheotomy scheduled. He cut the man's throat with apparent pleasure. I am relating all this exactly as it happened.

Bushuev had a unique way of accepting new patients. They would form a line alongside the building, in the snow. Bushuev would go out, straight from his nice warm room, and order, "Shirts off! Come on now, don't be bashful!" Then, never even touching the naked men, he would count off, "One, two, one, two," indicating which hospital they would be sent to, and his assistants would then lead the shivering men to wagons that would take them to the hospitals. Bushuev also had a peculiar approach to the sick and wounded. Whenever a medic informed him that one of the sick soldiers was "acting up," Bushuev's usual response was, "Give him one right in the mug." Dr. Vatslav told me this, with a laugh that hid deep indignation and contempt. "'Give him one right in the mug.' How do you like that?" And laughed. Probably he was thinking to himself, "Where do such useless people come from?"

*   *   *

Where was I all this time? The thing of it was that I had not yet had any leave, and it was time to take some. This was before Mackenzen's attack. A nurse and I left on leave and went to Lvov, where we stayed at the Saxony Hotel. The hotel had two glass baths, one blue and the other pink. I had been shamefully dreaming about them for a long time. I took the blue bath, and Nurse Liubov took the pink. After luxuriating in the bath, I fell asleep, and so did she. Suddenly there was a merciless knock at the door. Telegram. I read it and swore.

---

*The saintly Father John of Kronshstadt (1829–1909), one of Russia's most revered churchmen in this period, had a very large personal following and was widely regarded as a miracle worker (trans.).

"Bring dressings to Dembits." This was a code meaning "We have retreated to Dembits." Efim, my nephew, had sent the telegram, as we had arranged.

There's a furlough for you! Waking the nurse, I rounded up a government car from somewhere, and we set off for the IUZOZO base. Our driver, Alexander, was supposed to be in the garage with the car. When we arrived—horrors! Some of the gears and bearings had somehow loosened up, and Alexander had taken the whole engine apart. His extraordinary dedication to his job was truly commendable. After having traveled three hundred kilometers, instead of sleeping, he began cleaning the engine. He cannot even be called an obedient fool, because how could he have known what would happen? I said, "Alexander, what have you done? We have to return immediately!"

"What! To Tarnov?"

"No, to Dembits."

"What do we do now!"

"Put the car back together."

"It will take two hours."

"Even if it takes three. We have to leave."

A new page begins—the retreat.

*   *   *

General Field Marshal Alfred von Schlieffen, who died not long before the war, on January 4, 1913, left his successors a strategic plan for a two-front war—against France and Russia. At the beginning of the First World War, the Chief of the Great General Staff, Count Helmut von Moltke, began to carry out this plan. Moltke was the nephew of the Prussian General Field Marshal Helmut Karl Bernhard von Moltke, Bismarck's famous comrade-in-arms and Kaiser Wilhelm I's tutor, who died on April 24, 1891.

However, Schlieffen's doctrine of a decisive war came to grief in a large-scale battle between the main French and German forces on the Marne River, which ended on September 9, 1914, with the defeat of the Germans. This defeat was the turning point of the war. The disgraced Count Moltke was immediately removed from command and replaced, as of September 14, 1914, by Minister of War Falkenhayn, who had to redo the German strategy.

In February 1915, the new commander's decision matured—to turn the line of primary operations from west to east, toward Russia. The refusal of the German high command to adopt Schlieffen's idea of how to conduct the war brought Falkenhayn into a sharp difference of opinion with the army's field commanders, General Erich von

Ludendorff and General Field Marshal Paul von Hindenburg. The latter became President of the Weimar Republic and was responsible for handing the leadership of the country over to Adolf Hitler.

The winter operations to free East Prussia from Russian hands had barely ended when Falkenhayn, in April of 1915, made his main thrust into Galicia and there organized General Mackensen's battering ram for a breakthrough on the Russian front between the Vistula and the Carpathian Mountains. In two months the Germans dislodged the Russians in Galicia, thus shoring up the fighting effectiveness of the Austro-Hungarian army for a whole year, until Brusilov's breakthrough in July 1916.

The great retreat, during which we gave up twenty provinces, including ten Polish provinces, began during Mackensen's attack. However, that was what happened when one takes a large-scale view of events; on the small scale of my tiny detachment, it was the beginning of a wandering which ended for me somewhere outside the city of Kholm.

* * *

In Dembits I continued to move the wounded out, attempting to go as far as possible on my forays, although this was rather difficult because we were met by a flood of retreating troops, first the artillery and then the infantry. In all my expeditions I tried not to be taken prisoner. So whenever headquarters was in a house along the road, I would stop there.

The chief of staff, a colonel, was a sensible man, in contrast to the general, who despite his white medal of valor was too old to grasp things immediately. The colonel understood my zeal, but established boundaries which I was not to cross. He also notified me of the division's general position, saying, "The day before yesterday I had twelve thousand. Now I have six."

I was very surprised and said, "Colonel, in the past two days a thousand men have passed through my divisional station. You have six, perhaps, seven. Where are the other five thousand?"

He answered, "Since we are retreating, all the dead and wounded were left behind with the enemy. That is our main loss. Some managed to retreat, but as always during a retreat, discipline falls apart. Troops run away. Some will return, attracted by the kitchens. That's all."

I continued doing what I could to evacuate the wounded, but my expeditions became shorter and shorter. The enemy was advancing. Returning from my last expedition, I did not find my detachment where I left them, but at the railroad station. The detachment, ready to move, was waiting for me. Efim was sitting on his horse. I asked, "What's going on?"

He answered, "Vatslav went crazy with fear. He ran to the commandant, who evidently is also a bit touched, and the commandant wired a complaint about you to the corps commander, saying that you disobey the orders of the military command and will be taken prisoner. I refused to move until you returned."

I said, "Go on. After I get the wounded on the train, I'll catch up with you."

They set off. I dawdled quite a long time, but was able to get away, although only one-half of the bridge was still standing. The other was already in pieces.

* * *

We came to a small town with eighteen severely wounded soldiers on our twenty carts. The flat, wide carts were well suited for transporting wounded. I brought all the heavily wounded to our wood, where there were large sheds which had once been used for drying bricks. Now the sheds were empty, so we laid out our wounded in them on straw.

Everyone began carrying out his assigned task. Since these were seriously wounded soldiers, I went to a neighboring town for a surgeon, who turned out to be my old acquaintaince, Dr. Bushuev, who had escaped from work to the town. I brought him to our woods almost by force. While making his rounds, he said about one of the wounded, "Don't touch him. He has been shot clear through the head. He'll be done for in two hours." However, when the doctor walked away, a nurse said, "I'm going to bandage him anyway."

She had remarkably agile hands. As she worked she said about herself, "I'm a witch. Things listen to me."

And this time a "thing," that is, the wounded head, obeyed the bewitching hands. First she washed the man's face, which was covered with dirt. Black and blue marks appeared under the man's closed eyes. Then she took his head, which looked like a melon or a pumpkin, into her witch's hands and, passing it from one palm to the other, began to wrap it in an extremely complicated pattern with white gauze. This type of dressing was called, and continues to be called, a "Hippocratic cap," named for the famous physician of antiquity. Her juggling of a human head seemed miraculous, and a miracle did happen.

Contrary to Bushuev's prognosis, the man did not die in two hours. Not only did he not die, but in two days he was able to say his name, although barely audibly. After two weeks, he could walk with the help of a doctor's assistant. When we evacuated him, taking all possible precautions, he seemed to be out of danger.

One day, General A. M. Dragomirov, chief of staff of the southwestern front, found his way to our wood. He was a veteran cavalryman and easily jumped down from his horse. I ordered, "Officers, attention!"

Since there was only one officer, namely myself, Dragomirov laughed as he shook my hand, and said, "At ease. Go about your duties."

We offered him tea with wine, and during our conversation he brought up the question of Bushuev. I told him about the surgeon's transgressions. Everything I said was confirmed by Kira, the general's niece, by the other nurses, and even by Dr. Vatslav. When I finished, Dragomirov asked, "And what do you propose?"

"That he be court-martialed."

Then the general went for a walk in the woods with his niece, and she told him about Bushuev's feats in more detail. Then the general bade us farewell and left.

After a short while we were transferred to another division, but Bushuev, though he did not have any special "protection," remained at his post. Dragomirov was one of the best generals in the Russian army and, furthermore, was a decisive man. Why didn't he do anything about Bushuev? I don't know. Perhaps he too was affected by the indecisiveness that percolated down from the top. Our national inability to be decisive accounts for much in Russia's history.

A thought occurs to me somewhat unwillingly. If Bushuev had not mocked the gray masses but Dragomirov's loved ones—his wife, his children—would the general then have revealed the same spinelessness and indecisiveness? Reflecting on this question explains a lot about our history.

*   *   *

Leaving Dembits, we traveled along the railroad and eventually came to a station that had been abandoned not only by the Austrians but also by our troops as they retreated. I stopped at the station anyway and discovered more than one hundred wounded. They lay in various parts of the building, unable to walk. Whether they had been left behind by the divisional station or the regiment was uncertain, but it really did not matter. Since we were the ones who had come across them, we were the ones who had to move them out. But how?

Walking through the building, I saw dying men here and there, and others who were alive but seriously wounded. Still others were alive and in good spirits. They begged us not to leave them but couldn't walk because they had leg wounds. There were so many that even if we had left all our things—our tents, sheepskin coats, provisions, and so forth—there would not have been room enough for all of them on our carts and cars. We needed a train. There was once an English king who was willing to give his kingdom for a horse. Well, I had a horse, but it couldn't help me. A train! I had to get a train at all costs!

Unexpectedly a healthy noncommissioned officer came up to me and said, "Well, sir, we're under your command now."

"Who are you?"

"Telephone operators, there are four of us; there's a switchboard here. Everyone left, but there was no order to retreat. We don't know what to do. Tell us, sir."

I was thunderstruck by an idea—salvation!

"Are you still in touch with the next station?"

"Yes, sir."

"Call up the stationmaster. Tell him we have 140 seriously wounded and need a train to move them. Understand?"

"Yes, sir. We need a train for the wounded." He ran to his telephone. I returned to the station. There the doctors, students, and nurses had already begun their duties—cleaning and dressing wounds, and so forth. The primus stoves were working noisily. Tea would soon be ready. I walked through the rooms. Everything was in order. Now all we needed was a train. I returned to the telephone operators and asked, "How's it going?"

"Well, they promise to send one, sir."

"Good."

"Glad to be of service, sir!"

I returned to the station, where one hundred pairs of eyes gazed at me hopefully. The work continued. I ordered that the sheepskin coats be unloaded because it was going to be a cold night and we would have to cover the wounded. Summer was coming anyway, so there was no need to drag them along with us. Give them to the wounded; at least they would serve somebody for a time.

I again returned to the operators, who said, "Sir, they said that there weren't any closed cars, just open flatcars. And they would have to find them. And the locomotive was gone, but it will return, they said."

"Well, we'll wait—"

We waited a long time. The operators did their utmost, but something wouldn't click and no train was sent for us.

Finally, the operator informed me, "Sir! Either they've gone or the lines have been cut. They don't answer."

Then I said to Efim, "There's no point in going on like this. Take a car and go to the next station. Find out what's happening. Have they gone, or are they lying, or are they just all mixed up? If you feel that you can't accomplish anything at the next station, then go on to the main station, to army headquarters. Find Stakhovich. Tell him that 140 wounded and the third detachment of IUZOZO and I will be taken prisoner. We can't leave the wounded. Just say we'll be taken prisoner."

I knew exactly whom to send. My nephew was sometimes thoughtless and absent-minded, but he was perfectly suited for such a mission. He was energetic, eloquent, and charming.

Also, I knew that Efim would not spare any of the gory details in describing how we would end up as prisoners. He left. A long time passed. Everything was ready. The wounded had been tended to and given tea. Some of the soldiers died. They lay near a wall, waxen yellow, four of them. I was supposed to remove their paybooks with their names, so that their relatives could be informed of their deaths. This duty was the responsibility of the commander of the detachment, but I didn't do it. I was so busy trying to save the living that I did not tend to the dead, and I regret it to this day.

Time passed. It was 9:00 P.M., but still not totally dark. These were the longest days of the year. Suddenly the telephone operator appeared and said, "Sir, they want to talk to you."

I picked up the receiver. It was Efim. "The train is leaving now," he said.

And a train did actually arrive, with ten open flatcars. We began to load the cars. It was cold. We covered everyone with the coats. I inspected the station to make sure that no one was left behind. No. It was empty, except for the four corpses lying along the wall, motionless and stern. In ancient times they used to sculpt stone figures of the body lying in the coffin. These four looked like those figures.

Efim went on the train with the wounded, and met up with us later. I sent the cars on to an assigned meeting place, clamored up on a hunter, and set off, with the twenty carts stretching along behind me. We were on the move all night and covered forty kilometers. A horse's slow, measured gait puts one to sleep, and several times I almost fell out of the saddle. I say "almost" because I would awaken just as I was about to fall. To stay awake, I would gallop to the rear of the detachment, under the pretense of checking up on everything. Finally we reached the village where our cars were. There was an old wooden, shingled church, shining like silver here and there from the tinplate that had been used to patch holes. Many churches in Galicia were in that style, reminiscent of a Buddhist or Japanese pagoda. Astonishing!

Marveling at the church, I again fell asleep. Somebody helped me down from the horse and filled me with strong tea. I became a person again. A person? No, a pitiful nonentity! Once, when a saint fell asleep while praying, he despairingly plucked out his eyelids and threw them on the ground. Two bushes sprung up where they landed—tea plants. That is why tea is such a marvelous cure for sleepiness.

That saint was a person, not I. Instead of plucking out my eyelids, I applied myself to current earthly tasks. But I sometimes remember those four dead soldiers.

* * *

July 4 (17), 1915. I was standing at my tent near the woods, on a slope. Next to me was the large divisional-station tent. The road led away through the woods to the front; the thunder of artillery was not far off. Sensing that we would soon receive the order to move out, I alerted my detachment. A transport appeared out of the woods, moving slowly, as they do when they are carrying wounded. I thought, well, we'll have to cart them along. The transport crawled up to the tent, but there was only one wounded man in it. I looked in, saw officers' shoulder boards and a very pale face, and assumed that the man was unconscious. Then he spoke up, but in a whisper, "You must—amputate my arm—now—now—"

I looked closely and suddenly recognized him. It was Golosov, Captain Golosov, my company commander. I answered clearly, "Everything will be done immediately." I ran to the divisional tent. It was a good division in which everyone worked conscientiously, so naturally we did not have much work.

I had a good surgeon here, not Vatslav, but an older man, from Petersburg or Moscow, I don't remember. His only interests were difficult operations and horse racing. The totalizator was his passion and true calling. Bored in our detachment, he spent his time at the divisional station, which was why I went there to find him.

I said that I had an officer who demanded that his arm be amputated immediately. My doctor livened up and said, "That's interesting." But the commander of the divisional station shook his head negatively and said, "I've just received orders from headquarters. We're going to take to our heels."

I asked, "Please, this is my company commander."

Then the "totalizator" said, "Well, let's give it a shot!"

The commander ordered his assistants to bring the wounded man. He was almost unconscious, but still repeated, "The arm—immediately—"

I was not present for the operation. They amputated his arm at the shoulder, and as they were returning him to me, the "totalizator" said, "It's hopeless. He's going to die."

"Why?"

"He lost too much blood. His heart is stopping."

"Isn't there any hope?"

He pondered an instant, then answered, "There's no such thing as absolutely no hope. I give him a fifty-to-one chance."

To me these seemed enormous odds. We loaded him onto a very good truck, which had originally been a motor-car. The springs were excellent and the truck would not shake a passenger as much as the other trucks. Map in hand, I asked, "Where to?"

"The stationmaster named a village, adding, "A country estate."

I had everything ready. I put my assistant in charge of the detachment, lifted Golosov onto the truck and I, the doctor, and a nurse clambered on. In two hours we covered sixty kilometers and found the estate. The owners had gone, but the estate was not yet in ruins. We turned a large hall with a parqueted floor into our ward. We had brought only one cot, but there were sofas in the room.

We laid Golosov on the cot. The "totalizator" glanced at him, took his pulse, and said, "Alive. Surprising. I give him a twenty-to-one chance. Give him strong coffee and don't let him sleep." The nurse heard him. She was from Kiev. Her father and two brothers had served in Golosov's 166th Rovnenskii Infantry Regiment, so saving him became a matter of love and honor for her.

I sat down next to the cot. Immediately she began to pour coffee into his mouth. Having drank it, he whispered, "Thank you. What good luck!" After a few more cups of coffee he murmured, barely audibly, "I was there ten months—not touched—not a single bullet—not a fragment. Now they got me—they cut off my arm—but I'm alive—"

The nurse said something to him that evidently inspired him with hope. "You're not only alive but are going to Kiev."

He picked up the idea and said, "I'm going to Kiev—" She took care of him all night, offering coffee and sweet words about Kiev—who was there, what was happening there, things she didn't know herself, having gone nine months without a day off. At midnight the "totalizator," who did have a conscience, stopped by. "Four to one. Continue. Coffee and conversation." He left, and returned again in the morning, asking, "Alive?"

"Alive. He wants to go to Kiev."

He took Golosov's pulse and said, "Even money. Anything can happen, but he'll be out of danger if he is taken straight to Kiev. You may go also. After all, haven't you been summoned to the Duma?"

So the Kievan nurse and I went. She had saved the commander of my company. Now, perhaps, I too needed help, although of a different kind. Thus my military exploits began and ended with Captain Golosov.

*   *   *

Sometimes fate acts very purposefully, as though writing a scenario for the cinema.

I would not be fulfilling my debt to the reader if I neglected to inform him of the happy ending to this film. In the fall of 1916 in Petersburg I was visited by a certain officer. He introduced himself, "Golosov."

I said, "What! Captain Golosov was seriously wounded at the front. His arm was amputated."

"Yes. I am his brother. There are four of us brothers, all officers."

"Well, how is my company commander?"

"Mitia? He is in noncombatant service in Kiev. Quite happy and content."

That is why I said that this film had a happy ending.

Part III

THE YEARS

Vasnetsov's Child

THE CHRISTMAS PARTY that the publishers of the *Kievlianin* made for the children of the typesetters and the hawkers was a tradition. On Christmas Eve, 1902, aided by a certain pretty girl who was holding the ladder for me, I was fastening a six-pointed star to the tree. She was not quite twenty years old, but she behaved with so much dignity that she was addressed as Catherine Victorovna, not Katenka, which was proper. Catherine Victorovna Goshkevich and her mother rented an apartment from the family of Sofie Ippolitovna, the newspaper's secretary. The Goshkevich apartment and the editorial office of the *Kievlianin* were in the same building, which was how I began my acquaintance with Catherine Victorovna Goshkevich.

The famous artist V. M. Vasnetsov painted the murals in the Vladimir Cathedral between the years 1885 and 1896.* His *Kiev Madonna,* on the wall behind the altar, is beautiful. Evidently, it was inspired simply by the artist's creativity, but he searched for a model for the Christ child, and, if one believes the Kievan legend, Vasnetsov found his model in the Goshkevich family, in the face of their young daughter.

Thus the ageless infant whose all-seeing eyes shined from the walls of the Kiev cathedral was to a certain degree copied from the young girl who was gazing at me with boredom in her beautiful eyes. Unfortunately, I did not know this as I sat so stupidly at the top of the stupid ladder. If I had, I would jumped down, ignored convention, and asked straightforwardly, "Do you know who served as Vasnetsov's model for the Christ child in the Vladimir Cathedral?" And if she had answered yes, and she must have known, then we could have ended up as friends. But I didn't know and I didn't ask. No friendship was formed; on the contrary, I ultimately saw so much hatred in her tormented eyes that I was gripped with fear. But that happened in the end, and now we are only at the beginning.

* * *

---

*Victor Mikhailovich Vasnetsov (1848–1926), who specialized in realistic paintings on historical and legendary themes, revived the Byzantine genre of religious art in his murals for the Vladimir Cathedral in Kiev (trans.).

The Goshkevich family fell apart, the father going to the city of Herson, where he began to publish a leftist newspaper, and the mother remaining in Kiev. Since she had some medical knowledge, she became a midwife. There were still traces of a stern but ungodly beauty in her face. Mother and daughter would sometimes visit our house, that is, the *Kievlianin* family.

She was especially indifferent to me, but I was not the only one, for no one could break through the expression of majestic boredom on her young face. Even my wife Katia, who could rouse the dead, had no luck with the girl. Katia, by the way, could recite poetry beautifully. Once she recited some Nadson which I have retained in my memory.*

I kogda na okhote, za pyshnym stolom,	During the hunt, at a magnificent table
ot litsa imenitykh gostei,	Around which sat distinguished guests,
vstal prekrasneishii rytsar' i chashy s vinom	A handsome knight arose and raised his goblet of wine
podnial v chest korolevy svoei,	In a toast to honor his queen.
i razdalsia v lesu vdokhnovennyi privet,	And the forest resounded with the inspired compliments,
svetlyi gimn krasote i ventsu,	A fond hymn to beauty.
koroleva edva ulybnulas v otvet,	The queen barely smiled in answer
ne promolviv i slova pevtsu.	And did not say a word to the singer.

Although she was only a typist for a notary, earning twenty-five rubles a month, and owned only one decent dress, a black one at that, this twenty-year-old girl reminded me of the bored queen in the poem. Why was she so proud and so bored? Because she was more than a queen—she was a child of Vasnetsov.

One day the black dress brought her into society. The blackness of the dress made a startling contrast at the parties she attended, a noble shade to counterbalance tasteless wealth! The party I have in mind was a charitable function. Luxury was totally out of place at parties organized to help the poor, so the lady in black attracted attention. Some thought she was in mourning.

Be that as it may, Catherine Victorovna did not attend the charitable parties to have fun but to earn money, although not for herself but for the poor. Either the poor in general or poor students. There were very few rich students.

---

*Semyon Iakovlevich Nadson (1862–1887), a popular lyrical poet, wrote about brotherly love, the longing for ideological and spiritual change in Russia, and the meaning of life (trans.).

The lady in black sold champagne on a gaily decorated stage with a row of other ladies who were also dressed up but not all of whom were beautiful. Business was brisk near the black dress. Evidently people liked this strict-looking young girl who rarely deigned to smile. The champagne was sold by the goblet. There was no fixed price, but no one gave less than five rubles. Ten rubles was considered a good donation, but as far as I remember, she would only bestow a smile on those who donated twenty-five rubles. Those who gave one hundred rubles received, in addition to the smile, a sweet "thank you," accompanied by a gleam in her eyes. It was all somewhat touching.

A certain young Pole, a landowner not without means, was also touched by the beautiful girl in black who thanked people in the name of the poor. He thought, after all, that she too was poor. When the party ended he asked if he could accompany her home in view of the terrible weather. There was snow mixed with rain. She agreed. It was dark in the covered carriage, but her beautiful eyes glistened in the glow of the street lights outside, seemingly both promising something and refusing something at the same time. She said good night at the threshold of the *Kievlianin* building. He kissed her white-gloved hand. Nothing more? What else is there? He had learned where she lived.

* * *

| On ezdit stal k tebe, | He began coming to pay visits, |
| Pochtitelnyi vliublennyi . . . | The respectful suitor.* |

The notary typist did not belong to the circle of princesses and countesses about whom Apukhtin wrote, but she strove with all her soul to join it. For the time being, she fell in love with the young Pole, who was handsome, gentle, respectful. He proposed; she accepted. But the bachelor's mother announced that she would disown him if he married a Russian woman. In vain he pointed out that Goshkevich was a Polish name that had been Russianized. The mother did not agree, and Romeo withdrew his proposal.

Juliet took it badly and her heart filled with hatred. Revenge! She revenged herself by marrying a man who was no less eligible than the unfaithful Pole. Her intended was Vladimir Nicholaevich Butovich, a handsome and wealthy young landowner who had 960 hectares of land in Poltavshchin. He belonged to the Little Russian aristocracy. One of his ancestors had been a signatory of the Decree of Pereiaslav, uniting Kievan Rus with Muscovite Rus, on January 8 (18), 1654.

---

*The verse is from Alexis Nicholaevich Apukhtin (1841–1893), whose sentimental poems about the lost pleasures of youth were rather popular at this time (trans.).

Moreover, Butovich's star was rising. On December 15 (29), 1907, he joined the Ministry of Education.

The wealthy young couple began their career with Butovich assigned as an inspector of schools. It was an honorable position and interesting work. On their visits to the schools, inspectors became acquainted not only with the schools but with the district in general. They learned their needs, and could fulfill them, especially if, like Butovich, they had a direct line to the governor-general of the Southwestern Region.

However, neither wealth, nobility, nor sweetness of revenge brought happiness to Catherine Victorovna, for the simple reason that she did not love her successful husband or their child. She was as bored as before. She found neither pleasure nor warmth in their wealthy manor house. Her ambition, which had been temporarily satisfied, resurfaced.

Azor

THE FAMOUS RUSSIAN GENERAL M. I. Dragomirov retired in the fall of 1904. He had been the commander of the Kiev military district and governor-general of the Southwestern Region. His post was filled by his assistant, fifty-six-year-old Lieutenant General Vladimir Alexandrovich Sukhomlinov. It was the eve of 1905, a year of grim trial for the Russian government. One might think that all responsible administrative and military officials would have been at their posts in this difficult time, but the new commander decided to vacation abroad and went, if I am not mistaken, to Biarritz, in the south of France. There he met Catherine Victorovna Butovich, née Goshkevich.

In the meantime, in St. Petersburg, it was decided that it would be expedient to reunify the Ministry of War and the Departments of Military and Civil Service in Kiev, which had been separated following the departure of General Dragomirov. In April 1905 Sukhomlinov was notified of his appointment as governor-general, but he did not deem it necessary to leave France and part with Catherine Victorovna.

The so-called engineers' mutiny in Kiev broke out on November 18 (December 1), 1905.* It is described very briefly in the film *Pered sudom istorii* ("Before the Court of History"), in which I had a role.† In the last scene of the film, I meet the organizer of the mutiny, Fedor Nicholaevich Petrov, one of the last Old Bolsheviks, a Hero of Socialist Labor, and a member of the central committee of the Communist party since 1896.

The news about the disorders finally forced Sukhomlinov to return to Kiev. He relates, "My return to Kiev, in the capacity of governor-general, was the result of extraordinary circumstances. I was greeted by a horrible sight—broken store windows, damaged doors and gates, bits of merchandise in the streets, pools of blood here and there. I realized the seriousness of the task that had fallen on my shoulders, and I felt a sense of personal loneliness."

---

*The mutiny involved army field engineers stationed in Kiev; it was one of many local mutinies in the armed forces that year, of which the most famous occurred aboard the battleship *Potemkin* in the Black Sea (trans.).
†The film, which premiered in 1964, was based on Shulgin's earlier book of memoirs, *Dni* ("Days") (Leningrad, 1927) (trans.).

One way or another Vladimir Alexandrovich assumed his honorable post in Kiev, becoming both governor-general of the Southwestern Region and commander of the troops in the Kiev military district. Life slowly returned to normal. This period is now called a time of "deeply reactionary" government. We called it something else, but in any case, it was a relatively peaceful period, and Vladimir Alexandrovich was able to turn his attention to his personal affairs. He paid a visit to Catherine Victorovna and her husband on their estate in Poltavshchin, and then began visiting the Butoviches regularly. At first Butovich saw nothing wrong with these frequent visits, and perhaps was flattered that such an important statesman was coming to see him. However, in time the situation became more serious. Vladimir Alexandrovich began to behave in a way that was not fitting for a man in such a responsible position. It is true that this was his private life, but people in high positions do not have a private life. Everything becomes public.

For example, an event became known that damaged the governor-general in the eyes of his subordinates. On his way to Kiev after leaving the Butoviches, he was full of thoughts about the beautiful lady and even about her dog, whom the lady loved more than she loved her husband. It was an ordinary, nice dog, called Azor, which is an unusual name. Spelled backwards in Russian the name is "rose." At a station along the way, the general ordered his adjutant to send Catherine Victorovna a telegram. And he found no better signature for this tender telegram that intensified the conspiracy than the dog's name, Azor. Of course the story became known the following day, first in military circles, and then throughout the city. By this time, Vladimir Nicholaevich, her husband, already knew how the matter would end. He knit his brows. He ultimately had been told of the affair, and his wife demanded a divorce. Later, considerably later, I became more friendly with Vladimir Nicholaevich, and he told me, "I would have given her a divorce. Let her go if she wanted, but when Sukhomlinov, the governor-general and commander of the troops, tried to threaten me, demanding the divorce, I remembered that my ancestor Butovich had signed the Decree of Pereiaslav. No one threatens a Butovich or tells him what to do! And I refused. I would not give her a divorce!"

V. A. Apushkin, Sukhomlinov's biographer, confirmed these words in his personal impressions.* He said,

> Sukhomlinov was approaching his sixth decade when he became enamored of the wife of V. N. Butovich, a Kievan landowner. She was

---

*V. A. Apushkin, *General ot porazhenii* (Leningrad, 1925) (trans.)

half Sukhomlinov's age and tried to obtain a divorce from her husband. The latter adamantly refused. Sukhomlinov threatened to have Butovich banished from Kiev and threatened to have him committed. . . .

The governor-general's love affair and all its peripeteia were widely publicized in Kievan society and compromised Sukhomlinov.

Catherine Victorovna left her husband and moved into the governor-general's house. This is how he himself describes his residence in Kiev:

The entire estate covered seven desiatins—orchard, for the most part. Two kitchens, winter and summer, washhouse, stable, sheds, seed-bed, conservatory, and the various other buildings in the midst of the greenery transformed the house into a genuine country estate. On the outskirts of the estate there was a ravine in which there were several springs. The idea of damming it up occurred to me. A strong dam was built, and soon there was a deep pond, one square desiatin in extent, with two islands, a pier for two boats, two black swans, fish; a pavilion for meals, and a fountain in front, completing the impression of a life outside of the city.

The former typist for a Kiev notary came to this elaborately prepared estate as its new mistress. Azor the dog very likely followed her there.

The Skating Rink

A N ASTONISHING THING HAPPENED: the Kiev police reported to St.
Petersburg that the commander of the Kiev military district was
surrounded by spies. The leader of the spies, they said, was an Austrian citizen, Alexander Altschiller. Counterespionage agents had decided to put him under surveillance as a possible spy for several
reasons: his frequent trips to Vienna and Berlin, his close relations to
the Austro-Hungarian consul, and the medal he had received for
performing some mysterious deeds in the name of the Austro-
Hungarian monarchy.

The agents were prevented from decisively exposing him only because. of his friendship with Sukhomlinov, in whose house he was
considered "one of the family." Kukuranov, the public procurator of
the Kiev courts, said that he did not understand how the commander
could have accepted Altschiller in his home, since this gave "his
friend" access to information that would compromise him. Nothing
could interfere with the governor-general's friendship with Altschiller. They went abroad together, played cards, and Sukhomlinov said
that time never dragged for him in the company of his friend.
Sukhomlinov's study was wide open to Altschiller, who was able to
rummage through his friend's papers as much as he wanted. Everyone was asked to speak freely in Altschiller's presence, even about
military matters—after all, he was "one of the family"!

* * *

On December 2 (15), 1908, V. A. Sukhomlinov received the following royal summons: "Vladimir Alexandrovich, valuing highly your
extensive official and military experience in your previous work on
the General Staff, I find it necessary to appoint you to the responsible
post of Chief of the General Staff. . . . You remain as always in my
favor."

At the bottom was written, in His Imperial Majesty's hand, "Grate-
fully, Nicholas, Tsarskoe Selo, December 2, 1908."

Since I do not want to rely solely on my own memory, I will relate
some reminiscences of Major-General Vladimir Alexandrovich

208

Apushkin. On March 15 (28) 1917, the Provisional Government appointed him Chief Military Procurator, and two days later assigned him to the Special Investigative Commission* which interrogated Sukhomlinov. Besides being acquainted with secret documents, Apushkin met several times with the former Minister of War and learned much from him personally, so his short biography of a general in defeat is a documentary tale.

Apushkin relates the following:

> Butovich, finally exhausted by Sukhomlinov's persecution and fooled by his wife's simulated suicide attempt, agreed to grant her a divorce. Divorce proceedings were started. "Reliable" false witnesses appeared, and false evidence was given about Butovich's infidelity.
>
> Realizing he had been deceived by his wife, who had forced him to grant a divorce, and humiliated by the accusations, Butovich withdrew his agreement and brought a suit against the false evidence.

Sukhomlinov arrived in Petersburg weighed down by this ugly business, which immediately put him into an ambiguous, false, and distressing situation. As you can see, Sukhomlinov was in no frame of mind to concern himself with the defense of Russia. First he had to settle the matter of his future wife's divorce, which, thanks to Butovich's persistence, took a more and more threatening turn for Sukhomlinov and Catherine Victorovna. Only the royal will could bring about an outcome favorable to Sukhomlinov, and the royal will could be earned only if the monarch found him pleasant and useful. Therefore Sukhomlinov devoted all his efforts to gaining the Tsar's favor.

The Minister of War at the time was Alexander Fedorovich Rediger, an infantry general who had assumed the post in July 1905. He was honest, respectful, conscientious, and businesslike, but had a serious manner, a prosaic way of expressing himself, and an ugly face that was totally devoid of breeding. The Tsar, disliking his long, detailed reports, found him irksome but did not know how to get rid of him.

Rumors about Rediger's retirement had surfaced as early as 1908, coinciding with Sukhomlinov's arrival in Petersburg. A lively, superficial, playful mind, witty speech, felicitous, apt remarks, good manners, a pleasant readiness to fulfill His Majesty's every request, and an ability to predict His Majesty's needs—all these attributes made Sukhomlinov an interesting and clever companion for the Tsar. The new Chief of the General Staff was a complete contrast to Gen-

---

*A special tribunal set up on March 4 (17), 1917, after the February Revolution, to interrogate and try former ministers and officials of the tsarist government (trans.).

eral Rediger. The replacement had been found. And so, on March 11 (24), 1909, Catherine Victorovna's future husband assumed the post of Minister of War.

*   *   *

My life as a member of the State Duma was rather pathetic. All Russia had its eyes on the Duma, but serving as a deputy was like being buried in the remotest depths of the provinces. In what sense? Because we were so busy that we were completely cut off from the brilliant life of the capital. There was simply no time. For example, in ten years I went to the opera only three times and never went to the ballet at all, not even to see the famous *Swan Lake.* The same with the theater. The only recreation I allowed myself was an occasional film or a half-hour at the skating rink at Marsov Field. On weekdays, when the rink was empty, I would skate for half an hour to limber up my frail body, which was completely stiff from constant sitting.

On one of these weekdays I saw a beautiful lady skating, surrounded by elegant young officers. She recognized me and smiled graciously. It was the first time that she had ever smiled at me! Naturally I skated closer. She gave me her hand and we skated around the rink together, as was customary. I said, "Do you remember the Christmas party for the children?"

"Of course. How things have changed. And how is your nephew?"

"He lives here and is attending the Academy of Arts. He's a prize-winning sculptor now."

"He was always a clever boy. It was all so long ago and so nice."

We completed our circuit around the skating rink, and realizing that it was enough, I gave her over to her husband's young adjutants. But that's not all.

Zazor

LET US RETURN to the time when the remorseless Azor, as though a character in Ovid's *Metamorphoses*, changed into a horrible monster simply by adding *z* to his name. Thus was born "Zazor."*

Since Vladimir Nicholaevich Butovich had categorically refused to grant his wife a divorce, the newly named Minister of War and Catherine Victorovna decided to resort to means that were absolutely improper and even shameful. Everyone knows that there is, strictly speaking, only one official reason for divorce in church law—marital infidelity. In a gentlemanly divorce, the husband usually takes the blame on himself, even when the wife is guilty. It is not as disgraceful for a man to admit infidelity. Anything can happen in life! But, of course, it would be a stigma for a woman. At any rate, that's how it used to be.

However, since Vladimir Nicholaevich, having endured the threats of a highly placed statesman and the deceptions of his wife, did not wish to take a nonexistent blame on himself, Catherine Victorovna accused him of infidelity. With whom? After all, one must indicate the object of the infidelity, if I may use that expression. This the Sukhomlinovs did. The Butoviches' son had a French governess. After living for a while in the Butovich house, she had returned to her native country. The Sukhomlinovs decided to blame this young girl. Who in Paris would ever check?

Thanks to the testimony of false witnesses, the Butoviches were divorced. After some time had passed, Catherine Victorovna married Vladimir Alexandrovich Sukhomlinov, becoming the wife of the Minister of War of a great power. At this point the scandal was revealed.

* * *

The Western papers observed Russia closely, giving special attention to such personages as the Minister of War. Suddenly an article appeared in the Western newspapers about a French girl named so-

---

*The name Zazor comes from the Russian root of the adjective *zazornyi*, "dishonorable, shameful." The change in the dog's name reflects the metamorphosis Sukhomlinov himself underwent (trans.).

and-so accused of adultery with a certain Vladimir Nicholaevich Butovich. One can well imagine the embarrassment and bewilderment of this young girl, whom a foreign Minister of War had shamed in front of the whole world! Defending her honor, she demanded nothing less than a medical statement, in which doctors certified that Mademoiselle so-and-so could not have committed adultery because she was a virgin. The young Parisian girl then submitted a request asking her government to take steps to restore her honor. The French government ordered its embassy in Russia to do everything necessary in this vein. The ambassador went to S. D. Sazonov, the Russian Minister of Internal Affairs, who discussed the matter with I. G. Shcheglovitov, the Minister of Justice. Within a reasonable space of time, the latter was supposed to start court proceedings against Sukhomlinov.

The State Duma was disturbed by all this, but for the time being we held back from making any public statements. However, something happened that caused the cup of patience to overflow. All the compromising documents in the court's file on V. A. Sukhomlinov were stolen from the offices of the Minister of Justice. Everyone knew who was behind the theft.

*   *   *

The Duma was so shaken that it didn't just speak from the rostrum, it roared. This is what Vasilii Alexevich Maklakov, one of the leaders of the Cadets, said about the incident on May 2 (15), 1912, at the 122nd session of the Third State Duma, during the discussion of the budget commission's report on the expense estimates for the Ministry of Justice:

> We all know about a certain well-publicized divorce and the untruth that was perpetrated during the divorce proceedings. But none of this is shocking. After all, even the priests moan that the divorce process is imperfect, and they themselves admit that it cannot take place without deception, falsehood, and forgery. And if the falsehoods sometimes go beyond what is decent, that is well within the normal order in such matters, and thus that too is hardly shocking.
>
> We also know that when the consistory was gathering evidence, two officials of the Ministry of the Interior turned up: Colonel N. N. Kuliabko, chief of the Kiev Corps of Gendarmes, and D. G. Bogrov, the agent of the Kiev Okhrana who assassinated Stolypin. We know that they were the ones who maneuvered Butovich into a position where it was possible to establish his "blame." Once again, since we are accustomed to the tactics employed by the Okhrana, we are not at all shocked.
>
> But then, when we learned that the person who had been slandered in this proceeding, the woman whose name had been disgraced, had signed a complaint against the Minister of War, accusing him of inventing this

lie and of giving false testimony in the divorce proceedings, what did the Ministry of Justice do? . . .

When the plaintiff, hoping for justice, seeking and demanding justice, gave the procurator a document attesting that certain high-ranking persons had lied, what happened to that document? The Ministry of Justice destroyed the file, and the compromising documents disappeared. We know that an attempt was made to blame foreign institutions, maintaining that the documents had been sent abroad and never returned. . . .

. . . But that is not true! There are records proving that the documents were never sent abroad. And now let the Ministry say what it did with them.

But the Ministry did not say, although its representative, I. G. Shcheglovitov, who spoke immediately after Maklakov, said much in his own defense and still could not clear himself. He concluded his speech with an original if ambiguous phrase, "I go my own way, and let people say what they wish."

Our faction, the Russian Nationalists, was especially indignant at the course of this case. We felt that such scandals did great harm to the Russian nation. But who was to speak for us? My comrades could think of no one better than me, unfortunate soul! In vain I tried to show that it would be extremely awkward for me, since I knew Catherine Victorovna personally and we had lived in the same house. My comrades answered, "It is incumbent upon you to speak precisely because you know her so well."

And so I spoke, and when I did, I saw the rostrum of the State Duma as my Golgotha. That day, May 4 (17), 1912, the Duma was still discussing the budget of the Ministry of Justice. Since V. A. Maklakov had given a long speech on this issue at the previous sitting, I had to polemicize with him, criticizing the dangerous political attacks of the Cadet leader, who was trying to introduce the poison of doubt into the thinking of the government and the parties that supported it. I put off the unpleasant matter of Catherine Victorovna till the end, but the hour finally struck, and I had to do my duty. I said,

There is one issue remaining. It stands by itself. All the other speakers have touched upon it, but I would have spoken about it even if they had not. I am referring to the sensational Sukhomlinov-Butovich divorce case. Gentlemen, I assure you that we are not hostile to the government. On the contrary we support it, as far as our consciences permit.

But it must be said here and now that there are some things to which we will never acquiesce. One of those things pertains to the matter of the lost documents—and I hasten to add that in my opinion the Minister of Justice is not involved. I am referring to the most shocking aspect of the case. In itself, the fact that the documents were stolen is not really shocking; what is, is the fact that it was in someone's interest to steal the documents, and that this someone—or so rumor has it—is of such high station that he could only be a Russian aristocrat.

As far as I am concerned, that is the shocking aspect of the case. And even more shocking is the likelihood that the rumors may be unfounded; it may well be that this man, this Russian minister, this Minister of War—and I hope so with all my heart—it may be that he is not involved in any way. And yet, and this is what is so shocking, the finger of suspicion does not point at him without a reason, and that reason, as we all know, finds its basis in a certain unwarranted, unseemly piece of business that has already been perpetrated and thus can no longer be set right.

Amidst prolonged applause from the right, I concluded my speech, turning to the Minister of Justice, who was sitting only two steps away from me.

At the end of the sitting he approached me and said, "I understood perfectly what you were saying." He said nothing else, but simply squeezed my hand. This meant that Minister Shcheglovitov also felt that the act in question had been improper.

*　*　*

What was the outcome of all this? First of all, two ministers of the same government had contradicted each other. But there was something else. After all, everyone knew what the problem was. If there had been any normal degree of law and order, the Minister of Justice would have made the Minister of War answer for the theft of the important documents, but he could not do so, and this meant that the theft went unpunished.

This was the beginning of the great anarchy which preceded the fall of the empire. When Rasputin was killed, then not only theft but also murder went unpunished. That was the end. Authority had ceased to exist. That is why the prophetic words that were uttered at the time were so portentous: The shot fired at Rasputin killed tsarist Russia.

The Miasoedov Group

WHEN SUKHOMLINOV, the newly appointed Chief of the General Staff, came to St. Petersburg, he was accompanied by the cabal of spies, headed by Altschiller, that had surrounded him in Kiev. My information about this comes from Anatolii Ivanovich Savenko, member of the Kiev Duma, journalist at the *Kievlianin*, and member of the State Duma, who discussed it at length with the Kiev police. There was also information from sources unrelated to Savenko.

Alexander Ivanovich Guchkov had formed close ties with many of the young officers in Petersburg, and they told him about the Russian army's problems. From them Guchkov received precise information about the espionage ring surrounding Sukhomlinov. This is upheld by V. A. Apushkin, the ill-starred general's biographer, who relates some interesting details about Altschiller.

Upon his arrival in Petersburg, Altschiller opened an office for the nonexistent "Southern Russian Machine-building Plant." No financial transactions were conducted there, no bookkeeping was done, the firm had no customers, and only suspicious-looking personages visited the office. There was letter paper of the best quality with the watermark of the Austrian government. Sukhomlinov used some of the firm's stationery to make rough drafts of the papers pertaining to the divorce. And there was a portrait of Sukhomlinov, with a friendly inscription, on the desk in Altschiller's study.

Altschiller offered Nicholas Mikhailovich Goshkevich, Catherine Victorovna's cousin, the position of head of a department in his office. Until Catherine Victorovna's arrival in Petersburg, Goshkevich had occupied a minor post in the Ministry of Commerce and Industry. At first he took the husband's side during the Butoviches' marital conflict and ran various errands for him, but he changed sides after talking with his cousin. His wife even testified against Butovich during the divorce proceedings. Taking advantage of his close ties with the Minister of War, Goshkevich offered the V. A. Berezovskii firm, a military supplier, a contract to deliver rifles for the Poteshny Regiment in Petersburg, promising to arrange the purchase through Sukhomlinov and the Ministry of War.

Through Altschiller, Catherine Victorovna's cousin met a certain

Vasilii Dumbadze, who claimed to be the grandson of the famous governor of the city of Yalta. Introducing himself as a passionate admirer of the Minister of War, Dumbadze offered to write his biography. Through Goshkevich, the flattered Sukhomlinov gave his aspiring biographer a listing of all the measures the Ministry of War had taken from 1909 to March 1914, including secret information about its war plans.

Having won the confidence of the naive and light-minded Minister of War, Dumbadze told him about a scheme he had in mind. Making his way to Germany, Dumbadze would pretend to be an enemy of Russia who wanted to free the Caucasus from Russian rule. In this way he would find out all about the German government's plans to foment disturbances on the fringes of the Russian Empire. Sukhomlinov told the Tsar about Dumbadze's scheme and obtained his permission for the spy to go to Germany.

Although the counterespionage department of the General Staff had grounds for questioning Dumbadze's identity, and despite a warning from General M. A. Beliaev, the Chief of the General Staff, Sukhomlinov permitted Dumbadze to leave. He returned to Petrograd on June 12 (25), 1915, the day Sukhomlinov resigned as Minister of War, bringing a substantial amount of money and an account of his activities. When a special committee of General Staff officers examined this account, they labeled it fictitious and pronounced its author a German spy. Dumbadze and his accomplices, Goshkevich and his "dear friend Baller," as well as a Captain Ivanov of the artillery, were accused of evincing a willingness to carry out secret commissions, under Sukhomlinov's patronage, and were convicted of treason.

* * *

Meanwhile, what about agent Altschiller, the patron of this gang of spies? According to V. A. Apushkin's book, V. A. Berezovskii, the publisher and proprietor of a large military-book depot, once telephoned the office of the Minister of War and asked for Sukhomlinov. After a short pause, someone on the other end said, "Here I am." Recognizing Altschiller's voice, Berezovskii hung up. Thus, in the role of a "close friend," Altschiller would interfere in attempts to deal with the Minister of War by telephone. Also, he was the one who gave Sukhomlinov the idea of changing the route of a strategic railroad that was supposed to run in a direct line from Petersburg to Constantinople. On the insistence of the Minister of War, the route was changed so that it passed across land belonging to Count Pototskii, a member of the Austrian Reichstag. This change proved very helpful to the Austrians, enabling them to obtain information about the strategic railroad, and furthermore, an enormous sum of money went into the count's pocket for the right of way across his land.

All this happened at the same time that counterespionage agents in Kiev, having intercepted information sent to Vienna by Austrian agents in Petersburg, notified the government that Altschiller was the head espionage agent. The Austrian spies were extremely well-informed about everything that went on in the Ministry of War, including the Minister's talks with the Tsar.

In 1913, Altschiller suddenly began to liquidate his assets in Russia, and in March of 1914 he went abroad.

* * *

In 1909, the Minister of War met a man who would play a fatal role in his life—Colonel Serge Nicholaevich Miasoedov, a German spy. This was the man to whose health Kaiser Wilhelm II raised his glass at a dinner on his estate in 1905. At that time Miasoedov was commander of the Verzhbolovskii border detachment of the Warsaw railroad police department.

Suspected of doing espionage work for Germany, with whose rulers he was closely connected, Miasoedov was transferred to a province deep in the Russian interior, but he soon left his post there. With Samuel and David Friedberg, who were tried later for treason, Miasoedov founded the Southwestern Steamship Line, which transported passengers and cargo to Hamburg, Germany, and to America. Since the firm chaired by Miasoedov was engaged in "vital" activities, it was kept under special surveillance by the Ministry of Internal Affairs.

Miasoedov lived in grand style, but since he no longer had any connections in police or military circles, he had no way of obtaining information for his superiors. To make up for this deficiency, he was introduced, at a friend's salon, to Sukhomlinov, who was asked to find him a suitable position.

The Minister of War never denied anything to a flatterer, but no matter how much he wanted to take the spy into his service, he found it difficult to do so. The Okhrana gave Sukhomlinov an official report indicating that Miasoedov was suspected of engaging in espionage. When the Minister of War ignored the report, A. A. Makarov, Deputy Minister of Internal Affairs and chief of the Okhrana, warned him twice about the danger of developing close relations with someone whose past was so shady.

But as we have already seen, Sukhomlinov was not the type of man who could be dissuaded from doing what he wanted or from having things his own way.

Having learned from personal experience that obsequiousness and

218 THE YEARS

flattery open any door, he resorted to those means in this instance also. In order to undercut all the opposition at one fell swoop, he went straight to the Tsar and asked permission to take Miasoedov into his service, and, of course, his request was immediately granted.

The spy, who now became quite friendly with Sukhomlinov, was reappointed to the Corps of Gendarmes attached to the War Ministry. Since the Chief of the General Staff still had his doubts about Miasoedov, and Sukhomlinov wanted to allay his suspicions, he entrusted his new friend with the responsibility of delivering to the General Staff some extremely important secret military reports on the Entente with France.

Miasoedov's wife became friendly with Catherine Victorovna. The two couples would travel abroad together and stay in Karlsbad, Germany. The Sukhomlinovs greeted the New Year of 1911 at a party at the Miasoedovs' apartment with many other guests. One of the guests commented on the fact that during dinner the host continuously changed the topic of conversation with the Minister to military matters. Colonel Bulatsel, Sukhomlinov's adjutant, who also had been asked to the dinner, turned down the invitation and notified Catherine Victorovna that he would have nothing to do with such people.

Many of Miasoedov's acquaintances shared the colonel's feelings toward Miasoedov. More than once the Minister was warned about his new friend's suspicious actions, but in vain, even after the start of A. I. Guchkov's campaign against Miasoedov both in print and in the State Duma. Sukhomlinov's stubbornness and his disregard of both public opinion and the demands of highly placed officials can be explained only by the fact that he was unswervingly convinced that he had the support and favor of the Tsar. In this he was not mistaken.

It was also said that the Empress Alexandra Fedorovna liked the Minister of War because of his ability to amuse the incurably ill heir to the throne with various children's games.

Thus, in spite of the shocking things going on at the Ministry of War, and in spite of the extremely bad relations between Sukhomlinov and two of our Prime Ministers—P. A. Stolypin and his successor, V. N. Kokovtsov—Sukhomlinov felt secure in the post of Minister of War.

As Vladimir Nicholaevich Kokovtsov relates,* the fatally wounded Stolypin called him to his bedside and ordered him to inform the Sovereign of the necessity of replacing Sukhomlinov, "in view of the muddle in his ministry." Stolypin said, "Our defense is in the hands of a man who is unsuitable, unreliable, and unable to gain anyone's

*V. N. Kokovstov, *Out of My Past: The Memoirs of Count Kokovtsov* (Stanford, Calif., 1935) (trans.).

respect." Also in Kiev, the Chairman of the State Duma, M. V. Rodzianko, told Sukhomlinov to his face that he considered him harmful to Russia in the post of Minister of War.

This occurred at the very beginning of September 1911. Three months later, on December 6 (19), by royal decree, Adjutant General and Cavalry General Vladimir Alexandrovich Sukhomlinov was appointed to the State Council.

Here is how A. I. Guchkov explains the surprising appointment of Catherine Victorovna's husband to the post:

> Despite sensational scandals and compromising revelations, Sukhomlinov was the most influential member of the cabinet. This is because he knew how to exploit the Sovereign's weaknesses, using his reports to alternately worry and gladden him, catering to all his whims, and gratifying him as he had never been gratified before. He devoted all his talents to winning the monarch's favor, and he succeeded completely.

In connection with Sukhomlinov it is necessary to say a few words about his chief adversary, Alexander Ivanovich Guchkov, a very famous figure. He was born in Moscow in 1862 to a distinguished family of Old Believer merchants. His grandfather, Fedor Alexevich, a peasant by birth, founded a cloth factory in Moscow in 1789, and by 1853 it had become a large plant employing 1,850 workers. His father and uncle, Ivan and Efim Fedorovich, were members and founders of a commercial bank in Moscow. Alexander Guchkov's older brother, Constantine, headed E. F. Guchkov and Sons, the family firm, founded in 1859, and was on the board of directors of two Moscow banks.

Alexander Guchkov received a very good education, spoke excellent French, and had elegant manners, learned from his mother, who was French by birth. He became famous at an early age, during the Boer War. A significant part of Russian society at the time condemned the English for this war and sided with the Boers. Alexander Ivanovich, by nature a lover of freedom and adventure, went to South Africa as a volunteer, joined the Boer army, and after receiving a serious leg wound was left permanently lame. Ever since then he had been quite interested in military matters, and especially in the Russian army, although he was neither a soldier nor an officer.

Guchkov entered the political arena in 1905, when he asked the Tsar to make peace and found the zemstvo council. Then he very emphatically defended the honor of our army against the abuse of the many critics who had no understanding of military affairs. Guchkov, who had worked in the Red Cross during the Russo-Japanese War, maintained that even if some army commanders were guilty, the army itself was not, and on the contrary deserved gratitude and praise, since it had fought so gallantly in the Far East under terribly adverse conditions.

On November 10 (23), 1905, Guchkov and two other Menshevik leaders, P. E. Geiden and D. N. Shipov, published a proclamation announcing the founding of the Octobrist party, the "Union of October Seventeenth." In May of 1907 he was elected a member of the State Council as a representative of business and industry, but in October he resigned from this high calling and was elected to the Third State Duma.

On March 6 (19), 1910, when Nicholas Alexevich Khomiakov resigned from the Chairmanship of the Third Duma, Guchkov was elected to the post by a vote of 201 to 137. His interest in the army did not flag even during his tenure in the Duma. On March 15 (28), 1911, he resigned from the Chairmanship in protest against Stolypin's law on the zemstvos in the western provinces.

After Russia's military defeat in 1915, Guchkov concentrated on improving the fighting efficiency of our army. Elected to the State Council again, he became a member of a special conference on defense, convened on August 10 (23), 1915, on the initiative of the State Duma and the War Industry Committee, and attended by representatives of legislative institutions and social-welfare organizations. As a member of the Progressive Bloc, Guchkov at the same time chaired the Central War Industry Committee, which regulated industrial activities in accordance with military needs.

Finally, after the February Revolution broke out, Guchkov and I, on his initiative, went to Pskov on March 2 (15), 1917, to persuade Tsar Nicholas II to abdicate, as I describe in detail in my book *Dni* ("Days") and in the film *Pered sudom istorii* ("Before the Court of History").

During the first Provisional Government, which lasted until May 2 (15), 1917, Guchkov served as Minister of War and Minister of the Navy. In 1918 he emigrated to Berlin, where he spoke out vigorously against the Soviet regime, which he could not accept. Alexander Ivanovich Guchkov died in exile in 1936 at the age of seventy-four.

This was the man who intrepidly spoke out against the then-powerful Sukhomlinov.

*   *   *

When the rumors about spies penetrating the War Ministry began to be substantiated, Guchkov bluntly and straightforwardly announced this fact to the commission on national defense, naming Colonel Miasoedov as the head of the gang of spies and stating that his close relationship with the Minister of War was totally unacceptable and a threat to the empire. The Octobrist leader's speech made a great impression on everyone, as did B. A. Suvorin's assertion, in an article on intelligence and counterintelligence in the *Vechernoe vremia* ("Evening Times"), that our military secrets were easily obtained abroad. Around the same time Guchkov published a speech in the newspaper *Novoe vremia* in which he confirmed Suvorin's article and named the spies who were sheltered and protected in the War Ministry.

No one had any doubts about why Miasoedov needed Sukhomlinov, but it was natural to wonder what need the Minister of War had for a man who was making him the object of so much unpleasantness and suspicion. The fact of the matter was that when Sukhomlinov became Minister of War, he had decided to create a special unit within the military political-investigation department to investigate the political loyalty of the army, especially of the officers. His purpose in doing this was to curry favor with the Sovereign by cunningly demonstrating his loyalty to the throne and his zeal in the battle against the revolution, and at the same time to make his own position even more secure in the face of his many powerful enemies.

Sukhomlinov's idea was to appoint one particularly trustworthy staff officer, who would report only to the Minister of War, to command this Okhrana, constituted as an independent gendarme corps with officers assigned to the headquarters of every military district, and officially charged with counterespionage duties—that is, fighting foreign spies. Sukhomlinov's expanded system of political surveillance in the army was consolidated in special memorandum no. 982 of the Minister of War, issued on March 24 (April 6), 1910, and sent to the headquarters of every military district.

It goes without saying that Miasoedov was the "particularly trustworthy staff officer from the War Ministry" through whose hands passed everything pertaining to the new unit. That was why Sukhomlinov needed him. A spy had become the head of an organization that was supposed to fight spies!

After making his statement in print, Guchkov turned his attention to Prince P. Shakhovskii, chairman of the Commission on National Defense, and warned him that he intended to begin an inquiry about the Minister of War at the commission's next meeting. Prince Shakhovskii was able to persuade Sukhomlinov to appear personally before the commission to provide the necessary explanation. The meeting took place on April 19 (May 2), 1912. Guchkov elaborated on the accusations, demonstrating that our counterespionage system was in unreliable hands and that many of our military secrets had been obtained by the German and Austrian General Staffs. He concluded his speech with a severe denunciation of Sukhomlinov's system of political investigation.

Later Guchkov said,

After my presentation, the minister's dismay knew no bounds. A sort of pitiful babbling followed.

First he attempted to exonerate himself by claiming that there was no such memorandum.

At this I handed him a copy of it. Sukhomlinov explained, "But this is no longer applicable; it has expired."

It was reasonably pointed out to him that since the memorandum had not been superseded, it followed that it was still being applied in situations in which questions pertaining to the honor and careers of our officers were being decided. The Minister of War concluded his explanation with a promise to revoke the memorandum."

Guchkov continues,

That same day, I was visited by two officers acting as Colonel Miasoedov's seconds. They demanded that I repudiate the accusations I had made against Miasoedov in my article in *Novoe vremia*. When I refused, stating that I would not repudiate something that I had every reason to believe true, they challenged me to a duel. I replied that I was free to refuse, because as far as I was concerned, Miasoedov was a man without honor, but since the Minister of War thought it possible to allow him to wear the shoulder boards of a Russian colonel, I was obliged to grant him the right to obtain satisfaction.

The duel took place on April 22 (May 5), 1912. Guchkov was wounded in the hand. When he appeared at the Tauride Palace with a bandaged hand, the State Duma gave him a standing ovation, with both the right and the left participating. Thus, the State Duma gave a standing ovation to the man who had denounced Colonel Miasoedov, a close friend of the Minister of War, as a spy. What followed? Did the Minister of War resign? Was he removed? Were charges brought against him? No. The Minister of War remained peacefully in his post, as though nothing had happened.

What was the fate of Miasoedov after he wounded Guchkov in the duel? In the end, the Minister of War was forced to part with his beloved friend. A. A. Makarov, Minister of Internal Affairs, sent him an official letter informing him that when Miasoedov entered the service of the War Ministry he had not broken off his relations with a certain Dentser, a secret agent of the German General Staff. Sukhomlinov was forced to ask for Miasoedov's resignation, but he retained his good feelings for him and continued to serve as his patron whenever possible.

When the war began, Sukhomlinov officially announced that he saw no reason to prevent Miasoedov from serving in the army. Miasoedov did in fact enter the army, and there he found his dishonorable end. Grand Duke Nicholas Nicholaevich, Supreme Commander of the army, ordered Miasoedov arrested and brought to trial. A military court attached to the Warsaw fortress found him guilty of espionage in time of war, and on March 18 (31), 1915, sentenced him to death by hanging. The sentence was executed.

When Sukhomlinov learned of Miasoedov's arrest for espionage, he wrote in his diary, "God punished this scoundrel for blackmail and various other terrible crimes which he attempted to perpetrate against me because I did not support him."

Shells

AT THIS POINT I have to say a few words about Grand Duke Nicholas Nicholaevich, grandson of Emperor Nicholas I. His association with Sukhomlinov began before the latter became minister. At the time Grand Duke Nicholas Nicholaevich was chairman of the Council on National Defense. Knowing the Grand Duke's difficult character, quick temper, and rudeness, Sukhomlinov foresaw that it would be difficult to maneuver between him and the Sovereign if he ever became Minister of War.

Furthermore, the Grand Duke was on good personal terms with the Chief of the General Staff, General F. F. Palitsyn, who was not subordinate to the Minister of War, and had an equal right to report to the monarch personally on matters pertaining to national defense. In a word, there was a triumvirate running the War Ministry, and this was one of the things that A. I. Guchkov so severely criticized, because he saw the triumvirate as the main reason for the army's disorganization. Undoubtedly he could not foresee that a general would soon appear for whom even the Grand Duke would not be a hindrance, and who would quickly return sole power in the ministry to the Minister of War. And it is even more unlikely that Guchkov could have foreseen that the sole power in the ministry would fall into the hands of a man who would bring the inventory of army supplies into total disarray. That is exactly what happened when war broke out.

Now when Sukhomlinov set his sights on the post of minister, he was not pleased to have General Palitsyn, a close friend of the Grand Duke, as a spy and critic. Taking advantage of his good relations with the Sovereign, Sukhomlinov put all his efforts toward destroying the existence of the triumvirate running the War Ministry. He found this very easy, since his wishes coincided with those of the Tsar, who had no special liking for Grand Duke Nicholas Nicholaevich. On July 16 (August 8), 1908, the Sovereign dismissed him from his position as chairman of the Council on National Defense. In November, he forced General Palitsyn to resign and appointed Sukhomlinov Chief of the General Staff. This was the last step before attaining the post of Minister of War. As Count Witte recalled, "Sukhomlinov destroyed the defense committee and pushed aside the Grand Duke, so that in the course of a year and a half he lost all his influence with the Sovereign." One can imagine Nicholas Nicholaevich's feelings toward Sukhomlinov!

The war began. Grand Duke Nicholas Nicholaevich was appointed Supreme Commander of the army, while Sukhomlinov remained as Minister of War. How was this possible? How could the country's two most responsible posts during time of war be in the hands of men who had long been openly hostile toward one another? But that was how it was.

On July 19 (August 1), 1914, the day the war began, the Minister of War wrote in his diary: "The Sovereign told me that he is contemplating appointing me Supreme Commander."

Maurice Paléologue, the French ambassador, wrote on the topic, "For a long time Sukhomlinov had been seeking the high post of Supreme Commander, and he was furious when it went to the Grand Duke. Unfortunately, he is the type of man who will seek revenge."*

It is well known that the army ran low on shells soon after the war began. I was at the front at the time, and the shortage of shells made a painful impression upon me. The Germans rained fire on our positions, while we remained silent. For example, the unit to which I was assigned had orders not to fire more than seven shells per gun. Naturally this infuriated the ranks. The soldiers became suspicious. Their frame of mind and fighting spirit drooped. And thus the seeds of revolution germinated. From the fronts the Minister of War received the demand "Shells, shells, shells!" It was a wail of despair. Everyone was preoccupied with thoughts of shells.

The director of munitions on the southwestern front sent the following telegram to headquarters on August 28 (September 10), 1914: "Fierce battle rages along entire front. Expenditure of shells extremely high. Situation desperate. Help us!"

Count Illarion Ivanovich Vorontsov-Dashkov, vicegerent of the Caucasus, informed headquarters on October 25 (November 7), 1914: "The lack of cartridges will put the army into a hopeless situation." Adjutant-General N. V. Ruzskii, commander of the northwestern front, reported on November 25 (December 8), 1914: "The command does not have any supplies left."

General N. N. Iakyshkevich, who referred to the question of cartridges and guns as "bloody," wrote to Sukhomlinov from the headquarters of the Supreme Commander: "Our hair stands on end at the thought that because of lack of cartridges and rifles we will be forced to surrender to Wilhelm. . . . The Germans dropped three thousand

---

*Maurice Paléologue, *An Ambassador's Memoirs*, trans. F. A. Holt, 3 vols. (New York: Doran, 1925) (trans.).

heavy shells on a single sector of our regiment. . . . Everything was demolished. We fired barely one hundred shells. . . . The Twelfth Division of the Seventh Corps has twelve thousand bayonets and no rifles."

The office of the Minister of War was filled with similar dispatches. How did he react to them? Here are several selections from his diary from those terrible days which shook the entire country.

After the catastrophe at Soldau,* followed by the hurried retreat of General P. K. Rennenkampf's First Army from East Prussia, Sukhomlinov wrote on September 6 (19), 1914: "It would be interesting to know whether Rennenkampf still has the medal that Prince Beloselskii-Belozerskii gave him."

A week later he writes: "A. I. Guchkov is spreading rumors about the shortage of shells in the army. It is poor judgment to give such information to our enemies."

Another week later, after seeing the Tsar off on his trip to the front, Sukhomlinov writes: "A cool but nice day. . . . The Sovereign was in excellent spirits. It is pure rest for me. There is little to do."

The note for December 6 (19), 1914 is: "The enemy has taken the initiative, while in our army the complaints have begun: reinforcements arrive slowly, shortages of shells, boots, and so forth. The usual occurrences after losing a battle."

In March of the following year Sukhomlinov added several notes to his diary.

> A long line of scoundrels, including Polivanov, Guchkov, and K, are involved in rumor, slander, and intrigue in the heat of the war, when the country is in need of the cooperation of the people. . . . What is headquarters doing? It is forbidden to talk about military matters, to ensure that valuable information does not fall into the wrong hands. And suddenly a rumor that we do not have cartridges, shells, or rifles floats out of General Headquarters. Everyone is shouting about it; telegrams arrive from everywhere. . . . If it is true that we do not have enough shells, then we must retreat, not advance. . . . Headquarters complains about the lack of shells but decides to advance, and furthermore, across mountains!!

Even from these few selections one can understand why the outcry about shells was only a voice in the wilderness. Sukhomlinov rejoiced at the misfortunes of his personal enemy. He rejoiced, because the man had assumed the post that he himself aspired to, and that the Sovereign himself, so he claimed, had promised him!

On April 26 (May 9), 1915, when Supreme Commander-in-Chief Nicholas Nicholaevich sent still another personal telegram to

---

*The Battle of Tannenberg, August 26–30, 1914 (trans.).

Sukhomlinov, demanding that a supply of shells be sent to him immediately, Sukhomlinov wrote: "Grand Duke Serge Mikhailovich, the Inspector-General of the Artillery, has special powers in this matter. My interference would only make things worse." Thus the irresponsible minister hid behind two other irresponsible men, upon one of whom he was cruelly seeking venegeance. Not in vain did Maurice Paléologue call him a man who gets his revenge.

* * *

But why, after all, were there no shells? I received my first information about this from Alexander Ivanovich Guchkov. As I have already said, even before the war he was the chairman of a Duma committee on national defense. Since all military appropriations had to pass through the State Duma, as did any outlay, the committee discussed the most important and top-secret matters in detail. When the question of the number of shells to be issued per fieldpiece came up, the War Ministry requested five hundred. Guchkov was astonished. "In Western countries," he said, "the military ordinarily overstates its needs in the expectation that Parliament will reduce the amount. And you? Why are your estimates so low? After all, you know that we won't give less than you ask for; on the contrary, we will meet all your demands. Five hundred! What's five hundred shells! You should ask for at least a thousand." They agreed to request a thousand, and it was this amount, Guchkov later told me, that accounted for our early successes. But since the enemy had a substantial superiority in weapons, the shells did not last very long.

I learned more details about the reason for the inadequate supply of shells at the beginning of the war from Councillor of State Vladimir Petrovich Litvinov-Falinskii, director of the commerce department of the Ministry of Trade and Commerce. He had the special trust of Grand Duke Nicholas Nicholaevich. From the fall of 1915 I worked with Vladimir Petrovich on the special committee on defense. After a meeting one day he said, "I'd like to tell you something that I want you to remember."

We went to a cafe, where he told me the following story: "In February 1915 I received a telegram from Grand Duke Nicholas Nicholaevich requesting that I go see him immediately at headquarters, which was then located in Mogilev on the Dnepr River. I found the Grand Duke quite confused. He said to me, 'I am in a difficult situation. Look here.' The Supreme Commander-in-Chief opened an enormous ledger which covered the entire table, and continued, 'It says here that I'm supposed to receive so many shells this month and so many that month. The list covers the whole year. It looks good on paper, but in reality I'm not receiving any shells at all.

"'Quite frankly, I don't understand the calculations. I asked for an explanatory note, and got it, but it still doesn't make any sense. I understand only one thing: either they themselves don't know what's going on or they're lying and cheating us!

"'I trust you. Please, take all these papers, the ledgers, the explanations, and try to find out what's wrong.'

"I carried out his order and studied the information for an entire week. Then I again appeared before the Grand Duke and said, 'Your Highness, I am sorry to inform you that the shells will not arrive on time.'

"Then I explained the situation. At the very beginning of the war, Sukhomlinov had placed orders with American manufacturers to provide so many shells in so many months, exactly as noted in the records. But they could not fulfill their promises. Why? Because American and Russian shells are of different calibers, and in order for American plants to produce Russian shells, the dies would have to be changed. No matter how fast they worked, they could not possibly do this by the agreed-upon date, so the shells would not arrive at the scheduled time but much later."

Vladimir Petrovich told me all this that evening in the cafe. I will add that it was all true. After a great delay, American shells began to arrive in Vladivostok in such quantities that they blocked the entire Trans-Siberian Railroad.

A question arises: How could the Minister of War sign such an unfavorable contract? The weight of Sukhomlinov's thoughtlessness, if one may call it thoughtlessness, was made even more oppressive by the fact that he gave the Americans an enormous advance in gold when he signed the contract. As a result, since the advance covered all their expenses, the American manufacturers would only have broken the contract if we had begun urging them to speed up the order.

* * *

When I was preparing to leave the front to go to Petrograd for the opening of the Fourth State Duma on July 19 (August 1), 1915, I paid a farewell visit to General Abram Mikhailovich Dragomirov, who at the time was commanding a corps. In parting he said, "Goodbye. Whip them well, and send us shells."

That was the mood of the high command. Duma members wanted to reassure the troops, to tell them that they were not being betrayed, that the home front cared about them, that the State Duma would take care of their interests. When I left, a general's voice tormented me, saying, "Make sure there are no more Miasoedovs and Sukhomlinovs, only shells. We don't want to die with sticks in our hands."

At the front I saw it all, saw the unequal battle that weaponless

Russians were putting up against the Germans' hurricane fire. In Petrograd I did not consider myself merely the representative of one of the southern provinces. Like many others, I brought with me the sadness of unending roads of retreat and the army's simmering indignation against the home front. I considered myself the representative of an army that was dying dishonorably, in vain, and I heard the words "Send us shells!" ringing in my ears. The wound Sukhomlinov had inflicted upon the empire was fatal.

"How long, Catiline, will you abuse our patience?"* Thus Marcus Tullius Cicero began his accusatory speech against Lucius Sergius Catilina in the Roman Senate in the year 63 B.C., after the latter had organized a conspiracy to take power.

The cry of "how long?" was on everyone's soul. It was clear to everyone that things could not continue in the same way—clear to everyone except Sukhomlinov. He could not imagine that the power on which he depended could betray him. It was equally clear that the minister's activities would be subjected to merciless criticism at the Duma's opening session.

"What happened?" writes Sukhomlinov in his diary on June 7 (20), 1915. "I am told to follow the orders of the Duma, not of the Sovereign?"

Michael Vladimirovich Rodzianko, a man of destiny who was fated to destroy several ministers, went to see Sukhomlinov.

"The assembled Duma members curse you and accuse you of everything," said Rodzianko. "I again advise you to resign."

On June 8 (21), Sukhomlinov noted, "Guchkov is working around the clock and is carrying out his program persistently and underhandedly. Rodzianko is acting as his battering ram." After the Duma Chairman's visit, Sukhomlinov notes, "These representatives of the people evidently are under the influence of German provocateurs and wish to create chaos here."

However, Rodzianko had not yet exhausted his weapons. Obtaining an audience with the Sovereign, he so clearly described the situation created by Sukhomlinov that the Emperor agreed then and there to have Sukhomlinov resign. On June 12 (25), 1915, during a meeting of the Council of Ministers, a courier from headquarters gave Sukhomlinov the following handwritten letter from the Tsar:

> Vladimir Alexandrovich! After long contemplation I have come to the conclusion that the interests of Russia and the army require your immediate resignation. After a talk with Grand Duke Nicholas Nicholaevich, I am completely convinced of this. I am writing to you myself so that you will learn it from me first.

---

*Cicero, *In Catilinam*, 1, 1 (trans.).

It is difficult for me to tell you of my decision, since I saw you only yesterday. We have worked together for so many years and never had a disagreement. I sincerely thank you for your work and for the energy you have put to the use and organization of the Russian army. Impartial history will pass its sentence, which will be more lenient than the condemnations of your contemporaries. For the present time, Vernander will occupy your post. The Lord go with you. Respectfully yours, Nicholas.

On receiving the Tsar's letter, Sukhomlinov wrote,

Informed sources state that Grand Duke Nicholas Nicholaevich played the main role in my removal from office. Russia is greatly indebted to him: for October 17, for the leftist movement, for removing ministers from office at the most critical moment, and for all the losses of 1914 and 1915 which he blames on others. . . . Grand Duke Nicholas Nicholaevich has found a scapegoat in me.

* * *

At this point I will break off my discussion of Sukhomlinov. One may ask, Well, now, you said that the Duma finally did react to the minister's pernicious deeds or, more accurately, to his inaction, and finally, after great delay, irreparable delay, after millions of lives were sacrificed to his inaction, managed to topple him from his position. But there was a contemporary of Sukhomlinov's who was even more odious than he—Rasputin. Did no one ever speak about him in the Duma? Wasn't anything ever done about him?

People did speak about him in the lobbies, of course, and quite a lot was said, but it was too dangerous to speak about him from the rostrum, because that would have threatened the very existence of the Duma. Furthermore, one would need grounds for such a speech, not simply indignation. But one day, when there were grounds, there was an attack on Rasputin from the rostrum of the State Duma.

Its initiator was none other than Alexander Ivanovich Guchkov, and it happened to coincide with his attack on the Minister of War. And the Rasputin problem, like the Sukhomlinov problem, united all the factions in the Duma. By the way, Maurice Paléologue says that Sukhomlinov was on good terms with Rasputin and was considered one of his followers. It could not have been otherwise if Sukhomlinov really "never had a disagreement" with the Tsar.

* * *

A notice was given to the Chairman of the State Duma, with Guchkov as the first signatory, containing a letter from M. Novoselov, editor and publisher of the *Religiozno-Filosofskoi biblioteki* ("Religious-

Philosophical Library"). This notice had been published in issue no. 19 of the newspaper *Golos Moskvy* ("Voice of Moscow") on January 24 (February 6), 1912, and was reprinted in part the same day in issue no. 50 of the *Vechernoe vremia* ("Evening Times"). Both newspapers were confiscated by order of the Central Office of Press Affairs, and the editors were haled into court. It turned out that the editors of all the papers in Petersburg and Moscow, by royal command, were prohibited from printing anything about Gregory Rasputin. It is significant that Novoselov's letter had as its heading Cicero's dictum, "How long will you abuse our patience?" "These indignant words are involuntarily torn from my breast," the letter said, "by a sly conspirator against all things sacred, against the Church, an evil corruptor of people's souls and minds, Gregory Rasputin, who impudently uses the Church itself as a cover."

Further down in the letter the author expressed extreme indignation at the inaction and silence of the Holy Synod, which was well aware of the activities of this "bold fraud and corruptor." The author asked why the bishops remained silent when some of them openly called "this servant of lies" a "*khlyst*, erotomaniac, and charlatan."

The letter was appended to an application to A. A. Makarov, the Minister of Internal Affairs, for an inquiry into the unlawful confiscation of the newspapers that had published it. The letter was read in its entirety on January 25 (February 7), 1912, by the assistant secretary of the Duma, Michael Andreevich Isreitskii.

No one opposed an immediate inquiry, and two members spoke out in favor of an immediate inquiry—Guchkov and Vladimir Nicholaevich Lvov. The Duma applauded them loudly. Just as there are questions now which unite people of the most diverse political and religious convictions, so at that time there were issues so inarguable that they remained above mere political disagreement.

*   *   *

Guchkov said,

Russia is going through dark, difficult days. The public conscience is deeply aroused. Some sort of evil spirit from the Middle Ages has risen before us. Something is wrong in our country. Danger threatens our sacred things. And where are the protectors of these sacred things? . . . Why are the bishops' voices silent, why are the government authorities inactive? . . .

Duty demands that we raise the voice of our conscience so that it will allow public indignation, which is steadily growing, to be heard. . . . We have performed our duty today in requesting and supporting this inquiry.

V. N. Lvov asked,

What kind of strange personage is this Gregory Rasputin, that he is beyond the power of the press and is placed on a mysterious and inaccessible pedestal? It is to pull him down from his pedestal that we call for an inquiry. . . . In my opinion, silencing the press, which is our only means of uncovering the truth in this dark matter, is unworthy of a great country, and therefore I hope that you will agree to the necessity for haste and, indeed, for an official inquiry.

Both motions were approved unanimously.

*   *   *

I return to Sukhomlinov. At a closed session of the Duma in January 1915, six months before his dismissal, the Minister of War and his assistant, A. P. Vernander, gave a favorable account, quite contrary to the truth, about the army's supply of war matériel. This disturbed and angered the deputies, many of whom had served at the front, as I had, and knew the truth.

Everyone in Russia knew the horrifying truth about the lack of shells, cartridges, and rifles, from stories told by the wounded and letters written by soldiers. All Russia knew that our defeats at the front were mainly due to a lack of weapons, knew of the War Ministry's criminal negligence in the matter of national defense.

The political emotions of the masses were anxious and disturbed. Among those of low rank and of high, seeds of suspicion were sown; rumors spread of betrayal and treason and of the possibility of Sukhomlinov's appointment to an even higher post.

The speeches of the deputies from the front who assembled in the Tauride Palace, from the opening session on, were full of indignation at the inaction of those in power and especially of the Minister of War, inaction that was viewed as an insufferable state crime. The speeches were interrupted by cries of "Put him on trial! He has betrayed us all!"

The minister's mere resignation would no longer satisfy either the army or the country. Only a judicial investigation could define the thin line that separated the innocent from the guilty. Sukhomlinov's fate was decided. On July 23 (August 5), at an unscheduled closed session of the State Duma, the deputies, by a vote of 375 to 345, recommended that Sukhomlinov and all other officials guilty of negligence or treason be brought to trial. Then, on July 25 (August 7), a royal decree was issued establishing an imperial commission chaired by Nicholas Pavlovich Petrov, member of the State Council, "thoroughly to examine the circumstances of the recent and insufficient replenishment of war supplies."

The commission's findings were presented for discussion to the First Department of the State Council, which on March 10 (23) resolved to open a preliminary investigation into the minister's unlawful inaction, his exceeding of his authority, forgery, extortion, and treason. Finally, Sukhomlinov was arrested and imprisoned in the Trubetskii Bastion of the Peter and Paul Fortress. However, as Maurice Paléologue noted in his diary, "in spite of his scandalous misdeeds, Sukhomlinov in some secret manner has retained the trust of certain highly placed people."

* * *

On April 8 (21), 1917, during his interrogation by the Special Investigative Commission of the Provisional Government, Prince M. M. Andronikov, a swindler and one of the minister's former friends, told how Catherine Victorovna Sukhomlinov, in the spring of 1916, had entered into an intimate relationship with Rasputin in order to obtain an introduction to a woman named Vyrubov. The latter arranged a meeting between Mme. Sukhomlinov and the Empress during which Mme. Sukhomlinov gave the Empress a note with the heading "Black and White." In it she condemned the State Duma and practically the whole government. According to Andronikov, Catherine Victorovna gave Rasputin and Vyrubov large monetary gifts. Her gifts secured a position for her in Tsarskoe Selo and also the release of Sukhomlinov from prison.

When the commission's chairman asked how Mme. Sukhomlinov was able to rehabilitate herself and her husband so quickly, the Prince replied, "She argued that they were honest, decent people, and that all the others were good for nothing. . . . That was written in her 'Black and White' note."

As a result of the visit, Rasputin, who only a year before had vilified Sukhomlinov, underwent an astonishing metamorphosis. He was transformed from an enemy to Sukhomlinov's defender, to such an extent that the general was released from the fortress and the whole case against him was almost done away with. Andronikov's testimony is confirmed by Ivan Fedorovich Manasevich-Manuilov, secretary to the Chairman of the Council of Ministers. He related the argument between Andronikov and Sukhomlinov, which began when the former informed his friend of his wife's intimate relations with a certain Mantashev, a wealthy acquaintance. An argument ensued, and Andronikov retaliated by antagonizing Rasputin against Sukhomlinov, playing a role in his removal from his post. When Sukhomlinov was imprisoned, his wife began to visit Rasputin, who fell in love with her. Rasputin said to Manasevich-Manuilov, "Only two women on this earth have ever managed to steal my heart—Vyrubov and Sukhomlinov."

And once Sukhomlinov's relationship with Rasputin improved, the former Minister of War was released from prison.

How did this occur? After all, it is no small matter to release an important military criminal from prison during wartime. This caused an uproar in the Duma, and one may imagine the reaction of the army, which had endured the horrors of a disgraceful retreat because of the criminal minister. A. D. Protopopov, Minister of Internal Affairs, described how the release came about during his interrogation by the Special Investigative Commission. When the Tsar decided to release Sukhomlinov from prison, he summoned Protopopov.

Nicholas Constantinovich Muraviev, chairman of the commission, asked Protopopov if he remembered when this occurred.

The former minister replied, "During the visit of the commandant of the Peter and Paul Fortress, Nikitin."

"Did you come to meet with Sukhomlinov?"

"On the Tsar's orders. The Sovereign said that the Sukhomlinov case had been going on for a long time and asked if I really believed that he was a traitor. Perhaps he was simply thoughtless. I said, 'Yes, Sire, perhaps that's true. A person's soul is a mystery, but in this case there is a bad side—a matter of money—' 'Yes, there is. I feel sorry for the poor fellow. What would you think if his sentence was changed? Perhaps to house arrest.' 'Your Highness, I don't think that would be appropriate. The investigation can be speeded up, and he can be given more comfortable quarters, the right to go for walks in the fortress but not to leave it.' Then the Tsar said, 'Do you think that is possible?' 'At any rate, Your Highness, it will be kept quiet. You can improve his situation somewhat, and in the meantime there will be no scandal.' 'Well,' he says, 'go see Nikitin.' That was why I visited General Nikitin, but nothing came of it. Measures beyond my control were taken."

On November 11 (24), 1916, A. A. Makarov, the Minister of Justice, received a royal telegram from the newly appointed Chairman of the Council of Ministers, A. F. Trepov, about the termination of the Sukhomlinov case. Makarov said during his testimony, "Alexander Fedorovich asked me to come see him. I handed him the telegram and said, 'This is the type of royal decree I received for your debut.' We talked about the matter and decided that it could not be carried out, and that all possible measures should be taken to ensure that the Sukhomlinov case would not be terminated. We agreed to go to headquarters with a report, but first sent the Sovereign a telegram requesting that he not carry out the royal command before he received our report. Trepov and I gave our report to the Sovereign at General Headquarters on November 14 (27). . . . I did not receive a reply, and upon the Tsar's arrival here, I was removed from office." So ended Makarov's testimony.

In the meantime Sukhomlinov had long been walking the streets of the capital, giving rise to much indignation in the Duma. After his release the only step taken was to forbid his leaving Petersburg.

*   *   *

When the February Revolution broke out, on February 28 (March 13), 1917, I witnessed Sukhomlinov being brought to the crowded Catherine Hall of the Tauride Palace. His punishment began. Soldiers rushed at him and began to tear off his shoulder straps. Kerenskii hurried over, tore the old man from the soldiers' hands, and, shielding him with his body, led him to the Ministers' Pavilion. But as he was opening the door, several particularly violent soldiers rushed at them with bayonets. Then Kerenskii pulled himself up very straight and said with the authority for which he was known, "You will take him over my dead body."

The soldiers stepped back, and the former Minister of War was returned to the Trubetskii Bastion, to cell no. 55, which he had occupied before the revolution. Catherine Victorovna and Anna Alexandrovna Vyrubov were also being held in the bastion.

When the investigation ended in June, an accusation was made, and on August 10 (23) Sukhomlinov and his wife were brought before jurors in a special Senate court. The former Minister of War was charged with not doing what was necessary to increase the extremely low production of shells, powder, and explosives in government factories, thereby consciously aiding the enemy in his hostile actions against Russia; with failing to provide personal leadership to the main artillery department in undertaking measures to supply troops and fortresses with guns, artillery, reserves of ammunition, and other arms, thus lowering the fighting strength of our army; with passing confidential information to Miasoedov, whom he knew to be a German agent, information which for the security of Russia should have remained confidential; with passing similar information to Altschiller, whom he knew to be an Austrian agent; with playing a role, after Germany's declaration of war on Russia, in assigning Miasoedov to active service in the army, and enabling him to continue his treasonous acts, thus knowingly aiding Germany in its military actions against Russia; with knowingly and falsely stating in the press, in the name of the War Ministry, that Miasoedov did not have access to secret documents or receive any assignments related to military counterespionage, and deliberately and falsely informing the former Emperor of the same in a report.

Those were the main points of the accusation. His wife was charged with aiding him by introducing him, through friends, to Altschiller and Miasoedov.

Sukhomlinov was so hated by the soldiers that he was attacked not only in the Tauride Palace but also in court, where a crowd of soldiers demanded that he be handed over to them. "The court of our regiment will decide this case fast enough!" they shouted. The officers in charge had great difficulty persuading them not to overstep the law.

* * *

On September 14 (27), 1917, the trial ended with the jurors finding Sukhomlinov guilty on all counts of the indictment.

The court sentenced him to the highest punishment—life at hard labor and deprivation of all rights of property, rank, and honor. Catherine Victorovna was found innocent of any wrongdoing and immediately released from prison. Sukhomlinov again was brought to the Trubetskii Bastion.

G. E. Rein, a member of the State Duma, also served some time in the Peter and Paul Fortress, as did many other leading political figures. Rein was imprisoned at the same time as Sukhomlinov and later told me that an "angel" with a large basket fed all the prisoners. On being asked who the angel was, he answered, "Madame Sukhomlinov. First she would feed her husband, of course, and then the rest of us. Since she had also spent some time in the prison, she knew all the exits and entrances, and was able to get through all the locks and gates. A magnificent woman! I tell you, she's an angel!" This angel not only fed her husband but obtained his transfer to the Kresty Prison.

Sukhomlinov recalled, "I was taken out of a gloomy, damp, ramshackle bastion, and suddenly found myself in a light, dry, warm, newly constructed building, with central heating, a bath, hot water, and a kitchen."

There he met many other imperial ministers and officials, among them Purishkevich and members of the Provisional Government. Sukhomlinov was released on May 1 (14), 1918, by a decree of the Petersburg Soviet granting amnesty to those who had been arrested and sentenced for political reasons. However, he heard rumors that many imperial ministers had been taken from the Kresty Prison to Moscow and shot. Not trusting the Soviets, he hid for a time in Petrograd, not even appearing at his wife's apartment. Finally, on October 5 (18), 1918, he managed to cross the border to Finland, and then went to Germany. There Sukhomlinov wrote his memoirs,* which ended with the following words:

> I see a guarantee for Russia's future in the fact that she is ruled by a government that is self-sufficient, strong, and guided by great political idealism. . . . That my hopes are not quite utopian is proven by the fact

---

*Vladimir Sukhomlinov, *Erinnerungen* (Berlin: Hobbing, 1924) (trans.).

that certain of my esteemed former colleagues, such as Generals Brusilov, Baltiiskii, and Dobrovolskii, are wholeheartedly supporting the new government in Moscow. There is not the slightest doubt that they are doing this because they are convinced that Russia is on the right path to rebirth with the new regime.

* * *

And what happened to the "angel" of the Peter and Paul Fortress, Catherine Victorovna? She died at quite a young age, in Biarritz, France, where she had met her destiny—General Vladimir Alexandrovich Sukhomlinov. Fate spared Vasnetsov's child long years of wandering in emigration.*

---

*Shulgin was probably mistaken. According to Robert Massie in *Nicholas and Alexandra,* Mme. Sukhomlinov "returned to Russia to marry a young Georgian officer. They died together in the Bolshevik terror" (trans.).

Part IV

THE EVE OF DESTRUCTION

The Progressive Bloc

I HAD NO SOONER RETURNED from the front to Petrograd in the summer of 1915 than I visited Miliukov. He did not recognize me right away, because I was in my military uniform. Besides, to tell the truth, I had changed somewhat. War turns everything upside down. I learned that the Cadet party was not planning to change its program and, as before, still insisted that we fight the war to a victorious conclusion. "But," explained Miliukov, "we are no longer on the rise. Our losses have taken their toll. The underlying cause of our retreats has had a particularly detrimental effect. . . . And there is the greatest anger at our incompetent rulers."

"Do you think the situation is serious?"

"I do. First of all we must vent this anger. The people expect the Duma to expose the guilty parties. And if we do not use the State Duma as a safety valve, the anger will explode through other channels.

"I haven't spoken with everyone yet, but it is quite likely that we will all be of one mind in this matter. We who have been at the front are in no mood to appease the government. We have seen too many horrors. But that is one side. On the other side, we cannot allow morale to die. We have to find something positive, something to rekindle the hopes of the first days.

"Yes, in order to revive the dream, we have to guarantee that all the sacrifices that have been made already, and all the future ones, will not be in vain. There are two things that must be done."

"Go on."

"First of all, those who are considered guilty must resign, and be replaced by decent, competent, trustworthy people.

"You want a responsible ministry?"

"No. I'm reluctant to even use the term, and in any case we probably aren't ready for that yet. But something along those lines. The main thing is that Goremykin is totally incompetent. He was appointed a half-year before the war broke out and simply cannot continue as head of the government during wartime. His advanced age and his old-fashioned thinking make him unequal to the challenge. Why, the Western democracies have put the flower of their nations in their ministries in this war!"

"And the second thing?"

"This: To raise morale, we must give the people something to look forward to. I am trying to say that if we are victorious, people will dream of change, of course, different politics, freedom—"

"As a reward for their sacrifices?"

"Not as a reward but as an inevitable consequence of victory. If Russia wins, it will not be the government that is victorious but the entire nation. And if the nation knows how to win, then how can it be denied the right to breathe freely, think freely, govern freely? Therefore the government in turn must demonstrate that it is willing to sacrifice part of its power."

"How can it do that?"

"By taking certain steps. Of course, war is not the time for fundamental reforms, but something can be done."

*   *   *

This conversation was the prologue to what later came to be known as the Progressive Bloc. It actually came into being at meetings in the home of M. V. Rodzianko, where amid heated and serious arguments a new agreement was drawn up. In the end, some of the members of the State Duma "unanimously resolved to leave the Russian Nationalist faction and form a group founded simply on a program of national unity, presenting Count Vladimir Alexevich Bobrinskii as its head."

This declaration was signed by the journalist A. I. Savenko, Gentleman of His Majesty's Court D. N. Chikhachev, the engineer V. I Demchenko, and the landowners A. A. Kikh, K. E. Suvchinskii, myself, and several others. Representatives of three factions in the State Council later joined the new bloc. On August 14 (27) and 15 (28), 1915, representatives from the Duma and the Council met at the apartment of Baron Meller-Zakomelskii to draw up a program, which was possible only because the different factions yielded to each other's demands.

For example, although Miliukov wholeheartedly supported equal rights for the Jews, he softened his demands to a rather modest formulation that was acceptable to us of the right wing: "to embark upon a course of removing limitations on the rights of Jews."

As for the question of agrarian reform, Miliukov did not want to touch upon it at all. He maintained that if that question was brought up, peasants would come running from all parts of the front to claim their share of land. I was more to the left on this issue, since I considered it feasible to announce the allocation of land to our war heroes and to the families of soldiers killed in combat.

In a word, quite modest "reforms" were proposed in several spheres: rural zemstvos, village government, the granting of equal rights to peasants, a reexamination of the zemstvo situation, several civil laws, and so forth. Although both the government and the Tsar found the program on the whole to be acceptable, they regarded one point as totally unacceptable: the appointment of government officials with the Duma's consent. This smacked of parliamentarism, which the crown would not accept.

During the First World War, in the parliaments of Western Europe, opposing parties united in the interests of the country. This now occurred in Russia. On August 22 (September 4), 1915, six factions of the State Duma (Progressives, Progressive Nationalists, Union of October Seventeenth, Zemstvo-Octobrists, Cadets, and centrists) and three factions of the State Council (center, academic, and nonparty) united under the name of the "Progressive Bloc." Together they elected twenty-five officers, with Baron Meller-Zakomelskii as chairman. Because the Progressive Bloc had a majority in the Duma (235 to 187), its officers took control of the Duma. Including members of the State Council, the bloc numbered more than three hundred persons. Since we considered the government totally useless, we had to put pressure on it through this three-hundred-member bloc.

Earlier, on July 10 (23), 1915, the so-called Zemgor was created. It was the Central Committee of the All-Russian Zemstvo Union and the Union of Cities for Army Supplies. These unions became one of the fulcrums of the Progressive Bloc, and their representatives attended special conferences. The Zemstvo Union and the Union of Cities were headed by Prince G. E. Lvov and the Cadet M. V. Chelnokov, respectively. The two unions held conferences in Moscow on September 7 (20), 1915.

A book by M. K. Lemke, *250 dnei v tsarskoi stavke* ("250 Days at Tsarist Headquarters"),* relates a conversation between the Emperor and the Supreme Commander-in-Chief, General Alekseev, about the conferences.

"Your Majesty, aren't you going to order that a timely greeting be sent to the conferences—both zemstvo and city?"

"Why bother? After all, their work is no more than a systematic attempt to undermine my rule. I understand these things. They should all be arrested, not thanked."

"But Your Majesty—"

"Well, all right, all right. Send them a greeting. The time will come when I will reckon with them."

The conferences sent the Sovereign a delegation to inform him of the necessity of "replenishing" the government's ranks with "persons who inspire the country's trust." The Tsar, however, would not receive

---

*Petrograd, 1920 (trans.).

the delegation. Moreover, in December of 1915, displeased with the Zemgor's interference in politics, and suspicious that its members were aiming to seize power, the government prohibited a meeting between the two unions and the War Industry Committees. A year later, Zemgor conferences in Moscow were dispersed by the police. The Tsar intended to show his desire to preserve his sole right to appoint the country's ministers.

* * *

The Progressive Bloc's program was published in the Petrograd newspapers on August 26 (September 8), 1915. That evening, at a historic meeting, members of the bloc sat at one table with representatives of the government. The representatives of the bloc included D. D. Grimm, I. I. Dmitriukov, I. N. Efremov, P. N. Krupenskii, V. N. Lvov, Baron V. V. Meller-Zakomelskii, P. N. Miliukov, S. I. Shidlovskii, and myself. Representing the government were Prince N. B. Shcherbatovskii, head of the Ministry of Internal Affairs and commander of the Gendarme Corps, and A. A. Khvostov, Minister of Justice, among others. Nevertheless, nothing came of the talks, except that we found several of the ministers to be completely on our side and ready to give in. Give in to what, specifically?

It was clear that it was necessary to ask the Cadets to form a cabinet. In 1905, when the Cadets had sided with the left, they could not have been entrusted with this responsibility, but now they were patriots, so let them form a cabinet. Some feared that they would be too liberal? Nonsense! Radicals had become ministers in the past, but had there ever been a radical minister?

But those at the meeting that evening did not understand this. By not agreeing on this point the two sides brought on their doom. Consequently, both the dynasty and the Russian parliament perished.

However, confronted by an impending retreat, the ruling powers wished to gain the support of the people's representatives, and from their patriotism draw the strength to continue the war to a "victorious conclusion." The fact that the War Ministry had gone bankrupt and we found ourselves weaponless in the face of a superbly armed enemy played an enormous role in this decision. In a similar vein, Duma Chairman Rodzianko's tour of the front influenced the decision to summon the Fourth State Duma. He found that the army was not satisfied with the government and felt that only the Duma could help the situation. In a sense, those at the front were right.

On August 17 (30), 1915, as a result of Rodzianko's trip, a law was passed creating four special councils, namely: a council on national defense, under the chairmanship of the head of the War Ministry General Alexis Andreevich Polivanov; a council on transportation, under the chairmanship of the Minister of Transportation, Privy

Councillor Serge Vasilevich Rukhlov; a council on fuel, under the chairmanship of the Minister of Commerce and Industry, Councillor of State Prince Vsevolod Nicholaevich Shakhovskii; and a council on foodstuffs, under the chairmanship of the Director of Land Tenure and Agriculture, Alexander Vasilevich Krivoshein. These special councils were copied from certain Western parliaments, where they are called parliamentary commissions.

One must say that the work of the special councils was, in general, constructive. On August 19 (September 1), 1915, I was elected to the special council on defense, which successfully solved the extremely difficult problem of shells for the army. The other councils also completed their respective tasks. In this respect our consciences were clear. We did everything possible, fulfilling our responsibilities not out of fear but out of conscience.

But there was another aspect. There were times when I had my doubts about our work. We had agreed not to fan the flames but to put out the fire. In this respect, I wondered whether we were fulfilling our intention. Were we quelling the revolution? The State Duma could not cope with the fundamental political problem as a whole.

*　*　*

Russia's discontent, which stemmed from the terrible retreat of 1915, was redirected to the safety valve called the State Duma. The boiling revolutionary energy was transformed into words, fiery speeches and ringing but superficial words, "transition to the matters at hand"; that is, reprimands of the government were substituted for blood and destruction.

Another intention also met with success. On the basis of these sharp public "reprimands" the Duma succeeded in remaining in agreement with the government on the most important issue—the war. Throughout this period a bright placard reading "Everything for the war!" was firmly affixed to the dome of the Tauride Palace. No matter how much Markov called the Progressive Bloc a "yellow bloc," the fact of the matter was that we were a tricolor bloc—white, blue, and red.*
It was national; it was Russian!

But didn't the red of the tricolor emblem spread and swallow up the other colors? Sometimes it seemed to me that although we had been appointed firemen and given the task of extinguishing the revolution, we involuntarily became incendiaries. We were too eloquent, too talented at expressing ourselves. The people trusted us too much when we said that the government was good for nothing.

Oh, God! Why, the horror lies in the fact that it was truly so—it really was good for nothing.

---

*The colors of the Russian flag (trans.).

Bolsheviks in the Duma

S TRANGE AS IT MAY SEEM, my first speech in the Fourth State Duma, from the already familiar rostrum, was delivered in defense of the five deputies who composed the Bolshevik faction. In October 1912, five Bolsheviks—A. E. Badaev, M. K. Muranov, G. I. Petrovskii, F. N. Samoilov, and N. R. Shagov—were elected to the Fourth State Duma from the workers' ranks. Who were they?

Alexis Egorovich Badaev was born on February 4 (16), 1883, in a peasant family in the village of Iurev in the Karachevskii district of Orlov Province. On finishing evening technical classes, he became a metal worker at the Alexandrov factory in Petersburg and in the car shops on the Nicholaevskii (now Oktiabrskii) Railroad. In 1904 he joined the Communist party and became a party activist in the metal workers' union. He had been working on the Bolshevik paper *Pravda* when he was elected a deputy to the State Duma. At the beginning of the First World War he organized anti-war meetings in several cities.

Matthew Constantinovich Muranov was born on November 29 (December 11), 1873, and had been a member of the party since 1904. On being elected in 1912 by the Kharkov workers, he stated that he was a native of the village of Osnov in the Kharkovsk district, but it was later learned that he had been born in the village of Rybtsy in Poltav Province. He was a metal worker in a steamship plant. Muranov combined his Duma activities with illegal revolutionary work in Petersburg, Kharkov, and other cities, and also worked on *Pravda.*

The third in this pleiad of Duma Old Bolsheviks, Gregory Ivanovich Petrovskii, is a bit more famous, because in 1926 the city of Ekaterinoslav was renamed Dnepropetrovsk in his honor. He served as chairman of the All-Ukrainian Central Committee of the Communist party. It is unlikely that he would ever have guessed that Shulgin, his political rival in the State Duma, would turn up in Kiev in December of 1925, after illegally crossing the border with a false passport in his pocket. But enough has been written about this in Lev Nikulin's book *Mertvaia zyb* ("The Wave"). Petrovskii was born on February 4 (16), 1878, in the city of Kharkov, to the family of an artisan. He received his education in a school affiliated with the Kharkov semi-

246

nary. As a young man he worked in factories in Ekaterinoslav, Kharkov, and Nikolaev, and later was a lathe operator in the Providans factory in Zhdanov. In 1897 he joined the revolutionary movement and studied in a Social Democratic circle led by I. V. Babushkin. In 1899 he began active illegal party work, which was interrupted several times by his arrest and exile. After his election to the Duma, Petrovskii did not forsake underground party work, following Lenin's directives.

Theodore Nikitich Samoilov was born on April 12 (24), 1882, in the village of Golmylenki in the Pokrovskii district of Vladimir Province. He became a member of the party in 1903. He was a worker at the Pokrovsk manufacturing plant in Ivanovo-Voznensensk, where he carried out revolutionary agitation. He himself stated that he served mainly in administrative positions, as an inspector, counter, and foreman.

Information is scarce about the fifth Bolshevik, Nicholas Romanovich Shagov. It is known that he was a weaver who worked in the Krasilshchikov factory in the village of Rudnikakh, in Kostromsk Province. His health was ruined during a prison term and harsh conditions of exile. After the February Revolution he returned to Petrograd seriously ill and died in 1918.

The above information was given by the five Bolsheviks themselves when they were elected to the Duma by the workers, but I learned it much later—in fact, quite recently. At the time that I gave my speech I hardly knew anything about them. I only knew that they made up a single Social Democratic faction of the Duma, together with the Menshevik family: A. F. Burianov, I. N. Mankov, M. I. Chkhenkeli, M. I. Skobelev, I. N. Tuliakov, and V. I. Khausktov.

From November 15 (28), 1912, the opening session of the Fourth Duma, a terrible fight began between the Bolsheviks and the Mensheviks, principally concerning their different views on the role of revolution in Russia. Finally, on October 27 (November 9), 1913, the Bolshevik deputies broke off from the Social Democratic Mensheviks and formed their own group, the Russian Social Democratic Workers' faction. I later learned that the name was suggested by Lenin, who was close to the Bolshevik deputies and even wrote their speeches.

When the war began, there was a Bolshevik conference in the city of Ozorkow, south of Petrograd, which also was attended by the Duma Bolsheviks. On November 4 (17), all the participants in the conference were arrested, including the members of the State Duma who made up the Russian Social Democratic Workers' faction. Their trial took place on February 10–13 (23–26), 1915, with the special participation of the Petrograd Judicial Chamber. All five Bolshevik deputies were found guilty of belonging to an organization whose goal was to overthrow the government, and were sentenced to a lifetime of hard labor in the Turukhansk region of Siberia.

This was not right, since the members of the Social Democratic faction who remained in the Duma were also part of an organization which aimed to overthrow the monarchy. Only during the war did they begin to support the government, while the Bolsheviks spoke out against it even during the war, calling on the soldiers to throw down their weapons and go home. Therefore the court should have tried them for demoralizing the army during wartime, but it did not.

Only two Mensheviks were punished for anti-governmental activities, Andrew Fadeevich Burianov and Ivan Nicholaevich Mankov. The former spent two years in prison, sentenced by the Kiev Court Chamber for belonging to the Social Democratic faction and for attending the southern Russian party conference before his election to the Duma. Because of this, during the second year of the war, the Social Democratic faction of the State Duma consisted of only six Mensheviks: M. I. Skobelev, I. N. Tuliakov, V. I. Khaustov, N. S. Chkheidze, M. I. Chkhenkeli, and E. I. Iagello.

On July 20 (August 2), 1915, the day after the opening session, the secretary, Ivan Ivanovich Dmitriukov, said, "We have a received information from A. A. Khvostov, Minister of Justice, dated February 13 (26), 1915, concerning the case of the following members of the State Duma: Badaev, Muranov, Petrovskii Samoilov, and Shagov. By article 102 of part I of the Criminal Code, the sentence was upheld and put into effect."

Chairman Rodzianko explained that on the basis of article 19 of the rules of the State Duma, a deputy who was tried in court for treasonous activities and was subsequently deprived of all his rights was automatically expelled from the Duma. According to article 21 of the same rules, deputies could be expelled from the State Duma only by a resolution of the Duma itself. Because of this contradiction, on the basis of article 115 of the mandate, the announcement of the Minister of Justice had to be passed on to a membership committee.

On August 14 (27), 1915 a petition was sent to the Duma in the name of the Social Democratic faction, signed by thirty-two deputies, requesting that the membership committee present its recommendation on this matter at the next meeting. The Menshevik Akakii Ivanovich Chkhenkeli, the statement's first signatory, protested that the Duma had not yet reacted to the pressure exerted by the government on its members, by which its rights were most unceremoniously trampled. He announced, "Before saving your fatherland, you must save the honor and decency of the institution in which you serve."

The committee was faced with the extremely difficult task of finding some way out of the contradictory articles: either expelling the arrested and condemned Bolsheviks from the Duma or allowing them to remain as members of the legislative house, that is, not recognizing the decision of the Petrograd Judicial Chamber.

Markov, speaking for the rightist faction, which then consisted of fifty-two members, called on the Duma not to allow "people lawfully condemned by a court and sent to Siberia to sit on these benches. . . . I believe that there is nothing in the behavior of the SD's that would warrant a call for mercy by the State Duma . . . these people do not deserve any mercy."

The Cadet V. A. Maklakov, chairman of the membership committee, said that the matter of the five Social Democrats had not been considered because it was difficult to call a meeting during wartime, but of course if the Duma wished it, there would be no difficulty in obtaining a presentation of the report. However Maklakov opposed the request of the Social Democratic faction precisely because he agreed with its authors. He felt, as they did, that the government had made an enormous blunder by bringing charges against the five Bolsheviks, and that "condemning them under article 102, condemning them for a crime of which all their comrades now sitting here are also guilty, such a judgment is a sin against our judicial system." Feeling that this inequity should be rectified, Maklakov did not want to give the Duma grounds to consider the convicted deputies expelled.

Then Nicholas Semenovich Chkheidze announced that a telegram had been received from the five comrades in exile. It read,

> We consider it our duty before the country and the voters to declare that our disenfranchisement as members of the Duma will be a disenfranchisement of hundreds of thousands of workers at a decisive moment in the history of the peoples of Russia.
>
> Just as we were before the trial, so after it we remain deputies elected by the working class, always acting in total conformity with the thoughts and feelings of those who voted for us, and we declare that only they who gave us our mandate can deny us the right and responsibility of continuing to defend the interests of the working class.
>
> The State Duma's refusal to obey the creators of the process is a worthy response on the part of the people's representatives to attempts to deny the working class its representatives in the Duma.

* * *

Next was heard the resounding bass voice of Rodzianko: "On the subject of the vote, State Duma member Shulgin—five minutes." I was deep in thought about this entire matter. Of course, I did not agree with Markov. First I had to speak from the rostrum against the opinions of the right. I began,

We will be voting for the same proposal that was made by Vasilii Alexevich Maklakov. I have asked for the floor in order to quell any doubts about this question. We consider everything that has occurred in relation to the Social Democratic members of the State Duma a grave governmental mistake *(voices from the left: "Correct!")*, a mistake because the ruling powers must first of all be consistent, since a consistent path is the right path. There is no way to justify the accusation and conviction of people simply for belonging to a faction which has legally been given a place here. If we follow this path, we must go further and call upon these people, of whom there is a sufficient number, to respond— *(Voices from the left: "That's right!")* I would like to stress that the government should realize this. A mistake has been made, and all measures should be taken to correct it.

Gentlemen, I maintain that the deputy who has just spoken announced that the feelings of the working masses do not diverge from the tasks that remain before the country. Gentlemen, we must take advantage of those feelings; we must welcome, not insult, those who want to put their work and patriotism to the benefit of their fatherland.

I think that at first my words were drowned out by applause from everyone—the center, the left, and the right. In doing so, the Duma as a whole recognized the right of the five deputies removed by the government to take their places with their comrades, thereby condemning the unjust sentence imposed by the government. Of course, the ultra-rightists opposed this but did not dare to express their feelings.

Which deputy had I alluded to in my speech? The Trudovik Alexander Fedorovich Kerenskii, the procurator of the Petrograd Judicial Chamber, who was then thirty-four years old. He also expressed his extreme displeasure at the arrest and conviction of the five Bolsheviks. He spoke passionately and confusingly. There were many unnecessary words in his speech, but nonetheless one heard in it the characteristically effective appeal that would soon attract the revolutionary masses.

Kerenskii exclaimed,

I have a great request to make of you, gentlemen of the State Duma: now, when the situation in our country is becoming more and more grave, when the patience of the masses is wearing thin, when what is coming from the west draws closer and closer to our land, to our centers, we must forget our disagreements, forget our class affiliations, and think of the country, think of our native land, say to them: keep your hands off, you traitors and mercenaries!

* * *

Thus passed the day of my return to the Duma, when I had to take the stand in defense of five Bolshevik deputies. In spite of their arrest and conviction, their seats were saved for them, and officially, as though nothing had happened, the "List of Members of the State Duma by Party" continued to include the Russian Social Democratic Workers faction, consisting of five members: Badaev, Muranov, Petrovskii, Samoilov, and Shagov.

The Tragedy of Battle

THE BIRTH OF the so-called Progressive Bloc was accompanied by a schism in the Russian Nationalist faction, chaired by P. N. Balashev. The Duma members who joined the bloc created a new faction, the Progressive Russian Nationalists, choosing Count V. A. Bobrinskii as their chairman, and myself as assistant chairman. Since Bobrinskii was often absent, however, it fell upon me to lead the newly born faction. The rightists constantly showered us with criticism and attacks.

At that time, the Duma was considering the question of military censorship. There had been censorship since the beginning of the war, but under Sukhomlinov it became stricter. For example, when the investigation of Sukhomlinov's activities was launched, the newspapers could only print something of this sort: "The Sukhomlinov case: At its most recent meeting, an investigative commission discussed the activities of former Minister of War V. A. Sukhomlinov." This would be followed by a blank space.

But no matter how real the question of military censorship, the members of the State Duma were more concerned with the formation of the Progressive Bloc. During the first discussion of a bill to establish military censorship, speakers would constantly jump to a criticism of the bloc, despite numerous appeals by the chairman not to stray from the topic of censorship. On August 28 (September 10), 1915, the Progressive Bloc came under an especially sharp attack by the Nationalist Peter Afrikanovich Safonov and the nonpartisan Michael Alexandrovich Karaulov.

P. A. Safonov announced that attempts by the Progressive Bloc to implement its program would be met by the "most energetic opposition" and characterized the schism in the Russian Nationalist faction as a grave political situation. He reserved his most forceful criticism, however, for the Jewish question, expressing himself in the following manner: "Instead of restoring the purity of the national unity program, on the basis of which it was resolved that 'equal rights for Jews are unacceptable,' the new group has written: 'to embark upon a course of removing the limitations on the rights of Jews.'" Despite the war, the rightist faction had not changed its position on the Jewish question and could not forgive me for defending Beilis.

252

In responding to Safonov, I had to begin with the censorship question. Those who spoke before me had done the same thing. I described a humorous scene I had witnessed when censorship was instituted at the *Kievlianin.*

A year ago, while serving as editor of the *Kievlianin,* I was summoned by a certain official who had been charged with familiarizing the local newspapers with the new rules established by the military censor. I found this man surrounded by a flock of newsmen who were listening to him fearfully and asking,

"Is this allowed?"

"The answer is no!"

"How about this?"

"Under no circumstances!"

"And this?"

"God forbid!"

There was a flood of questions, each one receiving a negative reply. Finally the completely frightened people began to ask nonsensical questions, such as, "Tell me, please, those mobilization proclamations that are posted on fences—could they be printed in the newspapers?"

To my horror, he replied categorically, "Under no circumstances." Then someone asked, "Precisely why would that be forbidden?"

The answer was even more interesting: "Don't you understand? A fence cannot be sent to Germany, but an issue of a paper could be!"

To my greatest disappointment, the same narrow outlook now characterizes a wider range of issues. We see that the same thing is happening in regard to vital governmental and social matters. The question of how to do it and when to do it has colossal significance and often pales even before the question of what to do. Just recently an event of enormous importance occurred precisely along the question of when to do something.

At this point I tried to respond to attacks on the Progressive Bloc. I warned that I would not engage in polemics. We had a common enemy—Germany—and would not fight with our fellow countrymen. "You may attack us, but we will defend ourselves only in cases of the utmost necessity. Perhaps you will still join us in this great struggle."

I continued, "I feel that unequal rights for Jews is a horribly heavy chain for both sides to wear. It is obvious why it is heavy for the Jews, but it is no less so for us, because it is based on a presumption of our weakness. The mark of the Jewish Pale cannot be removed simply because you, or we, or someone else desires it. It can be removed only by war, so there is no point even talking about it."

* * *

On January 20 (February 2), 1916, Hofmeister Boris Vladimirovich Stürmer was appointed Chairman of the Council of Ministers. He was considered by many to be absolutely unprincipled and a nonentity.

The famous poet Alexander Blok said about him, "The decrepit bu-
reaucrat Goremykin's replacement by Stürmer as Chairman of the
Council of Ministers will be cause for reflection. Stürmer has a very
majestic and cold-blooded appearance, and has said of himself that he
has 'an iron fist in a velvet glove.' In his new post he is nothing but an
empty shell* inhabited by a conniving character who does everything
'on the sly with bureaucratic subterfuge.' Rasputin called him an 'old
man on a string.' "

Because of his appearance he was called "Santa Claus," but this
grandfatherly old man, far from bringing order to Russia, carried
away its last vestige of power. Stürmer was a nonentity, and Russia was
waging a world war. In fact, while all the monarchies of Europe were
mobilizing their best powers, we appointed a "Santa Claus" as our
Prime Minister.

*   *   *

The Duma was not dissolved. Not only was it not dissolved, but on
its insistence the seditious Goremykin was removed. One had to imagine public opinion from the faces of the members of the legislative
houses of B. V. Stürmer, the new Prime Minister, and the new government. This led to the resumption of the business of the Fourth State
Duma, on February 9 (22), 1916.

"Santa Claus" and his ministers—Minister of War General A. A.
Polivanov, Admiral I. K. Grigorovich, and Minister of Foreign Affairs
S. D. Sazonov—went to the rostrum with explanations. In my reply to
the government the following day, February 10 (23), I could not
criticize Prime Minister Stürmer, because he had just been appointed
and had not yet had a chance to show his worth, so instead I tried to
ascertain where Goremykin had gone wrong, in order to help his
successor avoid the same mistakes.

What exactly was Goremykin's mistake? The phrase that "the people are running this war," which had become a commonplace
throughout Russia, and was clearly understood by everyone, never
reached the head of the government. Ivan Logginovich seemed to
think that the army was running the war, that the Minister of War had
the sole responsibility for its conduct, and that the government, and
he himself as its head, had nothing to do with it.

I tried to reveal the full extent of the horror that resulted from this
point of view as it found expression in the activities, or rather the

---

*The word *futliar,* "empty shell," used here by Blok has a derogatory connota-
tion derived from Chekhov's short story "The Man in a Shell" about a person
who has shut himself off from the world, absorbed in his own narrow interests and afraid of anything new (trans.).

inactivity, of the government. To make the horror of the situation even worse, everyone had known that Goremykin was hostile to the Progressive Bloc and was an obedient instrument of the court circle headed by Rasputin.

Against the background of cheers of "that's true!" from the left, I said that the government needed a head who was able to understand the great progress being made by the people during the war, so that the government would immediately help when it saw that something was needed, and so that he, in the role of lubricator of the government machinery, could add a few helpful drops of oil whenever friction made the gears spark and squeak.

"Are the authorities carrying out this task?" I asked. "Unfortunately, the former authorities did not even try, and in the whole Russian Empire there was no leader who would even have thought about all this."

I urged the new government to formulate a comprehensive program that would clearly describe the policies to be followed by all of its most important branches. This program would have to be flexible and readily adaptable to circumstances, taking into account the possibility that continued offensives and retreats might bring about changes in the country, and rejecting everything that was old and worn-out.

Was it really true that no one had the power to make them listen to reason?! Certainly we could not continue in the same old way; we could not keep angering the country and the people, spilling their blood without limit. Didn't that blood have rights? Didn't those voiceless victims have the right to a voice?

In the end it hardly matters that Stürmer was a Santa Claus. Let us assume that he was the most honest of men. Whether rightly or wrongly, the country was going mad over the idea of being governed by trustworthy people. Why not try them? Why not appoint them?

Let us assume that they were really untrustworthy. After all, there was no Stolypin on the horizon. Let us say that Miliukov was a nonentity. Still, he was no more of an nonentity than Stürmer. What need was there for this stubbornness? What reasonable basis did it have?

Something transcendentally irrational appeared.

Its name was Rasputin!

Rasputin

THERE IS SOMETHING before which one lowers one's hands power-lessly. He who wants to destroy will destroy.

There is a horrible worm gnawing away like a maggot at Russia's trunk. Already it has eaten the core; now the trunk is gone. Only the three-hundred-year-old bark still remains. There is no cure. There is no medicine. It is fatal.

* * *

On September 27, 1967, at the age of eighty, the man who has passed into history as one of the organizers of Rasputin's murder passed away. On May 30, 1965, in the twenty-second issue of the Soviet magazine *Ogonek,* I read an article by V. P. Vladimirov entitled "A Meeting on Pierre Geren Street." The article describes the author's meeting in Paris with this man. His full name and title is Prince Felix Felixovich Iusupov, Count Sumarokov-Elston. The Prince told Vladimirov about the terrible night of December 16 (29), 1916, when he killed Rasputin. It made me remember something I had chosen to forget. I remembered and reread what I had written about Rasputin in my book *Dni,* five years after that horrible event.

I recommend this text to the reader. At the time everything was still fresh in my mind, but now I would not be able to write it in the same way.

* * *

Setting: A fireside. Coffee (pure mocha) is being served.

Characters: "She" and "He."

"She" is a middle-aged lady; "He," a middle-aged man. The object of their thoughts hovers over vulgar Russia. Because they are decent people, they speak only about what it is now proper to speak about in Petrograd.

She says, "I heard this from (next there is a long Ariadne's thread of cousins and sisters-in-law), and I can tell you this: she is very smart. She is a cut above everyone in her circle. Those who try to talk to her are amazed by her mind, her ability to argue; she demolishes every-one's arguments. No one can persuade her. In particular she acts disdainfully toward us—in a word, toward Petersburg. Once someone spoke with her about this topic—about the Russian people. She asked sarcastically, 'Did you learn that while playing bridge? Did your cousin tell you that? Or your sister-in-law?' She scorns the opinions of the Petersburg ladies."

"Does the Empress really know what is going on?"

"Through Rasputin?"

"Yes, but besides. She corresponds frequently with various people. Receives bags of letters from, how do you say, simple people. And judges the people's attitude from these letters. She is convinced that the simple people adore her. And everything that others dare report to the Sovereign is lies, in her opinion. Of course you know about Princess V.?"

"V. wrote the Empress a letter. A very frank one. And was ordered to leave Petrograd. Is that right?" he asked.

"Yes, and her husband also. You know him. The former Minister of Agriculture. But V. was not expressing her own feelings. She said in the letter that it was the opinion of an entire group of Russian women. That it was a protest."

"Does she say anything about Rasputin?"

"Yes, of course. By the way, I wanted to ask you what you think of him."

"First of all, I don't believe what is said, nor what is unpleasant to repeat."

"You don't believe it, then? Do you have any facts?"

"Facts? How should I say it? First of all, it is so monstrous that those who believe it should know what they are talking about."

"But Rasputin's reputation?" she asked.

"What's a reputation? It doesn't prevent him from being a clever and sly peasant. Where it is necessary, he keeps within the bounds of decency. Furthermore, if it were so— After all, so many people hate the Empress. Wouldn't there be someone who would open the Sovereign's eyes?"

"And what if the Sovereign knows, but does not want to know?"

"If that is so, then there should be a revolution. Such lack of will in a monarch is unforgivable. But I don't believe it. Perhaps I seem overconfident in judging simply on the basis of such a short conversation; but I have formed my personal opinion about her, and it does not fit—no, it does not fit."

"You spoke with her?"

"Yes, once."

"What did she say?"

"Someone introduced me, explaining that I was from such-and-such a province. She extended her hand. Then I saw rather helpless eyes and a smile, a forced smile which made her English face suddenly look German. Then she said, with some despair—"

"In Russian?"

"Yes, in Russian, with an accent. She asked, 'What is your province like?' It caught me off guard."

"And what did you reply?"

"Some banality. After all, it's difficult to characterize your province without any preparation. I replied. 'Your Majesty, our province is characterized by softness. Gentle climate, gentle fauna. Perhaps that is the reason the people are also known for their gentle character. We have a comparatively peaceful people.' I stopped there. But from the expression on her face I saw that I should add something. Then, although it is not permitted to ask questions, especially stupid questions—but that is precisely the kind I asked."

"What was the matter with you?"

"Yes, because I asked, 'Your Majesty has never been to our province?' I should have known the answer."

"What did she say?"

"I did not expect such a reply. She burst out, 'Of course not, I haven't been anywhere. For ten years I have been here in Tsarskoe Selo, as though in prison.'"

"She said that? And you?"

"It only remained to say, 'We hope very much that someday Your Majesty will honor us with a visit.' She answered, 'Definitely.'"

"Did she?"

"She never made the visit. She was supposed to come from Kiev, but then Stolypin was murdered and it was canceled. What were we talking about?"

"You were saying that your personal impression is—"

"Ah yes. My personal impression is that she is at the same time both an Englishwoman and a German woman. She and Rasputin—no, it's impossible. Anything but that."

"I don't believe it either, but then what is it? Mysticism?" she asked.

"Of course. Her sister, Elizabeth Fedorovna, has the same inclination, but it did not take on such a horrible form for Russia because Elizabeth Fedorovna has a different character—less powerful and stubborn."

"Why?"

"Because if the Empress were soft and submissive—"

She replied, "Unfortunately, that cannot be said about Alexandra Fedorovna. She is, first and foremost, a great wit."

"So they say. But the wit of queens always causes some calamity for the monarchy."

"But queens are allowed to be simply smart, I hope?"

"Only that female mind—the highest sort, by the way—which in every situation knows how to ease the husband's difficult burden. Ease it, which does not mean meddle with his governing. On the contrary, meddling only gives rise to more difficulty. To ease his burden means to remove any cares that can be removed. And a Tsarina's first duty is absolute submission to the Tsar, because, although she is the Tsarina, she is after all only the first of his subjects. Think for yourself. Who shows obvious disobedience to the Tsar in front of the entire country? At any rate that is what everyone says. Who has not heard the phrase 'Better one Rasputin than ten hysterical scenes a day'?"

"And so? What is the conclusion?"

"It is not in mysticism, but in the character of the Empress. Mysticism by itself would not be dangerous if she were a woman without thorns. She would have sacrificed Rasputin even if she considered him a holy man. She would have cried a bit and parted with him immediately if suspicion of any kind fell upon her."

"But what if she is actually under Rasputin's influence? After all, they maintain that he is a powerful hypnotist. If she believes that he can save the heir, the Sovereign, and even Russia—"

"In ancient times they had a good word for such cases. They would have said that Grisha* Rasputin has 'bewitched' the Tsarina. And wizardry is dispelled by prayer. And praying is done best in a monastery."

"Monastery? Yes, that is done. But what if the Sovereign himself is bewitched?"

"If so, then nothing can be done. We will perish. If he is bewitched, than it comes from within him."

"How?" she asked.

"He can't not know what is happening. He is told everything. His eyes are open."

"Why do you think so?"

"Because out of weakness the Sovereign daily, hourly, insults his people, and the people insult their Sovereign."

She asked, "How?"

"This way—is it not an insult to all of us, is it not the greatest scorn toward the entire nation and especially toward us, the monarchists, this receiving of Rasputin? I believe totally—how can I say this—well, that the Empress is totally pure. But nevertheless Rasputin is a filthy debaucher. How can he be permitted into the palace when this disturbs, worries, the entire country, when this allows its enemies to

---

*Russian diminutive for Gregory; the other common diminutive is Grishka (trans.).

throw mud at the dynasty, while we, its defenders, have no possible means of deflecting the attacks? And all this during the most difficult war that Russia has ever waged, when everything depends on the state of mind of the soldiers. Think how defenseless we are in this respect. We can't even talk about it. An officer cannot assemble his company and say, 'They say this and that about Rasputin, but it's all nonsense.' That is not possible, especially since some naive soldier will always say, 'Allow me to ask, sir, what is it they say about Rasputin? We haven't heard it?' The officer would have to explain, wouldn't he? Terrible, terrible. A hopeless situation. And how many officers believe it?"

"Who cares about officers? Why, all Petersburg believes it. People who explain it the way you and I are doing are few and far between. The majority accept the simplest, dirtiest explanation."

"Yes, I know," he said. "That is the other side of the drama. Every day, every minute, the Sovereign is insulted by his people. The Sovereign insults the country by allowing into the palace, to which access is difficult for the best people, a known debaucher. And the country insults the Sovereign by its terrible suspicions. And the centuries-old ties that have always sustained Russia are being torn apart. My God, my God!"

"What! What!"

"Only this. How terrible it is to have an autocracy without an autocrat."

*　*　*

That is what Petrograd hummed about day and night. Despite the unceasing babble, in essence we knew very little about this man who was bringing death to us. We simply did not know anything about him. At the same time, it was considered the highest form of indecency to have any sort of relations with him. For that reason, for example, I never met him myself. Thus I have no personal impression. It would be good to have one.

*　*　*

Here is the story of a certain R., from Kiev, and well-known there. In my opinion, he is honest, not stupid, although not very intelligent. This is what he said.

"Before His Majesty the Emperor and Her Majesty the Empress and Stolypin arrived in Kiev, I received a telegram that said that Gregory Efimovich Rasputin would be staying at my apartment. I had never met Rasputin and was not very happy, to tell you the truth. First of all, I already had plenty of extra worries, and you know how many cares I have. Because I, as chairman, was supposed to post my fellows around the Sovereign's train, so that everything would go as it should.

And now Rasputin on top of that. And besides, you know what they say about him, and I have a wife. Well, I think, nothing can be done about it, I cannot refuse him. He came. He behaved himself. A simple man, spoke familiarly to everyone. I made him as comfortable as possible. He says to me immediately, 'My dear man, make sure you get me the best place, so that I stand right next to the Sovereign's train.' I went straight to the Kurlov Hotel. Whatever Rasputin demands. They gave me a ticket for him and said that I had better make sure nothing happened.

"So I and my fellows were posted on Alexandrovskii Street, in the front row. I placed Rasputin between my boys and told them to watch him. And I knew that if the Sovereign noticed anyone at all, it would be us. Because when my fellows shout 'Hurrah!' as they have been taught, it is impossible not to turn around. They shout from the heart, all together. And that's how it was. Here comes the carriage, and when my fellows hurrahed, the Sovereign and the Empress both turned around. And the Tsarina recognized Rasputin and bowed to him. And he, Rasputin, began to wave his arms in the air."

"Blessing them?"

"Yes, as though he were blessing them. He stretched out to his full height in the front row, waving his arms, waving. And so they passed by. That evening an officer came to my apartment, sent by the Empress to see Rasputin. Her Majesty, he says, asks that Rasputin visit her. And he asks, 'And who is the aide in attendance?' The other replied. Then Rasputin got angry and said, 'Tell the Little Mother–Tsarina* that I will not come today. That aide is a dog. I'll come tomorrow, tell her.' Well, that's it, I have nothing more to tell you. He behaved properly at my apartment, and when it was over he was very grateful and left. A simple man; I see nothing marvelous about him."

* * *

Here is a story about the same events, but in altogether different tones. In the fall of 1913 I was visited in Kiev by a certain man whom I did not know. He said he was a postal clerk. At that time I used to see many people. I invited him to sit down and fixed a rather exhausted gaze upon him. He was an ordinary clerk, only there was something unpleasant in his eyes. He began like this: "I read about all this in the papers and often think about you. It must be hard on you."

Everything really was going wrong for me at the time, but I still did not understand what he was talking about and waited for him to continue.

---

*Peasants often affectionately referred to the Tsar and Tsarina as "Little Father" and "Little Mother" (trans.).

"Now your friends are against you. Mr. Menshikov in the *Novoe vremia* attacks you often. As do others. And you know that you're right, but you can't prove it. That is why they can attack you. And if you could prove it, then there wouldn't be any more of these unpleasant occurrences."

Suddenly I realized what he meant. He was talking about the uproar against me in the rightist press when the *Kievlianin* did not approve of the attempt to use the Russian judicial process as a political tool on the Jewish question. He was referring to the campaign against me because of the Beilis case.

He continued, "You have to prove the truth. I also know that Beilis did not kill the boy. You have to find out who did."

I answered, "Yes, it's true, and it is not only important for me to learn who killed Andrew Iushchinskii. But how can this be done?"

He gazed at me as though he were trying to penetrate my brain. I thought, what an unpleasant gaze.

He said, "There is such a person."

"Who?"

"There is a man who knows everything. He knows this too."

I thought he would name some fortune-teller, but he said, "Gregory Rasputin." He said it triumphantly, lowering his voice.

"Rasputin?"

He gave me a look that mingled condescension and pity. "Like all the others, you're frightened. Rasputin. But he knows everything. I know—you don't believe it. But you should listen. Once I was walking with him in Kiev along a street in the Pecherska Monastery. A totally drunk woman passes us. And he gives her five rubles. I said, 'Gregory Efimovich. What for?'

"He says to me, 'Poor thing, poor thing— She doesn't know— Her baby just died. When she goes home she'll find out. Poor thing.'"

"And did her baby really die?"

"Yes. I checked. I checked purposely; I asked her address. And when the Sovereign-Emperor was in Kiev, riding down Alexandrovskii Street, I was standing next to him."

"Where?"

"On the sidewalk, in the front row. I saw everything. When the Sovereign's carriage came by, the Empress recognized Gregory Efimovich and nodded, and he blessed her. Then, when the second carriage approached with Stolypin, Gregory Efimovich suddenly began to shake, crying, 'Death is following him! Death is riding behind him! Behind Peter!' Don't you believe me?"

His heavy gaze pressed down upon me. I can't say that I thought he was lying. I said, "I have no right not to believe you. I don't know you, after all."

"Believe me, believe me. I was with him that night. Rasputin slept in the next room and we were separated only by a thin wall. All night he kept me awake. He groaned, wailed, moaned, 'Oh, there will be a tragedy, a tragedy.' I asked, 'What's the matter, Gregory Efimovich?' He would only say, 'Oh, calamity, death is coming.' And he carried on that way till daylight. And the next day—you know yourself—they killed Peter Arkadevich—in the theater. He knows everything, everything."

His stare began to choke me and make me want to sleep. He continued, "You need to go to him. He'll tell you who killed Iushchinskii. It will help you. Go see Gregory Efimovich."

No, what is happening to me? His look choked me. I wanted to sleep. And suddenly it occurred to me that I was being hypnotized. I summoned my strength and shook off something. That instant he grabbed my arm and said, "My, are you a nervous man, Vasilii Vitalevich!"

I rose. "Yes, I am. Therefore it is better that I do not see Gregory Efimovich, who is just as nervous as I am and as you are. Goodbye."

But could this man's story be connected with R.'s story? It could. The clerk could have been one of R.'s "fellows," could have been staying at his apartment that day, could have been standing with Rasputin while the Sovereign's carriage drove by.

* * *

"Tell me the truth about Rasputin. Does he really have any influence? Is it really true that his scrawls are as powerful as Holy Writ?"

V. has an elegantly rough way of speaking that is ill-suited to someone who holds the office of Deputy Minister of Internal Affairs.

"Here is the truth—Rasputin is a scoundrel, and he writes his scrawls for other scoundrels. There are all sorts of scum who take his scrawling seriously. He writes it for them. He knows perfectly well who he can write for. Why doesn't he write for me? Because he knows that I will abuse him roundly. There is no such thing as Rasputin— only rapaciousness.* Rubbish, that's all. And he has no influence whatsoever on decent people."

"Still, they say he influences ministerial appointments."

"Nonsense! The fact is, the heir to the throne is fatally ill. Constant fear forces the Empress to throw herself on the mercy of this man. She believes that the heir is still alive thanks only to him. And in the meantime everything is turned into a pigsty. I tell you, Shulgin, he's a scoundrel. We—"

* * *

---

*In the original, using the Russian word for "libertinism, debauchery, dissoluteness," V. makes a pun on Rasputin's name, saying, in effect, "There is no such thing as Rasputin, only *rasputstvo*" (trans.).

Here is a story of a different sort.

One of my young friends, a journalist, said to me, "Yesterday I met Rasputin."

"How was it?"

"Like this: He looked at me, laughed, and thumped me on the shoulder. And said, 'You're a rogue, brother.'" I must say that my young friend is not a rogue at all, but a clever fellow, a descendant of the Don Cossacks, with a university education.

"What did you do?"

"I said, 'We're all rogues, And you, Gregory Efimovich, are a rogue too.' He laughed and said, 'Well, let's go have some vodka.'"

"And did you?"

"Yes. He can really put it away."

"What kind of a man is he?"

"You know, he's just a clever peasant, nothing else. He drank, he laughed."

"Who else was there?"

"Oh, a whole crowd. People gave speeches. All in his honor, of course. He didn't react; he only listened. Only once, when my patron, whom you know, said that the Russian land had been dark and unenlightened, and now the sun has finally risen, Gregory Efimovich suddenly said, 'Lie, brother, lie, but not too much.'"

*   *   *

Duma member E. evidently does not have the prejudices that entangle the rest of us. Yesterday he went drinking with Grishka. "He talks only about vodka and women."

"Which women?"

"Not demimondaines, alas. Rasputin is a function of the dissipation* of certain women in search of sensations. Sensations lost with degeneration."

*   *   *

"There was a mother—very beautiful; Natasha—simply gorgeous. I of course am not pretty."

"Will you allow me to disagree?"

"No need. And so, there were three of us and Grishka."

"Where was this?"

"At the archpriest's. His services were excellent, and he was in general a very good man. They often asked him, 'Why don't you invite Gregory Efimovich?' He did not want to answer that he would have

---

*Another instance of the word play explained in the preceding footnote (trans.).

had nothing to say to him. Well, finally, he invited him. And we were also there."

"Did you meet him?"

"Well, of course. We had dinner together."

"What is he like?"

"He is so broad-shouldered, red-haired, with greasy hair; his face is also greasy. But his eyes! Small, really tiny, but what eyes!"

"Unpleasant?"

"Terribly unpleasant. It's hard to tell what color they are, but when you look at him it's very unpleasant. Natasha said the same thing. She saw him another time, and he looked at her in such a way that she ran to church for confession again, in order to purify herself. He dresses finely, in silk shirts and so on."

"Did he behave decently?"

"Yes, quite properly. He spoke with the priest the entire time about some spiritual matters. But I have to tell you this. There is a certain M.—"

"Is she Russian?"

"Of course. She's the daughter of Countess P. You know her?"

"Yes."

"Well, this M. wore a red skirt up to here, had short, platinum blonde hair, always made-up, in general a very vulgar woman. She is, as they say, completely dissolute, and it even shows in her face. And imagine, she visited the court. First she would pair off with one man, then another, until finally she got to Rasputin. And there is another woman, G., the daughter of a senator. She's a little better, but also has stooped very low. But at least one can talk to her. And she once told me about Rasputin, that he is a unique man, that he gives her such sensations—"

"So she had, how do you say, intimate relations with him?"

"Well, of course. And she said that all our other men are good for nothing."

"What, has she tried all our men?"

"Almost. And she said that Rasputin is incomparable. I asked her, 'Then you love him very much? How can you not be jealous? He sees M., and others, everybody.' Of course, I was a fool. She laughed at me and said that I was an excitable little fool, and said that there are many who are so absorbed in mysticism that they don't understand anything and don't even suspect what Rasputin really is."

* * *

And so there it is. The round dance of "lost souls," unsatisfied with life and love. In their search for the secret of happiness some fall into mysticism, others into debauchery, some into both. Alas, they do their dance of death at the head of our nation. This grand circle, or better yet, this vicious circle, whirls through the entire capital—from palaces to churches, from churches to foul dens and back. This round dance in the capital naturally draws the lowest of the lowborn, kindred spirits from the depths of Russia. There, in the lower depths since ancient times, they have played these devilish games that mix mysticism with lust, false faith with genuine debauchery. What is so astonishing in the fact that the St. Petersburg garland—mystical and depraved—attracted Grishka Rasputin, a typical Russian cultist! Against this background the long-awaited union of intelligentsia and people occurred! Grishka joined the chain; holding a hysterical mystic with one hand and a hysterical nymphomaniac with the other, he adorned the Petersburg ballet with his two faces—wizard and satyr.

The horror lies in the fact that the round dance takes place too close to the throne—at the foot of the throne, one might say. Thanks to that, Grishka was able to wield his strange influence on several Grand Princesses, and they led him to the Empress.

A *khlyst* member is not necessarily an idiot. He can be a clever peasant. Grishka knew perfectly well when to present his different faces. The palace received him as a holy elder, a miracle-worker, a soothsayer. At all hours of the day and night the Empress trembled over her only son. The wizard knew this and would answer, "The boy Alexis lives because of my sinful prayer. I, humble Grishka, was sent by God to protect him and the entire royal family. While I am with you, no harm will come to you."

But no one realized that when this man stepped over the palace threshold, a man who kills had arrived.

He kills because he is two-faced.

To the imperial family he presented the face of a *starets*,* in which the Tsarina felt she saw the spirit of God residing in a holy man. But to Russia he presented his depraved mug, the drunken and lustful mug of a wood-goblin–satyr from the Tobolsk taiga. The cause of it all— All of Russia was indignant that Rasputin was in the Tsarina's chamber—

While in the Tsar's chamber there was indignation and deep mortification. What were the people enraged about? That this holy man was praying for the unfortunate heir, a seriously ill child threatened with death by every careless movement. This annoyed them? Why?

Thus this messenger of death stood between Russia and the throne. He kills because he is two-faced. Because of his two-facedness the two sides cannot understand each other. With each hour increasing the

---

*"Elder"; an unordained religious teacher (trans.).

mortification in their hearts, the Tsar and Russia lead each other, hand in hand, into an abyss.

* * *

The following scene took place in the palace of Grand Duke Nicholas Mikhailovich, in a large, well-lit room, which served as both study and drawing-room. Sometimes breakfast would be served on the round table. Very intimate.

That was how it was this time. Over coffee the Grand Duke told us exactly why he had called us, the Progressive Nicholas Nicholaevich Lvov, one of the founders of the Union of Freedom, and myself.

"The situation is this. I have just returned from Kiev. I spoke with the widowed mother of the Emperor. She is aware of everything, and after our conversation I decided— I decided to write the Sovereign a letter—totally honest—to the end. After all, I am older than he, I need nothing, I seek nothing, but I cannot remain indifferent—as we destroy ourselves. We are leading ourselves to our doom. There is absolutely no doubt. I wrote about all this. But I did not have to send the letter—I went to General Headquarters and spoke to him personally. But in order to be more definite, as it were, and furthermore, since I write better than I speak, I asked permission to read my letter aloud. And I read it."

The Grand Duke began to read us the letter. What did it say? It was written in a heartfelt, familiar tone, and set forth the general situation and the serious danger threatening the throne in Russia. There was much space allotted to the Empress. There was the following phrase: "Of course, she is not to blame for everything of which she is accused, and of course, she loves you. But—but the country does not understand or love her, views her influence on affairs as the source of all our troubles."

The Sovereign listened to the whole letter, then said, "Strange, I have just returned from Kiev. I felt that I was never before so well received there."

The Grand Duke answered, "Perhaps it is because you were with the heir—the Empress was not there—"

The Grand Duke continued with his story. Much of it has escaped my memory. I fear being imprecise. Finally, Lvov asked, "What do you think, Your Excellency, did your words make an impression?"

"I don't know—perhaps. I am afraid not—but no matter—I did it— I had to do it—"

* * *

"You're going?" I was leaving for Kiev, but Purishkevich stopped me in the Catherine Hall of the Tauride Palace. I answered, "Yes, I'm going."

"Farewell."

Suddenly he stopped me again. "Listen, Shulgin, you're leaving, but I want you to know. Remember the sixteenth of December—"

I glanced at him. The same expression had been on his face once before when he had told me a secret.

"What for?"

"You'll see. Farewell."

But he turned again. "I'll tell you. You can be trusted. We're going to murder him on the sixteenth."

"Who?"

"Grishka."

He hurriedly explained how it was going to be done, then asked, "What do you think?"

I knew he wouldn't listen, but I said anyway, "Don't do it."

"What! Why not?"

"I don't know—it's repulsive—"

"You're a weakling, Shulgin."

"Perhaps, but maybe it's something else. I don't believe Rasputin has any influence."

"No?"

"It's all nonsense. He simply prays for the heir. He has no influence on the ministers. He's a clever peasant—"

"So in your opinion, Rasputin is not bringing evil upon the monarchy?"

"Not only does he not bring evil, he kills it."

"Then I don't understand you."

"Why, it's perfectly clear. Killing him won't help. There are two aspects. The first is what you yourself have called the 'leapfrog' of ministers. The leapfrog occurs either because there is no one to appoint or because, no matter whom you appoint, you do not please anyone, because the country is wild about the idea of people who have the public trust, and they are precisely the people the Sovereign does not trust. Rasputin has nothing to do with all this. Killing him will not change anything."

"What do you mean, will not change anything?"

"Why, things will go on as before. The same 'leapfrog' of ministers. And the other aspect is that what Rasputin does will not be destroyed by killing him. It's too late—"

"What do you mean? Excuse me, but what are we supposed to do, sit idly by? Endure this disgrace? Do you understand what that means? It is not for me to say or for you to listen. The monarchy is perishing. You know that I'm not a coward. No one can scare me. Remember the Second State Duma. No matter how bad it was, I knew that we would come out of it. But now, I tell you, the monarchy is perishing, and we along with it, and Russia along with us. Don't you know what's happening? The movie theaters are forbidden to run films that show the Sovereign putting on his Cross of St. George. Why? Because when that comes on, one hears voices in the darkness, 'The Tsar–Little Father with George, and the Tsarina–Little Mother with Gregory!'"

I wanted to say something, but he would not let me.

"Wait. I know what you're going to say. You're going to say that all this about the Tsarina and Rasputin is not true. I know, I know. So it's not true, what but difference does that make? Go, prove it to everyone. Who will believe it? Julius Caesar was no fool. 'Caesar's wife must be above suspicion.' But in this case it is not suspicion, but—"

He twitched and said, "We cannot sit by, no matter what. We'll follow through to the end. It can't get worse. I'm going to kill him like a dog. Farewell."

* * *

On December 16 they actually did kill him. It was an attempt to save the monarchy in an ancient Russian way—by secret violence. The whole eighteenth century and the beginning of the nineteenth century passed under the sign of palace coups. When "accidents of birth" (Kliuchevskii's expression) exposed the monarchy to danger, some of the people around the throne would secretly correct the "accidents of birth" by forceful means. Sometimes this would occur without bloodshed, sometimes not.

At the start of the twentieth century there were fewer of such people. There weren't enough of them for a palace coup, so instead they murdered Rasputin. Of course, they did not achieve their goal. The monarchy could not be saved, because Rasputin's poison had already taken effect. Why bother to kill the snake after it has bitten? But for all its pointlessness, Rasputin's murder was a deeply monarchist act, and was accepted as such. When the news reached Moscow (it happened in the evening), the audiences in the theaters demanded that the national anthem be sung, and one heard, for perhaps the last time in Moscow, the hymn, "God Save the Tsar."

Three days later the Tsar and his whole family secretly attended what was, in his words, a sad scene not far from Tsarskoe Selo. At the end of the day he wrote, "The coffin with the never-to-be-forgotten Gregory, killed on the night of December 17 by monsters in the house of F. Iusupov, was already lowered into the grave, Father Alexander Vasilev conducted the service, and after that we returned home. It was a gray day; the temperature was 12 degrees centigrade. I took a walk before the reports."

After the February Revolution the remains of the "elder" were found by soldiers and burned, along with the coffin, in the Pargolov forest.

A Man of Destiny

ALEXANDER BLOK CALLED PROTOPOPOV a man of destiny. He felt
that Rasputin, on the eve of his death, somehow bequeathed his
work to Protopopov and that the latter, continuing it, involuntarily
played a decisive role in hastening the fall of the dynasty.

What sort of man was Protopopov? We members of the State Duma
knew him well, since he had served as Vice-Chairman when Rodzianko was Chairman. A landowner and industrialist of the Simbirsk
aristocracy, and a Gentleman of His Majesty's Court, Alexander Dmitrievich Protopopov belonged to the Union of October Seventeenth
(the Octobrists), and everyone assumed that he had joined the Progressive Bloc with the other members of his party. However, he later
denied any involvement in the bloc and fought against it. In a word,
he turned out to be a Judas.

Without breaking with his comrades in the bloc, or with the Duma
in general, he managed to penetrate the mystical circle of the Tibetan
doctor, Peter Alexandrovich Badmaev. This mysterious doctor had a
magnificently decorated villa-sanatorium south of Petersburg, where
he treated the aristocracy with Tibetan cures. Rasputin was a frequent
guest. There, far from prying eyes, people of high station transacted
important business of all kinds. The soul of the Badmaev circle was
the Empress' friend, Anna Alexandrovna Vyrubov, whom Protopopov called "a phonograph record of Rasputin's words and sug-
gestions," while the elder said he was "cut from the same mold."

An unknown nervous illness, and what some later called progressive paralysis, but most importantly, his acquaintance with Rasputin,
opened the doors of the Badmaev villa to the future minister. In
Rasputin he found an "astonishing perspicacity, sincerity, soft gentle-
ness, and simplicity."

Having done nothing, Protopopov began to acquire authority in
the matter of the food crisis. At that time his ambitions did not go any
higher than the post of Deputy Minister of Commerce and Industry.

* * *

In the summer of 1916 Protopopov accompanied a parliamentary
delegation of members of the State Duma and the State Council on a
visit to some friendly countries in Europe. He was lifted to extraordi-

nary heights and his head was turned by the audiences he was granted by the English King, George V, and the Italian King, Victor Emmanuel III. The parliamentary delegation returned to Petrograd on June 17 (30), 1916, but without the Vice-Chairman of the State Duma. At the request of P. L. Bark, the Minister of Finance, he remained in London to settle a question on a loan, and then went to Stockholm. There he had a secret meeting in a hotel room with a Dr. Barburg, an official of the German embassy and banker from Hamburg, who had been specially commissioned with this task by Von Liutsius, the German ambassador to Sweden. Count D. A. Olsufev, Protopopov's assistant in the parliamentary delegation and a member of the State Council, was present at the discussions. According to Protopopov, A. V. Nekiudov, the Russian ambassador in Stockholm, had asked him not to refuse a meeting with Barburg, in order to learn the terms for a separate peace. This meeting determined the fate of the man of destiny.

Upon his return to the capital, Protopopov was immediately summoned to General Headquarters, where he had a two-hour-long conversation with the Sovereign. The Tsar was very interested in the Stockholm meeting, and instead of being angry, reacted quite favorably. As Protopopov later said, he and the Sovereign charmed one another. The Tsar took an immediate liking to him and trusted him completely. And under the influence of such favor from the monarch, a sincere love for the master of the Russian people and his family suddenly flared up in Protopopov.

Protopopov then returned to his home in the country, with a promise from General Kurlov that he would be called back to Petrograd when he was needed. Rasputin began to reiterate that "whatever Protopopov says, will be, so you had better feed him again." The Tibetan wizard Badmaev informed General Kurlov that his friend had made an excellent impression on the "father" and that he thanked him.

On September 1 (14), 1916, Kurlov sent Protopopov a telegram asking him to come to Petrograd to accept the post of Minister of Internal Affairs in place of A. A. Khvostov, who had only served two months. On September 7 (20), the Empress wrote to her husband, "Gregory convincingly requests that you appoint Protopopov to this post. You know him, and he made such a good impression on you;— as it happens, he is a member of the Duma (not left-wing) and so will know how to get along with them. . . . He has known Our Friend for at least four years, which says much for him. I don't know him, but have faith in Our Friend's wisdom and advice."

By "Our Friend," of course, she meant Rasputin. And on September 16 (29), 1916, according to Protopopov, His Majesty wrote, "soon, God willing!"

At General Headquarters, Protopopov reassured the Sovereign

with his plans for resolving production problems. Toward the end of their conversation the Tsar asked if he had known Rasputin long. Protopopov's expansive gratitude toward the elder and his sincere love for him pleased the monarch.

Thus Protopopov's lucky star soared ever higher. He formulated a plan to save Russia, decided to put manufacturing matters under the power of the Ministry of Internal Affairs, reform the zemstvo and police, and solve the Jewish question. Joining the leapfrog of ministers, Protopopov attached himself so firmly that the leapfrog continued around him as though around some sort of mystical axis supporting the falling empire until its fatal hour struck. Three Prime Ministers were replaced during his ministry, but it did not worry him—why, he was the Tsar's favorite. He rarely attended meetings of the Council of Ministers, spending a good part of his time at Tsarskoe Selo. Despite numerous attempts by influential persons to force him to step down, he continued his work till the last possible minute.

* * *

From his very first step to the ministerial chair, Protopopov aroused the dislike not only of his comrades in the Progressive Bloc, which is understandable, but also of the members of the ruling circles, who regarded him as a parvenu. Donning a gendarme's uniform,* the former Octobrist, who held that "the genius of a whole people cannot be squeezed into the framework of official decrees," still felt a certain awkwardness. The State Duma and the Progressive Bloc were black spots on a background of mind-boggling successes, and so he wanted to smooth his relations with his comrades in the bloc.

On the evening of October 19 (November 1), 1916, I went to the apartment of Michael Vladimirovich Rodzianko. Ten other members of our bloc were there: from the centrists, Nicholas Dmitrievich Krupenskii, Dmitrii Nicholaevich Sverchkov, and Boris Alexandrovich Engelhardt; representing the Cadets, Paul Nicholaevich Miliukov and Dr. Andrew Ivanovich Shingarev; from the Nationalists, Dmitrii Nicholaevich Chikhachev, and finally, from the Octobrists, Duma Secretary Ivan Ivanovich Dmitriukov, Count Dmitrii Pavlovich Kapnist, Nikanor Vasilevich Savich, and Victor Ivanovich Stempkovskii.

Rodzianko warned us that we had been invited for an unofficial

---

*According to Peter Deriabin, in *Watchdogs of Terror* (New Rochelle, N.Y.: Arlington House, 1972), the Corps of Gendarmes had very flashy uniforms, "light blue with white accoutrements and white gloves." Protopopov was apparently something of a fop, and since the corps was part of the Internal Affairs Ministry, and therefore under his command, he evidently donned its uniform on public occasions (trans.).

meeting with the Minister of Internal Affairs, at his express wishes. Protopopov entered, dressed in a uniform. He said, taking a seat, "I have a request—that we keep this discussion private, so that nothing leaves this room."

"Alexander Dmitrievich, the time for secrets is over," Miliukov replied rather harshly. "I cannot give you my promise. I will have to report to the faction on everything that happens here."

"In that case I cannot say anything. I beg your pardon. Please forgive me for disturbing the Chairman of the State Duma and you other gentlemen. But tell me what's wrong. What has happened that you do not wish to hold a friendly discussion with me?"

"What?!" shouted Miliukov, jumping up and approaching Protopopov. "What has happened? You want to know what has happened? I'll tell you! A man who serves with Stürmer, a man who has freed Sukhomlinov, who is considered a traitor by the entire country, a man who persecutes the press and social-welfare organizations cannot be our comrade. And furthermore, they say that Rasputin is behind your appointment. Is that true?"

"I will answer in order. Concerning Sukhomlinov, he is not free; nothing has changed except the manner of his imprisonment—"

"He's in his own home," Miliukov interrupted. "Under house arrest, and he's asking for that to be removed too—"

"Yes. As for the press, I do not control the press. It falls under the War Ministry. But I have seen Lieutenant-General Serge Semenovich Khabalov, commander of the Petersburg military district, and have secured the release of the newspaper *Rech* ("Speech") from severe censorship.

"I would like to respond to the question about Rasputin, but that is a secret, and I have to speak here for the press. Paul Nicholaevich has shut my mouth so that I cannot explain myself to my comrades. I thought that our trip abroad together would improve relations. Evidently I was mistaken. What can I do? I wanted to come to an agreement, but if that is impossible, I will have to go it alone."

"Before we can hold a friendly discussion," said Shingarev, "we have to resolve the question of whether we can be comrades. We don't know how you were appointed. Rumors point to Rasputin's participation. Then you entered a ministry headed by Stürmer, a man with a definite reputation as a traitor. And not only did you not keep your distance from him, but on the contrary, we know from your interviews that you have announced that your program will be Stürmer's program, and that he will develop your program from the Duma's rostrum. You ordered another traitor freed—Sukhomlinov, and you have assumed the post of a man who was removed for not wishing to do that. During your tenure, Manasevich-Manuilov, Stürmer's personal secretary, about whom the vilest rumors are circulating, has also been freed.

"And finally, during the present workers' uprisings, or so rumor has it, your ministry is following the same provocative path as before. You spread every imaginable rumor among the workers. What are we supposed to think about all this? We would like to hear what you have to say before we decide what kind of relations we will have."

"I came here to hold a discussion. What do I see? I see that I am here as an accused man. Furthermore, you can say anything you deem reasonable, whereas Paul Nicholaevich has sealed my lips with his announcement that everything I say will appear tomorrow in print. Under these conditions I can't say many confidential things that would refute the rumors you so needlessly believe.

"For example, I met Rasputin several years ago, under circumstances completely different from the present ones. I am the personal candidate of the Sovereign, whom I have come to know well and love. But I cannot speak of the private side of this. For the police department I have taken a man who is known to me and is clean—"

Protopopov meant his friend General P. G. Kurlov, whom he had appointed Deputy Minister of Internal Affairs and chief of the Gendarme Corps. Voices interrupted.

"What about Kurlov's role under Stolypin?"

"The accusations against Kurlov were groundless."

"And Novitskii's note?" exclaimed Miliukov.

"Well, gentlemen, I see you put your faith in various notes. Kurlov was not to blame for Stolypin's assassination. Kurlov was appointed a senator before Peter Arkadevich's death. I have papers in my desk concerning this—"

I said to Protopopov, "First of all, we must decide what our relationship is to be. We have all condemned you; I have condemned you publicly and consider it my duty to repeat my condemnation in your presence. I warn you that there will be some painful minutes.

"We don't know what to think. Either you are a martyr, who went 'there' with the aim of accomplishing something when it was clearly impossible to accomplish anything, or you are ambitious, and have simply become engrossed in your glorious status, hiding from yourself the fact that you cannot do anything.

"What sort of position have you put yourself in? There were people who loved you; there were many who respected you. And now—now your credit has fallen very low. You have cut yourself off from the only people who could have supported you 'there.' We should have had this conversation before you took power.

"Under the circumstances it is understandable that Paul Nicholaevich does not consider it possible to keep our discussion a secret.

Tomorrow, when our group learns about this meeting, it may assume that we have made an agreement with you. We will not support you, for in so doing we would only destroy ourselves, just as you have destroyed yourself. I will admit the possibility of keeping it secret if we do not get anywhere today. Then we can say that we talked but did not come to an agreement. But if we agree to anything, then we are obligated to tell our group why we found it possible to agree."

Protopopov angrily answered, "If anyone here says that he does not respect me, my answer does not have to be given in public, but face-to-face, pistol in hand. As for my relationship with the public, I judge it by the large number of people who come to see me. I receive many who have been treated unfairly, many who are suffering, and no one leaves without being helped. The public values me. I came for your support but did not get it. What can I do but go on alone? Why, I was never even invited to join the bloc. I never attended even one of your meetings."

"That's your fault," objected Miliukov.

"I fulfill the wishes of my Sovereign. You want a change in the regime, but you won't get it, not while I can do anything about it."

"We now have a situation in which it would be harmful to do anything," said Stempkovskii.

"Not for long. Resign—but who would the power be passed on to?" continued Protopopov. "I see only one strong man—Trepov. My situation may be fatal, but I'll do what I can. Why did you welcome even Khvostov more warmly than me?"

Miliukov replied, "I said that since our meeting has political significance, I cannot keep silent about it before my political friends."

"Give me your word that nothing will appear in print."

"There is no way that I can give you such a promise. However, I can say that we will not reveal anything that is considered a government secret.

"Now to another matter. Why does Alexander Dmitrievich's appointment differ from Khvostov's? Because Khvostov belongs to a party that is indifferent to public opinion, but Alexander Dmitrievich took office as a member of a specific political organization. He stands in the shadow of his party's program and of the political meaning of the majority in which he is counted. He is considered a member of the bloc."

"As Vice-Chairman of the State Duma," replied Protopopov, "I regarded it as my duty to be nonpartisan, and thus I cannot consider myself a member of the bloc."

Count Kapnist objected, "But, if you'll allow me, that is surprising. How can Alexander Dmitrievich possibly feel that way toward the faction?"

Miliukov said, "I am very glad for this explanation, since it explains your acceptance of a ministerial post. The bloc has been blamed for it. But furthermore, you were Vice-Chairman of the Duma in this capacity before you became known abroad as chairman of our delegation."

"You do not know with what sympathy my appointment was met abroad. I received scores of congratulatory messages—"

"You did not receive them as Alexander Dmitrievich but as a man representing a party. As for the reports in the foreign press, we know how they get their information. I myself read your agency's telegram to Paris. What did it say? It said that your appointment was received with approval in parliamentary circles. How it was really received you now see for yourself.

"By the way, when we were abroad you said that you were a monarchist. I didn't discuss it with you at the time. After all, we are all monarchists, so there doesn't seem to be any need to emphasize the fact. But when they began to praise you as a monarchist, a question occurred to me which I put to you now: in what sense are you a monarchist? In the sense of an unlimited monarchy, or are you still a proponent of a constitutional monarchy? It is ambiguous."

"Yes, I have always been a monarchist. Now I know the Tsar personally and have come to love him. And I don't know why, but he loves me also." The expression on Protopopov's face changed, and he sighed heavily.

Count Kapnist said quietly, "Don't worry, Alexander Dmitrievich." But this expression of consolation angered him for some reason, and he said stingingly, "Yes, it's easy for you to sit in your chair, but how hard it is for me in mine! You have a title and connections, while I started my career as a humble student, giving lessons for 50 kopecks. I have nothing but the personal support of the Sovereign, but with this support I will go to the top, no matter what you think of me."

Miliukov said, "I'm not finished yet. I was starting to explain why we behaved differently toward Khvostov. As Shulgin has already said, we are responsible for you, whereas we weren't for him. But now the situation is different. We have a majority in the Duma, a majority with its own well-defined position. The government acted contrary to it, and now we have reached the point where the country has run out of patience and its faith has been used up. Now emergency measures are needed to restore the people's faith."

"A responsible ministry! Oh, no, gentlemen, this you will not achieve!"

Through Protopopov's exclamation one could hear cries of "a ministry of confidence, a ministry of confidence!"

"By the way, I heard a threat in your words," said Miliukov. "What do you mean by the phrase 'you will act alone'? Does that mean you will not summon the Duma, as some people say?"

"I am not vengeful. As for not summoning the Duma—that is simply hearsay."

"According to my information, which I consider trustworthy, several ministers have talked about that."

"At any rate, I was not one of them."

"You *were* one of them, Alexander Dmitrievich."

"Yes, yes, there have been rumors about your feelings on that subject," said several voices.

"No, I will not go that far. I am a member of the Duma myself, and am used to working with the Duma. I have been, and remain, a friend of the Duma. In your attitude, Paul Nicholaevich, there is reason but no heart. Your wife would have a totally different attitude."

"What does my wife have to do with this? I have already said, and I repeat, we meet here as political statesmen."

Everyone rose. The meeting ended. Above the din of conversation one heard Miliukov's words, "You are leading Russia to destruction."

* * *

After the murder of Rasputin, Protopopov's position not only did not worsen but on the contrary, to everyone's surprise, improved. Three days later, on December 20, 1916 (January 2, 1917), he was made Minister of Internal Affairs. The stabilizing effect anticipated by the perpetrators of the "patriotic terrorist act" never occurred. Everything remained as before. The Tsar and Tsarina believed in Protopopov as idolatrously as they had believed in Rasputin. Even more so, because Rasputin's final command was, "Listen to him. Do whatever he says." Nothing could be said. After obtaining the Sovereign's permission, Protopopov ordered the arrest of the Workers' Group of the War Industry Committee, on January 27 (February 9), 1917. Catherine Victorovna Sukhomlinov, whose husband Protopopov had released from prison, said that for this act of high politics he received a plus mark in Tsarskoe Selo. The cup of patience spilled over. M. V. Rodzianko took up his pen, wrote his final, completely subjective report, and went to Tsarskoe Selo.

He was received by the Emperor on February 10 (23), 1917, in the presence of Grand Prince Alexander Mikhailovich and the Tsar's brother, Michael Alexandrovich. While the newspapers reported that he was received graciously, Rodzianko himself said that his reception was "most difficult and stormy." A record of this conversation has been preserved.*

After the Chairman of the State Duma had read his report, the Tsar said, "You demand Protopopov's removal?"

---

*See M. V. Rodzianko, *The Reign of Rasputin: An Empire's Collapse; Memoirs of M. V. Rodzianko* (New York, 1927) (trans.).

"Yes, Your Highness. Previously I asked for it; now I demand it."

"And why?"

"Your Highness, save yourself. We are on the eve of an enormous upheaval, the results of which cannot be foreseen. Your actions and those of the government have incited the populace to the point of— Anything can happen. Any rogue can take charge. The public reasons, 'If a rogue can do it, why can't I, a decent person?" Then it will spread to the army, and there will be total anarchy. Sometimes you have listened to me and good has come of it."

"When?" asked the Tsar.

"Remember, in July of 1915, when you asked for the resignation of N. A. Maklakov, the Minister of Internal Affairs."

"And now I regret it," said the Tsar. "That one, at any rate, is not mad."

"Quite naturally, Your Majesty, because he has nothing to go mad from."

The Tsar laughed, "Well said, well said."

"Your Majesty, measures must be taken!" continued Rodzianko. "I recommend a whole series of measures. It's all written down. Do you want to shake the country with a revolution in time of war?"

"I will do what the Lord wills me to do."

"Your Majesty, at any rate you have to pray with all your might, and sincerely ask the Lord God to show you the right path, because the step you take now may prove fatal."

The Tsar rose and said something ambiguous.

Rodzianko said, "Your Majesty, I leave completely convinced that this will be my last report to you."

"Why?"

"For an hour and a half I have been reporting to you, and I can see that you have been led onto the most dangerous path. You want to dissolve the Duma. Then I will no longer be Chairman and will not come to you again. Even worse, I warn you, I am convinced that in less than three weeks a revolution will break out that will overthrow you."

"What makes you think so?"

"From all the circumstances. One cannot mock a people's pride and will, the way the men you have appointed have done. One cannot make all sorts of Rasputins the head of one's home. Sire, you will reap what you have sown."

"Well, God grant—"

"God will not grant anything; you and your government have ruined everything. Revolution is inevitable."

It was as though Rodzianko had gazed into a crystal ball. In only two weeks and two days, in Pskov, I was accepting the unfortunate autocrat's abdication from his own hands. However, despite his straightforwardness and courage, Rodzianko could not convince the Tsar. The very next day Maklakov was summoned to Tsarskoe Selo by Protopopov. Protopopov told Maklakov that the Tsar wanted him to write a manifesto that could be used if he decided to dissolve the Duma. Maklakov wrote a draft which basically blamed the members of the State Duma. The Duma was guilty of not increasing the salaries of clerks and clergy, and for that reason it was dissolved until new elections on November 15 (28), 1917. The manifesto concluded with the Tsar calling for unity in serving Russia. Thus, Protopopov, in hand-to-hand combat with the Duma that had elected him its Vice-Chairman, won in the end. But at what a price!

* * *

One can imagine the feelings of Duma members toward Protopopov at the fifth session, which resumed on February 14 (27), 1917. In the words of V. M. Purishkevich,

> Absolutely everyone, all Russia, is under suspicion. Our governmental system has resorted to slander. The aristocracy, zemstvo, Duma, Council, social-welfare organizations—everyone is under suspicion by those who are zealous servants of their own well-being and careers. Protopopov controls the entire Russian people at a difficult time, stifling the spirit of respect toward rulers, the spirit of faith in the future, the spirit of order.
>
> There is no name, gentlemen of the State Duma, for those who offer stones to a people asking for bread, who dabble in political blackmail, and who, despised by all Russia, nevertheless remain firmly at the helm. . . .
>
> Completely forgotten is history's lesson that domestic tranquility in any country is guaranteed not by the quantity of bullets controlled by the political rulers but by honor, by good administration, and by the government's ability to foresee imminent events. . . .
>
> And Russia? The Russia of honor, the Russia of duty, which admits the importance of this moment in its historical fate, this Russia opposes the ruling powers because they do not believe in her honesty, her patriotism. . . .
>
> Hanging over the Duma, gentlemen, is a Damocles sword of dissolution used to frighten the Duma. . . . The Duma is offered a choice—become the lackey of the Minister of Internal Affairs, obediently and servilely working for him, or preserve its present face, the face of honorable subjects and patriots.
>
> I realize that speeches from the Duma's tribunal are now to no avail, because between the supreme powers and the people, in these difficult, historic days—horrible even to think—stands a wall of egotistical careerists who live only for the good today might bring them.
>
> And Russia? What do they really care about Russia? *(From the left are heard voices, "Right! True!")* Russia? Gentlemen, Russia now stands, like

ancient Hercules, in a tunic saturated with the poison of the centaur's blood. He squeezes it, and it writhes in the torment of its powerlessness, and boils with rage that truth, Russian truth, has reached a point where it must be understood, valued, and obeyed. The dawn has not yet come, gentlemen, but it is not far off. The day will come—I feel it—when the sun of Russian truth will rise above a revived homeland in its hour of triumph.

Thus even the ultra-rightist deputy V. M. Purishkevich declaimed passionately from the Duma's rostrum. He had not heeded my words that it was senseless to kill the snake after it had already bitten but now realized that things had indeed gotten even worse.

Two days later, On February 17 (March 2), 1917, I had to make a speech. It was my last speech in the State Duma. The main theme was the food question, which the Minister of Agriculture, A. A. Rittikh, who replaced Count V. A. Bobrinskii, had already spoken about twice. But at the time Protopopov controlled everybody's minds to such an extent that I had to direct several seditious thoughts at him. I began,

> Gentlemen, members of the State Duma. It cannot be said that the speeches of the Minister of Agriculture were uninteresting. At any rate, I listened to them very attentively and was particularly interested in a certain theme to which the minister continuously returned—the theme that the trust of the people is as necessary as air to him.
>
> Gentlemen, if it is right not to talk about rope in the home of someone who has been hanged, then it follows that to come here with precisely such an announcement is not only irrelevant but rather unwelcome. We have been repeating the same thing for a year and a half, and we are tired of talking about it. And here the Minister of Agriculture brings up the same topic, with all the enthusiasm of a neophyte. I sympathize and agree with him totally, but I think he should make his speech in the Council of Ministers. That is where it belongs. *(Applause from right, left, and center. Voices from the left: "Even higher.")* It seems to me that the Minister of Agriculture should talk with certain friends—for example, with our former comrade Alexander Dmitrievich Protopopov, and say to him, "Please understand, Alexander Dmitrievich, as long as we are neighbors, no one can have faith in me." *(Voices: "That's right!")* True, Alexander Dmitrievich would probably threaten to challenge him to a duel, but I can comfort the Minister of Agriculture—he will threaten, but he will not challenge him— *(Applause from left and center, laughter and voices: "Bravo! Bravo!")* And what would happen if we did give the Minister of Agriculture the trust that he needs like air? What would be the result? Gentlemen, we know very well what the result would be—and I hope that Alexander Alexandrovich Rittikh will forgive my perhaps vulgar expression—that he would be dismissed. *(From left and center, laughter and voices: "Hear! Hear!")* In the past year and a half we have realized very well that Russia forgives everything. For example, even Sukhom-

linov has been half-forgiven, but success would never be forgiven. *(Voices: "Bravo, bravo!")* And for that reason I maintain that if the Minister of Agriculture did, by some heroic effort, win our trust, the same fate would befall him as befell Krivoshein, his former leader, and Sazonov, Polivanov, Ignatiev, and many, many others. *(Voices: "Bravo, bravo!")*

* * *

One might think that there would be no common ground between a coarse, uneducated, dissipated peasant and a cultured aristocrat who had graduated from the Nicholaevsk General Staff Academy and had been received by the Kings of Great Britain and Italy. Still, they did have something in common. The saying that Protopopov replaced Rasputin was true. The evil shadow of the holy elder cum satyr seemed to appear, as though newly risen, behind the face of the minister. His spirit appeared not only in the minister's servility at Tsarskoe Selo but also in his satanic talent for divining the country's feelings on the issues of the day and then going against those feelings with a sort of nasty joy. Thus he conscientiously fulfilled the behests of his confidant.

Two months after Purishkevich's speech, Protopopov spoke before the Special Investigative Commission and said:

"You understand, Mr. Chairman, I want to say that I feel the evil fate that Rittikh mentioned to me. He said to me in the Council of Ministers, 'You know, beware—that which the Romans feared is watching you— fate is watching you!' He said this two or three weeks before the end. . . . I felt it. I am not afraid of deciding my fate, you understand that, but I say, how strange! It actually is fate, actually fate!"

I happened to witness the fall of this man of destiny's lucky star, as predicted by the elder. It happened, I believe, on February 28 (March 13), 1917, in Rodzianko's study, which was full of people. People who had been arrested—helpless, pitiful—lined the walls and armchairs and benches, which during those days became very worn. An endless stream of arrested people was dragged to the Duma, where a group of Duma members was occupied solely with examining their cases. Kerenskii coined the slogan, "The State Duma does not shed blood." Thus the Tauride Palace became a shelter for anyone threated by the justice of revolutionary democracy. Those who, for their own personal safety, could not be released, were directed to the so-called Ministers' Pavilion, which grimacing fate had turned into a "pavilion of arrested ministers." There was an unspoken agreement between Kerenskii, who was in charge of this house of arrest, and us. We saw that he was acting out a comedy before the wild crowd, and we saw his reason. He wanted to save all these people, and to do so he had to pretend that the Duma, although it would not shed blood, would deal with the guilty.

Most of those who were arrested could be released, so we detained them in Rodzianko's study. Normally it took several hours to prepare the necessary documents. Everyone possible came through the doors.

One day, my strength exhausted from carrying out a thousand and one assignments, like all the other members of the Provisional Government, I lowered myself into an armchair in Rodzianko's study, opposite a large mirror. Reflected in the mirror I could see both that room and the neighboring one, the study of the Vice-Chairman of the Duma, Prince V. M. Volkonskii, where the same scene was occurring. Everything looked somewhat cloudy in the mirror.

Suddenly I sensed excitement in Volkonskii's study, and someone whispered the reason: "Protopopov is under arrest!" That same instant I saw in the mirror how the doors to Volkonskii's study were thrown open and Kerenskii tore in. He was pale, his eyes burned, his hand was raised, and he used it to cut through the crowd. Everyone recognized him and made way, frightened by his appearance. Then I saw soldiers with rifles walking behind Kerenskii, and between their rifles, a frail figure with a completely crestfallen face. I barely recognized Protopopov.

"Don't you dare touch this man!" shouted Kerenskii. The man in question was the great enemy of the revolution—the former Minister of Internal Affairs.

"Don't you dare touch this man!" Everyone froze. It seemed as if he were being led to his death. And the crowd stepped back. Kerenskii raced past, like the burning torch of revolutionary justice, followed by a frail figure in a wrinkled coat, surrounded by rifles. An eerie sight.

With those words, Kerenskii tore into the Catherine Hall, which was full of soldiers, future Bolsheviks. This is where the real danger began for Protopopov. People could have fallen upon this frail figure, killed him, torn him apart—feelings toward Protopopov had been brought to such a point. But nothing of the sort happened. Struck by the strange sight of the pale Kerenskii leading his victim, the crowd made way for him.

"Don't you dare touch this man!" And it seemed as if this man were no longer a man. Kerenskii cut through the crowd in the Catherine Hall and several other rooms and entered the Ministers' Pavilion. And when the door of the pavilion slammed shut behind him, the comedy which had demanded such great strength of will finally ended. Kerenskii fell into an armchair and said to the man, "Please sit down, Alexander Dmitrievich!"

* * *

Protopopov had come on his own, knowing he was in danger. He preferred to surrender to the protection of the State Duma rather than to hide and run from apartment to apartment. He came to the Tauride Palace and said to a student, "I am Protopopov!" The student, at his wit's end, ran to Kerenskii, but babbled to others on the way, and when Kerenskii arrived, Protopopov was surrounded by a crowd that promised him no good. Kerenskii knew what to do. He grabbed the armed soldiers closest to him and ordered them to lead "this man" with him.

And so "this man," who had triumphed over the Duma, came to the Duma to save his life. Fate led the "man of destiny" here. But he had wanted to kill the Duma, and the Duma could not save him. It no longer existed. In 1918, in Moscow, he and several other former ministers were shot.

The End of the Duma

I N KIEV I RECEIVED a worrisome telegram from Shingarev, asking
me to return immediately to Petrograd. I arrived on January 18
(21), 1917, and that very evening Shingarev came to see me.

I said, "What's wrong, Andrew Ivanovich?"

"It's bad. The situation worsens with each passing day. We are heading toward a precipice. Revolution is disaster, but there will be revolution. And even without revolution everything is coming apart with
unbelievable speed. The railroads are in catastrophic shape. So far
they are somehow barely holding together, but with these snow
storms—Everything is behind schedule. In Petrograd there already
are serious hitches in the food situation. In a day or two there will be
no more bread. The troops are discontented. The Petrograd garrison
cannot be depended upon."

"I'm afraid that if even if our foolish rulers make concessions, even
if a government of trustworthy men is created, they still won't be
satisfied. The general feeling is already to the left of the Progressive
Bloc. That will have to be taken into consideration. We will not be able
to restrain them. The country is no longer obeying us but those to our
left— It's too late—"

"If the power falls to us, we will have to seek support by widening
the Progressive Bloc to the left."

"How would this be done?"

"I would summon Kerenskii."

"In what capacity?"

"As Minister of Justice, perhaps. At the moment the post has no
meaning, but we have to tear the leaders away from the revolution.
Kerenskii is one of the only— It would be much more to our advantage to have him with us than against us. But we are only guessing
with tea leaves. In reality are there any signs that the government is,
in plain words, getting ready to summon us?"

"In reality, no. But on the eve, everything— There is great unrest.
We must be ready for anything."

* * *

While I was still in Kiev, on January 3 (16), 1917, the Council of
Ministers met under the chairmanship of its new Prime Minister. Who

284

replaced Trepov when Protopopov dismissed him? It was sixty-seven-year-old Prince Nicholas Dmitrievich Golitsyn. The very circumstances of his appointment reveal the extent of the confusion in the government.

The Prince said, "I am totally unprepared for a political role—I have always been a monarchist, a loyal subject, but have never spoken in the State Council."

Quite removed from political activity, and since 1915 controlling only the Committee to Aid Russian Prisoners of War, Golitsyn was suddenly summoned to Tsarskoe Selo. In vain did he beg the Sovereign not to appoint him Prime Minister. He said that he dreamed only of rest. The Tsar would not be swayed, and on December 27 (January 9), 1917, the Prince became the Chairman of the Council of Ministers. He was the empire's last Prime Minister.

Six days later, the Council of Ministers held a meeting on a matter of "high politics." What did this high politics consist of: resolving the food crisis, the transportation shambles, the catastrophic increase in dissatisfaction among the people, the low morale of the army? Nothing of the sort. The agenda for the day consisted of only one question—how to circumvent the royal decree of December 15 (28), 1916, summoning the State Duma on January 12 (25), 1917. There was a difference of opinion among the ministers. Five of them favored following the decree about the opening of the Duma on January 12 (25). In addition, they said, the possibility of summoning the Duma on time should be guaranteed by corresponding measures. The Chairman, Prince Golitsyn, and eight members of the Council felt that in view of the present feeling of the Duma majority, the opening of the Duma and the presence of the government would without doubt call forth undesirable and unacceptable demonstrations. The result would have to be the dissolution of the Duma and the designation of new elections. To avoid such an extreme measure the Chairman and other members decided it would be preferable to postpone the summoning of the Duma until January 31 (February 13). However, the question was decided by Protopopov, with the agreement of the Minister of Justice, N. A. Dobrovolskii, and the Senior Procurator of the Holy Synod, N. P. Raev. They demanded that the recess continue until February 14 (27), 1917, and their decision was upheld by the government.

* * *

One day I was visited by an officer. "Since I know you, I want to warn you."

"About what?"

"The mood in the Petrograd garrison. Don't you see the things they are "writing" in the snow on all the squares and streets? They've been disciplined, but they are incorrigible. Do you know what sort of men they are? They're mama's boys! They're the ones who hid behind all sorts of excuses to avoid mobilization. They don't care about anything, as long as they don't have to go to war. Besides, there are objective reasons for their discontent. Their quarters are terribly crowded. Three cots are stacked one on top of the other, like in a third-class railway car. The least little thing and they will mutiny. Mark my words. They should be chased out of here as soon as possible."

It was a clear, frosty day. Driving to the Duma, I actually saw the ranks of "writers" on almost every street. They marched back and forth, led by a noncommissioned officer, smoothing down the snow with wooden, automatic movements. Now I looked at them with different feelings. And I remembered how people had already complained to me in 1915 about a certain division from Petrograd, called the "St. Petersburg running society," no less. No matter where they were sent in battle, they would run away.

*   *   *

I don't remember exactly when the following scene took place. Probably toward the end of January. Where? I can't remember—somewhere on the Peska, in a big room. Everyone was there. First of all, there were the officers of the Progressive Bloc and other leading figures of the State Duma—the Cadets Paul Nicholaevich Miliukov, Nicholas Vissarionovich Nekrasov, Andrew Ivanovich Shingarev, Nicholas Nicholaevich Shchepkin, the Progressive Ivan Nicholaevich Efremov, the Octobrist Serge Iliodorovich Shidlovskii, and Vladimir Nicholaevich Lvov from the center. Also A. I. Ruchkov, I believe, the president of the Zemstvo Union, Prince Lvov, and some others.

First there was some light conversation, then we sat down at the table. One could sense something unusual, secret, important. Someone said that the situation was getting worse every day and that it could not go on like this. Something had to be done. Boldness was needed, the essential big decisions must be made—serious steps. But no one was willing to say what he wanted, what he proposed. I didn't understand exactly, but I could guess. Perhaps the organizers of the meeting wanted to talk about the need for a revolt at the top so as to prevent one at the bottom. Or perhaps it was something totally different. At any rate, nothing was decided. We dispersed. I had an oppressive feeling that doom was near and any attempt to fight it off would be pitiful. My own powerlessness, and that of the people surrounding me, looked me in the eye for the first time. And its glance was contemptuous and horrible.

Finally, on February 14 (27), the session of the Duma that had been interrupted on the eve of Rasputin's murder reconvened. It was attended by the Chairman of the Council of Ministers, Prince Golitsyn, several members of the government, and delegates from the unions. We discussed the bread ration. There was a schism within the bloc on this question. The right supported the government, considering its plan correct. The left, presuming that nothing good could come out of Nazareth, refused the government's offer.

The Minister of Agriculture, Alexander Alexandrovich Rittikh, spoke convincingly, passionately, but too nervously. He begged us not to ruin everything.

Superficially things continued as before, but in reality it was different. This was noted in the newspapers, which commented that the first day of the Duma seemed pale in comparison with the country's mood. Anxiety and sadness spilled into the air. During speeches there was a pervasive feeling that all this was unnecessary, overdue, unimportant. Hopelessness peeked out from behind the white columns of the hall, whispering, "Why bother? What difference does it make?" It was said in the lobbies that day that Rittikh went into the Ministers' Pavilion after his speech and burst out sobbing.

On the morning of the eve of the revolution, February 26 (March 11), 1917, Peter Bernardovich Struve paid me an unexpected visit. He was worried and sick but suggested that we both go see Maklakov. "We will find out from Vasilii Alekseevich. And the Duma is nearby—" There was such intense anxiety in the air that it was impossible to sit at home—one had to be there.

We went. It was below freezing, a clear day. Not a single tramway—they had stopped. There were no cabbies either. We had to walk five kilometers to the Tauride Palace. Peter Bernardovich could barely walk. He had to lean on me.

The streets were completely quiet and empty. The quiet was unpleasant, because we knew perfectly well why the tramways had stopped, why there were no cabbies. There had been no bread in Petrograd for three days, and this quiet day was the lull before the storm that was lurking somewhere behind those wondrous bridges and palaces, hiding and growing. It grew either on the Nevskii Prospect, which could not be seen from here, or over there, toward the city of Vyborg, near the Finland Railroad Station.

The Neva River was especially beautiful that day. We stopped to rest, leaning on the railing of the Troitskii Bridge. The embankments, brightly lit by the sun, spoke of what had been done but only made it seem more terrifying, because, finished in their beauty, they could not answer our question about what was happening.

Vasilii Alekseevich was in a hurry because he had been summoned by Pokrovskii, who had replaced Stürmer as Minister of Foreign Affairs. Pokrovskii, reasonable and honest, was more favored in Duma circles, as vice-chairman of the Central War Industries Committee.

Maklakov, the most moderate and clever of the Cadets, was more acceptable in government circles. At the same time, because of his constant opposition to Miliukov, he was not a partisan of the Progressive Bloc. Maklakov could very well become the connecting link between the Duma and the government. His invitation to Pokrovskii could signify much, so in expectation of his return to the government we went to the Tauride Palace.

As always, the bloc, or rather, the officers of the bloc, were sitting in room no. 11. The chairman was the Octobrist Shidlovskii. Of the Cadets, Miliukov and Shingarev were there. The Progressives had all left. Of the Octobrists, Count Kapnist was there, Vladimir Nicholaevich Lvov, I believe, from the centrists, and Ivan Fedorovich Polovtsev and I of the Progressive Nationalists.

The windows were large, but at 3:00 P.M. it was already dark. We sat at a table covered with green velvet, lit by table lamps with dark shades. How many times we had sat like that! I do not remember what was discussed, but I felt we were not doing the right thing, as I had felt many times before. We all criticized the ruling powers but had no answer to the question, "Well, enough criticism—do it yourselves! So, what should be done?" We had the bloc's great charter, which said that it was necessary to pass several reforms, but it did not touch the central question, how could we better conduct the war?

More than once I had tried to come up with a clear, practical program. Since I could not formulate one alone, I turned to my friends on the left, but they put me off by various means. When I was too persistent, they would answer that a practical program consisted of obtaining trustworthy leaders who were intelligent and sensible, and would take charge. There was no such thing as a simple recipe for good administration, they maintained. Even in the West, the guarantee of good government was trustworthy ministers.

Then I tried to ascertain who these trustworthy ministers might be. The response: For the time being it is awkward to say, because it would give rise to rumors; the question will be decided when it comes up in earnest.

But that evening it seemed to me that the question had finally come up in earnest. The government's disarray was clearly felt. We sensed that any minute we might be asked to name a minister. In the meantime, were we ready to answer? Did we know who, even among ourselves? Not in the slightest. For that reason I made the following suggestion:

"It may seem awkward and improper and so on, but the time has come when that no longer matters. Our responsibility is too great. For a year and a half already we have been saying over and over that the government is good for nothing. What will happen if they finally agree with us and say, 'Give us your names.' Are we ready? Can we name trustworthy, concrete, living men? I maintain that it is necessary to compile a list of names of men who could form a government."

There was a pause, and I saw that everyone felt uncomfortable. Shingarev asked for the floor and, evidently speaking for everyone, said that for the present it was impossible. I insisted, asserting that the time had come. But no one supported me, and the list was not drawn up. Everyone, including me, was uncomfortable.

That is what we Russian politicians are like. Overthrowing the ruling powers, we do not have the boldness, or better yet, the saving cowardice, to think of the gaping emptiness, or as they say today, the "power vacuum." Powerlessness again looked me mockingly in the eye.

After the meeting we went out into the Catherine Hall, and I walked out with Maklakov, who told me that nothing special had occurred during his talk with Pokrovskii.

Alexander Fedorovich Kerenskii appeared at the other end of the room, in a hurry, as usual, head bowed, arms pumping. The Menshevik Matthew Ivanovich Skobelev hurried after him. Kerenskii spotted us, turned abruptly, and approached us, thin arms outstretched significantly. He said loudly, "Well, gentlemen, the bloc? Something must be done! After all, the situation is—bad. Are you planning to do anything?" We met in the middle of the hall.

It seems to me that until then we had never been formally introduced; at any rate, I had never spoken to him. We were in enemy camps. His attack was unexpected, but I decided to take advantage of it. I said, "Well, if you ask in that way, allow me, in turn, to ask you: in your opinion, what is necessary? What will satisfy you?"

A happy, almost boyish expression appeared on his bearded face. "What? In essence, very little. The important thing is that power be passed on to other hands."

"Whose?" asked Maklakov.

"It doesn't matter. But not bureaucratic ones."

"Why not bureaucratic hands?" retorted Maklakov. "I was particularly thinking of bureaucratic hands—smart, clean hands. In a word, the hands of good bureaucrats. The 'responsible' ones won't do anything."

"Why not?"

"Because we don't understand anything about these matters. We don't know the technical part. And there is no time to learn now."

"That's a petty problem. You'll be given the apparatus. Why else do administrative assistants and departments exist?!"

Skobelev interrupted, stuttering a bit, "How can you not understand that you have the p—p—p—public's f—f—f—faith—"

"Well, what else is necessary?" I asked Kerenskii.

Boyishly, even thoughtlessly, he waved his hand happily and responded, "Well, a bit of freedom also. Press, assembly, and so on—"

"Is that all?"

"For the time being. But hurry! Hurry!"

He sped off with Skobelev in his wake. Hurry where?! My comrades
in the bloc and I were born and raised under the wing of the rulers, to
praise or censure them. As a last resort, we could move easily from
deputies' benches to ministers' chairs, but only on the condition that
the Imperial Guard would protect us. But in the face of the possible
fall of the regime, in the face of a bottomless precipice, our heads
spun and our hearts quaked. Again powerlessness glared at me from
behind the white columns of the Tauride Palace, and its look was
contemptuous to the point of horror.

* * *

I was walking alone somewhere back home in Volyn, approaching a
village. It was twilight, neither day not night, but everything was
somehow colorless. Both the road and the village were very ordinary.
Here was the first hut, set off a bit from the others. As I walked past it,
a hot blue flame suddenly flared up out of the black wooden chimney.
I wanted to rush into the hut to warn the people, but it was too late.
The whole straw roof was engulfed in flames. Everything burned, to
the last straw. A huge, bright, reddish-yellow flame roared upward. I
shouted in horror. A woman calmly walked out of the hut. I ran over
to her and shouted, "Save the children!" I ran into the hut, but the
roof crashed down. The huge fire flamed and roared madly. The
sound became louder and turned into a constant, shrill ring.

I awoke. It was 9:00 A.M. The telephone was ringing insistently.

"Hello."

"Is that you, Vasilii Vitalevich? Shingarev speaking. We must go to
the Duma. It has begun."

"What's wrong?"

"It has begun. We've received the decree dissolving the Duma.
There are disturbances in the city. We must hurry. They're taking the
bridges. We may not be able to get through. They sent a car for me.
Come right over. We'll go together."

"I'm coming."

It was February 27 (March 12), 1917. For several days we had been
living on a volcano. The eruption had begun. The street began to
speak.

* * *

The night before, late in the evening, when Rodzianko returned to his apartment, he found on his desk the following decree:

"On the basis of article 99 of the Fundamental Government Laws, we order that the business of the State Duma and the State Council be stopped on February 26 of this year and designate the date of their resumption no later than 1917, depending on circumstances."

It was signed in His Imperial Majesty's hand, "Nicholas, Imperial General Headquarters, February 25, 1917."

Countersigned by the Chairman of the Council of Ministers, Prince Nicholas Golitsyn.

It was the last tsarist decree. It was the end of the Duma. The Tsar's tragic battle with the Duma was at an end.

* * *

Eshche odno, poslednee skazanie—	One final story
I letopis okonchema moia. . .	And my manuscript will be finished.
. . . .	. . . .
Na starosti ia syznova zhivy,	In my old age, I live anew.
minushee prokhodit predo mnoiu—	The past passes before me,
davno l ono neslos sobytii polno,	Has it been rushing along for a long time, full of events,
volnuiasia, kak more okiian?	Surging like the seas?

Finita la commedia. The shipwreck has occurred. The ship of state went down, taking with it its legislative organ, the State Duma. Two months later, on April 27 (May 10), 1917, at a joint session of the remaining deputies of the Fourth Duma, I said, "I would not say that the Duma as a whole desired revolution. That would not be true. But even though we did not wish it, we created a revolution. We cannot renounce the revolution. We are connected to it and have a moral obligation to it."

With these words I conclude my narration about what was for me a great tragedy in the history of humanity. Now, in the place where formerly there was the Russian Empire, a new life is evolving. I am already ninety-eight years old. I am passing on to another world, and send my greetings and a behest to the living. Learn from the past. Do not repeat our mistakes. Do not concern yourselves with that which is already ashes and decay. Let the dead bury the dead. You, the living, preserve your living souls!

Index